Harry Hathaway headed down the street, a silver necklace dangling from his fingers. As he walked, he examined it, talking to himself.

"Not bad, Handsome Harry, you old rogue. There isn't a woman alive who can resist your charms."

He turned up the side street, dropping the necklace into a small pouch, then withdrew a slender key. He had stopped at a door, ready to unlock it when he thought he detected a faint hissing noise. He paused, the key only partly inserted, listening intently.

Again the sound issued forth, and then a voice whispered, "Harry!"

"Who's there?" he cried out, his voice echoing down the street.

"It's me, Harry," came a familiar voice.

"You'll have to be a little more specific," he replied. "I know a lot of 'me's'."

"It's me, Nikki, Nikki the Knife."

"Nik?" he responded in surprise. "You've been gone a long time Nik, we all thought you were dead."

He moved toward the voice and was suddenly conscious of a stench that permeated his surroundings. "What's that smell?"

"I had to escape through the sewers, Harry; they'll kill me if they catch me."

Nicole stepped out of the darkness.

"By the gods, Nik, you look as bad as you smell. Who's after you? Did you upset another gang boss?"

"No, Harry," she replied, "it's much more serious than that. Can you help me or not?"

"Of course, come inside, and we'll get you cleaned up."

"No," she insisted, "I need you to come with me."

"Where are we going?"

"I have someone stashed nearby, but we must hurry before he's discovered."

"You intrigue me, Nikki. Lead on."

~

Also by Paul J Bennett

SERVANT OF THE CROWN, HEIR TO THE CROWN: BOOK ONE

Banished with little more than the clothes on his back, Gerald seeks a new purpose, for what is a warrior who has nothing left to fight for?

A fateful meeting with another lost soul unmasks a shocking secret, compelling him to take up the mantle of guardian. Bandits, the Black Hand, and even the king, he battles them all for the future of the realm.

SWORD OF THE CROWN, HEIR TO THE CROWN: BOOK TWO

Dame Beverly Fitzwilliam has trained for this moment since she first held a sword. From her relentless pursuit of knighthood to the day she single-handedly saves the king's life and earns her spurs, she has searched for someone worthy of her fealty.

Her destiny will be determined in a monumental clash of forces where success can save the kingdom, but failure can only mean certain death.

MERCERIAN TALES: STORIES OF THE PAST, HEIR TO THE CROWN: BOOK 2.5

In a land where true heroism is more likely to be rewarded with accusations of treason, comes a recounting of past adventures by the unsung heroes of the realm.

More than just a collection of short stories, it falls chronologically between books two and three of the Heir to the Crown series and can be read at any time.

HEART OF THE CROWN, HEIR TO THE CROWN: BOOK THREE

Alric dreamed of being a hero; of defeating a dragon and saving the princess, but his royal position would never allow it, until… the arrival of the Mercerian Emissaries.

From fighting unknown creatures to defending the life of a royal, he discovers that becoming a hero is much more dangerous than he ever imagined. No matter what the outcome, his life will never be the same.

SHADOW OF THE CROWN

Heir to the Crown: Book Four

PAUL J BENNETT

Dedication

To my father,
Harold 'Pip' Charles Bennett
(1923 - 1996)
~

You fostered my imagination and supported me in
everything I ever dreamt up.
~

You are, and always will be,
my hero!

ONE

The Banquet

SUMMER 961 MC (MERCERIAN CALENDAR)

~

L ady Nicole Arendale let out a tremendous sneeze, belatedly covering her nose with her kerchief. Mortified, she glanced around the room, only to realize no one had taken notice. Instead, those in attendance were digging into the succulent meal and toasting the newly returned Princess Anna.

It was difficult for the Lady-In-Waiting to come to grips with her present situation. Over a year ago, she had been recruited to join the entourage of the young Princess Anna, daughter of the late King Andred IV of Merceria. After spending months travelling through Weldwyn, which lay to the west, they had returned to the welcoming arms of the princess's brother, King Henry, recently crowned after the death of his father. So here she sat, released from the princess's service, yet unable to leave, lest her true master discover her dismissal.

Her eyes refocused, looking across the table to take notice of Sir Barnsley, one of the princess's knights, passed out in his chair. Dame Abigail, another knight of the Order of the Hound, sat nearby mocking the slumbering man's condition.

Nicole swept her gaze farther up the table to Princess Anna herself. She appeared tired while listening to her brother, let out a big yawn and then fell face first onto the table. This behaviour elicited a collective gasp from the crowd, and out of the corner of her eye, Nicole perceived a number of soldiers moving forward.

Now Dame Abigail was down, and then Nicole noticed that all of the princess's entourage were dropping like flies; she looked to her tankard, which sat, untasted, on the table before her.

From across the room, there was a yell of alarm as Dame Beverly tried to stand, only to fall weakly back into her chair. Strong arms gripped the red-headed knight, holding her firmly in place, until her head nodded forward, her chin coming to rest on her chest.

Nicole was worried; somebody had orchestrated the poisoning of the entire diplomatic entourage. As a member herself, she was most likely an intended victim. Desperate to avoid detection, she let out an exaggerated yawn and fell forward onto the table, keeping her eyes open barely enough to see around her.

Soldiers lifted the princess from her seat, along with the old warrior who usually sat to her side. Nicole was prepared to run, to rush from the room and save herself should an opportunity occur, but before such a chance came, she felt hands on her shoulders.

Firm hands gripped her arms, preparing to lift her, but a voice sailed across the room, "Not her, she's one of Valmar's."

Released, she fell back into the seat, eyes now squeezed shut, but still listening intently. A woman's voice rang out, one that she recognized as that of Lady Penelope Cromwell, the previous king's mistress.

"To the dungeons with them," she commanded. "Henry," she continued, "have them kept separate from each other, we don't want them conspiring."

Nicole felt a hand grip her face, lifting her chin and tilting her head back. She kept her eyes closed, still intent on playing her part. A stinging slap brought her eyes wide open. Marshal-General Roland Valmar, Duke of Eastwood, stood over her, his hand preparing for another strike. He waited while her eyes focused and then delivered the expected blow.

"You've performed your services adequately," he said, dropping a small bag of coins into her lap. "You are no longer of any use to me. Take your coins and disappear. If I ever set eyes on you again, it'll be the end of you."

She looked down at the purse, grabbing it and clutching it to her chest. It was more than she had expected for this particular job; even surviving was miraculous, but still, it felt wrong, being a part of what had transpired here this evening. She raised her face again to look at Valmar, to ask what was going to happen to them, but another stinging slap knocked her from her chair.

"Begone, harlot," he commanded, "or I'll give you even more marks across your back."

Nicole rose from the ground, her body shaking with fear. Valmar was not a man to be trifled with; the scars on her back were a constant reminder of that. Lowering her eyes, lest she provoke him further, she hustled from the room, avoiding the Royal Guards as they disarmed the fallen knights before pulling them from their seats. Nicole had to stop at the door to make way for two soldiers carrying an unconscious Dame Levina through the doorway.

She fled down the hallway, concerned only with escaping before Valmar changed his mind, finally halting to compose herself after weaving through the twisted halls of the Palace. She leaned back against a wall, looking to the ceiling for inspiration but it was all for naught. She shook her hands, trying somehow, to rid herself of any feeling of responsibility that lingered. Looking around, she found herself in a hallway, somewhere in the Palace, though in her haste to escape she had paid no attention to where she was going.

Footsteps approached from the end of the hallway, and her heart nearly burst from her chest. Spotting a door opposite, she pushed it open, revealing a small sleeping chamber. She squeezed through the doorway, closing the door behind her until it was only open a sliver. She peered out, watching as the noises drew closer. The heavy footfalls of the soldiers moved past the door, a body hanging between them, likely one of the Knights of the Hound.

'I must stay here,' she thought, 'there is nothing I can do now.'

As she turned to plan her own escape, she noticed the unconscious knight was none other than Sir Arnim Caster; her Arnim!

Before Nicole even knew what she was doing, she stepped from the room, hoisted her skirt and pulled the slim dagger from her garter. It took only three steps to close the distance and then she drove the knife into the neck of one of the soldiers. Her victim collapsed almost instantly, while Sir Arnim, now bereft of one of his supporters, crashed to the floor.

The second soldier cursed as his burden dropped. He looked to his right in astonishment when his companion fell to the floor alongside their prisoner. Nicole struck again with the dagger, this time slicing across the remaining guard's arm, but the chainmail links easily deflected the blade. He jumped back, drawing his sword as he did so, ready for her next attack.

Nicole leaned forward, attempting to stab him in the gut, but the soldier agilely twisted aside, his sword opening a huge gash on her right arm, causing the knife to tumble from her hand. She stumbled back, falling to the floor as her feet became entangled with the bodies on the ground. The soldier loomed over her as she scrambled to extricate herself, her hands searching left and right, struggling for support.

She kicked out violently at the man's groin. At the moment of impact, she watched his eyes bulge in agony as he bent over, grabbing himself. Taking advantage of his momentary distraction, she found her dagger, sat up and sliced it across the guard's throat. The wounded man grabbed his neck with both hands in a hopeless gesture to stem the flow of blood. She rolled to the side to avoid being pinned beneath him as he collapsed to the floor, gurgling.

Nicole looked up and down the hallway, but no one came running. She knew it was only a matter of time before somebody discovered the dead guards, so she moved quickly to inspect Arnim. He lay in a heap on the floor, his drugged state making him unaware of his surroundings.

Rolling him over, she grabbed him under the armpits and began dragging him. It was at this moment that she remembered the wound to her arm, for he was heavy and the cut throbbed painfully. Knowing she couldn't get far, she made for the closest room, leaning him against the wall while she examined the door. Thanking Saxnor it was not locked, she opened it to peer into a small room, seeing a bench seat with a hole in it, obviously a garderobe. Turning around, she grabbed Arnim and dragged him into the small confines, closing the door behind them.

Raised on the streets, she knew if she could only get them to the slums they would be safe enough, at least for now. The biggest question was how to get safely out of the Palace. Her time was limited; once the bodies were found, the search would be on. Inspecting the wooden seat before her, she lifted the lid to look into the space below. It was full of Human waste, but it was still big enough for them to hide in.

Nicole looked back to the fallen Knight of the Hound and made up her mind. Arnim was a toughened warrior; it would be hard to carry him and his armour too. She began undoing the straps of his chainmail, the better to lighten the load.

The armour dropped down into the filth, making a splash as it hit bottom. It appeared the sewage here was not as deep as it looked, and she silently thanked the Gods. Dragging him over the hole, she lowered him as best she could, holding his arms as his feet touched bottom, then she let go, his body splashing into the muck as he landed. She quickly climbed down through the hole, replacing the wooden seat, and dropped down beside him, grabbing him lest he fall over and drown.

The smell was overwhelming, even with her cold, and she silently thanked Saxnor for her stuffed nose. It was dark, far darker than she would have imagined. She felt around the edge of the pit seeking a hatch or doorway; surely someone had to clean out this area from time to time.

Pausing in her efforts to catch her breath, she heard the sound of running water. Drawn by the noise, she followed it with her hands until encountering a metal grate on the far wall. It ran from the floor, halfway up the wall and she realized it must lead to the sewer. She tried pushing and pulling, but it didn't budge. Running her fingers along the edges, she discovered a padlock.

Nicole's mind raced as she tried to think things through. First, she must free up her legs, and to do that she took her dagger and began cutting away at the hem of her dress. Once free of the cumbersome attire, she tossed the rags aside and reached for her right garter. Here, in a small leather pouch, lay her lock picking tools. Opening it carefully, she withdrew a slender pick but cursed as she nearly dropped it when her injured arm throbbed with pain. Grasping it more firmly, she reached through the grate and inserted the pick, twisting it to unlock the tumblers.

Sitting in the dark, it seemed to take forever, and she feared it might never succumb to her ministrations. An unexpected sound from above froze her. Someone opened the door to the privy, and then there were two voices, likely guards, and she held her breath. It was only a moment before they left, slamming the door shut behind them, but it felt as though her heart had stopped.

Nicole gathered her breath, the stench in her nostrils making it difficult not to gag. A few more twists of the pick and then a satisfying click indicated her success. The lock popped open, and then she reached through to unclasp it, pushing the grate away from her. She poked her head through, but the darkness still loomed; she could see nothing.

The task of moving Arnim was difficult. First, she had to position him so she could crawl past, and then grab him under the arms and pull him through, all the while coated in filth which lent a slipperiness to the whole procedure. By the end, the two of them were covered head to toe in sludge. With the two of them on the other side, she closed the grate, ensuring she clicked the lock shut.

She had done it, escaped the Palace, only to find herself still a prisoner in complete darkness. She tried to stand up but cracked her head painfully on the overhead bricks. Here, the sewer was short, not even tall enough for a man to stand, and she wondered who serviced these tunnels. A skittering sound echoed from the distance, and her first instinct was to discount it as rats. Were there other creatures that lived in the sewers? She doubted it, but one could never be entirely sure.

This tunnel ran in two directions, and Nicole had no idea of her bearings, but growing up in the slums in the capital, she knew safety lay to the south. She thought back to her escape. The great hall that housed the banquet had doors leading east and west. At the feast, she had been sitting by the western wall, and then her flight from the dinner had taken her into the western wing of the Palace. She reasoned that the privy was on the same end of the Palace, so this tunnel likely ran north-south. If this was true, it meant that after exiting through the grate she had only to turn left, and they would logically be heading south.

She found the grate once again and double-checked her bearings before proceeding on her way. It was a painstaking process; the tunnels were slippery, and she had to drag a full grown man. The lack of light here, combined with the low ceiling, made the effort all the more difficult.

She was sure there would be a call of alarm and half expected soldiers to descend into the sewers with lanterns, but none arrived. All of a sudden, she felt a slight breeze and then saw a faint light coming from above; a sewer cover. It was a simple metal grate with moonlight drifting through, illuminating the close confines of the tunnel. She laid Arnim down carefully and pressed her face to the cover. Hearing no sound, she lifted the grate, standing straight up, her back protesting. Her head was just above the level of the road, poking out of the hole. She glanced around, seeing the moonlight glinting off shop windows in the unlit streets. In front of a business nearby she could just make out a hanging sign in the shape of a boar's head.

It was all Nicole needed, for the Boars Head was a well-known tavern within the city. She had made more progress than she realized, though she had little concept for how much time had passed. The sewers didn't run all the way to the slums; in that part of the city sewage was dumped, raw, into the streets. She resolved to travel south as far she could using the tunnels, and then find somewhere to stash Arnim until she returned with help.

By the time the early morning light began to trickle down, she had come to the end of the line. The sewer here was so tight she had to crawl, dragging Arnim by the arm. Pushing the grate aside, she emerged in front of an abandoned candle shop, looking around nervously. The street appeared completely empty, thank Saxnor.

The combination of his weight and her injured arm made the task of pulling Arnim out of the sewer almost impossible. Once she manoeuvred him, he sat, still unconscious, in the opening, waiting for her to lift him out. She struggled with it for ages until his feet finally cleared the hole. Dragging him into an alleyway, she returned, dropping the grate back into place.

Now, she needed to find a spot to hide the knight until she returned. The derelict candle shop was the best choice, so she quickly ran around to the back door. It only took a few twists of her pick for the lock to spring open and she soon had Arnim safely inside.

· · ·

Harry Hathaway headed down the street, a silver necklace dangling from his fingers. As he walked, he examined it, talking to himself.

"Not bad, Handsome Harry, you old rogue. There isn't a woman alive who can resist your charms."

He turned up the side street, dropping the necklace into a small pouch, then withdrew a slender key. He had stopped at a door, ready to unlock it when he thought he detected a faint hissing noise. He paused, the key only partly inserted, listening intently.

Again the sound issued forth, and then a voice whispered, "Harry!"

"Who's there?" he cried out, his voice echoing down the street.

"It's me, Harry," came a familiar voice.

"You'll have to be a little more specific," he replied. "I know a lot of 'me's'."

"It's me, Nikki, Nikki the Knife."

"Nik?" he responded in surprise. "You've been gone a long time Nik, we all thought you were dead."

He moved toward the voice and was suddenly conscious of a stench that permeated his surroundings. "What's that smell?"

"I had to escape through the sewers, Harry; they'll kill me if they catch me."

Nicole stepped out of the darkness.

"By the gods, Nik, you look as bad as you smell. Who's after you? Did you upset another gang boss?"

"No, Harry," she replied, "it's much more serious than that. Can you help me or not?"

"Of course, come inside, and we'll get you cleaned up."

"No," she insisted, "I need you to come with me."

"Where are we going?"

"I have someone stashed nearby, but we must hurry before he's discovered."

"You intrigue me, Nikki. Lead on."

He followed her as she turned down an alleyway. They cut across a number of streets, finally emerging half a dozen blocks away.

Nikki pointed at the candle shop, "He's in there; I had to put him somewhere to keep him safe."

She led him around to the back, opening the door. Arnim lay sprawled on the floor, unmoving.

"For Saxnor's sake, Nikki, did you kill him?"

"No, I didn't kill him, Harry. He's been drugged."

"Here's a tip," offered Harry, "if you don't drug people, they can walk."

She punched him in the arm, "I didn't drug him, someone else did."

Harry rubbed his bruised limb, "Who is it? He looks kind of familiar, but he's covered in shit."

"Never mind that," she said. "Help me get him to your place and out of sight."

He sighed and moved around to lift Arnim, "You make sure the way's clear, I'll carry this sleeping baby here."

"Thanks, Harry, I owe you one."

"If I had a crown for every time you said that I'd be a rich man," he murmured.

"What was that?" asked Nikki.

"I said, it's my pleasure."

He lifted Arnim, hoisting him over his shoulders. "This man's heavier than he looks, and I thought YOU smelled bad. Who did you say he was?"

"I didn't," she responded. "Now let's get moving."

The early morning streets were mostly empty, and it wasn't long before they were safely indoors. Harry carried his burden upstairs and into a room, dropping him to the floor beside the bed. It was dark, and he searched around for his flint and steel to light the fireplace. As the sparks ignited the kindling, it gave the room an eerie glow. He blew on the fire, watching as it grew, then stood.

"I'll fetch some water so you can clean up. I'll be back in a moment."

Nikki knelt beside the fallen knight and began pulling the stinking clothes from his body. Harry soon returned with a bowl of water and some rags.

"I'll do that," he insisted. "You see to yourself."

He began scrubbing at Arnim's arms as he finished pulling the clothes off of him.

Nikki undid what remained of her dress. It had long sleeves, and as she pulled the right one off, blood poured from her wound. She gasped in pain.

Harry turned at the sound. "Nikki," he said, "what happened to your arm?"

"I was cut by a sword," she said. "I was lucky it didn't take my arm off."

He moved toward her to examine the wound, turning her to get more light on it. "You might still lose it," he cautioned. "You went through the sewers, it's likely to fester. Let me clean this up for you."

She waited while he cleaned the wound as best he could.

"I hope he's worth it," Harry said at last.

"He is," she replied.

"Are you going to tell me who this is?"

"His name's Arnim Caster, Sir Arnim Caster."

"He's a knight?"

"Yes, a Knight of the Hound."

Harry stopped what he was doing, "A Knight of the Hound? I've never heard of them before."

"They serve Princess Anna," she explained.

"Isn't that the queen's bastard? How do you fit into all this, Nik?"

She looked down at Arnim, "Look at him again, Harry, don't you recognize him?"

Harry knelt by the unconscious knight, using a cloth to wipe his face. "He certainly looks familiar, but I can't place him."

Nikki decided to put him out of his misery, "He used to be in the town watch. Of course, we were all much younger in those days."

Harry whistled, "He's the one you deceived, isn't he?"

"Yes," she answered, though her voice was barely audible.

"So why would you help him now?"

"I had no choice all those years ago, Harry. I had to betray him, it was my job. My life was on the line, but he never deserved what happened to him."

Harry looked at her closely, "You still love him, don't you?"

"Don't be ridiculous, Harry. I just owe him, that's all."

"Sure, Nik. You go on believing that."

TWO

Anna

SUMMER 961 MC

S creams echoed down the hallway, bouncing off the cold stone walls, making their way to where Anna, Princess of Merceria, lay huddled on the floor. She held her hands over her ears, but the sounds of agony pierced her heart. She could do nothing to end their suffering.

She was being held in a cell; a small room, barely enough space for her lie down with no way to escape. The only entrance was a sturdy wooden door with a narrow barred window at the top and a smaller door below where food could be passed through.

She shivered, her thin shift doing little to protect against the dampness of the chilly stones. The screams began anew, this time a much higher pitch; a woman. The princess brought her legs to her chest and wrapped her arms around them, trying to eke out what little warmth she could while her breath frosted in the cold air.

When footsteps echoed down the hallway, she ran to the bars, straining to see who was coming. Two armed guards appeared carrying spears, and then two more who dragged someone between them. Closer they came, and then one of the spearmen aimed the point of his weapon at her, motioning for her to back away. The second pulled forth a key ring and unlatched the cell door while the first kept his spear at the ready. With a creak, the door opened, and the last two men dumped the prisoner onto the floor.

"This is a gift from the king," one of them said. "He thought you'd like to watch him die."

He chuckled at his own words, and then he and his partner withdrew. Without another word they locked the door, disappearing down the hallway, their footsteps blending into the distant screams.

Anna crawled forward, toward the body in front of her. It was slumped, face down, but she instantly knew who it was.

"Gerald!" she cried out, her coldness forgotten.

She rolled him over. His face was battered and swollen, with a large gash over his right eye. Blood seeped from his mouth, while his body was covered in cuts and bruises. What clothes he still wore were tattered; his shirt, ripped front and back, revealed deep lacerations to his flesh.

She rolled him onto his side to let the blood flow freely from his mouth, afraid he might choke to death on it. She put her ear to his chest and thankfully heard a faint heartbeat.

She tried to think, but the numbing cold and the drowsiness that clouded her mind were working against her. Forgetting her own misfortune, she began pulling at the remains of his shirt to bind his wounds in a vain attempt to stem the flow of blood.

"Stay with me, Gerald," she begged. "Please don't leave me here alone!"

Unsure how much time had passed, she was awoken by someone else screaming; a man's voice this time. He kept begging them to finish it, but his tormentor merely laughed and bragged about how long the torture was going to last.

Anna was numb; her fingers and toes had lost their sense of touch in the cold, harsh environment of her cell. Her attempt to bind Gerald's wounds had had a limited effect, for there was not enough material left for all his injuries. He now lay on his side, the blood from his mouth oozing out to create a small red pool beneath him.

Once again, the sound of footsteps attracted her attention. It didn't take long for a guard to appear and unlock her cell, the door protesting with a familiar squeal as he pushed it open. Behind him, two guards stood by with spears while her brother, King Henry, entered. Dressed in his most elegant clothes, he carried a kerchief close to his nose to ward off the stench of the dungeons. Looking down at Anna, his face wore a mask of contempt.

"Our father, King Andred was murdered," he began. "I rule Merceria now, and I will see to it that you, his murderer, are brought to justice."

"I didn't kill him, Henry," she pleaded. "Please, you must believe me."

Henry chuckled, "Oh, I know full well who is responsible, but I can't hold onto the crown if I don't have someone to blame. That's where you come in, my dear sister. I intend for you to confess to plotting the murder of our dear, departed father."

"Never," spat Anna. "Why would I confess to such a thing?"

Henry stared at her for a moment, thinking. "No doubt you've been entertained by the screams of agony I have provided for you; your precious Knights of the Hound. I've decided to let you listen to their cries of anguish as they die, one by one. I have a rather skilled torturer employed here; he uses a special elixir that prevents his victims from succumbing to the pain and lapsing into unconsciousness. I've been told it's most entertaining to watch. I'd let you see for yourself, but you might get the idea of escaping, and we can't have that, can we."

"Why are you doing this, Henry?" she implored. "What have I done to earn this?"

Her brother's face broke into a rage, "You interfered in things! If you had minded your own business in Westland, none of this would be necessary." He paused, took a deep breath, and then continued in a calm voice, "No, I'm afraid you've caused too much trouble for us. It's been decided; you have to be silenced."

"You can't do this, Henry," she exclaimed. "You'll never get away with it. When Weldwyn hears of this-"

"Weldwyn?" interrupted the king. "Don't make me laugh. Do you really think they can help you?"

"They'll hear of it," she responded. "The Weldwyn ambassador will surely report this."

"The Ambassador? I think not. He will not be returning home to report on anything." Henry smiled, throwing Anna into confusion. "That reminds me, I have a present for you." He fished about his belt, finally settling on a small pouch. He carefully opened it, withdrawing a crumpled package, then tossed it to the floor in front of her.

"That's what I think of your precious Weldwyn," he sneered.

Anna crawled forward, grasping the paper in her numb hands. She picked it up, opening it as carefully as she could. Suddenly she dropped it, shocked by what she saw. A finger rolled forth, the signet ring of Weldwyn still adorning it.

"This will mean war," she proclaimed.

"I doubt it," said Henry knowingly. "You see, Weldwyn, as you like to call it, is far too busy with problems of its own. Did you look at the wrapping? No? Too bad, it's your precious marriage proposal. Of course, I could offer you a choice, if you wish."

"What choice?" she asked, a small sliver of hope present in her voice.

"If you don't want to be charged with the murder of the king, you could do my bidding."

"Meaning?"

"Meaning I would raffle you off to the highest bidder and then you would be used by whoever paid the most. I know a number of people that would be amused by such a prospect."

"You're sick, Henry," she spat out. "I would rather die."

"I thought you'd say as much. It's just as well; things are tied up nicely this way. Of course, I have a written confession from all your knights to support my claims."

"My knights had nothing to do with the king's death."

"True, but a confession is very compelling, especially when the prisoner is no longer around to argue the point. I've killed them all, Anna, every single one of them."

"You lie," she shouted, "I can still hear their screams."

"Oh, yes, I forgot, we're not quite done yet. I've saved the best for last. That harlot Fitzwilliam will be the last to die. I've been making her watch the rest. By the way, I've killed that nasty brute of a dog of yours."

He enjoyed watching all hope die on the young princess's face, smiling as he did so.

"You'll be dead soon enough, Anna, but not before you suffer. You've angered some very powerful people, people who've been planning this for centuries. You don't upset folks like that without paying a price."

"What people? What are you talking about?"

"I would tell you, but I'd rather you die in ignorance. You have some time left, perhaps you'll figure it out for yourself, but then again, you might not, it matters little either way."

He stepped back into the hallway, and then a guard closed the door, locking it securely.

"I won't come and see you again, Anna. I think it's better this way. Wallow in your despair, little sister, it's the only thing you have left."

He turned abruptly, straightened his tunic, and marched back up the hallway, the kerchief once again returned to his nose.

Anna ran to the barred window to watch him disappear down the hallway, and then the screaming resumed.

THREE

Revi

SUMMER 961 MC

R evi Bloom, Royal Life Mage, awoke to limbs that were painfully cramped, while his neck was pushed awkwardly forward. He tried to straighten it, but the top of his head struck something. Reaching out with his hands, he found himself surrounded by bars. The movement caused him to shift slightly, and he began to sway. He opened his eyes and let them adjust to the darkness, and then slowly, his surroundings emerged. He was sitting in a small cage, big enough only for him to squat with his legs crushed against his chest. Twisting his head up, he saw chains dangling the cage from above, and he assumed they were attached to the ceiling.

Uttering the words of power to summon his magical light, he was rewarded with... nothing. In shock, he concentrated again, trying to draw forth the magic that lay within him, but he was unable to find it. A momentary sense of panic gripped him, and then his intellect took control.

"Magebane," he muttered. He knew of the herb but had never experienced its magic draining effects first hand before.

The arrival back in Wincaster had been glorious, with a celebratory feast. The king had even toasted to their health; oh, how he had fooled them all. Revi swore. He should have known better. Now, he was hanging here, a prisoner, unaware of the fate of his friends.

As his eyes grew accustomed to the dark, he could make out shapes and outlines. Off to the side, light seeped through small cracks in a shuttered window, slowly revealing the room in more detail. One wall was curved, and he took it to be the outside wall of a tower. The small size of this room meant it could not be one of the towers on the city walls, so he surmised that it was, in fact, likely one of the small towers that decorated the top of the Palace. The room was a half circle, with a straight wall opposite the curve, containing a doorway.

Shelves lined the wall to either side of the door, and on the curved side, where his cage hung, there was a work table of some sort, littered with papers and other oddities. He strained his neck trying to get a better view, but his cage was a tight fit, and the table was behind him; he couldn't move his head enough to see it all.

Revi considered himself an educated man, perhaps even one of the most learned men in the kingdom, though he was too humble to admit it. To his mind, one thing was perfectly clear; whomever captured him wanted him alive for some reason, and that meant he still had a chance of surviving his current predicament. Closing his eyes, he tried to relax, breathing deeply to calm his rising panic, concentrating on each muscle. When he finally felt the pressure leave him, he began to look inward, to find his own inner sanctum in his mind.

As peace descended, he imagined himself standing in his home in Wincaster, looking about his library. Why did the king capture them all? They had speculated about a darkness behind the throne. The witch Albreda had even warned them, but they had returned from Weldwyn in triumph, forgetting about the shadow that gripped the land.

He tried to look at it dispassionately, separating his feelings from the situation. He was a Life Mage, and though his training had been incomplete, he knew his very existence threatened something. Did the unknown shadow understand how to use gates? He thought it unlikely. No, it was more probable that his existence as a Life Mage was the problem and, to his mind, there was only one explanation; the presence of a Death Mage, a vile necromancer.

His presumption led him to his next train of thought, for why would such a person be interested in him? His master, Andronicus, had not completed his apprenticeship before the old fellow had succumbed to death. Now, he wondered if the demise of his mentor had been natural after all. Was it a necromancer that had slain him? He knew they had ways of carrying out their objectives without detection, but little more.

In Weldwyn, they had concluded that warriors bane was the ingredient used in two poisonings. Could Andronicus have been killed in a similar manner? He thought back to the old mage's final words. The man had been out of his mind, surely not the symptoms of warriors bane, though he couldn't rule out a different poison.

Revi had to accept that at least he was alive, for now. If his captor wanted something, he would find out eventually. He must bide his time, try to gain what rest he could, and wait for the effects of the magebane to wear off.

A rattling of keys pulled him from his musings, and then the door opened, flooding the room with light. Revi blinked his eyes, letting them adjust. The outline of a person blocked most of the doorway, but beyond, he saw a curved hallway with steps leading up and down.

"I see you've awoken." The woman's voice broke through the silence of his prison. She stepped into the room, placing her candle holder onto the worktable, casting a flickering light throughout the tiny chamber. Revi twisted in a vain effort to make out her features, but the cage kept him still.

"You're an enigma," the woman announced. "You're barely trained, and yet you exhibit sparks of inspiration. One moment you're scarcely able to cast a simple healing spell, the next you're the close confidante of the princess. Or at least, you were. That particular chapter of your life has been closed."

"Why am I here?" Revi demanded.

"Why, indeed?" she mused.

He heard her fumbling around at the work table, seeking something, but his close quarters prevented him from seeing any details. Suddenly, her face loomed in front of him as she stepped from behind the cage. He instantly recognized her features; Lady Penelope Cromwell, mistress to King Andred, the late King of Merceria. She stared back at him for a moment as if sizing him up.

"You have something I want," she said at last.

"What could I possibly have that would be of value to you?" he responded. "I have little in the way of belongings."

"Foolish boy," she said. "It is not your possessions I covet; it's the location of the tower. Give it to me, and I will allow you to live."

Revi was confused, surely everyone knew of his tower. "It's in town," he replied, "I'm surprised you didn't know."

"Don't play games with me, Master Bloom. It is the tower of Andronicus of which I speak."

Now everything fell into place. Andronicus had told him of a tower but had died before revealing its location. He was about to say as much, then checked himself; the only thing keeping him alive was knowledge he didn't possess. If he were to reveal his ignorance, his life would be forfeit.

"I shall not divulge it," he stated.

A look of anger exploded on Penelope's face. "How dare you refuse me," she said. "I could have you killed for that."

"Then kill me," Revi retorted, "and you'll never know its location."

"You are too smart for your own good, Life Mage. You seem to forget, some of your companions are still alive, under lock and key. Will you be so glib, I wonder, when I haul them up here and start killing them?"

Revi remained calm, he had expected as much, but at least now he knew at least some of his friends were still alive. "I hadn't thought of that," he replied. He must buy time, let her think she was making progress, "I shall consider your words."

Lady Penelope stood there staring at him. Revi stared back, noticing she didn't blink.

"Very well," she said at last, "I shall give you some more time to consider your circumstances."

She disappeared from his view, and then he heard her at the workbench. She appeared a moment later, a small vial in her hand.

"Before I go, you must drink this; we can't have your magic returning."

"I'd love to oblige," replied Revi, "but I can't move. I'm afraid I'll have to decline the kind offer."

Penelope's face broke into a wicked grin, "A minor inconvenience, soon remedied."

She moved behind him. He heard the rattling of chains just before he felt his cage lifted on one end while the other dropped, leaving him lying on his side. A hand reached through the bars to hold something beneath his nose. His immediate reaction was to cough, but as he did so, she poured the contents of the vial into his mouth and pinched his nose.

He coughed and sputtered, but the damage was done; the harsh liquid found its way down his throat.

"See? Now that wasn't so hard, was it?"

A knock at the door interrupted her, and she turned in irritation.

"What is it?" she yelled.

"News, my lady," came the reply.

She wheeled back to face the young mage, "I'll come back and check on you later; it seems I have more pressing affairs that need my attention."

"I'll be here," promised Revi, "though if you're coming back, I'd appreciate some food."

Penelope glared at him before turning to the door, which opened to reveal a member of the Royal Guard. She exited the room, closing and locking the door behind her, but the candle still burned on the workbench, illuminating all within.

Revi strained to listen, as the voices rose in the hallway.

"Spit it out, man," she hissed.

"There's some trouble, my lady. One of the princess's entourage is unaccounted for."

"Who?" she demanded.

"The captain of her guard."

"Fools," she fumed, "no one was to escape. Search the city, leave no stone unturned, and seal the gates. No one goes in or out until he's found."

"Yes, my lady," replied the man.

Revi heard their footsteps receding. It appeared not all of his friends had been captured!

FOUR

Arnim In Danger

SUMMER 961 MC

~

Feet moving, the sound of drawn steel, shouting...
   Sir Arnim Caster, Knight of the Hound and Captain of Princess
Anna's Bodyguard, opened his eyes, the sounds of his capture still echoing
through his mind. He was lying in a bed, its rough sheets draped across
him. The sound of street hawkers could be heard in the distance.

Looking up, he noticed the ceiling was old and yellowed with age. His
eyes scanned his surroundings, trying to determine where he was holed up.
The room was small, barely large enough to hold the bed and a small fireplace. The arched ceiling sat above a window at one end, from which the
sounds of the street entered, while the other end had a door. Without warning, an arm came out of nowhere, and then a cold compress was placed
upon his brow. He struggled to focus as someone loomed over him.

Lady Nicole Arendale's face hove into view, but something didn't look
right. He concentrated all his efforts on the task. Her face finally snapped
into sharp relief, and his mind struggled to understand what he saw. She
gazed down at him with a concerned look in her eyes.

Arnim blinked, willing the fog to leave his embattled mind. He remembered the shouts, the feeling of losing control of his limbs. They were all
gathered about the great hall as the king made speeches, then, one by one,
all the Knights of the Hound began to fall. Treachery!

He pulled his mind back to Nicole. She had re-applied the compress, and he was struck by her paleness. She was wearing a simple dress, but he noticed where blood soaked through the sleeve on one arm.

"What happened," he croaked out.

"You must rest, Arnim," she soothed. "You've been drugged. It'll likely be some time before it completely wears off."

He struggled to rise, but Nicole placed her hand on his chest to stop him. "The princess?" he asked.

"They're all gone," she answered. "I could only save you. Now you must sleep, I'll be in later to check in on you."

She rose from the edge of the bed, making her way to the door.

"Wait," he called out, "you must tell me, what happened?"

Without answering, Lady Nicole Arendale exited the room, closing the door behind her.

Arnim tried to focus his mind, but his thoughts kept straying, random memories drifting in and out. He closed his eyes. Perhaps she was right, he mused, sleep might clear his head. Someone whispering in the hall forestalled any chance he had for slumber. That, and his curiosity.

"You shouldn't have brought him here, Nik," a man said. "They'll be looking for him."

"Where else could I go, Harry?" she asked. "I had no one else to help, and you owe me."

"Calm down, Nikki," responded Harry. "I didn't say he couldn't hide here, but I don't have to like it."

"Thank you, Harry."

"Don't thank me yet; you're in bad shape. How's our guest?"

"He's resting. The drugs haven't worn off yet."

"Saxnor's beard, how much of the stuff did they give him?"

"Far too much, I'm afraid; I believe it was in the wine."

"Lucky for you, you weren't drinking."

"I'm not sure lucky is the word I'd use."

"Get some rest, Nik, I'll take care of our guest."

The sound of the door opening was enough to convince Arnim to open his eyes again. He watched the man enter. There was something about him, something familiar, but he struggled to pull the memories from his drug-addled mind.

"I see you're awake," the man said.

"Who?" stammered Arnim, struggling to find the words.

"I'm Harry," the man responded. "We don't use last names around here. I suppose you're wondering where you are?"

Arnim nodded.

"You're nowhere; that is to say, you're in a building in the slums. It's best you don't know the actual address for now."

"How did I get here?"

"Nikki and I brought you here," he said, "but, only the Gods know how she got you out of the Palace in the first place."

Arnim's head was beginning to clear. "Why would she do that?"

"You honestly don't know?" Harry challenged. "I find that difficult to believe."

"I know you," said Arnim, "your face is familiar. Give me a moment."

His host waited, a smirk growing on his face.

"You're Handsome Harry," he said. "You ran with the Maitland Street Runners years ago."

"I'm flattered you remember me," Harry responded.

"You're a con-man; what's your game here? You don't do anything without an angle."

"Hard as it is for someone like you to understand, even con-men have friends. I've known Nikki for many years. She asked me for help."

"Listen," said Arnim, "I'm trying to make sense of all this. How did I end up here? I remember being at the Palace; there was a welcome home feast in honour of the princess. After that, none of it makes sense."

"You were drugged," Harry responded, "all of you. Nikki was nursing a cold, so she decided not to drink, likely saving your life. When your friends started collapsing, she somehow managed to get you out."

"They didn't stop her?" he asked.

"They most certainly tried, but they don't call her Nikki the Knife for nothing. I'm not sure how many she killed, but she's likely got a death sentence on her now, thanks to you. She fought off guards, dragged you through the sewers to escape. I still don't understand how she managed that with the wound she suffered."

"Her arm," said Arnim, now understanding.

"More than that," added Harry, "she took a deep cut. Running through the sewers didn't help. The wound is festering, but we've no healer here to help. I'm afraid there's little I can do for her, she'll likely lose her arm, but she insisted on staying by your side while you slept."

"Why would she do that?" asked Arnim, his mind working hard to digest all this new information.

"You, of all people, should know that," said Harry. "Now get some rest, you look like death warmed over."

With a start, Arnim awoke to the sound of fists rapping on doors.

"Open up, in the name of the king!" the voice echoed from down the street through the open window.

He ran to the window; soldiers were marching along the lane, peeling off, two by two, knocking on doors and searching each hovel. He watched as they came closer, and knew it wouldn't be long before they were at the very house he was in. Making his way into the hallway, he heard scurrying about downstairs and started down, only to stop as somebody came up; it was Harry.

"The guards are coming," he announced. "You need to hide."

"I saw them," replied Arnim. "Where's Nikki?"

"Back up the stairs, second door on the right. You have to hurry; if they find you here, it'll be the death of us all."

Arnim turned, making his way to her room. The door opened to reveal a space much like his own. Nikki lay in the bed, but if he hoped they could make a quick getaway, he was sorely disappointed. She was tossing and turning, the nightshirt clinging to her sweat covered body.

Shouting erupted from downstairs, and Arnim heard Harry yelling back at the soldiers. He must get Nikki out of here as quickly as possible. He walked over to the window, opening the shutters to reveal an angled tiled rooftop. He poked his head outside to look around at his options. The street below was flooded by troops, but thankfully, they were all occupied with searching inside the houses, not the roofs.

He returned to Nikki, lifting her under the legs and back, clasping her to his body. He thought of wrapping her in a blanket, but the sound of the door crashing downstairs girded him into action. To the window he went, throwing the shutters wide open, allowing him unfettered access. He stepped outside, onto the tilted roof, careful to test his footing before transferring his weight. With Nikki in his arms, he struggled to steady himself. Moving to the side of the window, he began slowly making his way toward the peak of the roof.

Nikki mumbled something, but he didn't have time to listen. Almost at his destination, his foot slipped on a tile, and he crashed to his knee, causing pain to shoot up his leg. He struggled to maintain his balance, clutching her tightly, desperately praying to Saxnor for their safety.

Taking a deep breath, he heaved himself back up, and continued climbing, his bare feet gripping the tiles for all he was worth. He had initially planned to hide on the reverse side of the roof, but as he crested the roofline, he saw soldiers on the next street over. He silently cursed and turned back to the window. The peak of the dormer was lower than the top of the building. He manoeuvred his way so that he straddled it, sitting down, his legs splayed to either side of the structure.

More shouts emanated from deep within, and then a man yelled from the window beneath them. Another soldier returned his call from the street below; Arnim leaned back as far as he could, hoping he wasn't visible. They were tossing the place; he heard furniture scraping across floors and things being broken, more shouting and then finally the voices began to recede.

He looked down at Nikki, her pale skin covered in sweat. He tried to comfort her, held her close to him, but all he could feel was the fever that burned through her body.

"You can make it, Nikki," he soothed, keeping his voice as low as possible. "I thought I was over you, but I was wrong."

She muttered something, and he put his ear to her mouth, but nothing more escaped.

"What happened, Nikki? After everything we've been through, why did you save my life?" he implored.

It felt like they sat on the rooftop for ages. Arnim's knees ached, while his arms, holding Nikki, were numb. He was only keeping her safe through sheer willpower.

Finally, Harry appeared at the window, calling out in a quiet voice. "Where are you? They're gone now."

Arnim rose, coming carefully down the tiled roof to the window. Harry took Nikki, laying her gently on the bed as the knight climbed back in.

"She's not looking good, Harry."

Harry shrugged, "I'm open to suggestions."

"Can I trust you?" Arnim asked.

"It's a little late to be asking that, don't you think?"

"There's another knight, a former ranger. She knows how to apply warriors moss; she helped when the princess was wounded in Weldwyn."

"What are you suggesting?"

"If I can send word to her, she might be able to help. She could pick up some moss at the herbalist and meet us somewhere, then we would bring her back here."

"Do you know where this knight is?" asked Harry.

"She's staying at her uncle's farm, just outside of town. Her name's Hayley Chambers. I seem to recall the uncle was on her father's side."

"I see what you're getting at. I can arrange for a messenger to travel to the Chambers farm. You write it down, and I'll see it delivered."

"Any idea how long it would take?"

"I can't say. I need to find someone trustworthy," explained Harry, "and with the price on your heads, that will be difficult."

"You have to find someone, Harry, it's our only chance. Get me some ink and paper, and I'll write a note."

"I hope this works, Arnim. Nikki's life is on the line."

"You don't have to remind me," replied the knight, rather testily.

Harry left to get the supplies while Arnim thought over his message.

FIVE

Anna's Escape

SUMMER 961 MC

~

Anna stared down at Gerald. She had manoeuvred him until he lay in a fetal position, his breathing shallow, but alive. She had hoped it would at least give him some warmth against the cold stone floor, but the reality was it made little difference. She sat there, next to him, watching her closest friend bleeding to death from scores of cuts, and there was nothing she could do about it.

Echoing down the hallway came a scream of such agony, she froze. Something in that terrible wail was different; she had just listened to someone utter their last breath. Anna closed her eyes while tears of despair rolled down her cheeks.

Next, muttering came from down the hallway, and then the crank of some devilish device. This was not the first time the sound had been heard. There would be a break in the torture while they removed the body from the rack, and then...

The young princess pressed her face to the bars in a vain attempt to see down the corridor, but, like each previous attempt, it was unsuccessful. Moving to the rear of the cell, she collapsed to the floor, her back against the cold stone, staring at what might be her last friend left alive. She bowed her head, her shoulders slumping in defeat.

A noise caught her attention; not the screaming of tortured souls or the clanking of the rack, but rather the soft footfall of padded feet. She rushed to the bars and looked out of her cell to see the grey wolf. It stared at her, unblinking and then loped down the hall, out of sight. It resembled the same wolf she had seen when Gerald was missing in Weldwyn! It was Gerald; it had to be!

The sound of the torturer's art drifted once more through the corridor. A guard approached, the jangle of his keys making a distinctive sound. He would often wander up and down the hall, making sure his victims were aware of his presence, but this time a low snarl interrupted his progress, and the guard's footfall ceased.

A moment later, the wolf reappeared, clutching the arm of the jailer, dragging the body toward her cell. Closer and closer it got until Anna reached through the food door and grabbed the man's belt, pulling it even closer. The key ring was her objective, and she soon had it in hand.

She struggled to unlock her cell, her numb fingers finding it hard to grip the keys. Finally, the key slid into place and she used all her remaining strength to turn it, relief written all over her face as the door finally swung open.

She paused to listen for a cry of alarm, but the noise of the attack had been drowned out by the torture down the hallway. She grasped Gerald under the arms and began to pull, but she wasn't strong enough. She needed help, and by the sounds coming from the down the corridor, at least one of her friends was still alive.

The wolf followed along as she made her way down the hall, past a series of empty cells. At the far end was an immense door, lit from within by a flickering light. It was from here the endless screams emanated. Anna took a deep breath, building the courage to open the door; there was nowhere else she could go.

Ever so gently she pushed it open, peering around the edge, remaining as quiet as she could. The sight that met her eyes was gut-wrenching, for just inside was a pile of bodies, naked, heaped on top of each other. Levina's sightless face looked back at her; her eyes plucked from her body. It was as if the knight was staring directly into Anna's soul and the princess froze in fear.

An unbearable scream brought her back, and she poked her head in farther to inspect the rest of the room. A bulky wooden construction lay in the middle, with someone strapped to it, face down. A tall, beefy man, obviously the torturer, bent over the body holding a heated poker, while a shorter thin man stood nearby, watching.

"She didn't last long," the observer remarked. "You're getting impatient. I called it, that's three shillings you owe me."

"I should have given her less elixir," the beast of a man confessed. "I think she died."

"I thought it was supposed to keep them awake?" questioned his partner.

"It is, but they can still die if they drink too much." He tossed his poker to the floor. "Give me a hand here; we'll toss it with the others, then the real fun will begin."

His companion smiled, "The Fitzwilliam bitch? I've been waiting for this."

"Come along, then; these bodies are heavier than they look."

The two men began unstrapping their latest victim, Dame Abigail. Anna glanced to the side and noticed a wooden pillory with someone locked within. The red hair gave away the occupant's identity immediately; it was Beverly.

Engrossed in their chore, the men had their backs to the doorway. The wolf glided past Anna, launching itself across the room. The torturer, catching a glimpse of movement out of the corner of his eye, turned as the beast attacked. Teeth sunk in the arm he used to defend himself, and he fell back onto the rack. The thin man backed up, confused by what was happening.

Anna ran into the room, grabbed the poker and struck at the short one, the red-hot iron sinking into his head while the torturer struggled with the wolf. Anna pulled the poker free and ran toward the stock calling out the knight's name. Beverly was unresponsive, but Anna spotted the padlock that held the wooden boards in place. She dug in with the end of the poker and pried it upward, the metal snapping as the lock came loose.

Freed from her imprisonment, Beverly fell backwards, collapsing to the floor with a groan. Anna came up beside her, slapping her face, desperately trying to get her to wake up.

The red-headed knight shook her head, "Highness? Is that you?"

"We have to get out of here, Beverly, we have to hurry."

With the help of the princess, Beverly staggered to her feet. Behind them, the wolf bit into the torturer's arm, his screams now replacing those of his victims. A table full of instruments sat nearby, and the knight reached over and grabbed a knife, then stumbled over to the rack.

The massive man had managed to throw off the wolf, sending it sailing through the air when Beverly stepped forward and drove the blade through their tormentor's chest. He looked down at the knife, buried to the hilt, while blood gushed from his mouth and then he fell backwards, onto the rack.

Beverly staggered, barely able to stand, her body weak from the effort.

"Bastard!" she yelled. "He killed all of them, wouldn't let them pass out."

"What do you mean?" cried Anna. "How could he do that?"

"He had some sort of drink he gave them. It kept them awake while he tortured them. It was horrific." She turned back towards Anna, "We have to get you out of here, Highness."

"Wait, we have to help Gerald," she pleaded.

"Gerald? Where is he?"

"He's in my cell. He's unconscious; I couldn't move him, he's too heavy."

Beverly rushed back to the table. "It's here somewhere; I saw him using it. Here it is." She pulled forth a small metal flask and shook it beside her ear. "It doesn't have much left. Let's hope it works for Gerald. Show me where he is."

Anna led her back down the hallway to where her old friend lay. The knight tipped the contents of the flask down his throat, and a moment later he sputtered awake.

"Anna?" he croaked.

"I'm here, Gerald, and Beverly, too. We have to get out of here. Can you walk?"

He nodded, and Beverly helped him to his feet.

"Where do we go?" asked Anna. "I don't know where we are."

"I do," said Beverly. "We're in the dungeons below the Palace. They exit through the barracks. If we can make it to the courtyard, we can escape through the sewers."

"But we'll never make it through the barracks. There's bound to be lots of soldiers up there, and we haven't any weapons."

Beverly looked at Anna and smiled grimly. "We have all the weapons we'll need, Highness. They stripped us of all our equipment after they brought us down here. There's a room the other side of the torture chamber chocked full of our gear."

"Then we'll make them pay for this," uttered Anna.

"No, Highness, not today. We're going to get you to safety. We'll make them pay eventually, but I swore an oath to protect you, and that's what I'm going to do. I won't have all those brave knights die, only for you to throw your life away."

"But where shall we go? Henry controls the kingdom."

"Then we'll leave the kingdom. Maybe we can go to the Darkwood or ask the Dwarves for help, but we'll worry about that later. Right now, we have to get you out of this dungeon."

"You have to get her out of here," said Gerald, looking directly at Beverly. "Leave me, I'll just slow you down."

"That's not going to happen," said Anna. "We're in this together, you and

I. We started this friendship years ago at Uxley Hall, I won't let it end this way."

He grasped her hands, "The future of the kingdom is at stake, Anna. Right now, you are the most important person in the land. I'm just a burned out old warrior who'll slow you down."

"NO," she declared, "you're my friend, and I won't leave you here. Either we both get out, or we die here, together."

He looked at Beverly for sympathy, but none was forthcoming.

"I know better than to argue with the princess," she said. "We lost you at Bodden when you were wounded. I won't let us lose you again."

"Fine," grumbled Gerald, "I see I'm outnumbered." He staggered out of the cell, using the walls to steady himself, looking up and down the corridor. "Which way do we go?"

Anna smiled as the old fire began to burn in Gerald once more. "This way," she said.

They made their way back to the torture chamber and soon found the armoury. Beverly was happy to see her armour and sword, though her hammer was missing. Anna helped Gerald pull his old chainmail shirt over his head and then strapped on her Dwarf blade. She partially drew it, examining the masterful workmanship. "I'm surprised they didn't take this," she said.

"They likely didn't get around to it and why would they," said Beverly. "They must have taken it for a child's blade."

"I have an idea," said Anna. "I know where we can hide once we get out of here. Before we exit the city, I mean."

"Where?" asked Beverly.

"Herdwin," she replied.

"Where's that?"

"It's not a where, it's a who. Herdwin is a Dwarf weaponsmith, a friend of Gerald's. He made this sword. I'm sure he'd help us."

"And you know where to find this Herdwin?"

"I do," said Anna, "in the merchant district. But we'd have to move at nighttime, or we may be recognized."

"Oh, I don't know," mused Beverly, "a red-haired woman, an old man and a young lady. Don't you see them everywhere?"

"Can we get out of here," mumbled Gerald, "before I bleed to death?"

"Yes, of course," said Anna. "Follow me."

"What about the wolf?" asked Beverly.

"He's gone now that Gerald's awake, just like in Loranguard," explained Anna. "We need to get moving. Lead on."

Beverly took them through a second corridor on the other side of the torture chamber, which paralleled the first. It ended at a set of stairs that led upward.

"I remember this from when I was brought here," said Beverly. "These stairs come up beneath the barracks."

"Shouldn't there be more soldiers here?" asked Gerald. "It seems very lightly guarded."

"I suspect," offered Anna, "that Henry doesn't want to advertise the fact that he's got me locked up. He's still hoping to convince me to support him."

"That makes sense," added Beverly, "but there's bound to be lots of soldiers in the barracks."

"What time of day is it?" asked Gerald. "I've lost track."

"There's no way to tell," said Anna. "I suspect they would have fed us once a day at dinner time. That being said, it's likely the middle of the night."

"Let's hope so," added Beverly. "We need the darkness to mask our escape."

"How do you want to proceed?" asked Gerald.

It was Anna that made the decision, "I think Beverly should go first. In her armour, she's less likely to stand out. She'll wave us through if it's safe."

They proceeded up the stairs, coming to a solid wooden door. Beverly pressed her ear to it and listened.

"I can hear voices," she whispered. "It sounds like someone's arguing over a game of cards, at least two people."

"Let me go first," said Gerald. "It's dark, and they're less likely to recognize me."

"Are you sure you're up to it?" asked Anna. "Your wounds..."

"They're painful, but I can move. I think I have a better chance of getting close to them. Beverly, you charge in if anything goes wrong."

Beverly was about to disagree, but Gerald opened the door, forestalling any further discussion. They were looking into a common room, the bottom floor of one of the barracks, where tables were scattered about, but only one was occupied. Four men, wearing quilted jackets, were swilling wine and playing cards; two of them argued over the rules as Gerald entered.

"I say that a king of cups beats the queen of swords," a bald-headed man disputed.

His companion, a dark-haired man with a bushy beard protested, his words slurred by his drink, "And I say all swords are high, I called it when we started."

Gerald moved slowly toward them. At least one, the shortest, was dropping his head, the drink having got the better of him. The fourth, however, a tall, lanky individual, looked wide awake and Gerald silently cursed as the man looked directly at him.

"Tell me, sir," the tall one said, in a friendly tone, "do swords trump cups?"

Gerald hadn't the slightest idea. He had always found cards too annoying, preferring instead, the tossing of dice. Thinking it unwise to show his ignorance, he decided to bluff. "It depends," he said, "are you playing with Shrewesdale rules or do you prefer the Wincaster variant?"

The two arguing men stopped squabbling to focus their attention on the newcomer.

"What's the difference?" asked the bushy-bearded fellow.

"In the Shrewesdale rules, the cups are more powerful."

"Why would they do that?" asked the tall man.

"Well," added Gerald, "it's a well-known fact that the Earl of Shrewesdale likes his wine, so naturally cups are high. On the other hand, in Wincaster the king rules and everyone knows the Order of the Sword reigns supreme."

"There, you see?" said the bushy-bearded man, "I told you. We're all Knights of the Sword, so swords are trump." He sat back down, a smile of satisfaction on his face.

"Glad to be of help," said Gerald. "Now, if you'll excuse me, we have a prisoner transfer coming up. I don't want to interrupt your game any more than we have already."

"Nobody told us about a transfer," challenged the thin man.

"It was a last moment decision; you know how Valmar is."

The mention of the marshal-general's name brought the desired effect, and the man appeared satisfied.

"Very well," offered the more sober knight. "Do you need some help?"

"Managing a prisoner? I don't think so. I have a knight with me; I'm sure we can handle her."

"Oh, a woman?" slurred the drunken man. "Anyone of import?"

"One of the female knights," offered Gerald. "She's wanted at the Palace for some...special questioning."

"I'm sure she is," the man spat out, laughing at his own words. "You'd best get going then; you don't want to keep them waiting at the Palace."

"Yes, of course," added Gerald.

He returned to the door, opening it to reveal Beverly and Anna. Having listened at the door, Beverly had donned a helmet and was holding Anna roughly by the arm.

"Come along, then," bid Gerald, and Beverly pushed the princess forward.

There was only mild interest from the card players as the trio made their way past the table. They were almost at the exit when the sober man spoke up. He had watched them as the cards were dealt and now, instead of looking at his cards, he was staring at Anna.

"What's that on her waist?" he called out.

Gerald cursed. In their haste, they had forgotten to remove Anna's sword. He stepped up to the man, his hand on the hilt of his weapon. "Pardon?" he said, buying time.

"I said-"

The words were permanently silenced when, in one smooth motion, Gerald drew his sword, slicing it across the knight's neck. It cut his throat, and the man's eyes bulged in incomprehension as he toppled from his chair.

The rest of the group were suddenly scrambling. The drunken man staggered to his feet, but Beverly's blade sunk into his chest, felling him like a tree. The bald-headed knight fell backwards over his chair in his attempt to gain some distance from his attacker, giving Anna the time she needed to dart forward and pierce his stomach with her Dwarven sword. He groaned, grasping the wound as she withdrew the blade, blood gushing through his fingers as he tried in vain to stem the flow. He rolled to the side and lay clutching his wound as Anna struck again, this time finishing him off.

The last man had backed up and now raised his hands as if in surrender. Beverly was about to strike but held her sword at his throat.

"Sir Preston," she said. "It's been a long time since we were both inducted into the order."

The knight's face showed surprise at her voice, "Dame Beverly? I heard you were dead."

"Far from it," she responded. "I have no quarrel with you, Sir Preston. Give me your word that you will not raise the alarm and I will let you live."

"I swear it," the knight vowed, "as Saxnor is my witness."

"Can we trust him?" asked Gerald.

"I believe so," said Beverly. "He has always been a man of his word."

"Then let us be gone from here," said Gerald.

"Farewell, Sir Preston," said Beverly. "Fortune is with you this day."

Gerald opened the outer door to reveal the courtyard. He peered out into the darkness, allowing his eyes to adjust. "How do you know him?" he asked as Beverly came up beside him.

"We were inducted into the Order of the Sword at the same ceremony. He was knighted for fighting Norlanders."

"What can you see, Gerald?" interrupted Anna.

"Not much, it's very dark."

"You'll never get out the gate," called out Sir Preston. "There'll be guards on it."

"Do you have a better idea?" asked Gerald.

"Yes, there's a drain behind the well. Do you remember it, Beverly?"

"I do," remarked Beverly. "Without it, the practice ground would flood out every time it rains."

"Is it big enough to get through?" asked Gerald.

"It'll be a tight squeeze in this armour," said Beverly, "but it drops into a larger drain. We should be able to follow it out of the Palace grounds."

"I'll go first," said Beverly. "Scabbard your weapons, we don't want to draw attention."

Dame Beverly left the room, walking across the courtyard that lay beyond. She adopted a leisurely pace in case any guards were watching. She stopped by the well and then waved at Gerald.

Gerald took Anna's hand and prepared to leave, but Anna held back just a moment.

"Thank you, Sir Preston," she said. "Your assistance will be remembered." She turned back to Gerald, "All right, let's get this over with."

They entered the courtyard. There was no chance of fooling any guards who might be watching, for a young lady would stand out in the barracks. They moved quickly but didn't run, for fear they would create too much noise. They soon joined Beverly, who had been keeping a watchful eye on them.

She led them around to the back of the well and knelt. "It's here some-where," she said, feeling about in the pitch black shadows. "Here it is."

She grunted with the effort, but soon the metal grate came loose.

"You'd best go first, Beverly," said Anna, "you're in the best shape."

The knight nodded her agreement and then lowered herself through the hatch. Her toes reached the bottom far sooner than she would have thought, her head still protruding through the opening. "You'll have to crouch," she said. "It's quite cramped here."

"At least it'll make it easier to place the cover back on," said Gerald. "You go next, Anna."

Anna climbed down when Beverly moved out of the way. Gerald soon followed, replacing the grate.

"It's pitch black down here," stated Gerald. "How will we find our way?"

"We have to go north," said Anna. "We'll know when we've gone far enough; there'll be moonlight coming in the other grates. We'll have to feel our way."

"Keep your helmet on, Gerald," Beverly reminded him, "you don't want to knock your head here."

"I'll keep that in mind," he grumbled in response.

"Let me go first," offered Anna. "I'm the shortest."

"Good idea," said Beverly, pushing herself to the side to let the princess through. "I'll go second; I don't think Gerald can get past me."

"Keep a hand on her back," said Gerald, "so you don't bump into her, and I'll do the same with you."

They made their way in darkness, as silently as they could. Occasionally, they heard the scurrying of small feet, and the dripping of water, but little else. To Gerald, it seemed to take forever. He was growing tired, and bending over in the cramped confines of the sewer was making his back ache.

Finally, Anna's voice drifted back to him, "I see light ahead."

Soon, they were standing beneath a metal grate. Anna was holding the bars, pressing her face close to them to get a better view.

"I think it's an alleyway. I can see a building to one side."

"Let me go first, Highness," insisted Beverly.

Anna backed up, allowing the knight full access to the grate. It only took a moment for the cover to come loose, and then Beverly pushed it aside quietly. She poked her head out to look around.

"It's clear," she said, heaving herself up.

Anna and Gerald soon followed, and Beverly placed the grate back over the opening.

"Gerald," said Anna, "do you think you can find Herdwin's smithy from here?"

"Shouldn't be too hard. I just need to identify what street we're on." He moved to the end of the alleyway and poked his head around the corner. A moment later he returned, a smile on his face.

"We're in luck," he remarked, "I know exactly where we are; we're close to the Dove. I spent a coin or two there while I was stationed in the city. The merchant district isn't too far; we should be able to make Herdwin's well before sunrise, assuming he's still there, of course."

Anna smiled, "Then, lead on, Commander."

SIX

The Smith

SUMMER 961 MC

The Dwarven smith, Herdwin Steelarm, rubbed his eyes. It was dark out, but his late-night efforts had been rewarded by the masterful blade he now held in front of him. The runes on it had turned out beautifully, and he angled the weapon to see the light catch them. Satisfied with his fine work, he yawned, realizing for the first time how truly late it was.

He rose from the table, stifling yet another yawn, intent on making his way to bed when a faint knock sounded at his door. The Dwarf paused, not sure if he was hearing things.

"Who, in their right mind, would be knocking at my door this time of night?" he grumbled.

He grabbed the unfinished sword from the table and made his way to the door.

"Who is it?" he called.

"A friend," answered a man's voice.

"What kind of friend comes to the door in the middle of the night?" the Dwarf yelled.

"For Saxnor's sake, Herdwin, open up."

Surprise lit the Dwarf's face, "Gerald Matheson?"

"Aye, it's me," came back the response.

Herdwin opened the door slowly, the weapon gripped in his right hand as he did so.

Gerald stood at the door, holding a bedraggled girl's hand, while someone in armour stood behind him.

"Gerald? What are you doing here?"

"We need your help," the old man replied. "Can we come inside?"

"Of course, come in," he beckoned.

Once they had all entered, Herdwin poked his head outside, looking up and down the street. He withdrew back inside and then closed the door. "What's this all about?"

"Thank you," said Anna. "We didn't have anywhere else to go."

"You're Gerald's daughter," said Herdwin. "I remember you, though I daresay you've grown a bit. You, however," he turned to the third member of the party, "you, I don't know."

"My name is Dame Beverly Fitzwilliam," the red-headed woman responded. "I am the daughter of the Baron of Bodden."

"Are you now?" said Herdwin. "Should that name mean something to me?"

"I'm the princess's bodyguard," she explained.

"Princess?" asked the Dwarf. "What princess? What are you talking about?"

"This," interrupted Gerald, pointing to the young lady, "is Princess Anna of Merceria."

"I thought she was your daughter?" said Herdwin.

"It's a long story," replied Gerald. "Tell me, Herdwin, what do you know of recent events?"

"Not much," the Dwarf admitted. "I keep my nose buried in my work, why? What's happened?"

"We just returned from Weldwyn, what you would call Westland."

"I know where Weldwyn is," complained Herdwin. "I'm not stupid, but what has that to do with anything?"

"We arrived in Wincaster to a feast held in Anna's honour. King Henry arranged it, but he betrayed us."

"Betrayed? How?"

"He drugged the food," offered Anna, "and imprisoned us, but we managed to escape. Gerald is badly injured."

"Slow down," interrupted the Dwarf, "you're going too fast. Why would the king capture you?"

"He accused me of murdering King Andred. He killed all my knights, save for Beverly, here."

"This sounds very serious," pondered the Dwarf, "but I've little patience for politics. How can I help?"

"We just need to hide out for a few days," said Gerald. "We don't want to put you in harm's way."

"How long have you been at large?"

"We escaped the dungeons this very night," offered Beverly, "but we left bodies behind. I'm sure they've been discovered. Doubtless by now there are soldiers out on the streets searching for us."

"Perhaps we should leave?" asked Anna.

"No," insisted Herdwin, "you're safer here."

"But if the guards should come-"

"They won't find you; I have a place you can hide, and Gerald is in no shape to go much farther."

"Thank you," said Anna, "we shall never forget your kindness."

The sounds of marching feet were heard outside, followed by the yell of a soldier.

"They're still some way off," observed Beverly. "It sounds like they're going door to door. It won't be long before they get to us."

"Come with me, into the back room," urged the Dwarf.

They followed him through the doorway to see a forge and bellows. The room was a decent enough size, reminding Beverly of the smithy at Bodden. A small bed sat nestled against the wall opposite the forge, with a rough blanket thrown across it.

"I thought your forge was outside," commented Anna.

"Whatever gave you that idea?"

"When you gave me this sword, you were working at a stall in the trades district."

"That's just where I sell things," the Dwarf replied. "I do all my real work here."

"What's that?" asked Anna, pointing at a long lever that was connected to the bellows by what looked like a strange toothed wheel.

"That controls the bellows through a gear mechanism..." He saw the lack of understanding on her face. "I'll explain it later. For now, let's hide you away."

He reached behind the strange wheel, adjusting something they couldn't see and then he started pumping the arm. There was a brief grating noise, and then a section of the floor beside the forge moved, sliding to the side to reveal stairs leading down.

"How did you do that?" asked Beverly.

"It's quite easy, actually," explained Herdwin. "It's just gears and counter-weights."

"What are those?" the knight replied.

"Dwarven engineering," he said in explanation.

"Good enough for me," said Beverly.

"Here," said Herdwin, handing her a lantern, "you go down first. Mind your head now; it's not built for Humans."

Beverly descended the steps, the lantern revealing a fully furnished room below. "What is this place?" she asked.

"It's my home," explained Herdwin. "Dwarves sleep better surrounded by stone. Now hurry, before the soldiers come knocking. I'll close up the hatch once you're all down there."

Gerald and Anna followed, and soon they were looking around at the furnishings. The bed down here looked much more comfortable than the small cot up by the forge. Urns and jugs packed the shelves that lined the wall, while nearby a sizable open-topped metal container held water.

Anna made her way to a small table and sat down, collapsing in near exhaustion. Beverly sat opposite her while Gerald fell onto the bed. The door above slid back into place with a clanking sound, leaving them with only the lantern for light.

It wasn't long before they heard shouting from upstairs. The soldiers had arrived and, judging by the noise, they were sifting through Herdwin's belongings. The three of them sat in silence, Beverly gripping the hilt of the sword, lest the enemy find the entrance. The slam of a door announced their exit, and they all breathed a sigh of relief. Moments later the door opened to reveal a red-faced Dwarf staring down at them.

"They're gone," he grumbled, "though, as usual, they've trashed the place."

"When did that start?" asked Anna. "Dwarves have always been welcome in Wincaster. I even negotiated a trade agreement last year."

"That was under Andred," spat out Herdwin. "Henry, in his infinite wisdom, saw fit to cancel it. Ever since then, they've taken every chance they can to drive us out."

"Who exactly?" asked Gerald.

"The Royal Guards. They've made it quite plain we're not wanted here."

"But you've been here for years, haven't you?" asked Anna.

"Aye, I've lived in Wincaster for nigh on sixty years."

"How old are you, Herdwin," asked Anna, "if I may be so bold."

"I'm ninety-three," replied the smith, joining them in the basement, "though that's only middle-aged for a Dwarf."

"This is quite the place you have down here," observed Beverly. "How long did it take you to build it?"

The smith smiled, "I laid down the plan back in '23. Took me ten years to finish, although most of that was figuring out what to do with all the dirt I dug out."

He made his way to the shelves, reaching up to grab a clay urn. Removing the cover, he reached inside to grab something.

"Now, let's get some food into you shall we, then we'll see about your wounds."

He pulled something out of the urn and walked over to Anna, offering his opened hand. She looked down to see what looked like a lump of coal.

"What's that?" she asked.

"Stonecake," he answered.

Anna took the lump, banging it against the table, only to find it made a solid sound. "How do we eat it?"

"You hold it in your mouth for a moment or two. Your spit will dissolve the outer layer."

Anna looked dubious but popped it into her mouth. It didn't take long for a smile to break out. "It's quite good," she uttered through a full mouth. "It's soft and chewy."

Herdwin offered the urn around the room, "Only one, mind. It's very filling."

He returned the stopper and sat, waiting for them to complete their meal.

"Let's get you all rested, and then, once the sun is up proper, I'll go out and fetch some help."

"No," insisted Anna, "it's too dangerous."

"But Gerald needs help for his wounds," pleaded the Dwarf.

"Do you know Bloom's Herbalists?" asked Anna.

"Yes, I've heard of them. They're a few blocks from here, why?"

"If I were to give you a list, do you think you could purchase some herbs for us?"

"Certainly," said the Dwarf. "You just tell me what you need and how much and I'll see to it."

Gerald opened his eyes, looking around the room. He was lying on the bed, his body in constant pain. Beverly had parked herself in a chair and had fallen asleep, while Anna sat against the wall, her knees pulled up to her chest.

Herdwin was nowhere to be seen, and he assumed the Dwarf had left on his errand. The room was quiet, save for a sniffle escaping Anna's nose. He watched her intently, suddenly realizing she was crying.

"Anna?" he asked, rising from the bed. "What's wrong?"

She looked up at him, her tears having left a trail in the dirt that covered her face. "It's all my fault, Gerald," she burst out, the words tumbling forth like a waterfall. "If it hadn't been for me, all the Knights of the Hound would still be alive."

She hugged her knees even tighter, and he took her hands, holding them in his. "You can't blame yourself, Anna. You had no control over the actions of your brother."

"Can't I?" she responded. "If we'd only run away back in Uxley, none of this would have happened."

"And then," prompted Gerald, "the whole kingdom would have been at war, or did you forget the rebellion? We saved the kingdom, Anna. That was all because of you. You can't let this get to you."

"How?" she said. "It feels like I've had my heart ripped out."

"I know," he said, nodding in understanding. "I felt the same way when I lost my family."

"How do I survive this?" she asked.

"You endure it by swearing vengeance. We can't change what's happened, but we'll make sure those responsible for it are punished."

"I don't know if I have the strength," admitted the young princess.

He pressed his hands tight around hers, "You are the strongest person I know, Anna. You will survive this, we all will, and one day we'll return to Wincaster and destroy the dark shadow that has blighted our home."

She took a deep breath, letting it out slowly, "You're right, Gerald, it falls on us to defeat the darkness."

"There," he soothed, "that's the Anna I know."

She leaned forward, and he hugged her, holding her close.

"We'll get through this," he said, "I promise you."

The smith returned that evening with a small bag. He opened it to reveal a green moss with sparkles of blue. "I hope this is enough," he said. "I wasn't sure how much was needed."

"This will do nicely," said Anna, pouring the contents out carefully onto the table. She sectioned off a small amount. "Beverly, can you boil up some water? We'll need a cups worth."

"I thought the moss was applied to the wounds directly," the knight said.

"It is," replied Anna, "but I read it can have fortifying properties when brewed in a tea."

"What do we do with the rest," asked the Dwarf. "I've never done this before."

"I'm going to moisten it slightly. I'll need some strips of cloth to hold the moss to his wounds. Do you have anything like that?"

"I've got some light blankets I can tear up. Will that do?"

"Thank you, Herdwin, that will do nicely."

Gerald watched as the princess quickly took charge. It always amazed him how she commanded so much respect from others. She was the confident, mature Anna now, not the scared young girl she had been earlier.

It didn't take long for the preparations. She insisted that Gerald drink the brew first. It had a very stale taste to it, and the old man winced as he poured it down his throat.

"That was awful stuff," he complained.

Anna watched him carefully, "No doubt, but it should bring about a feeling of calmness."

Beverly watched as Gerald's pupils dilated. A look of surprise crossed his face as he looked around the room.

"Everything is...distorted," he commented.

"It's a known effect," responded Anna. "How is the pain level?"

"I feel rather numb," observed Gerald.

"Good," said Anna, "because we have to clean these wounds properly before we use the moss and it's likely going to hurt quite a bit."

Anna moved around behind Gerald, who was now sitting up in the bed. They pulled what was left of his shirt over his head, revealing the nasty looking scabs beneath. Anna placed a sharp knife over the first wound, ready to scrape it clean but hesitated. She wanted to help, but couldn't seem to find it in herself to hurt him. She looked to Beverly.

"I can't do this, Beverly. I know what has to be done, but I can't do it." Her hand shook as she spoke.

Beverly stepped forward, taking the knife from her. "It's all right, Highness, I'll do it."

The knight started removing the scabs, one at a time. Anna stood ready with a warm, damp cloth. As the first scab came loose, a yellow pus leaked out. She wiped down the oozing wound and then packed moss around it, almost troweling it in like a paste.

Gerald didn't seem bothered in the least. "How's it look back there?" he asked.

"It's not pretty," offered Beverly as she concentrated on another wound, "but it's working. Hopefully, this will hold until we get you to a healer."

"Where are we going to find one of those?" asked Gerald. "Revi is likely dead."

"Then we'll get you to Aubrey," said Beverly. "Now stop talking, this is delicate work."

It took quite some time to finish the job. By the time they were done, the brew had worn off, and Gerald felt the pain of his wounds once more. The final injuries on his legs required him to stand up for them to finish.

"Blood is seeping through the bandages," observed Beverly.

"That's good," remarked Herdwin. "It means you've cleansed the wounds, and they aren't likely to fester anymore."

Anna walked around her dearest friend, looking him over carefully. "Well, you won't win the country fair for your good looks, but you look much better."

"How long will I be wrapped up like this?" he asked in response.

"That's easy," replied the Dwarf. "Until you stop bleeding for more than two days."

Everyone looked at him in surprise.

"It's an old Dwarven rule," the smith stated.

"Well," said Beverly, "I don't know if Gerald has the constitution of a Dwarf, but it's as good a rule as any."

"What do we do after that?" asked Gerald. "That is to say, what will our plans be?"

"We have to get the princess out of Wincaster," said Beverly.

"I'm in full agreement with you on that, Beverly," said Anna. "The big question is how?"

"I have an idea on that topic," offered the Dwarf, "but it will depend on how alert the guards are."

"Let's hear it," said Gerald.

"Well," began Herdwin, "they'll be looking for a blond girl, a redhead and an old man travelling together. I propose we split up."

"That still puts us at risk," observed Beverly, "and I'm not sure I'd like the princess being left alone."

"The princess is small; I can hide her in my wagon."

"How do you intend to do that?" asked Gerald. "Surely the guards will inspect all wagons leaving the city."

"Yes," Herdwin agreed, "but here's what I have in mind..."

SEVEN

The Message

SUMMER 961 MC

〜

Dame Hayley Chambers, Knight of the Hound and former King's Ranger, threw the spade full of manure onto the ever-growing pile that sat nearby. Empty of her burden, she drove the shovel into the ground and leaned on its top, her arms crossed over its handle. It had been a busy morning, and she wondered how her uncle managed all by himself.

She looked over the modest plot of land that he called his farm. The fields were growing nicely, and she watched as her uncle hoed weeds from between the rows of grain. She walked back to the barn, content that her job was finished, only to hear the distinctive sound of a horse releasing its bowels.

"I give up," she uttered, "it can wait until tomorrow."

She made her way to the small stream that ran by the house, intending to wash, but movement on the nearby road caught her attention, and she halted to watch.

The Chamber's farm was located on the west side of Wincaster, outside the city itself, and just north of the king's road. Traffic here was rare and usually consisted of the locals going to or from the city, but the rider who approached wasn't dressed like a farmer. His clothes certainly made him look like a city dweller, and something about his demeanour nagged at her.

As he neared, he lifted his hand to wave, but his horse bolted slightly, throwing the man into a momentary panic. Hayley smiled as she realized what was nagging at her; this man was obviously no equestrian. The question remained, why he was so intent on riding now?

His mount finally halted, and the man cried out, "Hello there, is this the Chamber's farm?"

Hayley moved closer, "Who wants to know?"

The stranger reached into his tunic, withdrawing a folded paper. "I have a message for someone named Hayley Chambers. Do you know where I can find her?"

Hayley chuckled to herself. "Yes, as a matter of fact, I do know. Who's the letter from?"

"I'm afraid," the man responded, "that would be for Miss Chambers' ears only."

"Are you expecting a reply?"

"Yes, I was told to wait."

"Well, you better get off your horse and let me have the note. I'm Hayley Chambers."

"I think not," the man objected.

"Pardon?"

"I find it hard to believe that you are the person this note was intended for. I was told the woman is a knight."

Hayley put her hands on her hips, "I AM a knight. And a King's Ranger as well." She reached down the neck of her shirt to pull forth her ranger token. Each King's Ranger had one, with the symbol of the rangers on one side and their number on the reverse. Even though she was officially no longer a ranger, she still carried it, for an appointment to the order was considered a lifetime responsibility.

The stranger, humbled by this display, began to dismount. His horse edged sideways, and he struggled to control it. Hayley stepped forward, taking the reins.

"I rather gather you're not used to horses."

The man blushed, "No, I'm afraid not. I do most of my business in the city; there's little to bring me out here."

"And yet, here you are," Hayley pointed out.

"Indeed," he replied. He was waiting, clearly not used to his role as a courier.

"The letter?" she prompted.

"Oh yes, I forgot, sorry." He handed over the letter. It was neatly folded but bore no seal.

She began to unfold it, but the stranger cautioned her, "I've been told it is confidential. You are to share it with only those you trust."

Her interest peaked, she looked over the paper carefully, holding it so that the messenger could not read it. It was addressed simply to Hayley Chambers, which she thought strange, but she kept reading.

Hayley Chambers,

I am writing to you to inform you of a situation that has developed regarding a mutual young friend. It appears that she is attending an exclusive party for her and her closest associates, and cannot leave at this time.

I am hoping that you might assist by meeting with us to talk over plans for her upcoming trip, assuming she can get away.

It is important that this be done as soon as possible as I believe her host has other plans that might conflict with ours.

Please meet us at Aubrey's Quill when the bells announce the afternoon watch change this day.

Your friend,

Drake

At first, she was confused; perhaps the letter was delivered to the wrong person? But no, her name was explicitly written at the top, so it was definitely for her, meaning it must be in some kind of cipher.

"Is there a problem?" asked the courier.

"Where did you say you came from?" she asked.

"Wincaster, miss. I was paid good money to find you and deliver that."

"Are you aware of the contents?" she asked.

The man blushed slightly, "Of course not, I would never do such a thing."

Hayley smiled. The message was definitely a code; someone was afraid of it being intercepted. She read through the letter one more time. Obviously, the mutual young friend must be the princess, she thought. If she cannot leave at this time, she is likely a prisoner.

She tried to think who Drake might be. Back in Weldwyn, they had slain a drake, but everyone was there. She remembered Arnim cutting the pelt from the beast and everything fell into place. Aubrey's quill could only mean one thing.

"Tell me, is there a tavern called the Gryphon in Wincaster?"

"Yes," the courier replied, "it's just off of Temple Square, near the Cathedral.

"Thank you. You may tell your employer that I'll be there today."

The man nodded in agreement and then turned, grasping his saddle. He was plainly not comfortable with the procedure, for when he placed one foot in the stirrup and then tried to jump up the horse kept shying out of the way.

"May I be of assistance?" offered Hayley.

"Please," the man replied.

Hayley moved to hold the horse's bridle while he clumsily climbed aboard.

"I shall deliver your reply directly," he said, kicking the horse's flanks.

Hayley stood to the side as the horse bolted forward, the rider barely holding on. She watched him disappear down the road towards the city, and then she turned and made her way toward the house.

Uncle Wilfrid met her by the door, having just returned from his fields.

"I saw you had a visitor," he remarked, opening the door and waving her through.

"Yes," she replied, "it was a message, sent by some friends of mine."

"The same friends that dropped you off here?"

"Yes. Well, some of them, anyway."

He made his way to the table, dropping into a chair, "And now I suppose you want to go gallivanting off again."

"It's not quite like that, Uncle."

"What's it like, then? You're a ranger, Hayley; it's about time you got back into your work."

She looked him in the eye, trying to gauge his mood before continuing, "Actually, I'm not really a ranger anymore."

"What do you mean? I thought rangers were appointed for life. Are you not happy as a ranger?"

"Yes and no. The truth is for the last year I've been a knight."

Uncle Wilfrid laughed, "That's a good one, I'll have to tell Hannigan." His laughter died when he noticed the look on his niece's face. "You're serious?"

"I was knighted by King Andred and then sworn into service to Princess Anna."

"The young princess that saved the kingdom?"

"The very same, Uncle. Didn't you notice the carriage that dropped me off when I arrived?"

"I was busy in the barn if you remember, but you're not even a noble. You can't be a knight; it's not proper."

"The princess has many in her service that aren't nobles. Her closest friend is a commoner."

"It's not right," her uncle persisted.

"Why not? Are we somehow not worthy to serve royalty? We're more than capable of dying in the king's service, so why not as a knight?"

"But you haven't been trained as a knight. You'd need proper armour, learn to use a sword..."

"I've been training for the last year. I was in Weldwyn with the princess and her party."

"Weldwyn? Where's that?"

"Sorry, you call it Westland."

"Who's training you? You'd need someone highly skilled and experienced."

"I've had one of the finest warriors in the kingdom training me. She's quite accomplished."

"Come now, Hayley, what woman could train you to fight in combat? Women aren't fit for such things."

"Dame Beverly Fitzwilliam," she replied.

Her uncle stared back at her without blinking. "The baron's daughter? I heard she made quite a name for herself."

"She did indeed. She's been training all the Knights of the Hound."

"Just how many of these knights are there?" he asked.

"There were ten, including me, until we lost one in Weldwyn. Dame Beverly is in charge, but we've also trained under Gerald Matheson, though I doubt you've heard of him. He's a very experienced soldier."

She watched her uncle as he broke into a grin, "Well, I must admit to some surprise. Why didn't you tell me about this earlier?"

"I didn't want to burden you; I know how busy you are with the farm, especially since Aunt Belinda passed into the Afterlife."

"I'm proud of you, Hayley, I always have been. You've done far better for yourself than I thought you ever could."

"I'm not sure how to take that, as a compliment?"

"I know I can be grumpy at times. Your father was a right pain in my arse; I was always worried that you'd end up on the end of a rope for poaching. When you told us you'd become a ranger I was very happy for you. Your aunt must have told everyone she came into contact with how proud she was of you."

"I never knew," she responded.

"No, I don't suppose you did. You weren't here very often, off running around the woods of the kingdom, no doubt. It was a great surprise when you showed up here last week, a good surprise, mind you. And now you tell me you're actually a knight?"

Hayley smiled at the compliment, "Yes, but as a knight, I have certain... obligations."

"Go on," he urged.

"I received a note from a fellow knight. It appears that the princess may be in danger."

"That sounds very serious," said Wilfrid. "Can you be more specific?"

"He thinks the princess is being held against her will and that we might have to rescue her."

"And so you want us to go into the city?" he asked.

"Not you, Uncle. I would never put you in danger."

"Don't be ridiculous, Hayley. If your princess is in danger, I owe it to her to help in any way I can. She did look after you over the last year, didn't she?"

"Yes, of course."

"Then that settles it. The Chambers' men always pay their debts."

Hayley wanted to object but saw the look of determination on his face and surrendered, "Very well."

"So what's the plan?" he asked.

"I have to meet my friends at a tavern called the Gryphon, do you know it?"

"As a matter of fact, I do. It's in the merchant district. When are you supposed to meet them?"

"This afternoon, if it's possible."

Wilfrid cast a glance out the window, then rose from his seat. "That being the case, I better get the cart ready. Best gather what you need, and I'll meet you out front."

He started moving, but Hayley grabbed him by the arm, "Thank you, Uncle."

"No thanks are necessary," he replied, meeting her gaze. "Now, I'd best get those horses ready."

He wandered out the door, talking to himself as he always did, "My goodness, Hayley a knight. Next thing you know she'll be marrying a wizard."

Hayley let him go.

The streets were busy as Hayley approached the Gryphon. She halted at the entrance, taking a moment to view the room. Off to the side were a couple of empty tables, so she made her way to one, calling out for an ale. Once seated, she scanned the customers; they seemed a pretty typical lot, commoners all.

A tall, lanky man approached her, taking a seat, "May I join you?"

"I'm afraid I'm waiting for some friends," she replied, trying to be polite.

"Then I'll keep you company while you wait," he declared, turning away from her to order a drink.

"Don't get too comfortable," she said, "you're only going to have to move."

"And why would that be?" he enquired. "Surely it's not a sin to keep a girl company; you never know what dangers lurk in a big city like Wincaster."

"Are you trying to infer that I'm in some sort of danger?" she asked.

"It's in my nature to be protective," he calmly replied.

"Though I'm flattered by the offer, I assure you I can look after myself."

"Says who?" he asked.

Hayley reached into her tunic to withdraw her ranger token, "Says this." She brandished it before him.

The look of shock on his face was quite enjoyable. The man obviously knew the King's Rangers were charged with keeping the roads of the kingdom safe. As such, they had the power of judge, jury and, if needs be, executioner.

"My pardon," the man responded, rising quickly to his feet. "I have no wish to upset a king's man... woman, I mean."

In his haste to depart his foot hit a chair, eliciting an oath that would turn a bride crimson.

Hayley watched, amused as he decided to leave the tavern, most likely to get as far away from her as possible. A wench dropped a tankard on the table, and the ranger gave her a shilling. "Keep them coming; I'm expecting friends."

As the barmaid withdrew, another man sat down at the table. He was of average height, with a clean-cut, pleasant looking face.

"I'm not available," she started.

"I'm sure you're not," he replied, "but tell me; are you the ranger, Hayley Chambers?"

Her mild annoyance was replaced with intrigue. "Perhaps," she replied, "who wants to know?"

"My name's Harry," the man said. "I've been sent to bring you a message, but I need to confirm your identity."

"I see," she said, "and yet I have no way of confirming yours."

He smiled in amusement, "A good point, and one which was anticipated. I saw you dismissing the other fellow, so I know you're a ranger. Can you tell me the name of your friend's dog?"

"That's easy," she said. "It's Tempus, but anyone would know that."

"True," he admitted, "but there is a further question to follow."

"Is this to be some strange sort of question and answer game?"

"I'm afraid it's quite serious. There are forces at work here that would do my friends harm. I need to be sure you're not an impostor."

Hayley was suddenly struck by the seriousness of the situation, "Is it really as bad as you say?"

"It is," he replied.

"Then ask away."

"When you arrived in Weldwyn, who was it that brought the dog in to first meet the young prince?"

"That was in Falford," Hayley answered, "and it was me. We had just disembarked, and I brought Tempus into the banquet. The Westlanders were not impressed, at least initially, and they drew weapons."

Harry nodded his head, "That is the expected answer. Now, I assume you have questions for me?"

"Who sent you," she asked, "and have you any proof of this?"

He leaned forward to lower his voice, "I was sent by Arnim Caster and Nikki, though I suspect you know her by another name, Lady Nicole Arendale."

"Where are they?" she asked. "Are they at Lady Nicole's house?"

Harry grimaced. "No," he stated, "they are at mine. Something has happened, but we shouldn't discuss it here. I've been asked to bring you to them. Would you be willing to accompany me?"

"How do I know you're not trying to lure me into an alleyway to kill me?" she asked.

"Only a fool would kill a King's Ranger."

"Or a desperate man," she retorted.

"True enough," he admitted.

"So tell me something that proves Arnim is with you."

"He thought you might say that. I've been told you have an affinity for a man named Revi."

"What do you know of Revi? Is he with Arnim?"

"I'm afraid not," he said, "but I see my words resonate with you."

"I'm not sure I completely trust you, but I'll go with you to see Arnim. If this is a trap, you'll be the first to die."

"I promise you it's no trap," said Harry.

"Then I suggest we get going. If things are as bad as you say we have little time to waste."

She rose, downing the rest of her ale as she did so.

.   .   .

Harry's place was in a rundown building in amongst the squalor of the slums. He halted at the door, knocking twice, pausing, then two more times. He waited a moment longer, and then inserted his key, unlocking it.

"Just a precaution," he assured her.

The door led into a rather small lodging, with a staircase to the right of the hallway. He led the way up, and as her head cleared the level of the second floor, she spotted Arnim. He was waiting, knife in hand.

"Is that how you greet your friends?" she asked.

"Just being careful," he replied, tossing the knife onto a nearby table.

"Where's Lady Nicole?" she asked. "I heard she was with you."

"She's...not well," he replied.

She heard the hesitation, "What's happened, Arnim? Why all the secrecy?"

"That's a long story," he said.

"Perhaps," offered Harry, "we should sit down for this. If you'll follow me, we'll adjourn to my room," he indicated a door. Arnim pushed past him and entered into the small room. A bed sat to one side with a round table and two chairs against the other. Harry sat on the bed, indicating with his hands that they should take the chairs. "Have a seat and my associate here, will tell you all about it."

Hayley sat, waiting for the story to unfold.

"After we dropped you at your uncle's farm," Arnim began, "we carried on into the city. King Henry had prepared a magnificent feast in honour of the princess's return. Things were going well, there were toasts in her honour, and the mood was celebratory," he paused here.

"So what happened," Hayley pressed.

"We were betrayed. Someone drugged the wine, or the food, I'm not sure which. Our people started dropping. I saw the princess go down, even Gerald, but only those in the princess's retinue were affected. The last thing I remember were guards coming in to haul people away and then I, too, succumbed."

"If that's true, then how did you escape?"

"It was Nikki," he confessed. "Somehow, she managed to drag me out." Arnim waited while the words sank in.

"But how was it that she wasn't drugged?" asked Hayley.

"If you remember, she was nursing a cold and wasn't drinking or eating. It's the only thing that saved her."

"And she brought you here?"

"Yes, her and Harry have a common past."

"I'm confused," declared Hayley. "I thought she was a proper lady?"

Harry laughed, "Nikki? A proper lady? That's a laugh."

"I don't understand," said Hayley.

"Nikki was born and raised here in the slums."

"Then how did she end up with the princess?"

"That was my fault," offered Arnim.

"Care to explain?" asked Hayley.

"I was concerned for the life of the princess. The Black Hand has been trying to kill a royal for years. I thought if the princess had a Lady-In-Waiting who could use weapons, she would be safer."

"But how does someone go from the slums to serving a princess? It doesn't make sense."

"If I may interrupt?" said Harry. "You see, Nikki's specialization was impersonating maids and servants. Once she gained her employer's trust, she had access to their possessions, and she was very good at it."

"That still doesn't explain things," said Hayley.

"I knew her years ago," answered Arnim, "when I was a member of the town watch. I was the one that recommended to Valmar that he employ Nikki."

"Valmar? You work for the marshal-general?"

"I did, but no longer. I wrote to him a long time ago, long before we knew of the marshal-general's proclivities. I was the newly appointed captain of the princess's bodyguard and concerned for her safety. I rather gather that Valmar liked the idea and hauled Nikki in for training before he sent her out to us."

"That would fit what I know," offered Harry. "She disappeared more than a year ago. We all thought she was dead."

"Where is she now?" asked Hayley. "I was under the impression she was with you."

"Unfortunately," said Harry, "she was injured getting Arnim out and had to drag him through the sewers while she had an open wound. I'm afraid it's festering, she'll likely lose the arm."

"Can't Revi help?" asked Hayley.

"We have no word of Revi," said Arnim. "He was there, at the dinner. We have to assume he was captured along with the rest."

"I don't see what makes you so sure they haven't killed the princess," interrupted Harry.

"They used a drug to capture everyone," explained Arnim. "If they'd wanted us dead I wouldn't be here; they would have just used poison or killed us as soon as we passed out."

"That means there's still hope," said Hayley. "How do you propose we carry on?"

"She must be in the dungeons beneath the Palace. We need to get in there and find her."

Harry looked shocked, "The palace dungeons? No one ever gets out of there."

Hayley looked at him, "That's because no one has tried. After all, where would a royal prisoner go, even if they did escape?"

"And that," added Arnim, "is precisely our problem. Assuming we can even get to the princess, where would we take her? Where would it be safe?"

"Weldwyn," suggested Hayley. "I'm sure King Leofric would look after her."

"Even if it meant war?" asked Arnim.

"If not Weldwyn," argued Hayley, "then where? We can't take her to Bodden; the king would send an army."

"Perhaps the Elves or Dwarves?"

"And risk a war with Merceria? No, I don't think so. We'd have to get her as far away from here as possible."

"If we made it into Weldwyn we might be able to take a ship somewhere," offered Arnim.

"That might just work," agreed Hayley. "We'll use that as a plan for now, but the more pressing business is actually rescuing her."

"Yes," Arnim agreed, "and then getting her out of the city."

"I think that," interrupted Harry, "is something I can take care of. I'll work out a way of smuggling all of you out of the city, but you have to agree to take Nikki."

"Nikki?" questioned Hayley. "She'll just slow us down in her present condition."

"You can't leave her here," protested Harry.

"He's right," agreed Arnim. "If anyone found her they might be able to force the truth from her, and then we'd all be undone."

"My uncle has a farm outside of the city. I'll arrange for transportation from that point. Harry, here, will look after getting us out the city gates, and Arnim and I will investigate the Palace."

"How do you intend for us to do that?" asked Arnim.

"How likely are you to be recognized?" she countered.

"I'm afraid they've already had patrols out looking for me," answered Arnim. "Perhaps it might be best if you scout the area without me."

"That's a good idea. No one's come looking for me so I think I can assume I'm safe, at least for now."

"Just don't go rushing in," warned Arnim. "We don't want you getting captured like the rest."

"I'll be very careful," promised the ranger.

EIGHT

The Escaping Mage

SUMMER 961 MC

~

Light flooded the room as Lady Penelope threw open the shutters. Revi twisted his head, as best he could, to see what she was doing at her work table.

"It's interesting," she mused, "how simple it is to brew magebane. The recipe is easy to follow, but the measurements must be precise."

"Feel free to test it on yourself first," uttered Revi Bloom. "I'd hate for you to make a mistake."

She chuckled at the remark. "I see you maintain your sense of bravado, well done. Have fun while you can, Master Bloom, for I fear that soon you will be incapable of such diversions."

"Why is the tower so important to you?" he asked.

She appeared beside his cage, her task momentarily forgotten. Her gaze made him feel...vulnerable, and he swallowed in nervousness.

"It is of little significance," she said, "merely a moment of curiosity, though I daresay some of his research might prove of interest."

"Simple curiosity? I think not," declared Revi. "You're after his secrets. He was, after all, a very powerful mage."

"Is that what you think?" she responded. "Andronicus was a fool, easy to overcome and easy to deceive."

"And so you killed him." The words came out bitterly, and Revi immediately regretted losing his calmness.

"This may surprise you," said Penelope, "but I didn't kill him. I rather suspect he went insane when he delved into spells that were too powerful for his mind to comprehend. It's not an unknown thing for mages to get carried away with their experiments. I must admit though, that his timing was excellent. He not only eliminated a threat to my existence, he also neglected to pass on all his knowledge to his apprentice, a blessing in disguise."

"Surely," said Revi, "you were once an apprentice yourself. Who was your master?"

"Someone who died centuries ago," she retorted, "and his name need not concern you."

Revi was taken aback by the monumental implication. "You're immortal? I thought that was impossible."

For a brief moment she looked confused, and then a sudden understanding came upon her. "Oh, you poor boy, you just assumed I'm Human. I'm afraid the explanation is much simpler than you imagine. Yes, I am immortal, but not through mastery of my craft."

"Your craft? You mean necromancy? That's what you are, isn't it, a Death Mage."

"You're not as unintelligent as I first thought, though I daresay you've discovered this secret far too late to do anything about it. We now control the crown, and events will begin unfolding that will guarantee our supremacy over the entire land."

"You're an Elf," announced Revi.

"Very well done, Master Bloom. I am indeed, though I flatter myself that it is my magic that keeps me looking young."

"How is it that you don't have pointed ears?" he asked, trying to keep her talking.

"I do, you just don't see them. The spell I use lets you see what you expect. No one would imagine an Elf near the throne, and so they only see me in my current form."

"But why go to all this trouble? You could have controlled kings long ago."

"We've been planning this for centuries. If it hadn't been for the interference of you foreign mercenaries so long ago, we would have ruled here generations earlier."

"I'm afraid you've lost me."

"Allow me to elucidate. Before the founding of Merceria, we were a group of dedicated mages. We discovered the magic inherent in using blood."

"Blood Magic is forbidden," declared Revi.

"It is now, but back in those days, it was in its infancy. We learned how to harness it for dark purposes before the coming of man. The quest for power was long and difficult, but we discovered that the most powerful of spells required vast amounts of blood. An enslaved population would provide the energy we needed, or so we thought."

"It's not blood that powers the magic, is it?"

"No, it's the magical energy that beings possess. We feed off of it; absorb it to make ourselves more powerful."

"That's why you attacked the Saurians; they had more magical energy, but it didn't have the desired effect."

"We drove them to extinction," she continued, relishing in the story, "but it wasn't enough, we wanted more."

"And that's why you went after the Orcs."

She nodded her head, "Yes. The energy we absorbed allowed a group of us to increase our powers significantly, but the war with the Orcs was too expensive. We lost many troops and had to halt short of total victory. By the time we had regained our numbers, Humans had appeared. They were easy to manipulate, but then mercenaries arrived from across the sea. The tribes united to fight against the invaders, and then that fool of a King Loran had to go and outlaw our magic."

"And so you plotted your revenge."

"I like to think of it as preparing for our return. Humans are little more than tools, to fight and die at our command."

"If you think that Humans will allow Elves to rule over them, you are mistaken," offered Revi.

"Only a few of us," she clarified. "You see, we've been in positions of influence for generations, in some cases even centuries. The truth is we care little for the affairs of Humans. With us in control, few would even notice. I'm sure the average farmer would see no difference at all."

"And yet, you would use men to conquer and enslave those you deem suitable for draining energy from?"

"Of course, it is their lot in life."

"You'll never get away with this," said Revi.

"You're forgetting your current position," she replied. "You see, we already have."

Her speech chilled him to the very bone. At a loss for words, he simply waited, trying to organize his thoughts as she returned to her work table. A knock at the door interrupted her ministrations, and she walked across the room to open it.

"What is it?" she demanded.

A guard stood before her, his head bowed as if in defeat. "We have a problem, my lady."

"Spit it out, man," she commanded.

"The princess has escaped the dungeons."

Even from the cage, Revi saw the man cringing in fear.

"Fools!" she yelled. "Must I deal with everything personally? Move aside, imbecile, let me see for myself."

She stormed past the soldier, who fell in behind her. They were soon gone from sight, the door still open to the hallway.

As the footsteps receded, Revi looked inward. He knew Penelope had been preparing the magebane and that would mean he was due another dose. Perhaps, if he was lucky enough, he might be able to conjure forth a little of his energy reserves.

Closing his eyes, he dug deep, searching his inner strength to find a tiny spark that he could call forth. It was there; like a small burning ember, ready to be magnified into a bright flame of power. He combed through his mind, looking for the right spell and then settled on calling for his familiar. The snap of the spell taking effect sent his mind hurtling through the air, and then he was looking down to the city below through the eyes of Shellbreaker, his trusted companion.

He felt the bond, a strange magical link that called to him, connecting his mind to that of his bird. He beckoned it, and soon it was soaring toward the Royal Palace, flying around the towers until the link grew stronger. Finally, Shellbreaker flew into the window, landing on the work table.

Through the keen eyesight of the bird, he saw the room in great detail. There he was, suspended in the cage that was his prison. The bird rotated his head, revealing the full extent of the workroom to Revi.

Shelves lined the wall above the table, full of all sorts of objects; bones, feathers, jars holding strange looking creatures, but one item drew his attention more than all the others. A disc of stone, barely big enough to fit in the palm of a man's hand, covered in runes which Revi immediately recognized as Saurian. He had seen something similar to this in one of his books, and suddenly, he knew that this strange object was of monumental importance.

Remembering his present predicament, he had the bird turn its head to look at his prison. The chains that suspended his cage ran through loops in the ceiling and then down to a drum around which they were spooled. By turning a handle, the cage could be raised or lowered, but it was the release mechanism that drew his attention. There was a small lever that ratcheted each time the spool was turned, locking the chains into place, but the gear could be disengaged, allowing the drum to spin freely. He had Shellbreaker hop over to it, but the bird lacked the strength to move it.

Revi, fully aware his captor might return at any time, returned to his own body. He began tearing strips off of his robes, tying them together to make a loop at one end, and then sent his mind back into that of his familiar.

This time, the bird carried the end of the makeshift rope over to the mechanism, dropping the loop over the lever which held the wheel immobile.

Revi withdrew his mind back into his body, the effort causing him physical discomfort as his magical energy was nearly drained dry. He managed to keep his head, however, and maintaining a grip on the strip of his robe, he yanked it as hard as he could, to great success.

With the lever released, the cage fell to the floor with a crash, the structure splitting apart with the impact. Freed from his prison, Revi rolled onto his hands and knees, his body cramped and sore. As he stood, straightening his back, he felt his bones complain after such a long period of immobility. Struggling to make his body do his bidding, he staggered over to the work table, grabbing the stone disc before hurriedly looking around.

There were no sounds of returning guards or Penelope herself, but he knew this opportunity would not last long. He rushed to the window to see the sun beginning to set. Looking down, he clearly saw the rooftop of the Palace below, a drop of only ten feet or so. He sent his familiar out the window and then followed, perching on the small sill as he prepared to jump.

NINE

The Rendezvous

SUMMER 961 MC

〜

Hayley leaned against the wall of the building, pretending to empty a stone from her boot. From her present position, she had an excellent view of the rear entrance to the Palace. There were a good number of soldiers in evidence, and she assumed that someone had raised the alarm. She pulled her boot back on and started walking towards the back gate, hoping to learn more. The guard at the gate looked uninterested with her approach but soon changed his mind as she presented her ranger token.

"Trouble?" she asked.

"Escaped prisoner," he replied. "The whole guard's been called out."

"Did they say who escaped?"

"No, but it must be someone important. All the knights have been roused, not just the foot soldiers."

"Perhaps I can help," she volunteered. "I am a King's Ranger, after all."

He looked at her for only a moment and then nodded his head. "Good idea. You'd best report to the marshal-general's office, it's down that way." He pointed to a door at the other end of the courtyard.

"I will," she promised, passing through the gate.

She was in the barracks area now. To the right, she saw the cluster of buildings where Knights of the Sword were billeted. To the left was a well, along with a blacksmith's shop, though it appeared empty at the moment. Straight ahead was an archway that led into the Palace itself. She had heard

Dame Beverly describe the area before and stopped to look around as the light of day began to fade.

A commotion broke out at one of the barracks buildings and then a door opened, spilling a group of knights out into the courtyard.

"Get a move on," a woman's voice screeched, "and leave no stone unturned. I want them found, do you hear me?"

Hayley moved into the shadow of the smithy to watch, fascinated, as Lady Penelope Cromwell came into view, her face a mask of rage as she turned toward the Palace. Two men followed her, one of them barking out commands to the knights in front.

"We shall find them, my lady," the other promised.

"Be sure you do," she swore, "or the king shall have your head! As soon as you find anything, come to me, I will be in my tower."

"Yes, my lady."

The mention of a tower drew Hayley's eyes to the top of the Palace. There were four such towers and though they were not fortified like those that made up the city's defenses, they were still formidable in their own right.

She half expected soldiers to be clambering along the top of the Palace, but her scan revealed only a single individual. He was running along the rooftop, clutching his robes as he went and she instantly recognized the unusual gait; it was none other than Revi Bloom himself.

She immediately looked back to the courtyard, lest her staring draw attention. What on earth was Revi doing running across the roof? He was heading westward, she assumed, to avoid being seen from the barracks to the north where troops were often on guard. She waited until Penelope disappeared back into the Palace before returning to the guard house. The sentinel looked surprised at her sudden return.

"We've been ordered out to search the immediate area," she hastily explained.

He quickly waved her through, looking back into the courtyard, expecting more men to follow.

Hayley cut to her left, making her way along the outer wall, toward the western end of the Palace grounds, taking her past a stable where a group of knights were struggling with a horse. One of them tried to mount it, but the great beast was bucking and biting, resisting his best efforts. She paused when she realized it was Beverly's horse, Lightning.

One of the knights stepped forward with a saddle, but Lightning reared up, kicking out with his front legs. The hooves connected and a sound like a bell rang out as they hit the man's chest plate, sending him sprawling to the ground.

Hayley couldn't resist and whistled. The great beast surged forward, jerking the reins from the man who stood nearby. She waved her hands, and the horse ran straight towards her, its great bulk seeming to fill the street. Hayley had ridden horses before, had even helped Beverly with this very same beast, and yet, the spectre of the mighty Mercerian Charger coming directly at her was terrifying. She dove to the side of the road, coming up again to see Lightning patiently waiting for her. She scrambled to her feet and leaped onto the horse's back.

The knights recovered themselves and began waving their hands while yelling at her. "He's too dangerous," they warned. "Get off him before you get hurt."

Hayley squeezed him gently with her calves like she had seen Beverly do so many times, and the powerful horse exploded into a gallop. Fighting to hold onto his mane as he tore down the street, she hung on until his speed slowed and then she reached forward to grab the reins that dangled in front of him. Finally able to control him, she glanced back, and realized how far they had travelled; they were safe, for now.

She turned Lightning to the south, following along the edge of the Palace, looking up, trying to detect where Revi was. There, in the shadows, a dark shape moved. Halting Lightning, she dropped from his back and drew her bow, nocking her arrow the moment she landed. The mage kept climbing, growing ever closer to the ground, using the ornamentation on the Palace itself to slowly descend.

She carefully aimed and let fly, the arrow sailing across the open area, striking a stone close to the target. A pale face glanced in her direction, and she waved. A moment later, the figure dropped to the ground and started running toward her, revealing the smiling face of the Master Mage, Revi Bloom.

"Am I so glad to see you," he said, and then he noticed the horse. "And you brought transportation. How excellent."

"Come on," she urged, "we don't have much time. We still have to find the princess, she's somewhere inside."

"Forget it," said Revi, "the princess has escaped, I just heard."

"Then we'd best get you out of here."

She mounted Lightning, offering her hand to the mage.

"Where are we going?" he asked, as he settled in behind her.

"That's a complicated story," she replied, digging in with her heels. "First, we're going to stash this horse, then we're going to meet up with Arnim."

"Arnim? I heard he escaped. Have you found out about anyone else?"

"I'm afraid not," she replied, "but let's get you to safety, and then we will discuss things in more detail."

"Lead on," he urged.

The sound of Lightning's hooves echoed down the cobblestones.

Arnim fretted. He wasn't used to having to wait. He considered himself a man of action, taking fate into his own hands, but having to wait on someone else made him nervous, and he briefly understood how people felt when loved ones went off to war.

His thoughts were interrupted by Harry opening the door downstairs, and then footsteps grew closer, with Harry leading someone up the stairs, two at a time.

"Revi," called out Arnim, "you're the last person I expected to see."

The mage came forward to grasp the knight's hand. "Good to see you well, Arnim," he said. "I hear Nicole is injured?"

"Yes," confirmed the knight, "she's through here. She took a nasty wound rescuing me. I fear her arm has become infected."

Revi stepped into the room to see Nikki laying the bed, as pale as moonlight. Damp sheets clung to her heavily perspiring body, and her bandaged forearm leaked a brownish discharge.

The Life Mage immediately stepped forward, placing a hand onto her forehead. "She's quite sick," he pronounced.

"Can you heal her?" asked Arnim.

"Ordinarily, yes, but I've been dosed with magebane. What little magical energy I had was used in my escape from the tower."

A look of frustration crossed Arnim's face, "So it's all for naught then, Nikki won't make it."

"Let's not be hasty in making pronouncements," said Revi. "Even without my magic, I can do something, my parents are herbalists, you know."

"What can we do to help?" offered Hayley, coming through the door.

"We need to make her comfortable. Open the door, let some fresh air in and let's get this bandage off her arm. I'd like to bathe it, see if we can't remove some of the corruption."

"Will that work?" asked Arnim.

Revi halted his examination to look at the knight. "We only have to buy time, my friend. My power will return shortly, it merely takes time. It's like recovering from a night of celebration. Not long from now I'll be able to cast some healing magic."

"Will that cure the putrefaction?" asked Hayley.

"The flesh will be restored, but any disease that's taken hold will still be there. In any event, it will make her stronger, more able to resist its effects."

"Will she be able to travel?" asked Arnim. "We have to get out of Wincaster as soon as possible."

"Yes," said Revi, "though she won't have much stamina to begin with."

"I've arranged transportation," Hayley informed them. "My uncle stands by, ready with a horse and cart at one of the local stables."

"Yes," added Revi, "we also dropped a horse there."

Arnim looked surprised. "What horse?"

"Hayley found Dame Beverly's horse," Revi explained.

"Lightning?" enquired Arnim.

"Yes," confirmed Hayley. "I can only surmise that if the princess has escaped, as Revi indicated, that Beverly is with her. They probably assumed she might try to regain her mount."

"Hold on," interrupted Arnim, a look of annoyance on his face. "Did you say the princess escaped? You might have started with that."

"Sorry," said Revi, "I was more concerned with Lady Nicole's injuries. Yes, I heard the guards telling Lady Penelope that the princess had escaped. From the sound of it, I'd say there was a group that got out, though I can't be sure who that might include."

"I think we should assume that Beverly was with her, or else why worry about her horse?"

"Makes sense," agreed Arnim. "Let's hope they're still at large."

"The question now," remarked Revi, "is how we find them and then get out of the city."

"Getting out of the city won't be too hard," said Harry. "I have some connections among the gate guards. You'll go out the gate in two batches; Arnim and Revi will go with Nikki and Hayley's uncle while Hayley, you'll ride a horse."

"Won't they be looking for Lightning?" asked Arnim. "He is, after all, a Mercerian Charger, rather a distinctive breed."

"I've thought of that," said Hayley. "My uncle is going to discolour him and hook him up as a draft horse. I'll ride the real farm horse through the gate."

"What if they stop you?" asked Revi, a look of concern on his face.

"That's sweet of you to worry," she said, touching his cheek, "but I'm a ranger, remember?"

He smiled at her touch, "That's all well and good, but how do we find the princess? The whole city will be looking for her."

"We can't do anything for her at the moment, but she's very resourceful. I suspect that even as we talk, she's making her way out of the city," suggested Hayley.

"So how do we locate her?" Arnim pressed.

"If you were the princess," asked Harry, "what would you do?"

"I'd look for friends that could help me," Arnim answered.

"Yes, but who can the princess trust?" pressed Revi. "The people she knows best were captured with her, and she likely doesn't know we've escaped ourselves."

"She knows my uncle's farm," offered Hayley. "You dropped me off on the way into Wincaster."

"Do you think it's likely?" asked Revi.

"We can hope," said Arnim, "but hope is all we have to go on at the moment."

"So be it," declared Revi. "We'll smuggle ourselves out of the city and rendezvous with the princess at the farm."

"When will that be?" asked Harry, only to receive a look of annoyance from Arnim. "I only ask because I have to make some arrangements if you want to pass through the gates unmolested, and I have to know who's on duty to make them."

"Send your men to find out now, Harry," said Revi. "I should be able to cast healing shortly, at least enough to get Nikki moving. Once we're at the farm, I'll be able to do more."

"What about you, Harry?" asked Arnim. "You've been very helpful to us. I should hate to see you punished by the king."

"Don't worry about me, Captain, I can look after myself. Now, you'll have to excuse me, I've got work to do."

Harry left to make preparations, leaving Hayley, Arnim and Revi alone in the room. Revi was staring off blankly.

"Something wrong?" asked Hayley.

"I seem to have forgotten something," he mused.

"What?"

"If I knew that, I wouldn't have forgotten it," he chided her.

Hayley stood and began looking around the room. "We need to find you some clothes. A wizard's robe is a little obvious, don't you think?"

"But I like the freedom," he objected.

"There's some clothes over here by the bed. Come on, take off your robe and let's get you dressed."

Revi blushed.

Hayley, surprised at his reaction, gaped at him.

"Can you turn around?" he requested.

"Why?" she retorted. "It's not like I haven't seen a man naked before."

"You haven't seen THIS man naked before," he stammered.

"You're right, hurry up then," she leered at him.

"You're enjoying this far too much."

"I am," she smiled and then finally turned around.

He pulled the robe over his head, tossing it onto the bed. As he did so, they all heard the sound of something heavy hitting the mattress.

"What's that?" asked Hayley, turning around.

"That's what I forgot, the disc!" the excited mage shouted.

Hayley dug through the robes, "Just exactly how many pockets do you have in this thing?"

"Many," Revi replied. "It's how we mages carry everything we need."

She finally found the object; a flat stone disc. "What in the Afterlife is this?"

It was a round disc that easily fit the palm of her hand, embossed with strange looking symbols that appeared vaguely familiar.

"Where have I seen these markings before?" she asked.

"In Tivilton," replied Revi, "in the Saurian ruins."

"Where did you get this?"

"Lady Penelope had it in her study where she was holding me prisoner."

"Do you have any idea what it is?"

"I suspect it's a decoder of sorts. There are marks around the perimeter that remind me of ley lines. I believe it reveals the location of the Saurian city."

Hayley turned her attention from the disc to Revi. "That's incredible news," she said.

"Yes, I thought so too, but there's still one problem."

"Here it comes," remarked Arnim.

The mage, startled by the observation, looked to the knight.

"There's always some problem, Revi," continued Arnim. "You're always on the cusp of a great discovery."

"I realize that," admitted the mage, "but this is the final piece."

"So we know where the Saurian city is now?" prompted Hayley.

"Not exactly, no," said Revi.

"Make your mind up, mage," complained Arnim. "Either you know where it is, or you don't. Which one is it?"

"I have the reference points, but I need a map to overlay it on."

"So let me get this straight," clarified Arnim, "all we need is an ancient map that this stone is made to work with?"

"No," objected Revi. "It's much simpler than that. Any map of Merceria should do, as long as it shows the ley lines. I can adjust for scale."

"And where do we find such a map?" asked Hayley.

"That's the part you're not going to like."

"Let's hear it," said Arnim, crossing his arms.

"My house."

"Your house?" exclaimed Arnim.

"You can't be serious," remarked Hayley. "There'll be guards, it wouldn't be safe."

"Nevertheless, if we want to get away from here, I'll have to retrieve some notes from my house."

"We'll just flee west, Revi," said Hayley, "and avoid the roads."

"No," admitted Arnim, "the mage is correct. All the roads will be blocked. Heading south toward the swamp would never be expected, but it would be useless to attempt without the map."

"So we sneak into his house," stated Hayley.

"It would seem so," agreed Arnim.

"When?" asked the ranger.

"I would suggest as soon as possible," interjected Revi. "And let's not tell Harry. If he knew we intended to head south, it might be dug out of him."

"We have to go now, while it's still dark," uttered Arnim.

"Then we'll go now, grab your weapons," said Hayley.

"Aren't you forgetting one tiny detail?" asked Revi.

"What?" they both answered in unison.

"I still need to put some clothes on."

Their progress through the city was swift, aided by the deep shadows cast by the moon. Soon, they were behind Revi's house, looking at the two guards positioned at his back door.

"I'll take out the one on the left," Arnim whispered.

"No," said Hayley. "We need to take them both out at the same time, or they'll raise the alarm."

"How do we do that?" asked Arnim.

"I can drop one with my bow. Revi, do you have enough power to put the other one to sleep?"

"I doubt it, but I can make him drowsy."

"That's fine," said Arnim. "If he's drowsy, I'll have time to close the distance and finish him off."

"I'll move into that alley over there, it should give me a clean shot. Revi, you'll start the attack. As soon as you start waving your hands, I'll fire."

"I don't wave my hands," he objected, "I gesticulate."

"Are we really going to have this discussion right now?" she asked. "Fine, I'll attack when I see you gesticulating, will that work better?"

"Much," he smiled back at her.

"Honestly, Revi," she said, "you can be a real hand-full sometimes."

The ranger moved into position in the alley, giving her a clear field of fire while the others advanced. She watched Revi carefully, her arrow notched.

Soon, his hands began to move, and she recognized the familiar sparkles of light in the air as he traced intricate movements. She switched her concentration back to the targets to see the taller guard let out a yawn. She let fly the arrow, which sailed across the open ground, striking the man squarely in the chest. He looked down in disbelief, staggered forward a few steps, then dropped to the ground, dead.

The second one, hearing the arrow thud home, looked to see his companion fall to the ground. Placing his hand on the hilt of his sword, he was about to draw his blade, but his movement was too slow. Arnim had crossed the distance at a run, driving his sword through his helpless victim's throat. The soldier gurgled something unintelligible and then fell to the ground.

Hayley rushed forward, meeting the others at the back door. Revi pushed the door open while Arnim and Hayley dragged the bodies inside, out of sight.

The mage closed the door quietly and then drew forth what little arcane power remained within him, illuminating the room with a pale light. It drifted forward, in front of him, as he made his way to the library. Arnim remained at the door, guarding their avenue of retreat, while Hayley followed the mage.

Revi perused a bookshelf, carefully reading the spines as his fingers ran down the line. He stopped, withdrawing an ancient looking tome. He opened it, the small globe of light hovering over it for a moment.

"This is the one," he announced.

"Good," said Hayley. "Now let's get out of here before it's too late."

Arnim cracked open the door, peering outside. "It looks like we've got company," he whispered. "Two guards coming."

Footsteps drew close and then a voice cried out, "Hello, where are you? The replacements are here, stop messing around."

Arnim opened the door, "We're just inside," he said. "Is it time to change the guard already?"

One of the men, a sandy-haired fellow, stepped through the doorway. "For Saxnor's sake-"

His words were cut off by Arnim's steel as he drove his blade into the man's chest. His companion, a little more alert, backed up a couple of steps and drew his sword.

Arnim was left trying to dislodge his weapon as the guard had fallen forward. Hayley dodged past, emerging from the house just as the second man turned and fled yelling, "Alarm! We're under attack!"

Hayley let loose a shot, the arrow striking the back of the man's leg. He fell heavily to the ground, shrieking in pain but it was short lived. A second arrow dug itself into the centre of his back, silencing his calls.

The sounds of yells from the front of the house told them all they needed to know; the alarm was raised. All they could do now was run for it. Arnim dashed across the clearing, followed by the mage. Hayley waited, her bow ready, and shot off an arrow as someone appeared around the edge of the building. Whoever it was ducked back behind cover and then Hayley sprinted, rushing to join up with the others.

They ran as fast as they were able to in the dark, the sounds of pursuit soon dying off in the distance. Finally, they stopped to catch their breath.

"That was close," exclaimed Arnim. "I hope you got what you needed."

Revi held the book up, "I have it here." He stared at the cover for a moment, "Oops, I grabbed the wrong one."

Arnim stepped toward him, his fists clenched.

"Just kidding," said the mage.

"You can be such an arse at times," remarked Hayley.

"And that's why you like me so much," admitted Revi.

"We have to get back to Harry's," interrupted Arnim. "It's time to grab Nikki and get out of here. I assume your magic has returned?"

"A small part of it," admitted Revi. "I should be able to get Nikki into motion, but she won't have a lot of strength."

"Let's hope that's all we need," added Hayley.

TEN

Escaping Wincaster

SUMMER 961 MC

~

T homas Krickland had been a soldier most of his life. For the past five years he had been placed on the western gate, and though it wasn't the most demanding of jobs, it had its fringe benefits, for more than one person would tip a guard to let them pass unnoticed.

This evening had been particularly interesting, for no sooner had he come on shift than word came from the Palace ordering the gates closed. As a consequence, the farmers trying to return to their farms were backed up for three blocks.

It had taken multiple notes to the Palace to straighten out the situation and then, finally, a man named Sir Bullard had arrived to get things moving.

He was an imposing man, taller than most, with thick arms and a massive chest. Being a typical knight, he laid out, in no uncertain terms, what was required.

"There have been some important prisoners that have escaped," he was saying. "You are to let these people through, but observe them closely. We are looking for three individuals. A young girl of fourteen or fifteen years of age, an old man and a red-headed woman."

"That's a very distinctive group," Thomas observed.

The look of disgust thrown his way from the knight was enough to quiet him.

"If I find that anyone has let them through," glared Sir Bullard, "it'll be a charge of treason, and I shouldn't have to tell you what the penalty is for that."

The soldiers all muttered their agreement.

"Now, get to it and get this road cleared. There'll be knights coming through this gate later to search the king's road."

Thomas sighed, it looked like this would be a busy night after all. He waved forward the first in line and began asking them questions.

Some time had passed, and Thomas was growing thirsty. He waved through a woman returning to her farm with some cloth bundles and stepped over to the guard house. He bent over the water trough, using his hands to scoop a drink.

"You there," commanded Sir Bullard, looking at him. "Get over there and check that wagon."

Thomas looked up to see a horse pulling a two-wheeled cart. The back was covered by a tarp, but the overall shape indicated there was much beneath it for it looked as if it were top heavy.

He held up his hand to halt the wagon and the driver, a Dwarf, looked down at him, while his companion, an elderly man, sat beside him. "Problem?" asked the Dwarf.

"What's in the cart?" asked Thomas.

"Take a look if you like," offered the Dwarf, climbing down from his seat. "I'm a smith by trade. I'm heading out to Tewsbury." He lifted the tarp at the back of the cart. "I've got me a portable forge, some sample wears and a large supply of coal."

"Coal?" asked Thomas.

"Yes, we use it in the forge."

Thomas climbed onto the back of the wagon, tossing the tarp aside to reveal the contents. He saw some armour, a very nice looking breastplate amongst it. Picking it up, the soldier examined it in some detail; a small rose was embossed above a coat of arms, but it meant little to him. "This is very masterful work," he commented. "Did you do this?"

"Of course," the Dwarf admitted. "It's some of my best work."

"Why are you taking it with you. Shouldn't you have given it to whoever you made it for?"

The Dwarf seemed to hesitate. It was the old man up front that spoke. "The man that ordered it died," he said, though it appeared to take quite an effort to get the words out.

"A pity," said Thomas, "I suspect it represents a lot of work."

"It does," the Dwarf agreed, "but someone in Tewsbury might like it. I hear the earl there is equipping some new knights."

Thomas was just about to jump off the cart when a voice bellowed out, "Don't just stand there, you idiot. Check to see if anyone's hiding back there." Sir Bullard, who had been busy interrogating a young woman with dark hair, stepped across, pointing into the cart. "There's a cauldron there, it might have someone inside of it."

Thomas looked at the cauldron and made his way toward it. It was a difficult journey, burdened as he was by all the gear stacked into the back. He was about to reach into the coal on top when he remembered how dirty it was. He drew a dagger and poked the coal a few times, digging down the length of his blade. "It's just coal," he announced.

"Then get him moving," yelled the knight, "we haven't got all night."

Thomas waved them on, and they passed through the gate, the little wagon looking like it was going to fall over with its burden.

Sir Bullard returned his attention to the young raven-haired beauty that had initially attracted his interest.

"Tell me, have we met before? You look vaguely familiar?"

She smiled back at him, "Well, I do come into town fairly regularly. Perhaps you've seen me at market?"

"Perhaps," he mused. "What did you say your name was?"

"Evelyn, Evelyn Williams."

"Tell me, Miss Williams, what brought you into town today?"

"I went to market, though I fear there were no good sales. I was hoping to purchase some cloth to make my aunt a new dress."

"I'm sorry you were disappointed," the knight remarked. "Perhaps, if you were to return tomorrow, I might be able to assist you in your endeavours."

The woman cast her eyes to the ground in modesty, "That would be wonderful Sir..."

"Sir Bullard, but you can just call me Bull."

"Very well, Bull, do you know the Queens Arms?"

"Indeed I do," replied the knight, standing a little taller.

"I should be delighted to meet you there, kind sir. Perhaps at noon?"

"Noon it is then," exclaimed the knight.

He waved the raven-haired beauty on and then turned to the next in line. Tomorrow promised to be a most rewarding day.

The raven-haired woman rushed to catch up to the cart as it lumbered down the roadway toward the farms. "Everything all right?" asked the Dwarf.

"Fine," replied Beverly, "although I think Sir Bullard will be upset with me when I don't show up tomorrow. How long do you reckon my hair will stay this colour?"

"Can't say for sure," responded Gerald, "but it's served its purpose. Now, once we're out of sight of the walls, let's get off the road and get Anna out of that cauldron, I can't imagine it's very comfortable beneath that coal."

ELEVEN

On the Run

SUMMER 961 MC

The wagon rolled up to the southern city gate, the least busy exit that Harry could arrange for them to safely leave by. Hayley's Uncle Wilfrid snapped the reins, driving Lightning forward; the great beast was unburdened by the weight and trotted quickly. Arnim, seated beside Wilfrid, looked over his shoulder at Nikki, lying delirious in the back of the wagon, completely unaware that Revi tended to her.

Hayley, following along on her uncle's draft horse, noticed two soldiers come out from the tower. One of them held up his hand while the other stood by, looking bored.

"State your business," the first ordered.

"We're on our way back to my farm-" Wilfrid started explaining.

"I have, here, a letter from Marshal-General Valmar," interrupted Arnim.

"Indeed?" queried the guard, walking around to where the knight sat.

"Yes, here it is," Arnim said, pulling forth a small bag, and tossing it into the guard's hands. "I trust everything is in order?"

The guard poured the contents of the bag into his hand and gazed at the coins for a mere moment, then he snapped his hand shut, quickly concealing the crowns.

"Everything looks good," he declared. "Open the gate."

Hayley let out a breath as they made their way beneath the portcullis to the fields beyond the city walls. They kept heading south until the bulk of the city was enveloped in darkness.

"There should be a road that cuts west hereabouts," said Wilfrid. "We'll be back at the farm before sun up."

"Thank the Afterlife for that," added Hayley.

"Let's hope the princess has found her way clear of the city," said Arnim.

"What if she didn't make it?" asked Hayley. "What do we do then?"

"I suppose we should wait for a few days and then head south," offered Revi.

"Is that wise?" queried Arnim. "The whole region will be up in arms looking for her. The longer we delay, the greater the chance of our being discovered."

"We can't just leave the princess without at least giving her a chance," declared Hayley. "After all, we gave our oath as knights."

"I'm not suggesting we abandon her," Arnim insisted, "I'm just trying to be pragmatic. Yes, we will wait for her to find us, but we can't wait so long as to put our own lives in greater danger. That wouldn't help any of us."

"Fair enough," said Revi, "but let's not get ahead of ourselves. Perhaps she's already safely out of the city?"

"We'll know by sun up," added Wilfrid. "It's still quite a trip, you might want to catch some sleep if you can."

Arnim wasn't having any of it, "I'm staying awake; I'd hate to be surprised."

"Well, don't look at me," said Hayley. "I can't sleep while I'm on horseback. How about you, Revi?"

When the mage didn't answer, she turned her gaze to the back of the wagon where Revi was lying, already deep in slumber, beside Nikki.

Arnim barked out a laugh, "Now that's a sight for sore eyes. Our glorious mage has fallen asleep. Shall I wake him?"

"No," objected Hayley, "he's had a busy day, and we shall need his energy later. He may have more healing to do."

"Fair enough," said Arnim as the wagon trundled westward.

They turned north, and before long, crossed the king's road that led, eventually, to Kingsford. The trip had been uneventful since leaving the gate, save for the occasional snoring that erupted from the mouth of the mage.

They rolled up to the farm as the early morning light struggled to break over the horizon. Hayley dismounted and began walking the beast to the paddock and then stopped suddenly, for there, before her, was a cart, its pony still attached.

Just then, Lightning chose to rear up, making a ruckus, as a dark-haired figure emerged from the house.

"Lightning!" cried the stranger, and Hayley immediately recognized the voice.

"Beverly, you made it!" Hayley ran toward her, the horse all but forgotten, and embraced the knight.

"Good to see you too, Hayley," said Beverly.

"The princess?" asked Arnim, climbing down from the wagon.

"She's safe," offered Beverly. "She's inside with Gerald and Herdwin."

"Who's Herdwin?" asked a now awake and refreshed Revi.

"He's a Dwarven smith, a friend of Gerald's. He helped us get out of the city."

"And the rest of the knights?" asked Hayley, fearful of the answer.

"I'm afraid they didn't make it."

The group fell silent at the news.

It was the princess that broke the stillness when she poked her head through the doorway, "Come inside everyone, we have plans to make."

They filed inside, where Gerald sat in a chair, leaning against the wall. He raised his battered face and met them with a toothless grin as they all took seats.

Revi walked over to take a look at the old man's wounds. "You've taken quite a beating there, Gerald. Does it hurt?"

"That's a stupid question," grumbled Gerald. "How about I beat you about the face and cut you up and you tell me if it hurts."

"I see you're back to your old self," commented Revi, weaving his hands in an intricate pattern. "Now, hold still while I use a little Life Magic on you."

The air turned electric as magical forces built and then Revi's hands began to glow. He placed them upon Gerald's shoulders, and the light passed into the old man's body, gradually dissipating.

"That feels much better, thank you," said Gerald.

"I'm afraid I can't do much about the missing teeth, but you should regain your strength in a few days."

The old warrior cast his eyes about, noticing Arnim lowering Lady Nicole into the bed. "What happened to her?" he asked.

"She was injured rescuing Arnim," explained Revi. "I'm afraid her wounds are corrupted. Between you and me, I don't know if she'll make it."

"You'd best tend to her then," suggested Gerald. "Try to make her as comfortable as you can."

"I will," promised the mage, turning his attention from the old man to wander across the room towards Arnim, who was pulling a blanket over Nikki, a grave look to his face.

"How is she doing?" asked the mage.

"She's very pale," said Arnim. "I'm not sure why. You healed her, shouldn't she be getting better by now?"

"I've healed the flesh," reminded Revi, "but she's fighting some sort of sickness. The corruption of her blood is still raging through her body."

"You have to help her," pleaded Arnim, "we can't just let her die."

Revi bent over Nikki, pulling her eyelids open to examine her eyes. "She's not very responsive, but her eyes are clear. I'm hopeful that rest will restore her."

"She's been resting," complained Arnim. "That's all she's done since we escaped."

"Calm down, Arnim," said Revi, "getting upset won't cure her. She needs to sleep. Being trundled about in a wagon didn't help her either. Make sure she gets some water."

"How do you propose I do that? She's unconscious."

"Wet a piece of material and drip it into her mouth. For Saxnor's sake, get a grip, man."

Gerald turned his attention back to the rest of the room, but they were all talking at the same time. He finally got their attention by standing.

They fell silent while he waited, "Obviously, we have all managed to escape the city. I suggest that in the interest of saving time, we take turns. We'll start with the princess, she'll fill you in on what happened to us and then Arnim, or perhaps Revi can fill us in on your adventures. Highness?"

"Thank you, Gerald," Anna began. "With the help of the grey wolf, I managed to get out of my cell."

"Grey wolf?" said Hayley. "The same one you saw in Loranguard?"

"Yes, the very same. Once I freed myself, I found Beverly, but the other knights had been..." tears started to well up in her eyes. "They'd all been tortured..." her voice trembled, leaving her unable to finish.

"Beverly," asked Gerald, "perhaps you should continue."

Beverly stood, drawing the attention away from Anna, who moved beside Gerald where he put a reassuring arm around her shoulders.

"We made our way out of the dungeons and through the sewers behind the well in the barracks courtyard. Princess Anna remembered Herdwin. He's the person that made that short sword that killed the soul eater in Loranguard."

There were nods of appreciation around the room, for the beast of Loranguard had been a difficult fight.

"He smuggled us out in his wagon. Which is why, before any of you ask, I have black hair."

"It suits you, Beverly," complimented Revi.

"Don't get used to it," Beverly replied, "as soon as we're free of this town it's being washed out; it stinks."

"Um," said the Dwarf.

"Um, what?" asked Beverly.

"I might have forgotten to mention this, but the walnut juice we stained your hair with will take months to fade."

Beverly's disappointment was evident to all, but she recovered quickly. "Then I shall be raven-haired for the next few weeks." She stared back at the Dwarf, "Unless there's something else you're not telling me?"

"No, that's it," he said, suddenly taking an interest in a shirt button.

"Anything else to add?" asked Hayley.

"No, I think that covers everything. How about you? The last we saw of you was at the banquet."

"I'll go over the next part," offered Arnim. "Nikki, that is to say, Lady Nicole, pulled me from the banquet somehow. We also escaped through the sewers but underneath a privy."

They all made faces as they imagined the smell.

"I was unconscious for most of it. She dragged me to safety and then stashed me until she returned with a friend. We hid in the slums for a little while, and then I sent word to Hayley." He looked to the ranger.

"Yes," she continued, "I met up with Harry, he's the contact, and was taken to the safe house. We decided the princess would be held in the dungeons so I was sent to investigate as we thought it likely that Arnim might be recognized. While I was there, I saw Revi on the rooftop, rescued Lightning and then saved the kingdom."

Laughter erupted around the room. "Master Revi," asked Anna, "what happened to you?"

"I was held in one of the towers. Lady Penelope Cromwell had me in a cage. She's an Elf, by the way, and a Necromancer."

A look of shock passed through the room. "Are you sure?" asked Gerald.

"I'm afraid so. They've been planning things for centuries, it seems."

"Wait," said Anna, "Henry said I had upset some powerful people, that's why we were imprisoned."

"It would seem," added Revi, "that there's more to this darkness than just Penelope; she also used the term 'we'."

Hayley nudged the mage who looked at her in annoyance. "Go on," she urged, "tell them about the amulet."

"What amulet?" asked Anna.

"I found a round stone in Penelope's laboratory. It has Saurian runes on it. I think it reveals the location of the Saurian city."

"That's interesting," said Gerald, "but I fail to see what that has to do with our current situation."

"It's more than interesting," said Anna. She looked at Gerald, "Don't you see? It's our escape."

"I don't understand."

"We've nowhere to run," she continued, her excitement growing as she spoke. "Look at it this way. If you were Henry, or Penelope for that matter, and you wanted to find us, where would you look?"

"Bodden?" suggested Beverly.

"Weldwyn?" offered Arnim.

"Yes," Anna agreed. "That's where they'll expect us to go, but now we have another alternative. We'll head south, into the Great Swamp and find the Saurian city."

"What if the Saurians are hostile?" asked Arnim.

"What is the greater risk, Arnim? The Royal Army of Merceria, or a city of Saurians? I'll take the Saurians any day of the week. I can speak their language, and so can Revi, when he uses his spell of tongues, but it's our best chance at escaping the shadow of darkness that lurks behind the crown."

"Yes," agreed Arnim, "but then what? We'd just be stranded in a swamp city."

"That's where our mage comes in," explained Anna. "Revi, you once said you had almost unlocked the mystery of the gates. Surely, with an entire city at your disposal, you would be able to figure out how the gates work."

"I would hope so," admitted Revi.

"And if you did," continued Anna, "we could go anywhere a gate existed. We already know about the one in Uxley. Surely there are other gates that would still work."

"This is the beginning of a good plan," said Gerald, "but we must first cross hundreds of miles of countryside with a whole kingdom against us."

"Not the whole kingdom," said Herdwin. "I'm going with you."

"You can't do that, Herdwin," objected Gerald, "you have roots here, and a business."

"Nonsense," he answered gruffly. "The city's gone to shit under Henry. It's time to get out while I'm still able, and you can use my help, or have you forgotten you're short on funds?"

"Your help is greatly appreciated, Herdwin. Thank you," said Anna.

"We'll need to lighten the load," recommended Arnim. "It's bound to be rough going south as we won't be able to use the roads."

"We'll ditch the wagon," decided Gerald, "but take Herdwin's pony and Lightning, of course. Hayley, I assume you still have your own horse. Does your uncle have any he might spare?"

"I'll see what he can drum up, but we don't want to raise anyone's suspicions."

"The slower members of the group will be Herdwin, Anna and Nikki, so we'll keep them mounted as much as we can."

"I can walk," declared Anna. "It's you, Gerald, who'll need to ride for a few days, at least until you've recovered your strength."

"I'll head into the local tavern," offered Herdwin. "I've got some things I can convert into coins. Perhaps I can purchase a horse or two."

"How much time will you need?" asked Gerald.

"I'll be back by sundown, I expect.

The day drew on as they sat at the farmhouse, waiting for the Dwarf's return. Hayley watched from the window, lest guards show up looking for them, but it appeared their temporary refuge was safe.

"How are you, Hayley?" asked Beverly.

Distracted from her observations, she turned to see the black-haired knight. "It's odd," she remarked, "I can't get used to seeing you with black hair. I keep thinking you're someone else."

"I feel the same when I see my reflection," mused Beverly. "Tell me, Hayley, what do you think are our odds of making it?"

The ranger glanced around the kitchen, ensuring they were alone before answering, "Not good. We have a long way to go and dare not use the roads for fear of being seen. On top of that, we have wounded. Gerald's in bad shape, even with Revi's healing, and Nikki's even worse. It'll slow us down tremendously. Your thoughts?"

"I was thinking along the same lines."

"Perhaps we should leave some behind?"

"I could never leave Gerald behind," Beverly responded quietly. "I owe him too much."

"Yes," agreed Hayley, "and the princess would never allow it. What about Nikki, or the Dwarf?"

"Herdwin helped us," said Beverly, "and took quite a risk doing so. I trust him, and I think he adds something to the party. I suspect he's fought before. It's Nikki I don't trust."

"She did rescue Arnim," offered the ranger, "that must be worth something."

"Agreed, but she was serving her own interests."

Hayley tried to read her face, but couldn't decide where this conversation was going. "What makes you say that?"

"I overheard Arnim and Nikki talking when we were back in Loranguard. I've always been a little suspicious of Arnim. I know he has ties to Valmar."

"You think Arnim is a traitor?"

"No, I've come to accept his loyalty to the princess, but I don't trust Nikki's influence. She has some sort of hold over him, and I think it might affect his judgement. I just have this feeling that at some critical moment she's going to turn on us to save her own skin."

"If that's true, then we have to take her with us. If we left her behind, she might sell us out."

"I agree," replied Beverly, "but we'll have to keep an eye on her."

"Definitely," said Hayley.

"Have you ever been south?"

"No," admitted the ranger, "I've spent much of my time in the north, mostly along the road that runs through Uxley and up to Hawksburg. How about you?"

"I spent some time in Shrewesdale. I've also been through the Forest of Mist along the road from Haverston to Burrstoke."

"The Forest of Mist; that sounds a little ominous."

"It's likely to be very dangerous," countered Beverly. "It's one thing to traverse it on the road, but we'll have to cut through it."

"Couldn't we go around it?" Hayley asked.

"The area around the wood is open, too high a risk of being spotted. We shall have to rely on your ranger skills to keep us safe."

"I think it more likely we'll need to rely on your fighting skills."

Beverly smiled at the compliment, "Then between the two of us, we'll be in safe hands. What do you know of the forest?"

"My understanding is that it's perpetually covered in mist, at least the deeper portion. There's rumoured to be all sorts of strange creatures that live in those parts."

"Like gryphons?"

"I doubt it, they prefer rocky terrain. Why does everyone keep mentioning gryphons?"

"We're just teasing you, Hayley; we know how much you like them."

"It's a special interest of mine. Surely you have special interests?"

"I do, but nothing I like to talk about."

"You're thinking of Bodden," guessed Hayley.

"I am. I'd like to send a message, but it's too dangerous. If it were to be intercepted, it might be interpreted as treason. I'd hate to put my father in that situation."

"It may already be too late," advised Hayley. "With the arrest of all the knights, they've already signalled their intent to destroy any opposition. I'm afraid that puts your father in great danger."

"My father knows how to protect himself," said Beverly. "I'm also worried about my cousin, Aubrey. Do you think they'd go after her?"

"I doubt it," replied the ranger. "She wasn't with the party when we originally left Wincaster. There's a good chance they don't know she's apprenticed to Revi."

"Let's hope that's enough to keep her safe."

"How is the princess doing?"

Beverly turned her gaze to the room behind them. Anna was feeding a broth to Gerald, who kept complaining that he didn't have enough teeth to chew. "She's doing better than I thought she would be. Thank Saxnor that Gerald survived, I wouldn't want to think how devastating that would have been to her. It's bad enough that Tempus is gone."

"I didn't realize."

"King Henry told her he ordered the execution himself."

"I find that infuriating," said Hayley.

Beverly laughed unexpectedly, "How typical. People are killed, but you're more upset that a dog was slain?"

"Don't get me wrong, Bev. I'm angry that the knights were killed, but the princess was very close to Tempus. It must have crushed her."

"I'm not mad at you, Hayley; I just find it an interesting observation. I actually find myself a little numb from all the violence I've witnessed. I'd just like to climb into bed and stay there."

"No doubt with a nice warm man," added Hayley.

Beverly blushed, and suddenly the ranger understood. "There is a man, isn't there? I knew it. Who is it? Is it someone back in Bodden?"

The knight looked around to make sure no one was listening. "All right, there is someone, and yes, he's in Bodden, but I swear by Saxnor's beard, if you tell anyone, I'll kill you."

Hayley put her hand over her heart, "I swear by the ranger code I won't tell a soul."

"He's a smith. His name's Aldwin."

"Who else knows?" asked Hayley.

"Gerald knows, and my cousin Aubrey, but no one else, though I think my father suspects."

"A commoner? Interesting. I don't suppose that would go over well with the nobility."

"At this point in time, I don't care anymore. If we get through this, I'm going to tell my father how I feel. I'm not about to waste the rest of my life. There has to be something better waiting at the end."

"You think you're wasting your life?"

"No, not exactly. Serving the princess has been rewarding. I couldn't have asked for a more worthy sponsor, but it feels like we've been fighting against the darkness the whole time."

Hayley placed her arm on her friend's shoulder, "I know this has been rough, Bev, but we'll get through it. One day we'll make it back to Bodden, and you'll marry that smith of yours. I'll do all I can to make that happen."

"Thank you, Hayley, I needed that. What about you?"

"Me?"

"Yes, what is it you're looking forward to?"

She glanced across the bedroom to where Revi napped, "My hope is already here with us," she said.

TWELVE

The Race South

SUMMER 961 MC

Herdwin returned, as promised, before dark, but his news was not what they hoped for. Being eager to quickly rid himself of his wares, he had to take what he was offered. In addition, there was only one horse available for purchase and the sorry looking animal was far from ideal.

"It'll at least carry one person," explained Herdwin. "I thought it better than nothing."

"True," admitted Beverly, "but we can't wait any longer, we must get moving tonight, under cover of darkness."

"Where do we stand?" asked Gerald.

"We have four horses and eight people," stated Beverly. "Unfortunately, we can't take the horse from Hayley's uncle, he needs it to work the farm. Lightning is capable of carrying two, quite easily, and I suspect Hayley's horse can carry two for a short stretch. Herdwin's pony is good for another while the new horse will carry one more. The rest will have to walk. How would you like us distributed, Highness?"

"We'll put Gerald on Lightning with you, Beverly. Nikki seems to be doing a bit better with Revi's latest heal. Let's have her ride the new horse, with Arnim beside her in case she's unsteady. Hayley will take her mount and Herdwin his pony."

"That leaves you on foot, Anna," objected Gerald.

"For the first part of the trip, yes, but Arnim, Revi and I can switch out with other riders as we progress. We three aren't wounded and therefore unlikely to slow us down."

"How about weapons and food?" asked Gerald.

It was Hayley who responded, "Herdwin brought back some food, though it'll only last us a couple of days. We'll have to keep an eye out for water as we go. Luckily, we're well equipped with weapons. I have all my gear and you three managed to recover your armour, along with swords. Arnim has nothing, but the extra weapons Herdwin brought from his smithy will suffice for now. The bigger issue will be travelling in the dark."

"I can lead us the first step of the journey," offered Herdwin, "I see quite well in the dark. We should be able to travel a fair distance before sun up."

"Excellent," added Anna. "Once we've cleared the area, we'll take a rest. Then we'll travel by daylight, and hole up at night, but we'll have to forgo fires for the first few days."

"Good thing it's warm this time of year," grumbled Arnim.

They mounted up, with Herdwin taking the lead. Nikki was to ride the horse alone, but when she nearly fell off, Arnim ended up on the horse behind her, his hand around her waist to steady her. The first part of the journey took them out toward the perimeter of the farm and then they turned south, cutting across an empty field. Hayley brought up the rear, waving to her uncle as they departed. Their progress was slow, but they saw no sign of trouble. They passed three different farmhouses, the windows illuminated by lanterns, but then, as the journey continued, lanterns were extinguished and the inky black of the night engulfed them.

They rode on in silence, save for the occasional snort of a horse. Herdwin's pony was sure of foot, but the new horse proved skittish, scared by the many sounds in the night. The ground became rougher as they passed through the fertile farmland into the wilder lands. When they cleared a small cluster of trees, Herdwin stopped to take his bearings, calling Hayley to the front.

"Can you read the stars?" he asked.

"Yes," she replied, dismounting and walking forward to stand beside the Dwarf. "There's Malin's Hand," she said, "the five fingers are very distinctive."

"Yes," agreed the Dwarf, "and that over there looks like Gundar's Forge. If we head between them, we will be travelling southwest. It's some way off, but that should lead us to the edge of the Forest of Mist."

"I agree," said the ranger. "Highness, you should take my horse for a while, I'm going to proceed on foot to keep us on target."

"Very well," answered the princess, climbing into the saddle.

Gerald peered at her through the gloom. She was looking tired, and he was concerned for her health. The stress of the last few days had been telling on her. He was about to say as much, but the column resumed their march. Gerald sat behind Beverly, his arms around her waist to remain in place.

"We can't go much farther," he whispered, "the princess is tired."

"Good point," replied Beverly. "Hayley?" she called out, "how much longer till we rest?"

The ranger consulted with the Dwarf, and then her voice carried back across the darkness. "Herdwin says there's a slight rise up ahead. Once we clear it, we'll look for some cover. It shouldn't be long now."

Gerald hung on, though he had little energy to do so. Revi had healed his body, but he was still weak, his strength drained from him during his torture. It was with great relief that the old warrior heard the word to halt. He slid from the saddle to find his legs giving way beneath him. Luckily, Beverly was there to provide support.

Herdwin had located a fallen trunk in a small wooded area, and it was about this location that they now dropped themselves to the ground.

"We'll rest here till morning," the Dwarf announced. "Once the sun's back up, we'll continue on our way."

"How far are we going?" asked Anna.

"It's almost sixty miles from Wincaster to the edge of the Forest of Mist," declared Hayley. "It'll be days yet before we reach it, but we're well away from any roads now. The chance of discovery is slim."

"We must still be alert," said Revi. "Lady Penelope may have magical means of locating us?"

"Truly?" asked Anna.

"Yes," said Revi, "though not by a spell. She may have a familiar that can fly."

"Like Jamie?" asked Anna.

"His name's Shellbreaker, Highness, but yes, that's what I mean."

"Are we sure we weren't followed?" asked Arnim, lowering Nikki to the ground.

"I'll summon Shellbreaker in the morning and have him scout the area," offered Revi. "That should eliminate the element of surprise."

"An excellent idea, Master Bloom," said the princess.

"Yes," agreed Hayley, "that will suffice to keep us safe until we arrive at the forest. Once we enter that dark place, you'll want to keep him close. There may be large predators that would eat him for breakfast."

"Speaking of which," said Gerald, "the mention of breakfast is making me hungry. What do we have to eat?"

"My uncle gave us some cooked sausages," said Hayley.

Gerald groaned, "I can't eat sausages, I don't have enough teeth left."

"You can't bite them," said Anna, "but you can chew. I'll just have to cut them up for you."

Dawn came far too early for Gerald, who was awoken by the rising sun pouring across his face. He opened his eyes to see everyone scurrying about the camp.

"What's happening?" he asked.

"We're just packing up the gear," replied Anna. "You needed your rest, so we let you sleep."

"I'm fine," he declared, rising quickly to his feet, but then his legs wobbled, and he almost fell over. It was Beverly that saved him once again, grabbing his arm to steady him.

"You all right, Gerald?" she asked, her face a look of concern.

"I'm still half asleep," he retorted, "I'll be fine."

"Good," said Beverly, "because you'll be riding Lightning along with the princess." Her stern look gave him no option. She turned to Arnim, "How's Lady Nicole doing?"

"She's weak," replied the knight, "but doing much better."

"We'll put her on Hayley's horse today," said Beverly. "You'll need to watch her again."

"I can do that," said Arnim.

"Hayley, I'll want you up front with me. We'll be leading on foot, and I need you to keep an eye out for tracks and such. Sooner or later, we'll have to start hunting for food. If something comes our way, I'll count on your bow to catch it for us."

"Good idea," the ranger commented.

"Herdwin, I would like you to bring up the rear if you would be so kind."

"Hey," interrupted Revi, "what about me?"

"You're coming up front with us," answered Hayley.

"Why is that?" asked the mage.

"You have the familiar, remember? Shellbreaker's going to keep an eye out for trouble, or had you forgotten? It was, after all, your idea."

"Of course I haven't forgotten," Revi replied. "I was just busy thinking."

Hayley turned back to Beverly, "He's always doing that."

"I know," agreed Beverly, "it's because he's a mage."

Hayley chuckled, "Did I ever tell you about the strange mating rituals of mages?"

"That's not fair," interrupted Revi, "that was a complete accident."

"What's he talking about?" asked Beverly.

Hayley smiled, waiting, while Revi's face grew red with embarrassment. "Oh, nothing important really, he just decided he was going to sit on top of me when we escaped the watchtower in Riversend."

"That sounds like an interesting story, best told with a tankard of ale," the lady knight insisted.

"Indeed," chuckled Hayley, "but we should get moving before we while away the entire morning." She started walking, the others falling in behind.

Revi stood still for a moment, summoning Shellbreaker, who flew over a group of nearby trees to glide in and land on the mage's extended arm. Their heads touched, forehead to forehead, and then the creature flew back up into the air, circling the group before flying off to the southwest.

"All set, Revi?" Hayley called back.

"Yes," he replied, "Shellbreaker will let us know if he spots anything dangerous."

"I thought you had to see through his eyes," remarked Beverly.

"I can do that if necessary, but we have a mental link. If he sees any danger, I'll sense it. Sorry, it's a little hard to explain."

"I understand completely," assured the knight, "I can tell when Lightning gets nervous, it puts me on alert."

Revi ran to catch up, and then the group continued their journey.

As the day wore on, dark clouds appeared, and by late afternoon a light rain began falling, slowly enveloping them in moisture. The princess put Beverly in charge, freeing herself up to look after Gerald.

The clouds grew darker, with the sound of thunder in the distance warning of worse to come. They decided to make for whatever cover they could find, but the land was flat here, devoid of any trees that might provide shelter. Soon, the rain increased, drenching everyone, and the ground, which up to this point had proved easy to traverse, turned into a muddy quagmire.

The horses struggled, and to Beverly, it felt like the Gods had forsaken them. Even talking was impossible as the torrential downpour rattled against cloak and mail.

Gerald was miserable. Despite Revi's spells, he was still weak, and his missing teeth made it difficult to eat properly. Now he was hungry, sore and soaking wet. The only thing keeping him going was the fact that Anna sat behind him, her arms around his waist to steady herself on the great charger.

It was with some relief that they finally entered the edge of a small wood and were given a reprieve from their torment. He helped Anna dismount and then climbed down from the saddle, taking her hand to steady himself.

"Let's hope that's the end of it," he grumbled, "I'm soaked right through."

"I think we all are, Gerald," Anna agreed, "though I have to say Master Bloom looks quite comical in his thoroughly wet robes."

Gerald looked at the mage and laughed, "He looks like a drowned rat."

"So glad I'm entertaining you," the mage retorted.

"Come on, Revi," said Hayley, "let's get you out of those wet clothes."

"It won't matter," said Revi, "everything I own is wet. There's nothing dry to change into."

"Don't worry," Hayley soothed, "I'm a ranger. I can get a fire going anywhere. We'll have everyone warmed up in no time. Now, let's see about gathering some sticks, shall we?"

Revi and Hayley began searching the small woods while Beverly saw to the horses. Arnim, who had helped Nikki from the saddle, was laying out a blanket for her. She had not spoken much since leaving Wincaster, and his face wore a mask of concern.

Herdwin guided his pony to the makeshift paddock and then wandered over to Gerald, who was sitting on a log. The smith sat down beside him, digging into his pouch to pull forth some small stonecakes. He offered one to Gerald, who placed it in his mouth.

"What do you make of them?" asked Herdwin, indicating Nikki.

"I'm not sure what you mean," said Gerald.

"He means," said Anna, "what do you think their story is?"

"Oh," Gerald responded, "they obviously share a past."

"More than that, I'd say," observed the Dwarf. "I see the way that girl looks at the captain. It's more than just a shared past."

"What's that supposed to mean?" Gerald asked.

"It's obvious, isn't it?" said Anna. "She's in love with him."

"Is she?" said Gerald. "I hadn't noticed, not that it's any of our business." He watched them for a few moments before continuing. "I wouldn't say it works both ways. He appears more annoyed with her than anything."

"That's what I thought," said Herdwin. "I wondered if that was common among Humans."

"You've lived amongst us for years, my friend," said Gerald, "I would have thought you'd be used to Human behaviour."

"Not really," explained Herdwin, "I only dealt with Humans on a professional basis. You're one of the few I actually know reasonably well."

"I don't think there is a 'normal' among us," remarked Gerald. "Everyone seems to do things differently."

"Were you like that with your wife?" asked Herdwin.

"No," he admitted, "Meredith and I always got along, but I've seen others who didn't. I remember one of my men, a fellow named Harris, who got into a frightful row with his wife. Didn't go home for days."

"How terrible," remarked Anna. "A husband and wife should always get along, don't you think?"

Gerald looked at Anna, trying to gauge her train of thought. "Husbands and wives can still disagree, Anna, provided they're civil about it. One day you'll marry Alric and see for yourself."

Anna blushed, and Gerald smiled as he recognized the look. "I know it doesn't seem like it, Anna, but we'll survive this and come out the other side stronger than ever before."

"Saxnor's beard, Gerald, you're finally in a good mood," Anna beamed.

Gerald smiled back, "I suppose I am, even though I'm hungry, soaking wet, and aching all over."

The fire burned low, and Arnim placed more wood on the embers, watching as the flames grew higher. The camp was quiet, disturbed only by the gentle snoring of sleeping souls. He watched Nikki rise from her slumber, drawing her cloak about her shoulders to ward off the chill of the night.

She stumbled over to the fire and sat on the ground, across from Arnim.

"A cold night," she observed.

"Aye," he replied, "and likely to get colder. The season is turning; it won't be long before snow comes."

"What are we doing here, Arnim?" she asked.

He gazed back at her, carefully choosing his words, "We're going south, to the safety of the swamp."

"The swamp? To find some ancient long-dead race?" she asked. "Do you really think such a thing is possible?"

"You've met Lily, you know they exist," he replied.

"One Saurian does not make for a city," she said, pausing to put a hand to her forehead, wiping her sweaty brow and then continuing. "This mythical city of lizards is likely in ruins, full of nothing but emptiness, assuming we can even find it."

"Do you doubt Revi's wisdom?" he asked.

"He's young, not even a fully trained mage. Can we really rely on him?"

"The princess trusts him, which is more than I can say for you."

"Why don't they trust me?" she countered. "Ever since the visit to Loranguard I've been swept aside."

"Why should they trust you?" he asked. "What have you done to earn their trust? You spied on them for Valmar."

"That was your doing," she said, "I had no say in the matter. I paid a high price for your decision."

"Just as I paid a high price for your treachery," he angrily retorted, "or are you going to tell me that wasn't your fault either. Nothing is ever your fault, Nikki. You take what you want and leave chaos in your tracks."

She looked as if she was about to answer, but held her tongue, casting her eyes to the fire. "I wish I could undo the past," she confessed, "I never meant to hurt you."

"And yet you did," he said. "You can't change the past, none of us can, but you can build toward the future. You're not trusted because you don't trust anyone other than yourself. Until you let go of that, you'll always be alone."

"Do you trust me?" she asked.

"I want to," he offered, "but I can't, you haven't given me a reason to."

"I saved your life," she said.

"As I saved yours back in Weldwyn," he reminded her. "I pulled you out of the river, not because I thought you'd owe me, but because it was the right thing to do."

She rose to her feet, her eyes locked on his. "One day you'll know the truth, Arnim, and I pray that when that day comes, I'll still be here for you."

She staggered back to her makeshift bed and pulled her cloak tightly around her.

For two long days, they continued their journey. Fortunately, the rain subsided, and Hayley finally managed to hunt down a pair of hares, giving them fresh meat for the first time since they left the farm.

Late on the fourth day, the Forest of Mist came into view. The edge of the wood looked like any other, despite the ominous sounding name. They marched across the countryside, not following a path, and as they reached the edge of the tree line, they found the woods lined with thick undergrowth, preventing an easy entrance. Hayley suggested they follow the perimeter to the southeast, and so they turned, falling into single file.

Sometime later, the ranger found what she was looking for; a break in the underbrush. She halted, waiting for the others to catch up.

"You'll have to dismount, I'm afraid," she said. "The branches are quite low here, we'll have to lead the horses."

Gerald lowered himself from the saddle, "Finally. My arse was getting sore."

"What should we expect inside the woods, Hayley?" asked the princess.

"I have no idea," replied the ranger. "I've heard stories, of course, but I've never been down this way myself. Beverly's been here before, perhaps she has a better idea?"

"Don't look at me," said Beverly. "That was years ago, and I never left the road."

"Well, that was helpful," grumbled Arnim.

"Perhaps our mage can tell us more?" said Anna.

Revi placed his hand on his chin, giving him the look of a scholar. "It is said that the Forest of Mist is perpetually enshrouded in a thick fog."

"You don't need to be a mage to know that," commented Gerald. "It's common knowledge."

A slight look of irritation crossed the mage's face before he resumed, "Yes, well, there's more to it than that." He fell into silence.

"Please continue," urged Anna.

"It's not unusual to see a mist in the early morning," Revi continued, "but by all accounts, here, the mist never dissipates."

Gerald looked up and down the tree line as the rest fell into silence. "There's no mist here. Are we sure we found the right forest?"

It was Hayley who responded, "This is it. The mist doesn't linger at the edge, I suspect the sun burns it off. If we were to come back at dawn, we'd likely see more."

"Where does the mist come from?" asked Anna. "Mist has to come from water. Is there a lake or river nearby?"

"That's the most puzzling thing of all," admitted the mage. "No one has ever discovered a body of water of any significance within the woods."

"I suspect," offered the Dwarf, "that much of the wood is unexplored. The Elves tell tales of ancient creatures that dwelt in woods like this, generations ago."

"What type of creatures?" asked Gerald.

"I don't know, I never paid much attention. The Elves are always full of stories about things. I think it makes them feel superior. If you want to know details, you'd have to ask the Orcs."

"You trade with Orcs?" interrupted Nikki.

Everyone turned to look at her, for she hadn't spoken in days.

"What? I'm not allowed to ask questions?"

"It is a good question," remarked Revi. "Tell us, Master Smith, do the Dwarves trade with Orcs?"

"Of course, why wouldn't they? They're an intelligent race, aren't they?"

"I thought there was hatred between the Orcs and Dwarves," stated Arnim.

"No," defended the Dwarf, "you're thinking of the Elves. We Dwarves have never had any problems with Orcs. Why, in times past, we did a lot of trading. You see, they prefer hilly terrain, or deep forest, areas that we don't like; Dwarves have always felt most at home in the mountains. Of course, most of that ended with the Great War."

"I know there was the Elf-Orc war," said Anna, "but I've never heard it called the Great War before."

"It's called the Great War," continued Herdwin, "because it lasted so long. The fighting spread to engulf the entire land, bringing it into conflict for well over a hundred years. It devastated the area."

"How long ago was this?" asked Anna, her curiosity peaked.

"I'm afraid I'm not a scholar, but I believe it would have been about a thousand years before the founding of your kingdom, perhaps more."

"How did the war start?" asked Hayley.

"I don't know," replied Herdwin, "but I'm sure that after all these years each side has its own version of the story. The Orcs never forgave the Elves for the destruction of their great cities. They were driven to the ends of the land, eking out a meagre existence on the scraps of the world."

"So the Elves won," stated Gerald. "We thought as much."

"If you can call it winning," grumbled the Dwarf. "Their losses were so high they withdrew to the deeper forests of the land. Elves breed slowly, not like you Humans. Even to this day, their numbers are small. The war cost them more than it was worth, though I suppose you should be thankful."

Gerald looked at him in surprise. "Why would we be thankful for their loss?"

"If it hadn't been for the Elves low population, the Humans never would have been able to gain a foothold in the area. When your forefathers came to this shore, they found Humans already inhabiting the land. It would have been far different had they found Elves in their days of strength."

"How is it," asked Nikki, "that the Elves didn't go to war with the Dwarves?"

"Who says they didn't?" remarked Herdwin. He looked around at the faces reflecting disbelief. "All right, they didn't, but there were disagreements over the years. Dwarves are not territorial. Don't get me wrong, we'll defend what's ours, but we don't crave land the way others do; we have sufficient for our needs."

"If only Humans felt that way," mused Anna.

"The world would be a happier place," agreed Gerald, "but we must make do with what we are given."

"We should get moving, Highness," prompted Arnim, "it's getting late in the day, and we'll want to find a place to camp before dark."

"True enough," Anna agreed. "We have to enter the wood eventually; it might as well be now. Lead on, Hayley."

THIRTEEN

The Forest of Mist

SUMMER 961 MC

~

It didn't take long to find the mist. It started as a swirling white fog that covered only their boots but soon grew to envelop them from head to foot. At first, it was light, just blocking their view of distant objects, but the farther they moved into the woods, the thicker it became until they had trouble even distinguishing the person in front of them.

With the reduction in their visibility came nervousness, and to cover it, they talked. Soon, their voices were the only way to follow each other, the pace growing ever slower and slower until finally, Hayley called from up front.

"We won't get much farther in this fog," she said. "We need to make camp while we can."

"Good idea," agreed Beverly. "Perhaps a fire will burn off some of this mist."

"I wish Lily were here," commented Anna. "Even with her mist up, she knew which way she was going."

"Probably some sort of natural talent," commented Hayley. "They were an interesting race, the Saurians."

"They are," Revi corrected, "not 'were'. We found Lily, there must be more."

"Gerald and I found her," Anna defended. "I don't remember you being there, Master Bloom."

"My apologies, Your Highness," Revi replied with a blush.

"Where did you find a Saurian?" interrupted Herdwin.

"In a grotto, near the estate we were living in," said Anna.

"I had no idea you were a noble, Gerald."

"I wasn't, Herdwin. I was the groundskeeper."

"Is that so?" asked the Dwarf. "And you just naturally thought to introduce the princess as your daughter?"

"Don't look at me," defended Gerald, "that was Anna's idea."

"I'm not looking at you," said Herdwin. "In any case, I can't, even if I wanted to, this blasted fog is too thick. How are we ever going to find wood in this soup, let alone get a fire started."

"You needn't worry," said Hayley, "it's already taken care of." The sound of steel striking flint broke through their chatter, and then a small morsel of light appeared.

Gerald drew closer until he could make out a shadowy outline. Hayley was crouched over a pile of sticks, blowing on it to grow it into a fire.

"Nice work, Hayley. I see you've learned a thing or two in the rangers."

"Thank you, Gerald," she replied, "though it wasn't the rangers that taught me this."

"Then who did?" asked Revi.

"My father. He was a very clever man, but not quite clever enough."

"Why," asked the mage, "what happened."

"He was a poacher," she replied. "They hanged him for it in the end."

"I'm sorry," said Revi, "I hadn't realized."

"It's not your fault, Revi. It was years ago, and I was still quite young. After his death, I went to live with my uncle."

The fire was beginning to come to life; its flames leaping higher and higher. The group secured the horses to a nearby tree and gathered around the blaze where their visibility improved. At least, here, they could see each other's faces, and it was a welcome respite from the near blindness of the fog.

"How much of this do you reckon we'll have to put up with?" asked Gerald, to no one in particular.

"I suspect a few days, at least," offered Hayley.

"That would agree with my reckoning," said Revi, "though it depends on a lot of factors."

"Like what?" prodded Gerald.

"Like how easy it will be to find our way and not get lost," offered the mage. "If this mist persists the way they say it does, it'll be difficult to make headway. We'll have to be careful not to get turned around."

"What about Shellbreaker?" asked Hayley. "Surely he can fly above."

"He could," he admitted, "but there are unknown dangers here in the Forest of Mist. If I were to lose him, the effect would be devastating."

"I'm sure it would," said the Dwarf, "but people have lost pets before and still survived."

"It's more complicated than that, Herdwin," explained Anna. "Master Bloom is linked to the bird through magic. If it dies, part of him will die as well."

"Then we'd best not use your bird," concluded Herdwin. "We'll have enough trouble in these parts without the burden of a half-dead mage to look after."

"Agreed," said Anna. "Is there any magical way to get our bearings, Revi?"

"I'm afraid not, Highness. Were I not a Life Mage, we might have options, but I'm afraid my skills tend more toward healing."

"But you can produce light," Hayley reminded him. "Perhaps if you floated the light in front of us, it might be easier to make headway."

"That sounds like a good idea," agreed Anna. "It won't be perfect, but it should speed us up a little bit. We'll have to rely on Hayley's dead reckoning."

"Oh great," exclaimed the ranger, "no pressure there."

"We may have to revise our travel time," suggested Gerald. "Beverly, you said you travelled through here on the road?"

"Yes," she agreed, "there's a road that leads from Haverston to Burrstoke that cuts through the forest from east to west."

"So we must be to the north of that road," commented Gerald. "If we head roughly south, we should be able to find it. That will tell us we're on the right track."

"But we can't just take the road," said Anna. "The king may have sent word of our escape. There could be soldiers out looking for us."

"I doubt that," offered Herdwin. "They'd have to know which way we're heading."

"Don't discount magic," said Revi. "We know Lady Penelope is the real power behind the throne; the Dark Queen, if you will. It's not beyond possible that she's sent word to the others to hunt us down."

"Others?" asked Arnim.

"Yes," continued Revi. "She didn't get to her position of power without help. She hinted that there were others she was working with. We must assume a well-organized and magical group that is trying to advance its own agenda."

"Yes," agreed Anna, "and they've made it quite plain that they're upset with us for ruining their plans. We must be extra careful."

"What do we do if they find us?" asked Nikki.

"Simple," replied Beverly, "we fight. You do know how to fight, don't you, Nicole?"

"I think we're well past Nicole, call me Nikki, and yes, I know how to fight. Anyone have a dagger they can spare?"

Beverly withdrew her dagger and handed it to the woman. "Here," she replied, "I hope you know how to use it."

Arnim snorted, "They don't call her Nikki the Knife for nothing."

"Nikki the Knife?" asked Beverly. "I thought she was Lady Nicole Arendale."

"No," said Arnim. "That was a ruse, it was all my idea. I wanted someone near to the princess in case the Black Hand got too close. It was all arranged through Valmar, long before we knew what type of man he was."

Nikki took the blade, examining it thoroughly. "This is quite the weapon, where did you get it?"

"It was made for me by the smith of Bodden," answered Beverly. "A man named Aldwin."

"He does excellent work," she remarked.

"Wait," said Herdwin, "did you say a smith named Aldwin?"

"Yes," the knight replied, "Aldwin Strongarm, do you know of him?"

"As a matter of fact, I do," revealed the Dwarf. "He wrote to me. He wanted to know how to construct a hotter forge."

Now it was Gerald's turn to be surprised, "A hotter forge? What for?"

"Sky metal," announced the Dwarf as if all would understand. The looks of confusion around the fire made him realize his mistake. "It comes from the sky, falls to the ground. Surely you've heard of sky stone?"

"Yes," agreed Arnim, "lumps of stone that fall from the sky occasionally. It's rare, but not unheard of."

"Well," continued Herdwin, "that stone usually contains small amounts of metal. Dwarves learned long ago that a hot enough forge can melt it, allowing us to forge legendary weapons."

"Are you saying," asked Revi, "that this smith, Aldwin, could make a legendary weapon? That's preposterous. Only the oldest and most skilled smiths can forge such items, and it would take powerful mages to enchant them."

"You don't know Aldwin," said Beverly, "so I'll forgive the insult. He's the finest smith in the kingdom, save for perhaps the Dwarves. He has a natural talent for it; he made my armour and sword." She drew the blade, passing it, hilt first to Herdwin. "Tell me, Herdwin, is this the work of a skilled smith?"

The Dwarf took the weapon carefully, lifting its blade to his face to examine it in detail. "It's a well-crafted weapon, Dame Beverly. It appears this young smith of yours has an exceptional talent."

"I never said he was young," said Beverly.

"My apologies," replied Herdwin, "I just assumed so from his letters. Had he been older, I would have heard of his skill." He let his eyes drift up to the handle and cross guard. "Impressive," he continued, "he's actually embossed a rose onto the hilt. Such work is outstanding."

"So you think he managed to build this forge you spoke of?" asked Beverly.

"I'm sure he built it some time ago. It was last year that we began corresponding. I haven't heard from him in three months or so, so I assume he's completed the work. I must get out there sometime to see his workspace. He obviously took great care with this weapon." He returned the sword to Dame Beverly.

She held it before her, looking at the embossed rose and smiled. "The rose was my mother's favourite flower," she said, then returned the blade to her scabbard. "As to Nikki's earlier question, let us now take an oath."

"What oath?" asked Nikki.

"We must protect the princess, at all costs. If we should encounter the enemy, the first priority will be to get her to safety."

"Agreed," said Gerald, the rest nodding their heads in acknowledgement.

"To that end," Beverly continued, "if it is necessary, we will fight. Arnim, myself and Hayley will bear the brunt of fighting as we're the most experienced."

"What?" objected Gerald. "Surely I'm-"

"You're the one responsible for getting the princess to safety. If we go down, we need someone who will defend her and protect her. Your most important task is keeping her alive."

"Fair enough," he relented, "though I hope it doesn't come to that."

"Let's hope not," said Beverly, "but we must always be prepared. Now, let's get some sleep, and in the morning we'll see if we can navigate this nightmare of a woods."

"Wait, what about the rest of us?" asked Nikki.

"You'll just have to improvise and make yourselves useful," said Beverly, her tone ending any further discussion.

They settled down quickly for the night. Gerald insisted on taking the first watch while the others slept. He kept the fire going, occasionally tossing on more wood, but the forest was quiet. He was startled by the sound of approaching feet and turned to see Anna.

"I couldn't sleep," she said quietly.

"I can't blame you," he replied. "This place makes me nervous. You?"

"I feel a tremendous burden," she confessed. "All these people willing to give up their lives for me."

"You're their hope, Anna. You represent the future of this kingdom."

"Do you really believe that?" she asked.

He looked at her, trying to gauge her mood, "I want what's best for you, Anna, I always have. If you want to run away to Weldwyn and live a life of luxury, I'll be there with you. If you want to enter the gates of the Underworld to defeat Pherus, himself, I'm there with you, too. I'll be there till the end, one way or the other. We're family, Anna; that's what family does."

She hugged him, and he held her tight. The pressure of all this was building inside her, and he feared it would be the ruin of her. Finally, he felt her begin to relax.

"There, there," he soothed, "this will all be over soon enough. Look on the bright side."

She pulled back from him to look at his face, "Bright side?"

"Yes," he smirked, "you've seen the ocean, now you will see what a swamp looks like."

She laughed, "I suppose I have always wondered. Do you think Revi has really found the lost city of the Saurians?"

"Let's hope so," he said, "or it's going to be a long trip for nothing. Now, you should get some sleep."

"I'll help you keep watch," she replied. "I'll get some sleep when Hayley takes over."

"Very well," he replied, "but if we're going to stay awake we need to make plans."

"What type of plans?" asked Anna, her curiosity piqued.

"Why, your wedding to Alric, of course."

Beverly shook Gerald awake, "Time to get moving, it's morning."

"Are you sure," he replied, "it's still foggy."

"Yes," she admitted, "but it's a lighter shade of fog."

"Where's Anna?"

"She's over there with Hayley, there's nothing to worry about, just a call of nature."

He rose to his feet, his back protesting as he did so. "That was a very uncomfortable piece of ground," he complained. "Where is everyone?"

"They're gathering the horses. We're all ready to start moving. Hayley thinks she knows the way. Oh, I'm supposed to give you this." She dropped a bundle into his hands. Someone had taken great pains to wrap a kerchief around something. He opened it carefully to reveal sausage meat.

"The princess went to great lengths to cut that up for you," said Beverly. "I know the missing teeth are a problem."

Gerald's face broke into a grin, "I think we're going to be all right, Beverly."

"You'd best eat that quickly, Gerald," she said, "we're about to head off."

Revi was out in front with Hayley, having conjured a globe of light that hovered in the air slightly ahead of them. It moved with them, bright enough to act as a guide through the mist.

"How will you know if we're heading in a straight line," asked the Dwarf.

"If I imagine a line," Revi explained, "from the people behind us, through us, and ahead to the light, I have only to keep things aligned. That means we're heading in the right direction."

"And if it's not in a straight line?"

"Then we're lost. Either way, we keep moving."

"You're not exactly filling me with confidence," said Herdwin.

"I wasn't aware that was my job," Revi remarked.

Farther down the line, Anna spoke, "There's a lot of complaining."

"It's natural," said Gerald. "It keeps their minds occupied. As a leader, you have to be worried when people stop complaining. It means it can't get any worse."

"Those are wise words coming from my general."

"Hah," he exclaimed, "I'm a general without an army. Does this mean you've decided to fight?"

"We'll have to travel to Weldwyn first," she said. "I can't very well organize a rebellion if I'm on the run. I need a safe place to plan."

"You've been giving this some thought."

"I have," she admitted. "And I've come to some conclusions, though I'm sure others will be shocked."

"What kind of conclusions?" he asked.

"We're going to need allies, first and foremost. I want to contact the Elves, the Dwarves, and the Orcs."

"The Orcs? I didn't expect that."

"The Orcs know how to fight, and from what I've read, they're excellent at the type of warfare we'll be using."

"What type of warfare is that?"

"Scouting, taking out sentries, sneaking in and out of enemy camps, all sorts of things."

"Like raiders," said Gerald.

"Yes," she admitted, "but I think the Orcs are more disciplined than the Norlanders."

"And how, precisely, will you recruit these Orcs?"

"I haven't thought that through yet," she admitted, "but I know there are Orcs up in the Artisan Hills, we fought them at Eastwood, remember?"

"How could I forget, they would have slaughtered us; if it hadn't been for Beverly, we'd likely all be dead."

"Yes," she added, "but if you remember, the Orcs of the Greatwood, in Weldwyn, knew all about Beverly. I think they have a way of communicating over long distances. That could be a huge strategic advantage."

"You HAVE been thinking this over. What else have you come up with, aside from recruiting Orcs, that is?"

"I'm going to have Beverly form a new group of knights," she announced.

"Knights are terribly hard to control," suggested Gerald, "but if anyone can, it's likely to be Beverly."

"Perhaps knights isn't the correct word," Anna continued. "I want her to recruit soldiers, not nobles."

"You mean commoners? That won't go over well with the other nobles."

"You served at Bodden. Who was more reliable, the horsemen you commanded, or the knights?"

"The cavalry, obviously. The knights were excellent fighters, one on one, but they lacked discipline. What is it you're proposing?"

"I want to train professional cavalry, but arm and armour them as knights. The crown will bear the cost, and we can concentrate on making them highly disciplined."

"That's all well and good," mused Gerald, "but that's a substantial expense, and you don't have the crown on your head, yet."

"True," she admitted, "but I can plan, can't I? One day we'll defeat this great shadow and take the kingdom back, and when we do, I'm going to change a great many things."

"It sounds very noble of you, Anna, but I think we should concentrate on the task at hand. There's still the little matter of making it out of the kingdom alive."

"Of course," she said, "but keep in mind what I said, you're going to be a part of it."

"Me? How did I get picked?"

"You're my general, remember? And one day I'm going to make you a duke."

"Hah, now you're poking fun at me. I was born a commoner, Anna. I couldn't possibly be a duke."

"Of course you can, Gerald. If I was queen, I could do anything I wanted, and if I decided to make you a duke, no one could do anything about it. My father saw to that."

"You can't just dictate commands, Anna. That would make you very unpopular. Look what happened to your father, there was a rebellion."

"Good point," she admitted, "I'll have to win people over first."

"I think first you'll have to find an army, that's assuming we get out of our current situation."

"I know we'll get out of here," she stated.

"How do you know that?" he asked.

"Because we're together, you and I. I know things will work out as long as we're together, we look after each other."

"I suppose we do," he admitted, "though maybe next time I could do so without losing my front teeth."

The journey through the woods dragged on, but finally, after four days of mist-enshrouded travel, a road broke their path. The fog was thinner here, with small streaks of light penetrating from above, burning some of it away. The road was clear in both directions, so they quickly crossed, making their way once again into the underbrush on the other side.

With their spirits lifted after this affirmation that they were making progress, they looked forward to seeing the end of the forest, even though they knew there were still miles to go.

Gerald woke to the sound of a distant roar. He immediately spied Beverly, who was on watch, her sword drawn. She stared off into the mist while the others scrambled to pack their meagre belongings.

"What was that?" he asked.

"I'm not sure," Beverly replied, "but whatever it is, it's large. I'd say it sounds bigger than the drake we fought in Weldwyn."

"Then we'd best not upset it," said Gerald, buckling on his sword. "I'd suggest we head in the opposite direction as quickly as possible." He drew his weapon, peering into the mist.

A tremendous noise rang out as if trees had just been knocked flat. "Back," he yelled.

The others rushed into the mist behind him, while he waited, not moving, trying to discern where the noise was coming from. There, a dark shadow ahead of him! And then the massive flank of something barely visible through the swirl of mist; he turned and ran.

Through the woods he charged, his fear driving him onward. He saw

Beverly; the knight had turned and beckoned him forward. Gerald rushed past, Beverly falling in beside him.

"Where's Anna?" he asked.

"I put her on Lightning, she's safe."

Another crashing sound boomed out, while bits of twigs and leaves fell on them from above.

"What was that?" Beverly called out.

"I have no idea," he replied, "and we're not sticking around to find out."

Whatever it was began following them. He heard the sound of large feet striking the ground, felt a tremor in the earth. He forced himself forward, fought against his instincts to look back.

Another shudder of the ground spurred him on, faster than he had ever run before. His foot caught a root, and he pitched forward, sprawling. He had the presence of mind to hold onto his sword and roll, coming to rest, face up, in amongst some weeds.

As a large shape moved past him, Gerald had a brief glimpse of a creature the size of a ship. Its immense legs propelled it forward, the sight of its head blocked by the trees that surrounded it. He lay perfectly still, hoping to escape notice, but his actions proved unnecessary as the beast continued on its way, oblivious to his prone body.

He forced himself to wait, counting to ten slowly, then sprang to his feet, ready, if necessary, to run again, but the only thing he heard was his companions crashing through the trees. He rushed forward, his feet carrying him closer to their voices.

"Over here," Anna called out.

He saw the small group standing by a slab of rock and hurled himself forward, seeking shelter.

The crashing sound dissipated into the distance as the enormous creature, whatever it was, left them to their fears.

"What in the Afterlife was that thing?" he cursed.

"I have no idea," said Hayley, "and I don't think I care to know. I'm more than happy to let it go on its way."

"What's this?" said Revi.

Everyone turned to look in the mage's direction. He stood in a small clearing, looking about him in wonderment.

"What is it?" asked Hayley.

"These are standing stones," the mage explained.

"I can see these stones are standing," said Hayley, "but what does that mean?"

"There is great power here," said Revi. "Can't you feel it?"

"I don't feel a thing," said Anna, "but then again, we're not the wizards."

Gerald entered the clearing and began scanning the area. "These stones are all regularly spaced," he observed.

"Yes, they form a magic circle," said Revi. "This one looks extremely ancient."

"What does a magic circle do?" asked Arnim. "It doesn't seem to glow."

"It helps focus magical energies. I've never seen one this old before, but I can feel the power flowing through it."

"There's writing on this stone," added Anna.

Revi moved to her position, "Intriguing. There are runes of power here, but more than just that." He drew a dagger and scraped off some moss. His eyes widened, and he stepped back in disbelief.

"What is it, Revi?" asked Anna.

"Meghara," he said, his voice almost a whisper.

"What's a Meghara?" asked Gerald.

"Not a what, but a who. A great mage," he answered. "Perhaps the greatest the world has ever seen. She was known as a powerful sorceress; she brought the magic of the Elves to Humans."

"The magic of the Elves?" repeated Beverly. "I thought magic was common to all the races."

"It was," said Revi, "but it was Meghara who taught ancient Humans how to harness it."

"I hate to dull your sword," said Anna, "but there's some sort of writing on this stone. I don't think it's as old as you believe."

"Nonsense," the mage declared, "it's likely just Elvish."

"This isn't Elvish," she said, "I could read it if it were. This is some other language altogether."

Revi examined the writing in more detail. He stood back slightly and began to incant.

Gerald felt the hairs on the back of his neck bristle as the magic words spilled forth from the mage's mouth. The chanting stopped and then Revi Bloom looked back at the stone.

"It's Orcish," he declared.

"Orcish? How can that be?" asked Gerald.

"We know so little about the Orcs," explained Anna. "Perhaps this is left over from one of their cities."

"But to find Meghara's mark on a stone with Orcish letters is baffling," said Revi.

"Let me guess," said Hayley, "you're on the verge of a great discovery."

The mage, who had opened his mouth to speak, simply looked at the ranger, closed his mouth and smiled.

"I suppose you'll want to study it now," said Anna.

"Of course," said Revi, "but I realize we must make haste. I should like to return here at some point in the future, to unlock the secrets it holds."

"Certainly," said Anna, "if we should be so lucky as to live that long. In the meantime, we must continue our journey. We still have to make the safety of the swamp, and no doubt by now, the Dark Queen and her followers are out in force looking for us."

FOURTEEN

The Great Swamp

SUMMER 961 MC

F our days after leaving the magic circle, they finally emerged into the sunshine. From the edge of the forest, the land opened into a massive plain that stretched as far as the eye could see.

"To the south lies the Great Swamp," declared Hayley.

"How much longer do we have to travel?" asked Anna.

"Three or four days I would think," the ranger declared. "It's not like we have accurate maps."

"What lies between us and the swamp? Are there any towns?" asked Gerald.

"No," Anna quickly added, "just flat ground, though I'm sure there will be small groups of trees and whatnot."

"You know Merceria well," said Hayley.

"Of course she does," said Gerald, "she's been poring over maps for years."

"Master Bloom," said Anna, "once we make the swamp, how do we find the lost city?"

"By my calculations, it should be no more than a day or two past the edge."

"Can you be more specific? We'll be travelling through a swamp; we don't want to march right past it."

"I will be relying on Shellbreaker's eyes," said Revi. "As soon as the edge of the swamp is in sight I'll send him out scouting."

Herdwin spoke up, "What makes you think you'll be able to spot it?"

"We once had a chance to see through a magical flame," explained Revi, "and were looking over trees. I believe it was a great temple in the city. With that type of view, it must be obvious to a bird. Shellbreaker will find it, of that I'm certain."

"Let's hope you're right," said Hayley.

"I think it's about time we doubled up on the horses now that we're not encumbered by wounded or trees," interrupted the princess. "It'll allow us to make better time."

"An excellent idea, Highness," agreed Beverly.

"I'll ride with Herdwin," said Anna. "His pony is the smallest, and I'm relatively light. Gerald, you ride with Beverly, Revi will travel with Hayley, and Arnim and Nikki can go together on the last horse. With any luck, we'll be well out of sight of the woods by nightfall."

Gerald helped Anna up onto the pony while Beverly adjusted Lightning's saddle. There was a general mood of optimism, for the sun was out, and no danger was in sight. Hayley's next words caught their attention.

"Revi? What is it?"

The mage was standing still, looking to the north, his eyes staring at something far beyond the tree line.

"Revi," yelled Gerald, "what do you sense?"

"There's something dark coming," he said. "I don't know what it is. I feel as if someone is breathing down my neck."

"Hey, it's not me," said Hayley, "I was over there with my horse."

"I think we're being scryed," the mage warned.

"Scryed?" asked Gerald.

"Someone is using magic to detect us, to detect the disc I stole, to be more precise."

"Is there a way to protect ourselves?" asked Gerald.

"No, it's too late for that. She's figured out where we are."

"What do we do now?" asked Anna.

"We continue on," he said. "If she's detected us magically, then she's still not in the area. That buys us some time. We must hasten to the swamp with all speed."

He rushed to Hayley's steed, pulling himself onto the horse's back behind the ranger. They galloped off to the south, followed closely by Arnim and Nikki. Herdwin waited while Gerald climbed up behind Beverly and then the two mounts followed their companions.

Over the plains they rode, pushing the horses to their limits. Only

Lightning was unfazed, for the great warhorse was prepared to carry its burden to the ends of the earth. As nightfall approached, Gerald called a halt. Off to the side was a small copse of trees which boasted a narrow stream where they watered the horses while they set up camp.

Shellbreaker had been circling them all day, and the mage declared that they were safe, for the moment. They slept uneasily, resuming their journey at first light, for the prospect of being caught on the plain weighed heavily on their minds.

By the end of the second day, Revi's fear appeared to be unfounded. That evening, before sundown, he sent his familiar forth once again.

Revi grew quite excited as he looked through his bird's eyes. "It's there," he said, "I can see it."

"The city?" asked Hayley.

"No, the edge of the swamp. We should be able to reach it by tomorrow afternoon."

"Will that make us safe from the scrying?" asked Gerald.

"Her power should lessen with range, so the farther we are from her, the weaker her spell should be. We travelled at a very quick pace today, much faster than she could have pursued from Wincaster. I think we're safe."

"Let's hope so," added Gerald.

Nikki was awakened when someone shook her arm. She opened her eyes to see a dark figure looming over her. It took her a moment to focus, finally revealing the form of Dame Beverly Fitzwilliam.

"Come with me, Nicole," the knight said, "we have things to discuss."

"Now? It's the middle of the night."

"We need to speak privately, you and I, and this is likely the last opportunity we'll have."

Nikki rose from her slumber, stretching as she stood. She rubbed her eyes and looked at the knight, trying to discern her intentions. "Lead on."

Beverly led her away from the glow of the fire until they were far enough to talk without being heard.

"What's this all about?" asked Nikki.

"I need to know where your loyalties lie," demanded Beverly.

"What's that supposed to mean?"

"I saw you conspiring with Arnim back in Loranguard. You two share a connection with Valmar, and I don't trust you."

Nikki paled, thankful that the dark night concealed her discomfort. "Why would you say that?"

"I know that Arnim was originally assigned to the princess by the marshal-general, but he's proven himself over the last year. Your background, however, is a mystery."

"I was sent by the crown," she said defensively. "Decisions were made for me far above your station. If you've a problem with that, then I suggest you take it to your princess."

"Listen to me," said Beverly, stepping closer to emphasize her words, "I've seen good men and women tortured to death for their loyalty to the princess. I swore an oath to protect her, and I meant it. I'll fight to my last breath to keep her safe, and if you get in my way, you'll feel the wrath of my sword."

"And so by threatening me, you hope to do what, scare me? If you feel I'm such a threat, then go ahead and kill me right now," Nikki demanded. She waited, seeing the look of indecision on the knight's face. "I thought as much," she continued. "I've no doubt you could kill me, Beverly, but I'm not someone you can threaten lightly. I've spent years keeping myself alive by whatever means necessary. Trust me when I tell you that if I'd wanted to betray your precious princess, I would have done so by now."

"I shan't forget your words," said the knight.

"Nor I, yours," Nikki warned.

"Then it seems we are at an impasse. I shall be watching you closely, Nicole, don't give me a reason to act. Now let us return to the camp and speak no more of this conversation."

They rose early, ready to make the final push. Hayley was saddling her horse when she stopped to sniff the air.

Beverly noticed the ranger's actions, "Interesting smell, isn't it?"

"What is it?" asked the ranger.

"It's the swamp, we're getting close. It reminds me of when I first arrived at Shrewesdale."

"It's awful, how did you stand it?"

"You get used to it after a while. By the time I left I'd forgotten all about it until I got to fresh air again. They call it the Shrewesdale stink."

"It smells like something's rotting," commented Hayley.

"It likely is. The Great Swamp goes on for hundreds of miles. I'm told it covers the entire southern coast."

"And we're heading straight into it," mused the ranger, "lucky us."

Beverly laughed, "You can stay here if you want, I'm sure the Dark Queen would be more than happy to look after you."

"No, thank you. I'll take the stink of the swamp over imprisonment, any time." She finished her preparations and climbed into the saddle, "Shall we?"

"After you," Beverly replied.

By the time the sun was high, the edge of the swamp loomed in the distance. With a cry of victory, they pushed the horses almost to their limit, intent on making cover as soon as possible. A high-pitched, piercing shriek shattered their celebration. Gerald, holding onto Beverly's back as they rode, turned his head, and the vision that greeted his eyes shook him to his very core. There, in the sky, soared a dark cloud pursuing them. As it drew closer, it morphed into the form of a hideous giant bat. When it shrieked again, the air distorted around its mouth as the sound issued forth.

He looked ahead, to the swamp, but he knew they couldn't close the distance quickly enough. "Slow the horse, Beverly," he warned, "we have work to do."

Anna looked to Gerald in worry, but he cast aside her looks of concern.

"Rush to cover," he yelled, "we'll try to delay it."

The creature came swooping in, intent on the two riders. Gerald drew his sword, and Beverly turned her mount to face this new threat.

"It's not going after the princess," said Beverly.

"No," said Gerald, dismounting. "I suspect it's some sort of conjuration. It likely has no mind of its own; we can use that to our advantage."

Beverly drew her sword. "For Bodden!" she cried, urging Lightning forward.

Gerald waited for barely a heartbeat and then followed. He hoped the creature would attack the first thing it saw, leaving it open to a flanking manoeuvre.

He watched Beverly duck as the creature bore down on her. She clung to her saddle, her sword slicing overhead through the gaseous shape, its form dissipating in the wake of the blade. Lightning, with Beverly holding tight, thundered past the figure, arching to the right for a return attack. The creature, however, banked to the west in an effort to cut her off.

Beverly changed course, cutting east instead, the sure-footed Lightning handling the change remarkably well, but the creature altered its flight path, copying her. She used its innate seeking ability to her advantage, dodging back and forth. Gerald realized she was drawing it along, closer to him as she zigzagged through the field.

He waited for her to ride past, and then, when the great shadow zoomed overhead, he thrust his blade up, slicing directly into it. His weapon met no resistance, passing through what would be its belly, the smoke dissipating around his sword, but it continued its trajectory, colliding with Beverly even as she struck at it.

Her sword flew out of her hand as she was knocked from the saddle moments before Lightning tumbled from the force of the blow. Gerald watched them both land with a tremendous thumping sound, neither one of them moving.

Gerald ran as the conjuration landed, ready to finish the job it had begun. It raised its head skyward and let out a terrifying screech. As the thing lowered its head to strike a death blow, Gerald drove his sword into the creature's back, only to have his blade sail clean through it. He staggered forward trying to keep his balance. The entity turned, opening its mouth to wail again.

He twisted, striking without mercy, sending his sword plunging into the creature's head. This time, he held the weapon steady, as if impaling the thing, swinging it side to side, trying to dissipate the smoke even more. Opening its mouth to rain down an attack, it all of a sudden vanished, with only a popping sound.

He stood, looking before him, no longer seeing any sign of the strange creature that had been defeated. "What in Saxnor's name was that?" he asked out loud.

Beverly sat up, shaking her head, "I have no idea, but that was a lucky one. I wouldn't like to do that again. It felt like a giant hand knocked me down."

"It probably did," said Gerald. "That thing was obviously magical, and it was likely Penelope's hand that guided it. How's Lightning?"

The great horse was still lying on the ground. Beverly knelt by his head, placing her own head to his. "I think he's all right, just winded." A moment later she had him stand, his tail swishing in the gentle breeze.

"Let's catch up to the others, shall we?" she suggested.

The Great Swamp began as little more than a sunken landscape. They first had to make their way through a soaked plain. Soon, their horses were fetlock deep in water as they rode beneath a canopy of strange looking trees, draped in vines, with vegetation wrapped around them.

Despite the copious pools of stagnant water, their progress continued unobstructed on clear paths that ran between the trees. All that came to an end as Hayley's horse suddenly went flank deep into a hole hidden beneath the surface of the water.

The column halted immediately as she backed up her mount. The nimble Archon Light, withdrew, the mud clinging to its legs.

"Well, that didn't go well," exclaimed Hayley.

"The water's likely to get deeper," said Revi, dropping from the horse's back. His feet sank into the sticky mud beneath the surface of the water. He looked around briefly, then retrieved a stick that was roughly his height. "I shall go in front," he announced.

Stepping forward, he prodded the water with his newfound staff. It took a few attempts before he made his decision. "This way."

They were now reduced to a slow pace. The air grew fetid and still, as sweat began to soak their clothes.

"How can it be so hot here?" complained Nikki. "Just this morning we were all quite comfortable."

"There's no breeze," explained Arnim, absently swatting at an insect. "I suppose it will be like this for most of the way. How far to the temple, Revi?"

The mage halted and leaned on his staff. "Let me take a look. Hayley, can you come here a moment?"

The ranger, who had been following him with the reins of her horse, closed the distance. "What is it, Revi?"

"I need you to watch me closely. When I look through Shellbreaker's eyes, I will be temporarily disoriented; I shouldn't like to fall into the water."

"You're already soaking wet, Revi, I doubt falling in would make it any worse."

"Yes, but I'll lose contact with my familiar."

"Very well, I'll keep a close eye on you."

"Thank you," he said, closing his eyes.

Hayley watched in fascination. She could almost see the bird flying over the tops of the trees by watching Revi. He would lean from side to side as Shellbreaker rode the currents, and he would occasionally duck as his familiar dove. She carefully flicked an insect from Revi's arm, trying not to distract him. The spell lasted forever, and she began to worry that he was somehow caught up in the magic, so engrossed was he with his visions.

Revi's eyes snapped open, and a look of disappointment showed on his face.

"What is it?" asked the ranger. "Did you see the city?"

"No," he admitted, "something's wrong, I must have made a mistake in my calculations." He made his way to Hayley's horse and began rummaging through the bag that hung there.

Anna dropped down from Herdwin's pony and came to see what the fuss was about. "Is there a problem?" she asked.

"Just checking something, Highness," said Revi, opening the book. He laid it out on the saddle, carefully balancing it with one hand. Flipping through pages, his finger's came to rest on a strange looking map. He reached into his robes to withdraw the stone disc that was hanging around his neck.

"That map," said Anna, "there's something odd about it."

"It's a map of Merceria," explained Revi, absently, "but it doesn't show any of the cities, it's based on an old Elvish map."

"Are those faint lines the ley lines?" she asked.

He looked from the book to the princess. "They are, and this disc uses the ley lines as reference points. The difficult part is lining it up. The disc and the map are not the same scale, do you understand?"

"Of course," she said, "I've studied hundreds of maps; I know what scale is."

The mage returned to his work. He was holding the disc above the page in his left hand while his right finger traced patterns on the map.

Anna watched with great fascination.

"I don't understand," he said at last. "Shellbreaker should be able to see it."

"Could the image in the flame have been from the past?" asked the princess.

"I suppose anything is possible, but I don't think so. It felt so real as if we could have reached through and touched it. Everything I've discovered so far points to gate travel being in real-time."

"Real-time?" asked Hayley.

"Yes," he confirmed, "that is to say, instantaneous travel. It would be like stepping through a door but ending up far away."

"Perhaps the map isn't accurate," offered the princess.

"It's all we have to go on, I'm afraid. I had better maps back in Wincaster, but they would have been too hard to carry. This was all I could manage," he gestured at his beloved book.

"May I see the medallion?" Anna asked.

He removed it from his neck and passed it to her. She held it up to catch the light, examining it in detail.

"There seems to be some markings on the side here," she observed.

"Yes," he agreed, "I think they reference the ley lines. I'm using the Uxley estate as a reference point since we know of its existence."

"This map," said Anna, "it shows the known ley lines according to the Elves, doesn't it?"

"Yes, they were experts in such things."

"What if there is another, parallel ley line below Uxley. That would move the whole map down, wouldn't it?"

"It would," he admitted, "which would mean the city is farther into the swamp."

"We need an accurate fix on our location," she mused. "We've been assuming we came straight south from the forest of mist."

"We did," offered Hayley, "that was the easy part."

"Yes," replied Anna, "but what if we came out farther east than we thought? We were disoriented in the fog."

"That would make sense," agreed Hayley. "That would put us east of where we thought we were. We'd have to search more to the west."

"Wait a moment," said Anna. She was holding the disc up directly to her face. "There's a strange symbol here. It looks like a tiny circle. I think it's a reference of some type." She looked at the map in the book for a moment, then passed the disc to Hayley. "You have good eyesight, Hayley. Tell me what you see."

"I see it now that you've pointed it out," she admitted.

"If that's a marker of some type, and we assume those faint lines on the disc are ley lines, where would that likely be?"

The ranger examined the map, casting her eyes back and forth with the disc. "The only place it could be would be in the middle of the forest."

"Yes," said Anna, "that's what I thought."

"That must be the circle," said Hayley. "That means we'd have to shift the map eastward. The city must be far to the east of where we've been looking."

"Wait," said Revi, "that means that the magic circle must have existed when this medallion was created. How can that be? The sorceress Meghara lived long after the Saurians disappeared."

"Perhaps she knew of their city?" offered Anna. "Others have likely looked for it over the centuries, why not her?"

"Can we confirm its location?" interrupted Hayley.

Revi examined the map one more time. "I can send Shellbreaker, but it will take some time. I won't be able to maintain contact with him."

"How does that work?" asked Anna. "Won't you need to see the city through his eyes?"

"No," he replied, "I can send him with specific instructions. If he finds it, he'll return and tell me about it, in his own way, but we'll have to remain here, at least until he comes back. With this much coverage from the trees, we'd be hard to find if we moved."

"Very well," said Anna. "We'll camp here."

"It's very wet here," commented Hayley, "surely we should find a dry spot first?"

"Good point," Anna conceded. "We'll find a place to rest, and then you should send Jamie out."

"Shellbreaker," Revi corrected.

"I named him first, Master Bloom; he'll always be Jamie to me."

Revi bowed, "As you wish, Highness."

They eventually found a suitable place to camp, a small mound that protruded above the surface of the water. It was barely big enough to hold them, but Hayley managed to coax a fire from some damp twigs and soon they were all resting their legs while the horses ate some local plants.

Revi sent Shellbreaker on his way while Hayley tried to rustle up some food. They had seen the odd fish earlier in the day, and now the ranger stood, knee deep in the water, her bow strung and an arrow notched. She showed tremendous patience, holding still for what felt like an eternity before an arrow sailed forth. With a shout of glee, she returned to the camp, a strange looking fish impaled.

"It has whiskers," noted Anna, "how strange."

"It's still a fish," said Gerald. "I'm sure it'll cook up nicely."

Hayley proved adept at cooking as well as catching. The meat was somewhat chewy, but they all felt better for the food.

It was late evening by the time Shellbreaker returned. The first indication that anything was happening was when Revi suddenly stood up. Beverly began to draw her sword in alarm, but the mage simply shook his head. A moment later, he extended his left arm and his faithful familiar flew to him, landing on the proffered limb. The mage bent his head, touching his forehead to the bird, and closed his eyes.

Everyone watched in anticipation, and then Revi stood up straight, looking to the group.

"Well?" asked Hayley.

"It's good and bad news, I'm afraid," he declared. "Shellbreaker has found the city. It lies far to the east, as the princess said."

"What's the bad news?" asked Gerald.

"It's quite some distance away. We'll have to traverse the swamp the entire way."

"How far?" asked Hayley.

"At our current speed," mused the mage, "I should say somewhere in the range of two weeks."

"Two weeks? Are you sure?"

"I'm afraid so," he said.

Hayley sat down, obviously disappointed.

"We might be able to speed that up considerably," suggested Gerald.

Anna turned to her mentor. "How?" she asked.

"We could backtrack to the edge of the swamp and then follow the northern border of it eastward, covering a lot of ground, then cut down from the north again."

"Yes," agreed Hayley, "and we could stock up on food while we do so."

"What do you think, Master Bloom? Would it work?"

"Yes, I believe it would."

"Good, then it's decided," Anna declared.

"What about the Dark Queen," asked Nikki, "or had you forgotten?"

"That's a valid point," said Beverly. "Couldn't she scry you again?"

"I've actually given that some thought," said the mage. "I believe the creature she summoned took a lot of her power. If she were capable of finding me again, she would have done so by now. No, I think we are safe from her, at least for the moment."

"Then we'll move north in the morning," decided Anna. "It's far too late in the day to do so now, we'd end up moving through the swamp in the dark, and I don't think anyone wants that."

"Agreed," said Gerald. "Now let's pack it in, we need to rest up and be ready to move at first light. I'll take the first watch."

"Me too," said Anna. "The rest of you sleep."

"Easier said than done," grumbled the Dwarf. "I hate swamps."

It took them a day to make their way out of the swamp and then another five heading eastward along the northern edge. Each afternoon, Revi would send his familiar up into the skies to get his bearings until, at last, he announced that it was time to re-enter the swamp.

This time they prepared before entering. Hayley foraged ahead, and they took a day to cook and skin the game she caught. Each traveller carried a walking stick as they led the horses, single file, into the marshy terrain. Using Shellbreaker, they were able to scout ahead, to find dry spots to set up camp in. This became easier as the mage realized that certain trees only grew on these bare areas. For four days they moved south in this manner, drawing ever closer to their destination.

Finally, they were, by the mage's reckoning, only a day's march from the Saurian City. Revi, close enough now he could examine the temple through his familiar's eyes, discovered it was an immense pyramid structure, made of stepped stones, reaching far above the canopy of trees. Upon the flat top sat a large archway which held a green flame. At the base of the structure, Saurians were scurrying about smaller buildings, made of sticks and covered with moss and other vegetation, which he assumed were dwellings.

He came out of his trance to inform the others of his discovery. "How do you wish to proceed?" he asked.

"If we walk straight in," suggested Arnim, "they might think we're hostile."

"Good point," said Anna. "Revi, I'd like you to cast your spell of tongues on me."

"You already speak their language, Highness," the mage objected.

"Yes," she agreed, "but your spell will make me more fluent. I'll be better able to explain our situation."

"It might be better if only a few went at first," suggested the Dwarf, "less intimidating."

"Good idea," she agreed. "I'll take Gerald and Beverly with me. The rest of you stay here. Revi, you keep an eye on us using Jamie. If things don't go well, you'll just have to improvise."

Gerald smiled and turned to Beverly, "She likes that word."

Beverly coughed to hide her amusement.

"Once we make contact, we'll tell them about the rest of you, and we can signal you to come out into the open. Remember, we don't know much about these beings, but as long as we're careful not to antagonize them, we should be all right. If they're anything like Lily, this will go well. Are we ready?"

"I'm ready," said Gerald.

"Me too," said Beverly.

"Just waiting to cast the spell, Highness," added Revi.

"Good, then let's begin."

Revi started calling forth his magic.

Anna looked out from behind the tree to see a group of Saurians here, standing in knee deep water. They were holding rake like objects which they dipped into the water, presumably to look after crops of some sort.

She stepped from the tree, moving slowly, trying not to scare anyone. The Saurians kept working, their heads bent to the task at hand.

"*Hello,*" she said in Saurian, holding up her hands to indicate a lack of weapons.

Gerald watched, his nerves ragged. He clutched his sword hilt, fearful that Anna might be in danger. She stared at the lizard people, but when they failed to react, she turned to Gerald and shrugged her shoulders. He pointed back to the diminutive creatures and cupped his hands to mimic a shout.

Ann turned back and yelled out in Saurian, "*Excuse me?*"

One of the workers turned at the sound and went still. A moment later it dropped its rake, which fell, splashing, into the water.

"What?" it said. The other two looked up from their work to freeze in place.

"I mean no harm," Anna continued. *"I'm a friend. I'm looking for the person in charge."*

"Who are you," asked the first Saurian.

"My name's Anna," she said, her voice growing bolder. *"I come from a place called Merceria. Have you heard of it?"*

The Saurian walked toward her, stopping an arm's length away. *"What nature of creature are you? You look like an Elf, but your ears are different."*

"I'm a Human," she said. *"Have you ever heard of us?"*

"No," the Saurian admitted, *"I don't believe I have."*

"I'm not alone, I'm with friends. May I bring them out?"

The Saurian looked to the trees, but if it saw anything, it gave no indication. *"By all means,"* it said.

Anna waved, and Gerald and Beverly stepped out from the tree line. They kept their hands away from their weapons and walked slowly, so as not to upset the villagers.

"This is Gerald and Beverly," Anna announced.

"Strange names," the Saurian replied. *"I am Sliss. I and my companions are caretakers. We tend to the water grass."*

"Water grass?" asked Anna.

"Yes," said Sliss, *"it is one of our crops. How did you find us?"*

"We travelled a great distance to meet you," Anna continued. *"Who is in charge here?"*

"Our leader is named Hassus; he is the High Priest of the Flame."

"Would it be too much to ask that you take us to Hassus?"

"I should be delighted," he said. *"If you will come with me, I will show you the way."*

He led them through the murky water and then up three stone steps. He rose out of the water, leading them to a long walkway, made of grey stone.

"Where do you suppose they got all this stone?" asked Gerald.

"I don't know," said Beverly, "from Dwarves, maybe?"

He looked at the knight in surprise, "Why would you say that?"

"I have no idea. I suppose whenever I see something I can't grasp I simply attribute it to the Dwarves. It's a good enough explanation for me."

"I suppose it's as good as any," he agreed.

The walkway wound through the trees, where more dwellings were visible. Some were of stone, but these were overgrown with moss and weeds, and the vast majority were of a simpler construction. The trail turned ninety degrees to reveal a straight path to the foot of the pyramid, ending in an ornate doorway that led into a lit interior. They followed their guide through the archway.

"What is this place?" asked Anna.

"It is the High Temple," said Sliss. *"It's here that the High Priest tends to the flame."*

"The green flame?" asked Anna. *"We've seen that before."*

Sliss stopped to look at her,*"You've seen other flames?"*

"Yes," she admitted, *"does that surprise you?"*

"It does," he replied. *"We understood that all the other temples were broken long ago."* He resumed walking to a set of stairs that led upward to a balcony that ran around the room. At the top, they found another hallway with a similar stairwell, directly above the first.

"From here," said Sliss, *"we will exit onto the outside of the temple. The last set of steps will take us to the peak. It is there we shall find Hassus."*

They exited the room to a breath-taking view, high up on the side of the step pyramid, far higher than they would have thought. Gerald was almost overcome by a desire to run back inside. He took a deep breath and then resumed his trek.

Anna followed Sliss up the last set of steps to the platform at the top of the structure. In the archway was a pile of stones that reminded her of the flame they had found, so long ago, in the ruins at Uxley. The pedestal here, however, was slightly larger; the stones more ornate.

"High Priest," said Sliss, *"I have brought you visitors."*

The High Priest stepped out from beside the archway. He was slightly taller than Sliss, wearing a chain of stones about his neck that reminded Gerald of the symbol of office that Baron Fitzwilliam wore on special occasions.

"Greetings, strangers," intoned the priest with a melodic voice, *"you are most welcome."*

"You don't seem surprised to see us," said Anna.

"The arrival of strangers to our city was foretold long ago," he replied, *"though the exact nature of such visitors was unknown. It was only a matter of time before someone found us."*

"You don't seem alarmed," said Anna.

"Should I be?" he retorted. *"You don't look like Elves."*

"We have come seeking your help," she said, *"for there are dark forces at work in the land we come from."*

"Then you are in luck," said Hassus, *"for we have experience with dark forces. Come, let us retire to more comfortable chambers."*

FIFTEEN

Bodden

AUTUMN 961 MC

∾

Edgar Greenfield urged his mount forward. It had been a nice job while it lasted, but now, with the princess likely dead, his employment was over. Time to settle down and enjoy life. Luckily, he had managed to squirrel away some coins, and he thought back to the widow he had met in Stilldale.

He topped the rise, near the great elm tree, to look down on the Keep. It had been years since he'd been in Bodden, but this time he felt a great burden with the news that he carried. He rode on in silence, forgetting, for the moment, the widow and his savings. His service was over years ago, and yet he felt a certain responsibility to Baron Fitzwilliam, to fill him in on what had transpired.

The walls of the village grew closer, until, at last, he was before the gate. A bored looking soldier stood atop the tower, an archer by the look of things. He saw the man looking down at him but was startled by the pitch of the call.

"You there," said what sounded like a woman's voice. "Who goes there?"

He peered up from the back of his horse, shading his eyes from the sun. It WAS a woman!

"Edgar Greenfield, I've a message for Baron Fitzwilliam."

"Wait there a moment," she replied, disappearing from view.

Indistinct yelling wafted out from beyond the gate, and then one of the great doors swung open. Three guards stood by, though none had their weapons drawn. The first of them was a woman, younger he thought than her voice sounded. He was about to remark on her presence when one of the men stepped forward.

"Edgar Greenfield? Saxnor's sake, you look old."

Edgar looked closely to see familiar eyes peering back from a bushy face. "Blackwood? Is that you?"

"It is, man. I thought you were dead. Whatever happened to you?"

"I were too old to fight. I got me a nice job running letters and such. That's why I'm here."

"Let him in," Blackwood called out.

Edgar rode forward, to stop as Blackwood came near.

"I've a message for the baron. Is he hereabouts?"

"He's up at the Keep," replied Sergeant Blackwood. "You remember the way?"

"I may be old," Edgar replied, "but I ain't completely lost my wits. Who mans the inner keep?"

"The Knights of Bodden. A man named Sir Ambrose is in charge, have you heard of him?"

"Can't say I 'ave. Any advice?"

"Yes," warned Blackwood, "be respectful, he's rather full of himself."

"Thanks," said Edgar, "I'll watch me mouth."

He urged his mount on, leaving the gate behind as he made his way into the village, through the bustle of the mid-day business. He marvelled at the changes since his days of service, surely Bodden was doing well. He cut down a side street, avoiding the main thoroughfare, and was soon before the gates to the inner keep. The doors were open, the portcullis raised, with a soldier leaning against the stone wall. When the guard noticed him coming, the man ran back into the inner courtyard, out of sight. By the time Edgar reached the gates, a knight and three additional soldiers stood waiting.

"Who are you, old man," the knight called out, "and why do you come here?"

Edgar halted his horse before the gateway. "My name's Edgar Green-field, and I bear a message for Baron Fitzwilliam."

"I will take the message," commanded the knight, stepping forward. "Give it to me."

Edgar stared down at the man, an uncomfortable feeling growing in the pit of his stomach. "It's for the baron's eyes only," he declared.

The knight did not look amused. He was obviously debating something in his mind but finally made a decision. "Very well," he relented, "dismount and come with me. Parker, take his horse."

One of the soldiers came forward, and Edgar dismounted, passing him the reins. He reached back to pull the bag from his saddle and followed the scowling knight.

On to the inner keep they went, past the practice courtyard. Edgar noticed a strange looking structure to the right of the Keep, then realized it was a smithy housing a peculiar chimney. He thought no more of it as he moved past and entered the Keep proper. He was stopped in the great hall where another knight, this one richly dressed, intercepted them.

"What's this now, Sir Bentley, servants should be using the back entrance."

The chastised knight halted, "He claims to be carrying a message for the baron. Says he's to deliver it in person."

"Is he, now?" mused the other man. "He looks a bit rough around the collar for a courier." He looked Edgar up and down slowly. "I'm Sir Ambrose, and I'm in charge around here. I'll not put up with nonsense like this, give me the letter."

Edgar didn't reckon himself a brave man, but the years of service to the baron told him this knight was acting well beyond his purview.

"The message is verbal," he said, "and for the baron's ears only."

"Who is it from?" asked Sir Ambrose.

"I come from Wincaster," said Edgar, refusing to divulge more. The mention of the capital had the desired effect.

"Very well," said Ambrose, "his lordship's in the map room, it's this way."

"Oh, I knows where it is," Edgar replied.

Sir Ambrose gave him a look of surprise but decided to lead him anyway. His heavy footfalls echoed as they made their way up to the tallest room in the Keep. The knight stopped at the open door and rapped on the frame. The baron, who had been peering down at a map, looked up in mild irritation.

"What is it, man?" snapped the baron.

"This ruffian claims to have a message for you, Lord. From Wincaster."

"Then show him in, Sir Ambrose," the baron commanded. "We can't have couriers waiting in the hallways, now can we?"

The knight indicated, with a wave of his hand, for Edgar to enter. The old man stepped into the room, the bag still clutched in his hand. "Beggin' yer pardon, my lord. I don't know if you remember me..."

"Edgar Greenfield," the baron said, walking over to him. "Saxnor's beard, man, how long has it been?" He grasped the new arrival's hand to give him a firm handshake.

"Quite a few years, m'lord," mumbled Edgar.

"Come in, man, let's get you a chair. Sir Ambrose, go and get someone to fetch some wine, there's a good chap."

The knight nodded, but his face was a mask of fury as he stomped down the stairs.

"He don't seem to like that," Edgar observed.

"It'll teach him humility," said Fitz, "a trait I wish more knights had. Goodness, it's been, what? Five years?"

"A bit longer than that, my lord."

"Tell me, what have you been up to?"

"I been a courier, Lord. Makin' an honest living. I was hired on to carry messages for Princess Anna."

"Ah," said the baron, "then I trust you've seen my daughter, Dame Beverly?"

"'Fraid not, my lord. My courier duties were carried out mostly from a distance. I was a collector of information for the princess."

The baron took notice of the change in tense. "Was? What's that mean?"

"I'm afraid I've come with bad news, Lord. Princess Anna and all her friends have been imprisoned."

"Imprisoned?" said the baron, growing pale. "Tell me all you know."

"I 'eard down in Wincaster that the king, he threw a big party for 'em. 'Ad 'em arrested as they ate. I'm afraid it's said they've all been executed for treason."

Baron Fitzwilliam sat down, his eyes glued on the courier. "Are you sure of this?"

"I can't say for sure," Edgar continued, "rumours was flowing all over town 'bout it, so I tried to find out more. I couldn't see any bodies, but I did find this." He reached into the bag to withdraw the head of a warhammer. "It was said to be used by Lady Beverly, do you recognize it?"

Fitz took the hammer, carefully examining it. He immediately recognized the unmistakable smith's mark of Old Grady, who had worked the smithy before his untimely passing all those years ago.

Edgar watched as a tear formed in the baron's eye. The man was devastated, and now, the courier wondered if it wouldn't have been kinder to deny him the knowledge of the loss of his only child.

They sat in silence until a maid showed up bearing a tray with wine and tankards. She slipped into the room quietly, leaving her charge on the table and withdrawing in silence.

"My lord..." said Edgar, unsure of what to say next.

The baron held up his hand to forestall him. "It's not your fault, Edgar. You are only the bearer of bad news. Might I ask how you came to possess this?" he pointed to the hammer head.

"I was snooping 'round the Palace, you see, back in the rear where the barracks is. There was a bunch of soldiers with a heap of armour and weapons and such, they was sorting through them, arguing over who would get what. It were some marvellous stuff, mind you, terribly valuable. I realized at once that it were likely the equipment from the Knights of the Hound. I would've liked to bring back more, but I 'ad to pick something I could hide. Carrying a breastplate would 'ave been too obvious."

"I understand," said the baron. "You'll have to forgive my questions, but did the soldiers say anything?"

"Only that all the knights had been killed, Lord. I'm afraid they was laughing about it, said the women got what was coming to them for being upstarts. Their words, not mine."

"Thank you," said the baron. "You've been most informative." He poured some wine, passing a tankard to the courier. "Tell me, Edgar. Now that your courier duties are done, what do you intend to do?"

Edgar blushed, "I met an old widow down in Stilldale. I was thinking of settling down there, I've managed to put aside some coin over the years."

"Good," said the baron, "you deserve to live out your life in peace." He rose, making his way to the doorway. "Someone get me Sir Malcolm," he shouted down the stairs. He turned back to Edgar. "I'm afraid you must excuse me, I have arrangements to make."

Edgar stood, feeling helpless and unsure of what to say. He finally settled for, "Of course, Lord."

He made his way to leave, but the baron stopped him with a hand. "Wait a moment," he said, "Sir Malcolm will come to see you out."

The knight appeared a few moments later.

"This is Sir Malcolm," said the baron, "he's been with me for years. Sir Malcolm, this is Edgar Greenfield. He served me years ago and has brought me grave news from the capital. I'd like you to take him down to the kitchen and have him fed, then give him a hundred crowns and send him on his way."

"A hundred crowns?" replied the incredulous knight.

"Yes," said the baron, "I no longer have use for the money, I'd like to see some of it go to a good cause." He turned to face Edgar. "You go find that widow of yours, Edgar, and hold her tight; these are perilous times.

Edgar followed Sir Malcolm down the stairs, still puzzling over the baron's final words.

. . .

Aldwin Strongarm, the smith of Bodden Keep, examined his work. The forge had taken forever to heat up, but the finished product before him had been worth it. Finally, after more than a year of trial and error, he had forged a magnificent hammer for Beverly. He examined the head, its silvery surface catching even the barest of light and reflecting it back a hundred-fold. He raised it in front of him, feeling the weight in the head. It was a warhammer, made from the rarest of all ingredients; sky metal.

He hefted it; felt its weight, and yet it was perfectly balanced. He swung it left and right and then raised it over his head, grasping it in two hands, only to bring it down in a tremendous crash onto the anvil. A loud cracking noise erupted from the anvil as it split in two. He examined the head of the hammer to see there wasn't even a single mark on it.

A guard came running into the smithy to investigate the noises, but Aldwin held up his hand. "It's all right," he explained, "everything's fine. I was just testing a weapon."

The guard looked at the split anvil. "That's some weapon," he commented. "I hope you don't do that all the time, it would get expensive."

"No," admitted Aldwin, "just the once. What do you think?" he held up the hammer, offering it to the man to inspect.

"No, thank you," he replied, "that's a knight's weapon, I'm just a simple soldier. Now, if nothing's wrong, I'd best get back to my post."

Aldwin smiled and returned to examining his handiwork. It was, by far, his finest creation and he longed to see the look on Beverly's face when he gave it to her. He heard the soldier almost bump into someone as he exited, then, a moment later, Sir Malcolm entered the smithy.

"What can I do for you, Sir Malcolm," Aldwin began, "perhaps a new battle axe?"

The knight's face was a mask of sorrow. "I'm afraid not today, Aldwin. The baron wants to see you." His attention was drawn to the hammer, "What's that you've got there?"

"My newest creation, what do you think?" he offered it to the knight.

"It's marvellous," replied Sir Malcolm. "You do excellent work, Aldwin, we're lucky to have you."

"Thank you," he beamed. "Now, you said the baron wanted to see me?"

"Yes," Sir Malcolm replied, "he's in the great hall."

"Not the map room? That's strange. Did he say what this is about?"

"It's not for me to say," answered the knight, "but I would suggest you take that hammer with you. It might give the old man some pleasure to see it's finally finished."

"I will," Aldwin promised. "I'll go there directly."

He cleaned himself up as best he could, grabbed the hammer, and made his way to the great hall of the Keep. The guards outside ignored him, for he was a regular within the inner courtyard and everyone knew of his skill at the forge and respected him for it. He entered the large room to see the baron sitting by the fire.

"You called for me, my lord?" said Aldwin.

"Yes, my boy, come and sit down."

Aldwin did as he was beckoned but felt uncomfortable; never before had he been invited to sit in the presence of the baron.

"What's that you have there?" the baron asked. "Is it the hammer? Is it finally complete?"

Aldwin offered it to him, "It is, my lord. My finest creation."

Fitz took it, examining it closely, but Aldwin could tell his thoughts were elsewhere. He handed it back, "It is a weapon for the ages," he proclaimed. "You have done well."

"Thank you, my lord. Is that why you summoned me?"

"What? No. No, not at all."

"Then what is it, my lord?"

The baron leaned forward, entwining his fingers together as he did so. "I'm afraid I've received some rather distressing news."

Aldwin saw the pain behind the baron's eyes, and it struck him in the heart like a lightning bolt. "Please," he pleaded, "please tell me it's not Beverly."

He watched as tears formed in the baron's eyes, and then ran down his cheeks. "I'm afraid Beverly is dead, Aldwin."

Aldwin stood, his heart breaking, "No, it can't be. How did this happen?"

"She was arrested, along with all the princess's entourage. They were charged with treason. I have word that they've all been executed by the crown."

Aldwin's legs shook, and he sat back down, numb with pain. "No," he mumbled, "it can't be, are you sure?"

In answer, the baron reached down beside his chair to produce the head of a hammer. He tossed it to the smith, "Do you recognize this?"

Aldwin stared at the object before him, afraid to examine it, yet sure of what he would find. He finally forced himself to look, to see the telltale dents and scratches that he recognized so well. "This was Beverly's," he said, his voice dull and devoid of life.

"I'm sorry, Aldwin," said the baron.

"Sorry? What have you to be sorry for, my lord?"

"I'm sorry that I didn't allow my daughter to follow her heart. If she were alive today, I would permit her to marry whomever she wanted. I should have done that years ago, given her that choice, at least then she would have died knowing she was loved."

"She knew she was loved," said Aldwin. "And though we never married, I would like to think she knew my thoughts were with her when she passed into the Afterlife."

Baron Fitzwilliam wiped the tears from his face. "And now, my dear boy, there is something else of which I must speak."

"Yes, my lord?"

"The death of my daughter is a hard burden to bear. One, I fear, you shall carry for many years to come, for I know how deeply she cared for you. I cannot bring her back to us, but I can, in her name, protect you. She would have wanted that."

"What do you mean, Lord?"

"I mean, Aldwin, that I intend to keep you safe. My daughter was implicated in a plot against the throne. Real or imagined, this will come to Bodden. I fear my days as baron are numbered and I suspect even now they are dispatching men to place me under arrest."

"No, it cannot be," protested Aldwin.

The baron raised his hands to calm the smith. "I am at peace with it. My time here is drawing to an end. I have lived a long life, Aldwin. I have loved the woman of my dreams, and though my marriage was short, I was content, for she gave me Beverly. Here, take this," he tossed a bag toward the smith.

"What is it?" asked Aldwin, opening it to peer within.

"It's coins," he said, "a sizable sum. I want you to leave Bodden. You've a bright future ahead of you, but you need to get away from the stain that will haunt this place."

"Bodden is my home," declared Aldwin. "I'd rather stay and fight."

"I'm flattered," responded the baron, "but there will be no fight. Most of my knights are sworn to the king. Who would dare defy the ruler of Merceria? No, I'm afraid there will be only one ending to this. Gather your things, Aldwin. I'll give you a horse and wagon. Leave this place while you still can, I implore you."

"Though it goes against my nature, I will do as you command," swore Aldwin.

"Thank you, my boy. It does my heart good to know that at least some small part of Beverly will live on in this world."

"My lord?"

"You have her heart, Aldwin. I think you always did. Live your life for her, my boy, live your life for her."

Aldwin rose, tears coming freely to his eyes. "I will," he promised, "for Beverly, I will."

SIXTEEN

Imprisoned

AUTUMN 961 MC

~

L ord Richard Fitzwilliam, Baron of Bodden, stood in the great hall looking at the painting of his wife. Though she had died many years before, he still found solace in her image.

"I'm sorry, my love," he said quietly, "I'm afraid I've failed. I promised you our daughter would inherit Bodden, but now I find she is dead and, no doubt, I will shortly follow her. You would have been proud of her, Evelyn, for she was more noble than any knight I have had the privilege to know. Would that she could have lived to rule over Bodden. Now, I must prepare to surrender all I have, knowing that my ancestral home will be parcelled out to a sycophant of a murderous tyrant."

He looked down to his hands, to the small wooden figure he held. As the baron of Bodden, he often had to send out patrols and organize his troops. He had found it convenient to use tokens to represent the soldiers under his command. The one he held was a rather crude carving of a knight and, as his eyes examined it, they began to tear up.

He placed the figure on the picture, balancing it carefully on the thick frame. "She's with you now, Evelyn, look after her."

The sound of a door opening drew his attention. Sir Gareth was waiting, respectfully. "I'm sorry, my lord. I didn't wish to disturb you."

"It's all right, Sir Gareth, I'm done here. What is it?"

"Riders are approaching, Lord. They just crested the hill near the elm."

"Thank you, Gareth. Send word to Aldwin to get moving, I don't want him trapped here."

"Surely, Lord, we should resist?" offered the knight.

"Resist?" said Fitz. "The knights here are all sworn to the king's service. Most of them are from influential families. Do you think they would resist representatives from the crown?"

"Perhaps it's not as bad as you fear, Lord. Perhaps they simply bring news."

"How many are there?" he asked.

"Our lookouts spotted six, my lord. Five knights and a lord of some type, though we can't make out his standard at that range."

"If it were a simple message I would expect only one or two. No, they've come for me. The only question is how they will proceed."

"What should we do when they arrive, Lord?" asked Sir Gareth.

"I will await them in the great hall," declared the baron. "Bring them to me when they arrive."

"Anything else, Lord?"

"Yes, summon the knights. We shall have them present when our visitors arrive."

"Armed and armoured?" asked the knight, still hopeful.

"Saxnor's sake, no. Have them dressed in their finest clothes. We don't want to create a scene."

"Yes, my lord."

Sir Gareth turned, leaving the baron alone once more with his thoughts. Fitz took a last look at his wife's portrait and then steeled himself for what was to come.

He had never asked to be baron, never expected it, training his whole life to serve his brother, but when Edward died, Richard was forced to take over the responsibility. His life since had been dedicated to the preservation of his charge, and he took his obligation seriously. He had moved the farms closer to the Keep, extended the defenses and walled the town. Bodden had been sieged multiple times over the years but never had it yielded, and the thought of losing it now left a bitter taste in his mouth.

He took one last look around the great hall and then moved to his chair. As lord of the Keep, he was required to hold audience in this hall, to give orders and be heard. He had always preferred to go amongst the people and do his work, rather than dictate from a throne. For this day, though, he would make an exception. Today, when they came to arrest him, he would be seated on this chair, wearing his official chain of office; a rich, gaudy pendant and collar that hung from his shoulders.

The Knights of Bodden began to file in, taking their place to either side of him. All save Sir Gareth, who was waiting to escort the visitors. There were currently twenty such knights, though fully a third were brand new, having only arrived in the last few months. They all stood nervously, shuffling their feet and fidgeting.

Finally, there was a rap on the door, and then it swung open. Sir Gareth was accompanied by the noble and his knights. He paused to announce the visitor, "Lord Eglington, my lord."

Fitz waited as his guests filed into the room.

"Greetings, Baron," the man said, "I am here at the behest of the king."

"I see," mused Fitz. "Will you introduce your companions, that I might know who has come for me?"

Lord Eglington was startled at the request, and the baron suspected he had been expecting a fight. How strange, he thought, to meet his enemy with manners.

"My pardon," the lord continued. "I am Lord Godric Eglington. Allow me to introduce these fine knights. They have been sent by the Earl of Shrewesdale to accompany me. This is Sir Aigen, Sir Belvedere, Sir Heward, Sir Gilford, and Sir Lyndon."

"And the purpose of your visit?" pressed Fitz.

"We are here to execute a warrant for your arrest, signed by King Henry himself."

"On what charge?"

"On the charge of high treason. Specifically, that you did plot to kill the late King Andred IV, of Merceria."

"That is a serious charge," said Fitz. "Have you proof?"

Lord Eglington smiled and held out his hand. One of the knights passed a scroll case which the lord opened carefully, extracting and then unrolling a parchment. "This is the signed confession of Dame Beverly Fitzwilliam, Knight of the Hound."

Sir Gareth took the proffered document, carrying it to the baron. Fitz looked at it with only passing interest.

"An obvious forgery," he declared.

"It is enough to arrest you," his visitor countered.

The sound of drawing of swords to the baron's side interrupted the proceedings, and he looked to see Sir Gareth, his weapon halfway out of its scabbard. At least two other knights had acted likewise, but the rest were backing up, their hands away from their weapons.

"Enough!" declared Fitz. "Put down your weapons, there will be no blood shed this day."

He rose from his chair, feeling his age.

"Seize him," declared Lord Eglington.

The Shrewesdale knights stepped forward, grabbing the baron by the arms.

"Lock him up in the dungeon," the lord declared and then turned to Sir Gareth and the others. "Them too," he pointed at the resisting knights. "We'll hang them later."

"My lord," said Sir Heward, "are we not to take them back for trial?"

"Trial? What do you think this is, Heward, a banquet? We're here to carry out the king's justice. Now take them away!"

Richard Fitzwilliam, Baron of Bodden, was escorted from the room.

Aldwin halted the wagon and turned, looking back at Bodden Keep. It had been his whole life, ever since he was rescued from a raider attack, and now he was loath to leave it. Baron Fitzwilliam was a noble man, a man that was loved by those that served under him, and deserved a chance to live in peace and prosperity. Aldwin had even heard the tales of how the baron had made peace with the Witch of the Whitewood and ended the devastating attacks that had plagued the land.

He turned to the north, suddenly struck with an idea. The White Witch, Albreda, lived in these parts. He had heard how she had saved Bodden during the recent insurrection and knew she had visited the Keep many times since. Making up his mind, he urged his horse on, turning north, off the road, making directly for the Whitewood.

The ground quickly grew more uneven as he approached the tree line and he yanked back on the reins, bringing his horse to a halt. Pulling forth the hammer, he dropped to the ground and continued on. The wagon contained his entire wealth, small as it was, and yet he didn't even stop to consider it as he made his way into the thick underbrush.

The woods were masked in shadows, the high trees cutting off the sunlight. Aldwin waited for his eyes to adjust and then began walking. He hadn't planned this excursion and didn't know which direction he should go, but he hoped that would be irrelevant, for it was said that no one passed through the woods without Albreda knowing of it.

In no time at all, he was disoriented. There were small paths that led nowhere, and somehow he had lost his bearings. The branches seemed to leer down at him, mocking his attempts to save Bodden. Was he so foolish as to think this would work?

He heard a sound behind him and wheeled about to see a pair of eyes staring back at him from the shadows. Gripping the hammer firmly in both hands, he waited, trying to quiet his beating heart. A moment later, a large wolf stepped out, issuing a low growl.

Aldwin had never fought in a battle, was untested in a fight, but he knew that today, his actions might well hold the fate of Bodden Keep. He gripped his weapon tighter, feeling its weight.

The wolf came closer, pausing just out of reach. Aldwin was ready, expecting the creature to lunge, but instead, it simply sat, never taking its eyes off of the smith.

He looked around, fearful that other wolves might be stalking him, for he had heard of such things. Time stretched on for an eternity, and his arms began to ache, so firmly was he grasping the hammer.

A noise to his right startled him, and he turned as a woman appeared from the very trees. Aldwin blinked in astonishment and then watched as her dress changed colour to match its new surroundings.

"Lady Albreda," he said in awe.

"I have that honour," the woman replied. "Who are you that comes to the wood with a weapon in hand?"

"I am Aldwin Strongarm," he replied, "the smith of Bodden Keep."

"And what brings a smith to the wood?"

"Bodden is in danger," he blurted out. "The baron has been arrested."

"What is this nonsense?" she demanded. "Baron Fitzwilliam rules in Bodden. Why would he be arrested?"

"They executed the princess and all her guards, including Beverly." He felt his heart breaking anew as his tears began to flow freely.

"What? That's impossible! Surely there's been a mistake, I should have known, my visions would have told me."

"It's true," he insisted, "the baron told me himself. He said they were arrested for treason and then executed."

Albreda turned pale, steadying herself by placing a hand on a nearby tree, "And you thought to come here?"

"The baron told me to flee. He wanted me to survive so that part of Beverly would live on."

"Part of Beverly?" queried Albreda. She looked at him and then understanding dawned, "You loved her!"

"Yes," he admitted, "but they took her from me. This was for her." He held up the hammer.

She moved toward him, extending her hand. He gave the weapon to her, and then sat down on the forest floor, too numb to move.

"Where did you get this?" she asked.

"I made it," he replied. "It was meant for Beverly."

"A fine weapon," she said.

"The baron said it was a weapon for the ages, but I suppose now it will go unused."

"Unused? I think not! Is Baron Fitzwilliam still at the Keep?"

"Yes," he admitted, "though he's likely in the dungeon by now."

"Good," said Albreda. "It will make it easier to rescue him."

"Rescue him?" said Aldwin, rising to his feet.

"You don't think I'm going to let him languish in jail, do you?"

"But how will you do that? You have no soldiers?"

"Do you imagine that soldiers can withstand the force of nature? If so, I believe you underestimate my powers. What did you think I was going to do?"

"Get help? Send word somewhere to raise an army, perhaps?"

She smiled at him, "You poor boy, you've been locked away in a smithy for far too long. You and I will rescue the baron, that's all it will take."

"Me? What can I do? I'm not a warrior."

"I can't do it alone, and I don't see anyone else here, do you?"

"What about the wolf?" he said.

"I can't take a wolf into the Keep. What would people say?"

"I thought nothing could stop you."

"Good point. I suppose we'll have to take him. What do you think of that, Snarl?"

The wolf growled in answer.

"Now, before we head to Bodden, there is something else we must do."

"What?" he asked. "Surely time is of the essence."

"Don't be in such a hurry," she replied. "We have to enchant that weapon of yours."

"Enchant it?"

"Of course, it's of exceptional quality, Aldwin. Fitz even called it a weapon of the ages. Surely such a weapon deserves to be enhanced by the power of magic."

"You can do that?"

"Not here, I can't," she said, "but not too far from here is a stone circle. There, I can call forth the power of the earth to live inside the hammer. Come along, we have things to do."

She led him through the forest, in a seemingly random path, zig-zagging from trail to trail, until they came to a clearing filled with vertical stones, chest high, standing upright to form a circle. Aldwin noticed strange carvings on them, ancient symbols that were beyond his understanding.

"Stay outside the circle, Aldwin," bade Albreda. "And no matter what happens, do not enter. The spell I am about to cast takes some time and will unleash powerful forces. Do you understand?"

"Yes," he affirmed.

"Very well," she said, stepping into the centre of the circle. She lay the hammer down at her feet, then raised her hands in the air. After a moment of silence, she began speaking quietly. Aldwin strained to listen, but the sounds made no sense. They grew in volume, and as they did so, Albreda raised her hands up higher. He watched in amazement as the runes on the stones began to glow. The air around him buzzed, the hairs on the back of his arms standing up, and he instinctively ducked, lest branches start flying. A strong wind was building, and he looked up to see a dark cloud forming over the circle.

Albreda's voice roared out the strange words as lightning arced from stone to stone. The very ground shook beneath his feet, and then a tremendous boom issued forth as the earth inside the circle fractured; small cracks radiating out from beneath the druid. Albreda rose into the air as the magic enveloped her, her hands pulling the lightning toward her like she was gathering yarn. She let out a great yell and then threw her hands down; the ball of lightning leaping from them into the hammer.

For a moment it was as if time stood still. Aldwin could scarce believe his eyes; the very earth was growing roots, lifting the hammer from the ground. Vines appeared from nowhere, entwining the handle and then the entire weapon was covered in a thick green mass of leaves.

The wind swirled even faster, and he heard nothing but the sound rushing past his ears. Suddenly, Albreda crouched on the ground, and then a tremendous clap of thunder echoed through the woods, leaving Aldwin's ears ringing with the noise. The wind died, and he watched as Albreda rose to her feet, the thunder echoing off in the distance.

She beckoned him forward, and he took a hesitant step toward her.

"It's all right," she soothed, "it's over now. Come and retrieve the hammer."

He made his way into the circle, the runes in the stones dimming as he advanced. The hammer sat in the centre, its surface unmarred. He was hesitant to touch it, for the lightning had frightened him, but the thought of Beverly steeled his resolve. He grasped the handle, expecting a surge of power... but nothing happened.

"It feels the same," he said hesitantly.

Albreda laughed, causing Aldwin to look at her in surprise. "That's not how magic works, Aldwin. The power of nature has been placed in that weapon."

"What does that mean?" he asked. "What kind of magic?"

"These are questions I must answer later, I'm afraid. This casting has taken a lot out of me. I have given up much of myself."

"I don't understand," he said.

"A part of my power had to be sacrificed to enchant that hammer. That's why there are so few magical weapons in the land. Most mages would rather preserve their energy."

"Why? Why would you sacrifice your power when it is needed most."

"Because it needed to be done, Aldwin. Fate has sent you here, and you have an important part to play. Now, I must rest." She looked drawn and haggard from the effort, and lay down in the circle.

"Now? You're going to rest here?" he asked.

She looked up from her position, "Of course, where else would I rest? I'm going to sleep for a while. Don't go anywhere, Snarl will keep us safe." She closed her eyes.

Aldwin looked around, the hammer still grasped in his hands; this had been a strange day, indeed.

Hands shook him awake, and he opened his eyes to see Albreda looming over him. Startled from his slumber, he cast about, trying to get his bearings, then realized he was laying in the back of the wagon.

"Time to go, Aldwin," said the witch. "We'll ride toward Bodden, but I suspect we'll have to leave the wagon before we enter the town."

"What time is it?" asked the smith.

"It's morning, you've slept the night away, as have I."

"I don't remember returning to the wagon," he said. "Did you bring me here?"

"No," she said, "you came here yourself, but you were close to the ritual, so you were likely tired from the magic."

"Was I enchanted?" he asked.

"No," she replied, "but you held the hammer. It often takes some adjustment, getting used to an empowered object."

"I remember the ritual," he said. "What kind of spell did you put on it?" He cast his eyes at the weapon lying beside him, but it still looked the same.

"It will have the power of the earth," she explained. "You'll find it will inflict even more damage. In addition, once you start using it, your speed will gradually increase. It's a spell called animal fury."

"But I'm not a warrior," he protested. "Will it still work for me?"

"Of course, but a trained warrior will be able to take advantage of it to a greater extent."

"So it would have made Beverly invincible?"

"I couldn't guarantee that, but certainly she would have been able to harness its powers. Are you absolutely sure she's dead?"

"I was told so by the baron, he had a visit from an old soldier that served him years ago. As I was leaving, Sergeant Blackwood told me that

Lord Eglington had arrived with some knights to place the baron under arrest."

"Who is this Lord Eglington?" she asked. "I've never heard of him."

"Neither have I," he confessed, "but the sergeant told me he came from Shrewesdale. I rather gather he's someone important."

"Obviously important enough to be trusted to place Baron Fitzwilliam under arrest. Who, aside from the baron, was arrested?"

"I'm not sure, but I would think a lot of the soldiers would support him, but I doubt the newer knights would go against the king's command."

"You seem very sure of yourself."

"I know the knights, they all come to the smithy at some point."

"Good, that will make it easier," said Albreda.

She climbed up into the wagon and sat down, taking her seat up front. A murmuring escaped her lips that the smith couldn't identify, and then they began moving.

He sat up, worried the horse was bolting, but the creature was as calm as ever. "How did you do that?" he asked.

"I simply asked the horse to take us to Bodden," she replied.

They continued travelling until they were within sight of the village walls. Albreda stopped the wagon, and they climbed down, resuming the journey on foot. Aldwin clutched the warhammer tightly in his hands while Albreda carried naught but a staff.

"Is the staff magic?" he asked as they walked.

"No, it's simply for effect. I find people take me more seriously if I carry one, it helps set the tone."

Aldwin shook his head in disbelief. They were approaching the gate when he noticed the archer, Samantha, on the tower. As they drew closer, she called out.

"Who goes there?" she challenged.

"I would think by now you would recognize me," called out the mage.

They watched as Sam called to someone behind the gate and then, a moment later, the door creaked open to reveal three soldiers standing in the opening, resting their arms on their spears.

"We're not supposed to let anyone in," said the tallest.

Albreda kept walking, "And who's going to stop me?" she asked. "You?"

The man was about to speak, but a withering stare from Albreda cut him off. She walked right past him, ignoring the implied threat. Aldwin hurried to catch up to her, and they passed through the gate, unhindered. The archer, Samantha, had come down from the tower to join the others.

Albreda stopped as Sam joined them. "Well," said the witch, "what news have you?"

"The baron and three others are held in the dungeons," she replied. "Lord Eglington and his knights guard the Keep, but he sent the soldiers into the village; I suppose he doesn't trust our loyalties."

"We have come to rescue the baron," said Albreda. "We'll have to fight them."

"We're in," said the archer, with the others quickly nodding their assent. "We can get some of the soldiers from the village, they're all loyal to the baron."

"It's not that simple," explained Albreda. "The Keep is held by knights. If you help us, it will be going against the king, and that's treason."

"We owe the baron many times over," said one of the men. "I say it's time to pay our debt to him."

"Aye," agreed the others.

"The portcullis will be down," Samantha informed them. "How will we get in?"

"Leave that to me," said Albreda. "Now, Aldwin and I will continue on to the Keep. I need you to gather all the soldiers you can from the village and join us there. When you get to the Keep, the portcullis will be gone so you can man the walls. We'll be down in the dungeon releasing the baron and his knights, but don't enter the Keep until we have the baron. Does everyone understand?"

There were nods all around. "Good," she stated, "let's get a move on, shall we?"

They strode off toward the inner keep without any further comment, leaving the soldiers to begin the task of rounding up the others. Aldwin felt a sense of foreboding as if the fight of his life were about to take place. He remembered Beverly and resolved to take vengeance in her name.

The portcullis was indeed down with Sir Ambrose standing on the other side. As Aldwin and Albreda approached, he turned to watch them, his hand on the hilt of his sword.

"Go away," he warned, "the Keep is off limits."

Albreda halted just out of sword reach. "Do you know who I am?" she asked.

He looked her up and down before answering. "No, nor do I care. The smith, I recognize. Be gone from this place, or I will call the other knights and see you off."

"Hardly the way to greet visitors," she replied. "You could learn a lesson or two from the baron. He has manners, at least."

"Begone, hag, and stop your needless prattle," Sir Ambrose ordered.

"Open the portcullis, Sir Knight, or I will destroy it."

The knight laughed, "It's made of solid iron bars. You'd need a siege engine for that."

Albreda raised her arms into the air, "Don't say I didn't warn you," she rebuked, and then began to incant a spell. The air started to buzz, while small patterns of light appeared in front of her as if dozens of fireflies had arrived. The lights floated forward to disappear into the ground, like melting snowflakes.

"Hah!" roared the knight. "Is that all you've got?"

A low rumbling from the ground beneath his feet silenced Sir Ambrose. The earth shook, ever so slightly, and then something sprang forth. Aldwin watched as small tendrils appeared, growing into thick vines. They reached forward, like a pair of arms, wrapping around the bars that formed the portcullis. Sir Ambrose disappeared from view as the plant grew even more, and soon the entire entrance looked like a giant bush. With first a creaking noise, and then a popping sound as metal was torn from metal, the plants stopped growing, as Albreda lowered her hands, speaking a single word.

The vines shrivelled, growing ever thinner until they disappeared back into the ground. The portcullis was gone, reduced to nothing more than broken and twisted metal.

Sir Ambrose drew his sword, "Witch," he cried, rushing forward.

Aldwin reacted quickly, swinging the warhammer through the air in a wide arc. The head smashed into the knight, punching through his breast-plate with ease and sending him to the ground in a heap. The smith looked down, his opponent unmoving.

Albreda touched his arm, "Come, Aldwin. We must hurry before others can react."

The smith thought it strange that no other guards were manning the inner keep, but he supposed they were likely in the great hall, making plans. After all, who in their right mind would suspect that a portcullis could be breached so easily.

Across the courtyard, they went, directly toward the Keep. They were about to walk up the steps to the front door when Aldwin grabbed Albreda by the arm. "There's another door, round the side, that comes out near the smithy."

"Lead on," said the witch.

Round the side of the Keep they went, Albreda setting a brisk pace.

"The dungeons are beneath the barracks," said Aldwin.

"I know," she replied, "I've spent time there."

The smith halted in surprise, "You were a prisoner?"

"Yes," she confirmed, "though that was years ago. Hurry up, we haven't much time."

She opened the door, stepping inside quickly. "Now," she mused, "if I remember, it's down this way."

"Yes," he agreed, "the barracks room is on the left and the stairs down are just beyond."

They made their way in silence, ever alert to the danger of discovery. Soon, they were at the top of the stone steps, looking into darkness. Aldwin disappeared back up the hall, only to reappear moments later with a lit lantern.

"Where on earth did you get that?" asked the witch.

"From the kitchen, they know me there, and they don't ask questions. I'm told the knights are all in the hall. It sounds like Lord Eglington is planning something."

"We'll deal with that later," she said, "first things first."

Down the steps they went, and then emerged into a long corridor that ran to the left and right. "Which way?" she mused out loud.

"Pardon?" said Aldwin.

"There are two sets of cells," she replied. "To the left are the small cells I was originally held in, but Lord Richard had me moved to a larger room later. I'm trying to decide where they'd take him."

"He's a baron," said Aldwin. "Surely they wouldn't chain him up?"

"He is a traitor in the eyes of the crown," she said, "and as such, I would expect his punishment to be severe. We'll go to the right; there's likely to be a guard or two there, so be ready for a fight."

Down the hallway they went, finally emerging into a surprisingly empty circular chamber, some twenty feet across. Doorways lined the outside wall, each made of solid wood. Despite its size, the room made Aldwin feel uneasy and confined.

"Richard, are you here?" called out the witch.

"Albreda," came a voice, "what are you doing here?"

She made her way to the wooden door, "Step away, I'm going to get you out."

She backed up slightly and then began chanting. Aldwin watched as once again small lights floated before her. This time, they sunk into the door and then the strangest thing happened. The wooden planks that made up the door emitted cracking sounds as they began to buckle and twist as if swelling. The door splintered, falling to the floor, lying there looking like rotten wood on a forest floor.

Albreda beckoned to Aldwin, who passed her the lantern. She held it before her, peering into the room. "It seems we meet again," she said, stepping inside.

Aldwin stepped forward only to catch her embracing the baron and turned away in embarrassment.

"Where are the others, Richard?" she asked. "Surely you're not down here alone."

"We're over here," they shouted from another cell.

"This just won't do," exclaimed Albreda. She stepped back into the circular room, the baron following. Moments later, she repeated her spell and the other doors crumbled to the ground.

The baron looked at the ruins of the doors. "Why didn't you do that years ago?" he asked.

"I wasn't as powerful back then," she replied. "Now, explain yourself, Richard. Why didn't you fight?"

"I couldn't," he replied, "most of my knights are loyal to the crown. It would have been a bloodbath."

"Well," she declared, "you're safe now. Let's head back to the Whitewood."

"No," said the baron. "It's time we took back Bodden. I've had enough of this king and his lackeys."

Albreda turned in surprise, "Why Richard, I don't believe I've ever seen you so riled up."

"We'll need weapons," suggested Sir Gareth. "Malcolm and Basil can fight, Lord, even though the numbers are against us."

"Three knights, is that all?" said Aldwin.

"More's been done with less," the baron replied. "Now, let's get out of this dungeon."

Lord Fitzwilliam took the lead, with Albreda close behind, holding up the lantern. The knights followed, with Aldwin bringing up the rear. Soon, they were back in the barracks where Fitz halted.

"The armoury is on the other side of the Keep," he stated. "Normally, we'd cut across the great hall, but our guests are likely to be there. We'll have to go around."

Back toward the rear of the Keep they moved, with Aldwin going ahead as he proved to be the quietest of foot. He would proceed down a hallway and then, when the way was clear, wave them forward. They managed to avoid any servants, and Aldwin was struck by how eerie the place seemed, as if devoid of inhabitants. Was this the fate of Bodden, to eventually lie in emptiness for all time?

Finally, they arrived at the armoury. The weapons lay just beyond their grasp, protected by a locked metal grate. Fitz cursed himself for forgetting that small detail.

"You shall have to use your magic," he said to Albreda.

"It will make noise," she advised, "and they may come running."

"Then we'll have to be quick," he said. "As soon as the gate is broken, we'll rush in and grab some weapons."

"I'll hold them back," said Aldwin, gripping the hammer.

"You'd be slaughtered, my boy. You're a smith, not a knight, they'd cut you down easily."

"I have this," the smith said, hefting the hammer. "It's imbued with the power of nature."

The baron looked at Albreda, who simply nodded.

"Very well," he said, "let's be quick about it."

Albreda raised her hands, holding the pose as she gathered her thoughts. Soon, magical words began to spill out, and the air erupted with its customary buzz. This time, no lights appeared and Aldwin wondered if, perhaps, she had exhausted her power, but then there was a grinding noise and the iron gates fell forward, to be caught by Sir Gareth and Sir Malcolm.

Fitz ran into the room, grabbing a sword and passing it back. Soon, they were all armed except for Albreda who refused the offer. Aldwin studied the metal gate which the knights had quietly lowered to the floor. It was fully intact, and he tried to wrap his mind around it. He looked to the archway which had held the door and then understood; Albreda had used her magic to soften the stone, and the weight of the gate had done the rest. Now, he placed his hands to the spot where it had been attached. It looked like soft clay that had been pushed aside, but as his fingers traced across its surface, he realized it was hard as stone.

"How did you do that?" he asked.

"You'd be surprised what an Earth Mage can do when she puts her mind to it," Albreda replied.

"Time to put an end to this," interrupted Fitz. "Follow me."

This time there was no hiding. They made their way directly to the great hall, the baron kicking the door open.

Lord Eglington sat in the baron's chair, his knights gathered around him. In addition to those he had brought with him, some of the Bodden knights were also present.

Aldwin was shocked; he had expected more of the knights would have supported the baron, but now their small group of six faced more than a dozen adversaries.

"Well, well," said Lord Eglington, his attention caught by the sound of the door. "What have we here; the traitor returns."

"Your time is up, Eglington," said Fitz, "as is the time of your master. No longer will we submit to King Henry's rule."

Eglington looked around the room at his men, "It seems you are confused. From my point of view, you are vastly outnumbered. Surrender now, and I'll make your death quick."

"The only death this day will be that of you and your men. You have brought this on yourself."

"Me? How have I brought this on? It was your daughter that conspired against the crown."

"My daughter's confession was forged," declared Fitz, "as was this whole conspiracy. She served the crown loyally, protecting the king's own daughter."

The baron had been moving forward as he talked, his hand grasping the sword in a vice-like grip.

One of Eglington's knights backed up, a huge man, pulling a battle axe from his back. The rest drew their weapons, readying themselves for a fight, but the axe wielder surprised them all.

"I cannot condone this," he said, "I stand with Lord Fitzwilliam."

Lord Eglington, stunned by the revelation, turned on his man, "How dare you, Sir Heward. I took you to be a man of honour. Will you forsake your oath so easily?"

Sir Heward held his axe in front of him, daring the other knights to test him. "You call this honour? I knew Dame Beverly Fitzwilliam, she was an honourable knight. I cannot believe her guilty of the crimes you have accused her of."

"Then you will die with the rest," said Lord Eglington. "Kill them!"

The assembled knights rushed at the small group in force, weapons gleaming in the candlelight. Aldwin backed up, unsure of his weapon, swinging the hammer one handed as he tried to gauge his opponents.

The baron surged forward, heading straight for Lord Eglington, but the noble backed up, allowing two knights to fall into place before him. Fitz feigned a stab with his sword, and the first knight moved to block. The baron pulled back and stabbed again, this time beneath the man's guard, driving the blade into his foe's chest. It dug into the breastplate but failed to find purchase in his body. The baron cursed, withdrawing his weapon.

Beside him, Sir Gareth opened up his opponent's leg with a vicious slash. It cut deeply through the mail, producing a crunching noise as the weight of the blade broke bone. The enemy knight collapsed, grasping his leg in agony.

Sir Basil was fending off an attack from Sir Lyndon, who was beating on him mercilessly with a huge two-handed sword. Basil's blade shattered when he tried to use it to stop the powerful overhead strike from his opponent, leaving him defenseless to prevent the impending sword from cutting him in two.

Aldwin swung the hammer, a one-handed attack that appeared to have a life of its own. Basil's killer moved to block, a display of dexterity that was as impressive as it was ineffective, for the hammer smashed through the blade, sinking into the side of the man's breastplate, leaving a massive dent and knocking him to the ground. Aldwin advanced to finish the job, but Sir Malcolm grabbed his arm, pulling him back just in time as another blade flashed in front of him. His new opponent was short but fast. Aldwin saw no face, for the helmet had dropped its visor, and now he appeared as some strange metal creature, intent on the smith's demise.

Sir Malcolm struck, a glancing blow that rebounded off the enemy's shield. His opponent turned to face this new threat, giving Aldwin time to react. He whirled the hammer overhead, bringing it crashing down onto the man's helmet with a loud metallic ring, cleaving through the metal defense like it was nothing. Blood spurted out of the helmet's eyeholes, and the enemy fell to the ground, still unknown, his skull crushed.

Albreda had backed up as the fight began and now she ran for the large double doors that led outside. She was reaching for the door when a voice yelled at her.

"Not so fast, witch."

She turned to see Sir Bron.

"How dare you turn on your master," she said. "Lord Richard deserves better."

"Lord Richard is a traitor," he snarled, running forward and swinging his sword.

She sidestepped, bringing her staff down as she did so. Sir Bron, encumbered as he was by his armour, overshot, tripping on the outstretched weapon.

Albreda spoke the words of command and roots shot forth from between the flagstones, gripping Bron in a net of coarse fibres. All he could do was watch helplessly as Albreda returned her attention to the doors and opened them.

Sir Heward swung his axe low, slicing into the legs of Sir Aigen, whose feeble attempts to block the mighty weapon proved useless. He pulled the axe back, swinging it in an arc to come to rest in his hands. The rest of the Shrewesdale knights were busy engaging the baron, but Sir Belvedere glared at Heward with a look of disdain.

"You filthy traitor," he shouted, spittle spewing from his mouth, along with the words. His blade struck out, scraping across Heward's breastplate, sending a jarring sound echoing through the great chamber.

Heward replied with his axe, a quick jab to push his opponent back and gain room to use his weapon. It had the desired effect for Belvedere retreated a step, drawing his blade back for another stab, but instead of swinging, Heward stepped forward, head-butting the man in the face, their helmets clanging noisily.

Belvedere staggered, only to trip on the fallen figure of Sir Aigen. Sir Heward was a big man, perhaps the tallest in the kingdom, and he used his height to swing the axe overhead, driving it down with all his might. The blade cut into his opponent, ripping through his chest plate and driving deep. Sir Belvedere gasped for air, and then stopped, dead.

Lord Eglington stood back and watched the fight. He had been promised Bodden as his own, but now he watched as his knights, the best knights in all of Merceria, were cut down around him. He thought to flee and looked for an exit when soldiers appeared from nowhere, brandishing spears.

One of them stepped closer. "Drop your blade, Lord," the man said.

His lordship turned with a snarl, drawing his blade. It was an exquisite weapon, crafted by one of the finest smiths in all of Shrewesdale, but he never had a chance to use it; as he pulled back his arm to swing, an arrow took him in the eye, and he fell over backwards to lie, unmoving, on the floor.

The baron parried a blow and struck out, his weapon scraping harmlessly off his enemy's chainmail. His opponent struck back, slicing across his forearm and drawing blood. Fitz focused his anger, driving his blade into the man's groin. It didn't penetrate the chainmail, but the force of the blow caused his opponent to double over instinctively, and then Fitz raised his arm, bringing his sword crashing down through the man's neck. The severed head rolled across the room, coming to rest against the chair.

Aldwin looked around the room; the fighting had ceased. Dead and wounded men littered the ground, including Lord Eglington. Bodden's soldiers flooded into the room, Sergeant Blackwood and Samantha, the archer, among them.

Lord Fitzwilliam stood, catching his breath. Albreda walked over to him and began examining the cut to his arm as the soldiers gathered up the wounded.

"What should we do with them, Lord?" asked Blackwood.

Fitz looked around the room, noticing for perhaps the first time, the slaughter that had taken place. Sir Heward was still holding his axe as he moved across the room. He lay his weapon before the baron, kneeling.

"My lord," he said. "I knew Dame Beverly, served with her in the battle of Eastwood. I knew her to be most honourable and true of heart."

"I thank you for your help," said Fitz. "Remind me, Sir Knight, what is your name?"

"I am Sir Heward," he said, keeping his head bowed.

"I have heard of you," Fitz replied. "They call you 'The Axe', do they not?"

"They do, my lord."

"Then tell me what reward you seek for your assistance, and if it is within my means, I shall grant it to you."

"I wish only to serve you, Lord," said Sir Heward, "and atone for the sins of my past. I deeply regret having served the Earl of Shrewesdale and the tyrant king."

"And so you shall," said Fitz. "Very well, I accept you into my service, though it may be short. The king will eventually learn of what has happened today and will most definitely send an army to punish us."

"Then let them come," said Sir Heward, "and we shall fight to the death for our cause."

"Let's hope it doesn't come to that," interrupted Albreda. "Though I daresay, there will be more fighting." She turned to the baron. "Now that we have regained Bodden, what shall you do?"

Fitz turned to Sir Gareth, "Raise the red flag."

The knight dutifully left, leaving Aldwin confused. "What's the red flag?" he asked.

The baron turned to the smith, "Our ancestors were mercenaries, my boy. The army that came to this land was composed of many companies, each led by their own leader. They elected their own army commander and would follow him to the end of days, but if they disagreed with a decision, rather than argue, they would fight under a red flag, signifying their displeasure. Over the years it has come to be recognized as the flag of rebellion."

SEVENTEEN

Lucky Charm

AUTUMN 961 MC

Nikki sat on a woven reed mat, her back leaning against the stone wall of the temple. The Life Mage, Revi Bloom stood over her, holding her injured arm.

"How does it feel?" he asked.

"It aches," she replied, "constantly. Your healing magic doesn't work on it."

"The spell I cast knits the flesh, restoring it to its pristine condition. I would have thought that would at least alleviate the pain." He began unwrapping the wound, careful lest the strips of cloth pull on the injury.

Nikki looked away, instead examining the intricate carvings that decorated the chamber they were within. They depicted Saurians tending to the wounded and sick, and she wondered at the train of events that had brought them here.

"Strange how we came here, of all places," she said.

"Strange?" the mage replied. "We sought this place out if you remember. It was the only way to prevent the king from capturing us."

"No," she corrected, "I meant this room, not the swamp in general."

"Oh," he said absently, "I misunderstood." He looked around, "I suppose it's just a coincidence, after all, there aren't a lot of rooms in this temple."

"Coincidence," she mused, "or fate?"

"I don't believe in fate." Revi looked up, halting his ministrations, "Do you?"

"Perhaps, a long time ago I might have, but not anymore."

"You sound disillusioned."

"I've had a hard life," she continued. "I had to fight for survival on the streets. What about you?"

"Me?" he answered, suddenly paying attention. "What about me?"

"What was your childhood like?"

"Mine was pretty average, I suppose. My parents are both herbalists, I grew up working in their shop in Wincaster."

"How did you become a mage?" she asked.

"You ask a lot of questions."

"I live on information, it's what has kept me alive."

"A trait you share with the princess," observed Revi.

"Why would you say that? I'm nothing like her."

"Oh," said the mage, "I don't know about that. In addition to learning as much as you can, you're both extremely loyal to your friends. She to Gerald, and you to Arnim."

"Arnim is in my past," she defended.

"There's nothing wrong with making friends," he replied. "We're all one big family here."

"Friends can be used against you. Better to be able to depend on yourself."

"Like you are now?" Revi asked. He peeled off the last of the bandages, revealing her bare forearm. The skin was blistered, pus oozing out as he watched.

"It smells," she said.

"Yes," he agreed, "the flesh is corrupted again."

"Isn't your magic supposed to fix it?"

"It does," he said, "for a time, at least, but the toxins in your blood continue to corrupt the flesh. I'm afraid my magic will only prolong the inevitable."

"Meaning I'll lose my arm?" she asked, her voice cracking ever so slightly.

"I can stave off that eventuality for a while, yet. Were we not in the swamp, I'd be able to gather some herbs to help. Warriors Moss often works well in these cases, but I doubt I could find it here." He looked back up at her face, recognizing the look of fear.

"Once we unlock the gates," he tried to soothe, "we'll be in a better position. Until then, I'll keep healing the flesh. Now, if you've finished your worrying, I'd like to cast the spell, I have my research to return to."

Nikki nodded her head in acknowledgement, and the mage returned his concentration to her arm. She looked away once again, but this time she used her left hand to wipe the tears from her eyes before the mage noticed.

Revi began the incantation, soft words spilling from his lips. Soon, his hands were glowing, and then he placed them lightly on her arm, the light disappearing into her skin. The blisters began to recede, the skin returning to a healthier hue. He wiped the pus from her arm, revealing, once more, a smooth forearm.

"There," he said at last, "that should do nicely, I think."

"How long will it last this time?" she asked.

"I should think a week or so. I'll check it each day to make sure."

"You're lying," she accused, "you know the treatments are becoming less effective. You have to cast the spell more often to keep it in check."

A defeated look crossed the mage's face, "It's true, I'm afraid. Whatever substance you came into contact with, down in the sewers, is increasing its hold on you. Even spells have limitations, and I'm afraid we've discovered the extent of my magic. I'll do what I can for you, but we are hampered by our situation. If I had my library at my disposal, I have no doubt I could find a solution, but here, I'm limited by my lack of resources."

"Don't the Saurians keep a library?" she asked.

"They do, indeed. They keep their records on stone slates, but even with my spell of tongues, I can only understand a small portion of them. The princess, at least, has mastered their language, but many of their writings are difficult to decipher."

"I don't understand," she said. "You say she is fluent, and yet she cannot understand the writings? How is that possible?"

"She reads the language clear enough," he explained, "but some references will be missed."

"I still don't understand," she said.

"Imagine you were a newcomer to Merceria. You might learn the language easy enough, but references to the Warrior's Crown or the founding Mercenaries would be lost on you without knowledge of our history and culture."

"I see what you mean," she admitted. "Is there any way in which I could help?"

"You can pray to Saxnor," says Revi. "It's not something I do often, myself, but I'm given to understand it can give people peace of mind."

"I've prayed many times over the years," she responded, "but never have I seen the benefit of it. The world is ruled by people who serve themselves. No one cares about the rest of us, least of all the Gods."

"Not true," said Revi. "The world can be changed by people, that's how we evolve as a culture. It's what makes us different from other kingdoms."

"And yet," she continued, "it's still the strong that rule over the weak. Some things never change."

"Things CAN change," he insisted, "and I think, in time, that will change too; one day the strong shall look after the weak. Changes are coming, big changes that will have a huge impact on our kingdom."

"You're talking about the princess again."

"Yes," he replied, "I am. She'll make the difference in Merceria, I know she will. The only question is how we will get her into a position to do so. That's our job."

"To put a young girl on the throne?" she questioned. "We barely survived her last visit to Wincaster, and you want to return?"

Revi smiled before continuing, "Not right away, of course. All good things take time. Now rest up, I'm going to put you to work."

"Doing what?"

"Our ranger has mastered the art of fishing, and someone needs to gut her catch. You do know how to use a knife, don't you?"

"You know full well I do," she said. She looked down at the well-made dagger laying on the mat beside her and chuckled.

"What's so funny?" asked the mage.

"I wonder what Dame Beverly would think if she knew I was going to use her fine dagger to gut fish?"

Revi Bloom stared at the stone slates scattered around him on the floor. They were written in Saurian, but they all contained magic runes of some sort. He had decided that any mention of the gates must include magic symbols and had thus searched diligently through the library for all the slates that met his requirements. Now, he stared down at the massive quantity wondering if he wasn't facing a lifetime of searching.

He noticed a familiar rune and picked up the slate. The Saurian letters looked like scratches on the slab, and so he cast his spell, uttering the words of power that would unlock his understanding of this ancient language. The symbols began to take on meaning to him as the spell took hold and he started scanning through the ancient document.

A voice interrupted his study. "What's that you have there?" asked Hayley.

"It seems to be a description of a potion of some sort," he replied, "though parts of it look familiar."

The ranger came closer, looking over his shoulder at the slate in his hands.

The mage looked at her in annoyance, "Do you mind?"

"You know," she said, "if you cast the spell on me, I'd be able to help."

"You don't know magic," he said, "how would you be able to help?"

"Well, I could read the Saurian parts and likely figure out what the spell was for, even if I couldn't cast it. Of course, you can just read all these slates yourself if you feel so inclined."

He looked at her a moment before answering, "I concede the point. Hold still, and I'll cast the spell of tongues."

He moved back slightly, keeping her at arm's length and then raised his arms in the air, ready to cast. "Don't do that," he said.

"Don't do what?" she asked with an innocent expression.

"Don't look at me that way while I'm trying to cast a spell. It's too distracting."

"What way?" she asked.

"You have a mischievous look in your eyes as if you're undressing me."

"A girl can dream, can't she?" she said.

The mage blushed deeply. "I'm very fond of you, Hayley, you know that, but I can't cast the spell without absolute concentration."

"Very well, I'll be more serious."

"Thank you," said the mage, extending his arms once again. He began murmuring the spell and then moved his hands in an intricate pattern. Soon, the familiar tingle gripped the air and Hayley felt the hairs on her neck stand up. Revi stopped the incantation and lowered his hands.

"You can cast whenever you're ready," said Hayley.

"I already have," he said.

"Really? I don't feel any different," she said.

"Look at one of the slates."

She glanced down, and a look of surprise crossed her face. "I can read it," she said. "Fascinating."

"You've seen me cast it before," he said.

"Yes, but not on me. You're a remarkable man, Revi Bloom."

"Thank you," he replied, "but, much as I'd like to chat, we have work to do. You start on that pile over there, and I'll continue making my way through these."

"Of course," said Hayley, dropping to the floor into a cross-legged position, and grabbing the nearest tile.

They sat in silence awhile, each absorbed in their own exploration. The ranger was closely examining one of her assigned slates when she looked over at the mage.

"Revi," she said, "I think I may have found something."

"Oh?" he replied. "Did you find a reference to the eternal flame?"

"No," she said, "something else." She passed the slate to the mage. "This rune, what is it?"

"It's called Urdyll," he said. "It's often used in spells of healing."

"It mentions something about someone being stung by a creature and then curing them."

"Stung? Are you sure?" The light outside was starting to fade, and the room was growing darker. He moved the slate closer to his eyes. "So it does," he said. "It refers to poison."

"Is it a cure for poison?" she asked.

In answer he held up his finger, silencing her. "Not just poison," he said, "but any kind of toxin." He set the slate down carefully and looked over to her. "You've found it, Hayley. You've found a universal healing spell for poisons of all sorts."

"I have?"

"Yes, you magnificent ranger, you."

"Do I get a reward?" she asked.

A surprised look crossed the mage's face. "A reward? We have nothing, what could I possibly give you as a reward?"

"I'd settle for a kiss," she said with a wicked grin.

He rose to his knees, shuffling across the floor in his robes. It was an awkward movement, but the ranger didn't care, she had eyes only for her mage.

Revi leaned forward, letting his lips linger on hers as they kissed. He pulled back, leaving Hayley with a pleased look to her face. They smiled at each other in the ensuing silence and then the ranger began madly searching through the scattered slates at her feet.

"What are you doing?" he asked.

"Seeing what else I can discover," she said. "I like this reward system."

Hayley made her way through the temple, her footsteps echoing in the empty halls. Passing through the exit, onto the stone walkway, she noticed Nikki sitting at the edge, her feet dangling in the water.

"There you are," said the ranger. "I've been looking for you."

Nikki looked up, shielding her eyes against the glare of the setting sun. "Why?" she replied.

"We've found a solution," said Hayley.

"You've managed to unlock the gates?"

"No," answered the ranger, "but we found a spell that will cure your arm."

"Don't even joke about that," said Nikki, "I can't handle it right now."

Hayley sat down beside her, choosing her favourite cross-legged pose, her feet tucked beneath her. "No, it's true. The Saurians had Life Magic. We found a spell that will cure poisons and such; Revi's studying it even as we speak."

Nikki lay back on the stone walkway, letting out a deep breath. "That's a relief, how long before he can cast it?"

"I'm not sure," responded the ranger, "he said it takes time to master a spell. He has the instructions, but he'll need to perfect it. With any luck, I'd say he'd be able to cast it in a couple days."

"And without luck?" asked Nikki.

"He'll get it," assured Hayley. "You need to have more faith."

"You talk to me of faith? How am I to rely on him for a solution when he isn't even a proper mage?"

"What's that supposed to mean?"

"When I was picked for my assignment, Valmar told me all about our young mage, and how he wasn't even trained properly. Let's face it, we're in the care of an apprentice."

"It might be true that he wasn't properly trained, but he's proven his ability on multiple occasions. Without his help, we wouldn't have been able to defeat the invasion at Riversend."

"And yet," persisted Nikki, "he's lacking in so many areas."

"Is he?" replied Hayley. "He's overcome his weaknesses and proved more than capable of using his magic to our advantage. Look at the strides he's made in the last year."

"Like what?" asked Nikki. "Like failing to heal me properly?" She raised her injured arm, "I've been in pain for weeks."

"I'm sorry," offered the ranger, "but he hasn't had much time to pursue his research. Beverly told me the first time the princess met him, he couldn't even cast a simple spell of healing, and now he needs to learn how to prevent the spread of poison? You should be more understanding."

"Understanding?" She paused for a moment, then lowered her arm and sat up. "You might be right. Listen, I'm out of my element; I'm used to the city, and I feel like I have no purpose here. It's easy for you, you're a ranger, you're trained in this sort of thing."

"What sort of thing is that?"

"Being in the middle of nowhere, hunting, fishing, you know; providing for others."

"I suppose that's true, but everything I can do, I had to learn. It's the same for you. Were you always good with a knife?"

"No," admitted Nikki. "It took me years to become proficient."

"There you have it," said Hayley. "If there's one thing I've learned as a ranger, it's that there's always room to grow. I have skills now that I didn't have a year ago. Surely, if you think about it carefully, you'd have to say the same."

"I suppose," muttered Nikki.

"You suppose? Is this the same Nikki that dragged Arnim out of the Palace? Would you have thought that possible last year?"

"No, I wouldn't," she confessed. "I never really looked at it that way."

"We all grow as individuals," continued Hayley. "But we're all influenced by those around us. Can I ask you a question?"

"Haven't you asked enough already?"

"Just one more, I promise."

"Very well," Nikki hesitantly agreed.

"If Arnim hadn't been at the Palace, what would you have done?"

Nikki thought back to that terrible day. What would she have done? "I suppose I would have fled the Palace and returned to my life in the slums."

"So Arnim brought out the best in you."

"The best? I'm not so sure of that, sitting here in the swamp with a stinking arm."

"You can't undo the past, Nikki."

"You're not the first person to tell me that."

"And I probably won't be the last," said Hayley. "Do you regret saving him?"

"You said only one more question."

"You don't have to answer it," said the ranger, "but think it over, for your own sake. I believe there's something between you two and I'd hate to see you lose it."

"What would you know of us?" said Nikki.

"I see the look in your eyes when you watch him. I feel the same way about Revi."

Nikki eyed the ranger with a look of warning, "It won't work, Hayley. You can't have a mage as a lover."

"Why not?"

"Mages are dedicated to their study of magic, everyone knows that. You'd become a distraction and prevent him from reaching his full potential."

"I don't agree," defended the ranger. "I think that, if anything, I'll help him focus and become even more powerful."

"That's not the way they've done it for hundreds of years."

"Then maybe it's time for a change. I only want what's best for Revi. If I thought my love was a distraction, I'd end it right now, before anyone got hurt, but I think it gives him strength."

Their discussion was prematurely interrupted by approaching footsteps. They both turned to see the very topic of their conversation exiting the temple.

"Ah, there you are," said Revi. "I have some excellent news."

"You've made a tremendous discovery?" taunted Nikki.

A look of confusion crossed the mage's face, "How did you know?"

"A little bird told me," said Nikki.

"Shellbreaker?"

"No, Revi," said Nikki, "obviously Hayley, here, told me."

"Oh," said Revi, blushing slightly, "now where was I?"

"You were about to tell us about your amazing discovery," offered Hayley.

"Yes, and one which will benefit you immediately, Nikki. I believe I can remove the corruption that has afflicted you."

"I thought it took time to study a new spell," said Nikki. "Hayley was expecting you to take much longer to master it."

Revi smiled at the ranger before answering, "Rather the opposite, actually. The spell was quite simple, really, a minor variation on my normal healing. If I'd realized it was so simple, I would have mastered it years ago."

"Spare me the details, mage," insisted Nikki. "I'm eager for you to try it out on me."

"Certainly," he replied, kneeling by her side.

"Should I remove the bandage?" Nikki asked.

"No, I'll cast the spell first. The only question will be how much toxin I will need to remove. I may have to cast the spell multiple times."

"How will you know if it worked? Will your magic tell you?"

"I won't know for sure if we got all the poison, but we'll keep an eye on you for the next few days in case it manifests the symptoms again."

"You're not exactly filling me with confidence," chided Nikki.

"Nonsense," said Revi. "I'm pretty sure one casting will be more than sufficient, and I have my lucky charm with me to ensure it takes."

"Lucky charm?" asked Nikki, her curiosity peeked. "What mystical object gives you luck, Master Bloom; an enchanted ring, perhaps, or maybe an amulet?"

"No," said Revi, blushing yet again. "Nothing of the sort. My lucky charm is Hayley, here. She's the one that found the spell."

Nikki looked to the young ranger with a new opinion of her. "You did say 'we' found a cure. You were with the mage, weren't you?"

Hayley smiled before answering, "Yes, I was. I told you things don't have to remain the same."

"Can I cast the spell now," asked Revi, "or am I interrupting something?"

"No," insisted Nikki, "go ahead."

Revi raised his hands slightly, closing his eyes and began to chant the words of power. She felt the now familiar tingle of magic in the air, and then his hands began to glow with energy, this time a pale blue light. The muttering continued for a moment, the light growing brighter, and then he opened his eyes and placed both hands onto Nikki's arm. The blue light soaked into her skin and then her veins took on a bluish hue as the magic spread throughout her body. The light finally faded, and Revi let out a deep breath.

"How do you feel?" he asked.

Nikki twisted her arm, clenched and unclenched her hand. "I have no pain," she announced. "I think it worked." She looked at the mage with newfound respect. "I'm sorry I ever doubted you, Master Bloom. You are, indeed, a Master Healer."

Revi, pleased with the results, smiled. "Good. Now I have to get back to my research, those gates won't work themselves." He turned to leave but paused, looking back over his shoulder at the two women.

"Hayley," he asked, "aren't you coming? I can't resume my search without my lucky charm."

The ranger stood, the grin on her face evident for all to see. "Of course." She looked down once more to the patient, "I'll catch up with you later, Nikki."

Nikki watched them re-enter the temple, their footsteps echoing off into the distance.

"I don't know which is stranger," she said aloud, "the healing or their relationship."

EIGHTEEN

The Secret of the Gates

AUTUMN 961 MC

❧

"For Saxnor's sake," Revi swore.

Gerald, who sat leaning against the wall, looked up from cleaning the links of his armour. Beside him, Dame Beverly was oiling her sword, and he looked over to her with a slight smile, "It seems our mage is displeased."

Beverly grinned back, "I can't say I blame him. He's been examining this wall and all its markings for months. I honestly don't think he knows what he's doing. He doesn't seem to be getting anywhere."

"That's because," yelled Revi, "you two keep interrupting me. I need silence."

"Well," said Gerald, rising from the floor, "I can tell when I'm not wanted." He held out his hand toward Beverly. If it had been anyone else, she would have forsaken the offer, but she gripped his hand firmly, allowing him to help her to her feet.

"I suppose we could use some fresh air," she agreed, scabbarding her sword. "Where do you think the princess is?"

"She's in the room with all the rock slates," said Gerald.

"You mean the library?"

"It's hard to think of it as a library when there are no books," he remarked.

"They store all their information on those thin slates," she replied. "What else would you call it."

"A place where one can find silence!" roared out the mage.

They left the room, their chastisement complete. The main hall, as they had come to call it, was covered in the strange letters that they now knew as the Saurian language. Gerald had seen them before, in the grotto cave in Uxley, but never had he seen so much of it. The entire wall was covered in the symbols, written in a very precise hand.

Revi and Hayley had spent weeks perusing the slates in the library, only to come to the conclusion that the answer must lay here, on these very walls. To add to the burden, it had become apparent that the present day Saurians had forgotten much of their ancestor's knowledge; the sad truth was none of them knew how to work the gates.

Off the main hall was a series of corridors. To the west was the main entrance, through which they had originally entered the temple. To the north lay the living quarters of the High Priest of the Flame and his acolytes, while to the south led to the village itself. It had been the eastern hallway which had soon grabbed Anna's attention, for it held the hall of records and it was to here that the duo made their way.

None of the rooms had doors, a fact that made privacy all but impossible. They had tried to explain to their hosts the concept, but the Saurians never managed to grasp it. They settled on creating their own form of doors; a woven grass mat that they could hang when needed. There was one such mat hanging here now as Anna had taken this room as her own.

Gerald parted the grass to peer inside, "Anna? Are you in there?"

"Oh yes, Gerald, come in," she replied.

He entered, Beverly just behind him. "Anything of interest?" he asked, knowing full well the answer.

"This entire room is fascinating," she said, for perhaps the hundredth time. "I'm learning more every day."

They had been here for almost three months, and Anna had not only perfected her Saurian language, but she had also learned to read it fluently. Ever since then, she had been buried in this room, poring over records from dawn till dusk. He had insisted that she rest and eat, and eventually, they came to an agreement; she would begin and end each day with a walk around the village, but the remainder of her time was hers to pore over the endless knowledge found within.

She sat, digging through the slates, which were stacked like books on shelves.

"Would you care to be more specific?" he asked. "What did you learn today?"

"It seems the Saurians kept lots of records about the other races."

"Other races? Which ones?"

"Mostly Orcs, Dwarves, and a little about the Elves. There's also mention of Trolls and Ogres, though there's not much about them. They say the Trolls and Ogres had speech, but no written language, like the Orcs."

"Are we likely to run across them in the swamp?" asked Beverly.

"I doubt it," said Anna, "though Trolls do generally live in swamps, at least according to this." She held up a slate. "Ogres, on the other hand, prefer rough hills."

"Is any of this going to help us?" asked Gerald.

She turned her attention from the slates to her friend, "I suppose not, but it's exciting to think that I'm the first Human to ever see these records. They date back thousands of years."

"That far?" asked Gerald, genuinely surprised. "I had no idea."

"These dates are a little strange," she said, "but from what I gather, the Elf-Saurian war was waged more than two thousand years ago."

"Interesting," agreed Gerald, "but of little practical use."

"How's our mage faring?" asked Anna.

"As grumpy as ever, and still unable to find what he needs."

"Is it that bad?" she asked.

"The pedestal beneath the flame has more runes than the one at Uxley. The number of rune combinations is, how did he say it?" he turned to Beverly.

"Astronomical," she said, "his new favourite word."

"At this rate," continued Gerald, "it'll take years to locate the gates."

"Maybe not," said Anna. "I have an idea." She moved down the wall, pulling forth the odd slate, quickly looking at it and then replacing it. She finally settled on the one she wanted. "I found this in my searching," she said. "It references the gates. It gives them names, and I think this one is Uxley."

"How can you be sure?" asked Gerald.

She pointed at the runes, "I remember seeing this combination in the temple at Uxley. I think they form some sort of coordinates. In their language, it would be Ku-Mon-Tah. I think each word is a part of the coordinate."

"Perhaps we should take this to Revi?" said Beverly. "It might be the information he's been looking for."

"Good idea," agreed the princess. "Lead on."

They stepped out of the room, returning to the main chamber where Revi could be seen simply staring, not really looking at anything. He turned in annoyance at their return but quickly recovered his composure at the sight of the princess.

"Highness," he said, "I'm afraid I've little progress to report."

"I think I may have found something of use, Master Bloom," said Anna, holding out the slate.

"What is it?" he asked.

"A slate with the coordinates of Uxley, or at least I think that's what it is?"

He gazed down at the slate as she pointed. "See here? Ku-Mon-Tah. Those words are, I believe, some sort of coordinate system. I recognized the symbols from the temple at Uxley. Does that help?"

"Indeed it does," replied the mage, now smiling uncontrollably. "I have discovered how to activate the gate, but without coordinates, I haven't been able to focus on a location. We must try the gate immediately."

Revi was ready to rush off, but Gerald grabbed his arm to stop him. "We should summon the High Priest," he warned, "we don't want to upset the Saurians."

"Agreed," said Anna.

"I'll go find him," offered Beverly. "Why don't you three get up to the flame and look things over. I'll join you as soon as I find Hassus."

Anna's eyes were alight with interest, "Come on, Gerald, this is exciting!"

Beverly and the High Priest of the Eternal Flame exited the stairs to join them. Revi, who had been looking over at the pedestal, glanced up, waiting for consent to begin.

"Proceed," said Hassus.

"All right, first I need to awaken the flame by speaking each magic word and touch the matching rune on the pedestal. It requires my utmost concentration, so no interruptions." He gave a steely glare in the direction of Gerald and Beverly.

Revi took a moment of silent contemplation before starting the ritual. He began by placing his hand upon each rune, saying the magic words needed to activate the gate. They began to glow while the green flame leaped to life, growing higher with each stone touched.

Finally, Revi turned to the princess, "We should only have to put in the coordinates now, and the gate will hopefully open." He touched the next rune, uttering the word, "Ku." The flame shot much higher to become a tall, thin column of flame. "Mon," he uttered, touching another, and the column grew wider until it almost reached the stone archway which housed it. "Tah," he said, touching the last rune. A sudden flash of light burst forth, and then the centre of the flame grew dark. It now looked like something was outlined in a strange green magic flame.

"It didn't work," said Revi, "something's gone wrong."

"No, wait," said Anna. "Let your eyes adjust. We're looking into a dark room. There, something's moving inside."

Gerald stared at the centre of the flame. It was almost as if shadows were moving and then a pair of eyes came into view. He jumped back in surprise.

"It's Lily!" cried Anna. "She must be in the temple. She's looking back at us. Lily, can you hear me?"

There was no reaction from the other side. Anna waved, and the Saurian's face grew closer and waved back. "She sees us," said Anna.

"I don't think she can hear us," said Revi. "Sound must not travel through the gate."

"This is amazing," said Beverly. "I never would have thought it possible."

"Oh, it's much more interesting than that," declared Revi. "I mean to go through the flame."

"What?" said Beverly. "You can't be serious."

"We've talked about this before," said Revi. "We know the Saurians used these gates to travel, I'm sure it's perfectly safe."

"Very well," said Anna, "but be careful."

"Perhaps," said Beverly, "I should go first, it might be dangerous."

"Don't be silly," said Revi, "that's Lily on the other side, what could be dangerous?"

"The gate might be dangerous to travel," she persisted, "and we can't afford to lose our healer."

"I have to go," declared Revi, "I'm the only one who knows how to get back."

"Good point," agreed Beverly, "but be careful."

Revi reached down to the stone bricks one more time. "This rune, here," he said, pointing to a strange mark, "is the symbol of air. I believe it to be the rune that opens the gate for travel. Wish me luck."

He touched the rune, uttering the magic word for air. With the briefest of flashes to the flame, the image rippled, as though they were looking at a reflection on the water. Revi reached forward, allowing his hand to touch the surface. As soon as he did so, he was pulled forward, as if someone was grabbing his hand and tugging, disappearing completely into the flame. They all stared at the image, not breathing, until they saw him reappear on the other side, stepping out of the flame. They couldn't hear him but watched as he hugged Lily, then the enormous flame vanished from their pedestal, reigniting a moment later as a tiny flame, much smaller than it had been upon their arrival.

"What happened," exclaimed Anna.

"*The flame must rest,*" said Hassus. "*It must recharge, this we know from our ancient teachings.*"

"*How long will that take?*" asked Anna, this time in Saurian.

"*I don't know,*" admitted the priest. "*I have been told it varies with the individual's magical power and the distance traversed. He is the first to use the flame in more than a thousand years and the only Human to ever do so, as far as I know.*"

"Trust Revi to make a mess of things," said Anna.

"What happened?" asked Gerald. "Is Revi all right?"

"He'll be fine," advised Anna. "Hassus says the flame needs time to recharge."

"How long will that take?"

"He doesn't know."

Even as they talked the flame began to grow, and soon it was back to its original size.

"What now?" asked Beverly.

"We dial the address again," she said.

"I can't remember all the buttons he chose," complained the knight.

"No, but I can," said Anna as she touched the runes, but nothing happened. "Something's wrong," she announced.

Hassus reached forward and touched a rune, lighting it instantly. "*You must have magic,*" he said. "*Only one that has been trained knows how to articulate the mental images required.*"

"What did he say?" asked Gerald.

"He says you need magic to do it," said an obviously disappointed Anna.

Hassus continued the ritual until the image of Revi and Lily could be seen within the flame.

"I'm going through," declared the princess.

"No, wait, you can't," said Gerald. "You're the only one that can talk to the priest. Let Beverly go next."

The priest activated the portal with the last rune and, as the surface rippled, Beverly stepped through.

"*Can we go together?*" asked Anna.

"*That would be most dangerous,*" said Hassus. "*You might end up in one body, and it would kill you.*"

They waited while the flame recharged and then Hassus repeated the ritual.

Anna hugged Gerald before he stepped through. "I'll see you on the other side," she promised.

Gerald took a deep breath and then stepped forward, touching the surface; after a brief moment of coldness, he felt his whole body seize up as if frozen in ice. His vision blurred and everything went black. A moment later his vision returned, showing the dimly lit chamber below the fields of Uxley Hall. He staggered forward as the feeling in his limbs began to return to him.

Beverly steadied him, "How do you feel?"

"A bit disoriented," he said. "How about you?"

"The same," she agreed, "but it only lasts for a moment."

The room was illuminated by one of Revi's light orbs, its light casting eerie looking shadows across the chamber. "I just had a thought," said Gerald. "How are we going to get out of here. We're at the bottom of a well."

"Lily had to get down here somehow," said Beverly, "so there must be another way out."

After waiting for the flame to recharge, Gerald watched as Anna stepped through and then, a moment later, staggered into the room.

"That was fun," she declared, as she stumbled into Gerald's outstretched arms. She took a moment to adjust to her surroundings. "Only a mage can activate the gates, Master Bloom. You should examine the pedestal here before the gate completely closes."

"Already done, Highness. We'll wait for it to recharge, and then I'll open the flames again, we still have to return."

Anna had extricated herself from Gerald and now threw her arms around Lily. "*I've missed you so much*," she declared.

"*Things have been busy here,*" said Lily.

"*Why?*" asked Anna. "*What's happened.*"

"*Visitors have come to Uxley. There's someone staying at the hall.*"

"*Who?*"

"*I don't know,*" admitted the little Saurian, "*but I saw Sophie.*"

"*Sophie's alive? That's great news.*" She switched to the common tongue, "We have to rescue her, Gerald."

"Rescue who?" he replied.

"Sophie. Lily says she's here. I thought she was dead."

"Thank Saxnor for that. They likely didn't take her for anyone important and returned her here. Is the estate empty? It would be great if we could stock up on supplies."

"Lily thinks someone's staying at the Hall. We'll have to be careful."

"First we need to get out of here," said Beverly.

"*Lead on, Lily,*" said Anna.

The Saurian led them through the ruins of the temple. The entrance opened into the old abandoned well. Lily, who had been here for some time, had fashioned a knotted rope out of reeds that hung down the well, securely fastened at the top. Beverly climbed up first, moving aside the old wooden hatch that covered the well.

"It's still daylight," she said, "though it's getting late. I would suggest we don't approach the estate until darkness falls."

"Fair enough," Anna agreed, "but let's at least get out of this well and get some fresh air. I can still smell the swamp."

They were soon into the clear air of Uxley, languishing in a copse of trees. "I'd forgotten how sweet the fields smelled," said Gerald.

"Agreed," said Anna. She looked across at Revi, who was stretched out on the ground, napping beside Lily, then across to Beverly, who was standing on guard, ever alert. "Gerald and I used to walk the estate here quite often," she reminisced. "It's where we first met Lily."

"That must seem like a lifetime ago," said Beverly. "So much has happened since then."

"What's our plan here, Anna?" asked Gerald. "Do we just storm in and take Sophie?"

"No, if we do that it will alert people. We don't know who's living here or whether or not they have guards. We'll go in quietly and look the place over."

"We should have brought Hayley," said Beverly, "she's the stealthy one."

"We'll just have to make do," declared Gerald. He looked across the field. "We should probably get moving, we've still some ground to cover. By the time we get close, darkness will have fallen."

They rose, Revi complaining at his rude awakening. Lily chattered excitedly, pleased to be among her friends again.

The trip across the estate was short, and they were soon staring beyond the field at the familiar sight of Uxley Hall.

"We should go in by the servant's entrance," suggested Beverly.

"No," said Anna, "there's a door in the back, by the sun room. Do you remember it, Gerald?"

"Of course I remember it. We'll need to get to the servant's wing to find Sophie, that's always assuming she hasn't been reassigned."

"I hadn't thought of that," admitted Anna, "but we have to try something. Let's start by getting inside first, and then we'll just have to improvise from there."

"Oh good," remarked Revi, "my favourite word. Is that all you bunch ever do?"

"Hush, Revi," warned Beverly, "we have to be quiet."

They struck out across the field and around the hedge maze that had occupied Gerald's mind so many years ago. Soon, they were at the sun room entrance, and Anna peered in through a window. "It seems quiet inside. There's enough moonlight to see, watch out for the furniture though, it looks like it's been rearranged."

Gerald opened the outer door to the sun room, his sword at the ready. The door creaked, revealing the large, glass-windowed room. Years ago it had been unused, its furniture covered in sheets, but now he saw it had regained its former glory, for someone had gone to great expense to redecorate it.

He passed through the room without comment, entering the hallway beyond. It was a mudroom of sorts, which he knew led to the trophy room. He paused at the end as he noticed light flickering from under the base of the door. Anna came up beside him and peered through the keyhole then stood up straight. Looking directly at Gerald, she took a breath and then opened the door, stepping inside.

The room was much as Gerald remembered it, complete with its roaring fire and animal heads mounted on the wall. From this angle, he recognized the inhabitant who was sitting in the large armchair, drinking from a silver goblet.

"Hello, Margaret," said Anna, "I see you've made yourself at home."

Margaret, startled by the words, almost spilled her drink but regained her composure quickly. "My dear sister," she said, "I'm so glad to see that you're still alive."

"What happened, Margaret. How did you come to Uxley?"

"I felt it best to leave Wincaster. The atmosphere there was growing unhealthy, and I didn't want to cross our dear brother, he's so touchy of late. I heard what happened to you at the banquet, sister dear. I hope you'll believe me when I say I'm sorry it happened, though I must admit I'm not surprised. Henry's grown ever more erratic since he became king."

"I can't believe you're here, of all places," Anna said. "You must come with us, get away from this place."

"I can't do that," explained Margaret, "I'm being watched."

Anna cast her eyes about the room.

"Not here," she said, "but whenever I leave the estate. I'm a virtual prisoner."

"How terrible," Anna said.

"It's not so bad," her sister admitted. "I have a pampered life here, they look after me well."

The others filed into the room.

"I see you still have that old bodyguard," commented Margaret. "That reminds me, I saved that servant of yours. Shall I call for her?"

"Please do," said Anna.

Margaret rose from her chair, making her way to the other door. Gerald watched her closely, afraid she might give warning, but she simply opened the door and called out for Sophie.

"The sound carries so well here in the corridors of Uxley," Margaret said. "I'm sure she'll be here shortly. Oh, didn't I mention, I also saved your dog."

Anna's eyes grew wide, "Tempus? You saved Tempus?"

"Henry wanted him put to death, but the beast saved me back at Alfred's funeral. It was the least I could do. He's been kept in a cage; he won't let anyone near him save for your maid."

Gerald saw Anna beginning to tear up. "How do we know we can trust you?" he asked.

"You have no reason not to," replied Margaret. "Please, take your maid and your dog. I can give you some money if you need it, but don't ever speak of this to Henry, it would be the death of me."

A light tap sounded on the door. "Enter," commanded Margaret. A moment later, the door opened to reveal Sophie. She was startled by the sight of strangers in the room but then recovered quickly as she recognized her friends. "Oh, Highness," she said through tears, "I thought I'd never see you again."

Anna rushed to hug her, her own tears flowing freely. "We've come to get you," said Anna. "And now, it seems, we must get Tempus too. I've never been so happy."

"You must leave quietly," Margaret warned. "There are guards here from the king. Sophie, go and collect the dog and meet them out back, behind the hedge maze. I don't know how you got here, Anna, but you should return to your hiding place. The whole kingdom is out in full force looking for you. You won't be safe here."

"Thank-you, Margaret. I won't forget this," Anna promised.

"It's good to know I'll be remembered for something," her sister responded. "Now go, before the guards get suspicious."

While they were waiting behind the hedge maze, a dark shadow appeared off in the distance. It charged forward, only to reveal itself as the faithful Kurathian Mastiff bearing down upon them.

Revi backed up in alarm, but the dog only had eyes for one person, Anna. He stopped in front of her and nuzzled forward while she buried her face into him.

"Oh Tempus," she cried, "I've missed you so much."

"It's good to see you, old fellow," said Gerald, patting his head. "Now, come along everyone, we've still a gate to get back to."

NINETEEN

Unlikely Allies

AUTUMN 961 MC

~

Anna sat against the wall, Tempus beside her, the great dog's head lying on her lap. All around her were tiles laid out, and she picked one up to examine it.

"Now that we know how the gate works," she was saying, "we need to determine the coordinates of others."

"Yes," agreed Revi, who was pacing the room. "Though I suspect many of them will no longer be working."

"Why would you say that?" asked Hayley.

"I would think the Elves likely destroyed as many as they could," said the mage.

Anna looked around the room at all her friends who were gathered here, a group that had grown with the addition of Sophie, Lily and Tempus.

"We need to rebuild our strength," she said at last. "And we need allies. If we find a gate near Weldwyn, that would be nice."

"Right now," said Revi, "I'd settle for finding any gate. The only one we know that works for sure is Uxley."

"Our research should speed up now that we know what we're looking for, and Lily will be a great help, she knows the language."

"Yes," agreed Revi, "though I've wondered about that. How did she learn it? She was alone when you found her, wasn't she?"

"She was," said Gerald, "but that doesn't mean she was always alone. I would think she must have had parents at some time or other."

"*Lily?*" asked Anna, falling into the Saurian language. "*Did you know your parents?*"

"*I never knew my father,*" the diminutive Saurian replied. "*but my mother taught me the language of my race and how to write it. She told me I was the last of my people. I was still fairly young when she died, but I remember many of the things she taught me.*"

"*How old are you?*" asked Anna.

"*By the counting of the seasons, a little older than you,*" she replied. "*My mother died two winters before you first came to the grotto. At that time I had just finished my growing.*"

Anna returned her attention to the rest, "We met her back in '58, and she'd finished growing two years before. According to the Saurian library, they finish growing when they turn fifteen. That would make Lily twenty-one or so, depending when her birthday is."

"I noticed," offered Hayley, "that Lily looks slightly different from the Saurians here at the temple. Why is that?"

"We may be discussing two slightly different, but related species," observed the mage. "The slates tell us that at the end of the Elf wars, the Saurians closed the gates. They sent out Guardians, Saurians with special gifts, to protect and guard those that remained."

"What kind of special gifts?" asked Gerald.

"I'm not sure, but bearing in mind they were known spellcasters, I'd assume that those selected were mages."

"Lily's ability isn't a spell," said Anna. "It's an innate power. She wills the mist into existence."

"We know so little about their ancient culture," said Revi. "The Saurians that live here now know nothing of their history. If it weren't for the library, we wouldn't have a clue who they were. Perhaps magic came naturally to all of them?"

"We may never know for sure," said Gerald, "but however interesting Lily's background is, we have other things to consider, like what we will do with this gate."

"I suppose," said Revi, falling into silence.

"Why don't we use the Uxley gate to escape?" asked Nikki. "Surely we could blend in and live out our lives in peace."

"With the entire kingdom looking for us?" said Arnim with some annoyance. "I think not."

"We have to right this wrong," said Anna. "It's the obligation of the nobility to serve the people."

"What a load of godspit," said Nikki. "Who came up with that line?"

"Baron Fitzwilliam," said Anna.

"And who's he?" asked Nikki.

"My father, remember," said Beverly, turning red in anger.

"No offense," said Nikki, "but shouldn't we be concentrating on living, rather than revenge?"

"How can you be so self-centred," said Arnim. "Isn't there anything in this world you care for, other than yourself?"

Nikki, stung by the rebuke, lapsed into silence.

"We need allies," repeated Anna. "Weldwyn would be preferred, but perhaps we could negotiate a deal with the Dwarves and Elves. They helped us once, why not again?"

"Your brother cancelled their agreement," offered Herdwin. "Why would they help again?"

"This is different," defended Gerald. "She'll be the queen once this is over. There'd be no one to cancel anything."

"It's a valid point," conceded the Dwarf, "but it's a long climb to the throne, especially when you don't have an army."

"What about the Orcs," offered Beverly. "They might help. They seemed to enjoy helping us in the Great Wood of Weldwyn."

"Yes," agreed Revi, "and that still baffles me."

"That they helped us?" asked Gerald.

"No," admitted the mage, "that they knew who Beverly was. They must have some way of communicating over long distances."

"Not necessarily," offered Hayley, "they might have couriers or travelling merchants they deal with that carry news. Not everything has to be ascribed to magic."

"Regardless," said Anna, "we can't do anything until we unlock some other gate locations. Lily and I have narrowed down these slates to those that mention gates. We'll read through them thoroughly and try to identify anything that might be useful. In the meantime, I'd like Gerald and Beverly to take a look at this." She slid a slate toward them.

Gerald picked it up, "It's a map of Merceria. How would the Saurians have this?"

"They didn't," declared Anna. "I made it myself. Hassus showed me how they make their slates. It's quite interesting actually, they last much longer than paper would."

"Yes," said Revi, "but you would break your back carrying them around."

"I daresay you could break your back carrying books, Master Bloom. I saw some of the tomes you brought to Weldwyn, you'd need a strong man to lug those around."

Revi bowed, "You have made an excellent point, as always, Highness."

"What do you want us to do with this map?" asked Beverly.

"Sooner or later," continued Anna, "we're going to have to wage a war. I'd like you two to come up with some plans. We'll have to adjust them as we make allies, of course, so plan for contingencies as best you can. I'd like to have options once we begin."

"What about the rest of us?" asked Arnim.

"I'd like Hayley to arrange some supplies. Hopefully, sometime soon, we'll be travelling through other gates. We may have to travel days to get to destinations, and we'll need supplies for that; dried fish or plants or whatever we can get. We'll put the rest of you to work under Hayley. Lily will work with me, oh, and Herdwin, I have something special in mind for you. I'd like to see you set up here with a forge."

"There's nothing to craft with hereabouts," the Dwarf replied.

"No, but once we start travelling, we can gather what we need. One day we'll start forming an army, and for that we need weapons. Are you up to the challenge?"

"I'll see what I can do," he promised.

"Good," she declared, "then let's get to work. We have much to do."

"I've heard that phrase before," said Gerald.

"What's that?" asked Anna.

He smiled, knowing full well she had heard. "It's good to see you back in planning mode, Anna."

"Thank you," she replied, petting her dog. "Now that most of our friends are back it feels like we can move forward."

Revi sat before the gate, examining the bricks. He was scratching out marks on the stone floor in chalk while the High Priest looked on.

Beverly appeared beside him, peering down at his work. "Are you making progress?" she asked.

"Yes, between the princess and I, we've managed to calculate three possible addresses, but we won't know where they lead us until we try."

"So we'll have to explore," she said.

"I don't even know if they'll work. The ancient flames may have been extinguished."

"And so how do we check them?" she asked.

"I was thinking of invoking them without activating the gate. Using the flame as a means of scrying, if you will. Perhaps we'll see something on the other side that might indicate where it's located."

"It's worth a try," she said. "Is that why you wanted me here?"

He looked up at the knight, her red hair now returned to its natural colour, except for the ends. "Actually, there's always the chance that someone at the other end might be able to step through to our side. I thought it best to have someone who can fight, if necessary."

"Shouldn't we wait for the others?" she cautioned.

"We're just going to look, not step through, and there's no guarantee the other end is actually working."

"Let's get this over with then," she said.

Revi began the incantations, touching the runes in succession. The flame expanded and they peered through, letting their eyes adjust until they perceived movement on the other side; something moving past! A moment later a large green face stared back at them.

"It's an Orc," said Beverly.

"Why does he look so large?" asked Revi.

Beverly looked to the glowing runes about the base of the flame. "There's an extra letter glowing. Somehow you must have activated it. It's like we're looking up close."

"Fascinating," he mused, "I had no idea we could control the view." He reached forward to touch the rune, and its light extinguished. A moment later the image reduced to normal size.

Beverly was standing directly in front of the flame, her sword drawn, though she was holding it in a non-threatening manner. Her eyes met that of the Orc on the other side, and she saw something in there; recognition perhaps?

The Orc bowed solemnly and appeared to yell to someone nearby. He backed up slightly, bowing again, but kept his eyes on her.

"What do we do, Revi?" she asked. "This Orc seems to be taking an interest in me, how do I communicate with him?"

"You can't," replied the mage, "there's no sound, remember?"

"There's something familiar about him," she said.

"You recognize him?"

"No, not exactly, but there's something about the way he's dressed that comes to mind." She was getting closer to the flame, trying hard to examine the Orc's clothing. "There's a strange token around his neck."

Revi came closer to peer through the flame, "He seems to be a mage of some type."

"A shaman, likely," she said, absently, "they don't call them mages."

"Of course," he said, "but whatever you call him, he likely still knows how to use magic. Perhaps we should terminate the gate; he might be able to leap through."

She turned to the mage in surprise, "It took you months to discover how the gates worked, and you had the resources of this temple. Do you now think the Orcs knew all along?"

"No, I suppose not," he mumbled. "What do you think we should do now?"

As if in answer, another Orc appeared before them, walking into the viewing area. He was wearing a helmet, a chainmail shirt, and a torc hung around his neck, emblazoned with an arrow.

"I know him," said Beverly. "He's the chieftain of the Orcs we fought near Eastwood."

"That means the gate must be located nearby," said Revi. "There should be one in the Artisan Hills."

"That's where the Orcs came from," she said. "I think we've identified the location."

"Excellent," said Revi, "it'll make it even easier to identify the coordinate systems. If we can locate one or two more, I might be able to crack the code."

The Orc before her bowed and withdrew, leaving the chieftain occupying the viewable area. The Orc drew his sword, a broad-bladed weapon with a serrated edge that glowed faintly with magic. He held it up in front of his face in salute, then laid it on the ground. He stood straight again, holding his hands to either side.

"What's that mean?" asked Revi.

"I'm not positive," said Beverly, "but I think he's showing us he means no harm." She returned the salute, placing her blade on the ground. The Orc appeared pleased with the result.

"Now what?" asked Revi.

"Send me through," said Beverly.

"What? Are you crazy? They might rip you to shreds."

"The gate will shrink, you'll be safe enough here. I don't think they mean any harm. This is a golden opportunity we can't pass it up."

"We should get the princess," he replied.

"Then go and get her," said Beverly. "Fetch her while the gate is recharging. Send me through."

"All right," he said, "but at least take your sword with you, I'd hate to think of you unarmed surrounded by Orcs. Stand back, I have to take up a centre position to activate the gate."

She lifted her sword from the ground, and scabbarded it, all the while keeping her eyes on the Orc Chieftain. He duplicated her moves, returning his own blade to his belt. A moment later, Revi spoke, and the surface of the flame rippled.

Having previously passed through the gate, this time she was prepared.

She had taken a stance, firm on her feet, as she touched the surface. She experienced but a moment of disorientation and then she was standing in a cave, the flame behind her.

The Orc had moved back as she stepped forward. Now he nodded his head in greeting. "You honour us, Redblade."

"The honour is mine, Chief Urgon," she said, remembering his name.

"You have learned the secret of the flame," he said, "you are full of surprises. Tell me, do you still serve the child?"

"Yes," she confessed, "though she has grown much in the time since we last met. What do you know of the Human lands?"

"A little," he replied. "The affairs of man are not much of concern to us. Our paths cross infrequently."

"And yet," she said, "your mastery of our tongue is outstanding. Surely you have had many dealings in the past."

"We have, though they have not all been beneficial to my people. My shamans tell me you appeared in the Great Wood and were of assistance to our brethren."

"How did you know that?" she asked. "That was many weeks of travel from here."

"The spirits tell us," he replied, "but that is the purview of the shamans. Come, we must drink to celebrate your return. It has been a very long time since the flames have brought visitors."

"How long, Urgon?"

"Many generations ago. Not since the lizard folk tread the world."

Beverly was about to follow when she had a thought. "Sorry, I cannot leave the flame. I am at the mercy of the mage that sent me here."

"Surely the mage has not imprisoned you?" he asked in alarm.

"No, but he's the only one that can control the gate, at the moment. I have to rely on him to get back."

"Understood," said Urgon. "Then perhaps you should return and bring back your mistress. We would be honoured to host her, though we are a simple people."

"I would be delighted to convey that message," said Beverly. "And thank you, Chief Urgon, for all that you did for us at Eastwood. We owe you a debt of gratitude."

"As we owe you," said the Orc. "Now, you must signal your mage friend. When shall we expect your return?"

"Shall we say this time tomorrow? It will give everyone time to prepare."

"Then tomorrow it shall be, Redblade. May your sword be guided true."

She bowed her head in acceptance. Turning to the flame, she waited until Revi came back into view. The flame had grown back to its full height, and the mage looked relieved to see her. She nodded to him and then the ripple appeared. She touched the surface and was transported back to the swamp.

"And you believe we can trust them?" asked Arnim.

"I think their chief is honourable," said Beverly.

They were gathered in the great chamber, the only room big enough to house them all. Anna had asked High Priest Hassus to join them. The old Saurian was learning to understand the Human tongue and listened intently as they discussed their options.

"Hassus tells me," said Anna, "that the Orcs were once friends and allies of the Saurian people; one of their greatest trading partners. Much of the stone you see here was from the great Orc cities." She waved her hand around to emphasize the point.

"That still doesn't mean we should trust them," warned Arnim, "after all, they turned on the Earl of Eastwood. Who's to say they wouldn't turn on us?"

"A valid point," offered Gerald. "We still don't know much about them."

"We know they have magic," said Revi. "That in itself could be to our advantage."

"How so?" asked Hayley.

"There are few mages in the world. Orc shamans are known to practice the healing arts. Having more healers is always a good thing, especially when you're going to war."

"I wouldn't trust them," offered Nikki.

"You don't trust anyone," said Beverly, perhaps with a little more venom than was warranted.

Anna absently rubbed Tempus' ears while she cast her eyes around the room. Everyone waited, knowing full well she was mulling things over. "I think we should at least talk to them," she said at last. "Perhaps nothing will come of it, but we're not exactly overwhelmed with allies at this point in time."

"There's a big difference between talking to someone and becoming allies," warned Arnim.

"Then we'll take things one step at a time. We'll go through and meet Chief Urgon. He has nothing to fear from us at this point in time and can, perhaps, provide us with valuable information."

"What will he expect in return?" asked Gerald. "We have little to offer."

"We can offer him a future for his people," said Anna.

"Assuming we win the war," offered Revi.

"That's not much of a deal," said Nikki. "He needs something now. People want compensation, and we have none. You can't raise an army without coin."

"Not everyone is motivated by gold," remarked Arnim, turning an intense stare toward Nikki.

"We'll ask him, then," said Anna. "I'm sure he'd tell us what he wants. If the price is too high, we're no worse off than we are now."

"Actually," offered Arnim, "we're considerably better off. Now that we know the coordinates of the Artisan Gate, we're closer to understanding how the system works."

"The Artisan Gate?" asked Gerald.

"Yes, I named it," said Arnim. "It's located in the hills that bear that name, it only seemed logical."

"How far is that from the Elves?" asked Hayley. "Isn't the Darkwood near there, somewhere?"

"That's got to be, what, a hundred miles or so from the Elves," said Revi.

"Yes," agreed Anna, "but if we travelled down the foothills, we'd be well away from the roads. It might be worth looking into."

"Yes," said Gerald, "I'm sure the Elves would help us. Lord Greycloak was instrumental in saving the kingdom."

"I wouldn't count on that," said Herdwin. "The Elves have been treated as badly as the Dwarves under your brother's rule."

"It's worth a try," said Gerald.

"Yes," agreed Anna, "though I doubt the Orcs will allow Elves to travel through their gate."

"I hadn't thought of that," said Gerald.

Anna continued, "Gerald, you and Beverly were looking at some war planning. What did you come up with?"

"We think our first foothold should be Kingsford. The duke there is likely to remember our support during the uprising. Even if we have to fight, the resistance is apt to be minimal. Of course, we can't even begin to contemplate such a move without troops, and therein lies the problem."

"We thought," added Beverly, "that, given a base of operations, we might be able to train and recruit from the local population. The issue becomes a matter of arming and armouring them; we can't just send spearmen into battle with no armour, they'd be slaughtered by royal troops."

"This looks grim," offered Herdwin. "Is there no one that can help? What about the land to the west?"

"Weldwyn?" asked Gerald. "We know King Leofric didn't want to get involved with the last uprising in Merceria. We should expect a similar result this time, though I think we have something to our advantage."

"Which is?" asked the Dwarf.

"We now know that there's a Death Mage controlling the throne, and we have Anna. The prospect of uniting the kingdoms through marriage must be immensely appealing to him. It would give him sovereignty over the entire area."

"I will not give up the crown," said Anna. "It will be a Mercerian that will rule here, I will have it no other way."

"Yes," agreed Gerald, "but eventually you would have children. If you married Prince Alric, your children would be both Weldwyn and Mercerian."

"But she'd have to give up the crown when she married, surely," said Nikki. "The law of the land says so."

"Then we'll change the law of the land," said Anna. "I will not give up control of the kingdom. I'll not see it fall into this state again. Merceria needs to change, to prevent this sort of thing from happening again."

"That's all well and good," said Gerald, "but surely we should concentrate on the task at hand. We can't even begin to worry about a war at this point. We're still operating in survival mode."

"Gerald's right," said Anna. "We'll make contact with the Orcs. I'd like to convince them to start scouting the land. Eventually, we'll need to know what Henry is doing. The more information we've gathered, the better our plan will be. We'll take a small group and go and visit Chief Urgon and see for ourselves what we can accomplish."

"Who shall go?" asked Hayley.

"Myself, Gerald, and Beverly," said the princess. "And of course Revi, so he can activate the gate."

"What about Tempus?" asked Gerald. "Don't you want him by your side?"

"I can't risk it," she replied. "It broke me when Henry told me he was dead. I want him here, safe, at least for now. Sophie and Hayley can take care of him."

"And the rest of us?" asked Herdwin.

"I should like you here, Master Smith, along with Arnim and Nikki. If anything goes wrong, it'll be your job to get to safety in Weldwyn."

"And what of the Elves?" asked Arnim. "Are they to be contacted on this trip?"

"We'll play it by ear," she replied. "If the opportunity presents itself, we'll see what we can arrange. You'll take your leads from me. Until I decide otherwise, the topic is off the block, at least while we're among the Orcs. Agreed?"

They all nodded their heads.

"Now, let's get ourselves cleaned up as best we can, we have a diplomatic mission to attend to."

Beverly was the first to enter the gate, stepping from the flame to find a large delegation waiting for them. Chief Urgon and his shamans welcomed her as they waited for the flame to reset.

It took some time for the party to fully arrive, for each time a traveller stepped through, the flame would need time to replenish its former strength. Revi's was perhaps the longest, for Hassus had said the magical power of the person passing through would determine the recovery time, and Revi's journey almost extinguished the flame. He stepped through, completing the party, and then the Orcs led them from the cave, exiting into the bright sunlight.

The four of them looked down from the Artisan Hills, a rough ground that extended from the mountains to the west, into the fertile valley of the Eastwood vale. They wound their way down the incline, their distant view soon obstructed by trees and hills, to find the village that the Orcs called home.

They lived in huts made from grasses and sticks, thatched with leaves and vines. Though the appearance was unique, the construction was not unlike houses that Humans lived in all throughout the land. Each structure was a single room dwelling, with fire pits that could be seen within as they made their way past.

The Orcs had turned out to view the visitors, standing in mute silence as the small group made their way toward the central fire pit. All of the huts were laid out in a circle, and Gerald was reminded of a wagon wheel. At the hub sat an open area, while around it was arranged the larger dwellings of the shamans, the chief and the warriors. Gerald had to remind himself that the Orcs didn't see themselves as warriors but as hunters. He must be sure to mind his words.

They were led to a large fire pit, upon which roasted an immense boar.

"The hunting has been good," said Urgon. "Our ancestors have seen fit to bless us this fine day. Come, sit around the fire that we might talk."

They sat on the ground, forming a ring around the fire. Joining them were a host of shamans and hunters who the chief introduced, though the names flew by too quickly for Gerald to remember them all.

Finally, the introductions complete, the chief asked his shaman to bless the assembly. The old Orc brought forth a bowl with a milky liquid which was passed around. Remembering his episode in the Greatwood, Gerald declined the offer, but no one seemed to take offense. Finally, the bowl returned to the shaman, and Urgon spoke.

"It is customary, when we have visitors, to speak of great deeds that we have accomplished," he said, "but perhaps, with so many visitors, we shall limit our stories to just a few."

The look of relief on the faces of the princess's party was short-lived when the shaman spoke his next words.

"Young princess," asked Urgon, "who among you boasts the greatest accomplishments?"

Anna looked around carefully, her eyes finally settling on Gerald and he knew his chance of escaping was gone. "I choose Gerald Matheson," she said. "General of all my forces and my lifelong friend."

"We are honoured," said Urgon. "Tell our ancestors of your greatness."

Gerald turned red. He was not a man to boast of his accomplishments and found himself unable to speak. Beverly nudged him, "Tell them about your first siege, Gerald."

"I was young," he started, "much younger than I am today. Raiders came to Bodden that year..." He continued his tale as an Orc translated his words.

His story finished, he sat down. He hadn't meant to tell so much of his past, but the words had come unbidden and the loss of his family, that had been with him so long, still lurked in the corners of his mind. He sat down in embarrassed silence and looked around the fire, only to see tears streaming down the faces of most of the Orcs. He knew in that instant that these people had suffered, much as he had, and his heart went out to them.

An Orc, sitting on the other side of Beverly, leaned forward to speak. "Your story is touching and quite close to us, for we, too, have suffered much in the past. I noticed that you have been injured more recently. Have you not been healed?"

"I don't understand," said Gerald, "of course I've been healed."

"And yet, you are still missing your teeth. Does your shaman not have the skill to replace them?"

Gerald looked in astonishment to Revi, "What say you, Master Bloom?"

"I think he's talking about regeneration, Gerald. I've never had the opportunity to learn that incantation."

Gerald turned back to the Orc. "Are you saying you can give me my teeth back?"

"I am," he replied, "though it will take many days. Do you wish me to proceed?"

"What? Here? Now?" he stammered.

"Here will do as well as any other location. With your permission, I shall prepare."

"By all means," he said, unsure of what to expect.

The shaman stood, moving around behind the old warrior. "It is simple enough magic, but it can only be cast once a day on any given individual. We will not know for sure how long it will take to restore you completely, but I've known Orcs to complete the process in three or four days."

"It will not hurt," added Urgon. "Kraloch is our most gifted shaman. I have been subject to his skill numerous times." He pointed to a large Orc on the other side of the fire pit. "Perhaps Redblade will recognize Volgar. She destroyed his knee in single combat, and yet he walks today, uninjured."

Kraloch began the spell, and Gerald's mind flew back through the years to the day that Andronicus had healed him. He watched, fascinated, as the Orcs hands began to glow and then he placed his palms to either side of Gerald's head. The old warrior felt a tingling sensation and then it was as if something was stretching him, there was no other word for it. It wasn't painful, but felt strange, as if he were a piece of cloth being pulled. The feeling was only momentary, and then the shaman withdrew his hands.

"How does that feel?" asked the Orc.

"Strange," said Gerald, his tongue slipping into the gap in his smile. He touched his finger to his mouth, feeling his lower jaw. "I can feel small teeth," he remarked, "like when I was a child."

"Yes," said the Orc, "it is the beginning. A few more treatments and it will be complete."

"Fascinating," remarked Revi, "you must teach me this spell."

The shaman looked over at the young mage, "It would be my honour," he said, "but I fear it would take some time. Time which, I think, you do not have."

"What does that mean?" asked Revi, looking toward the chief in alarm.

"It means," said Urgon, "that you have other things to keep you occupied, like contacting the Elves."

"How did you know we wanted to contact the Elves," asked Revi.

"You fought with them at Eastwood, did you not?" asked Urgon.

"We did," the mage agreed.

"Then it only makes sense that you would seek them out now when you need allies."

"Who said we needed allies?" asked Anna.

"We occasionally trade with Humans," replied Urgon, "and news travels quickly. If you seek to talk to the Elves, we will not stop you."

"Thank you, Urgon," said Anna, "but there's more. We would seek your hand in friendship."

"You have that already," he replied, "but I sense you want something else."

"Yes," she agreed. "Eventually, we'll raise an army to retake the kingdom. When that happens, we will need information about our enemies; your hunters can provide that. You could scout out their locations and report on where their troop's march. The prowess of your hunters is great."

"You flatter me with your words," said Urgon. "We shall consider your request carefully before deciding whether the Orcs will accept it."

"Thank you," said Anna.

"In the meantime, I will arrange hunters to escort you to the edge of the Darkwood, but they will not enter."

"Understood," she said, "you have been most gracious. When would we depart?"

"We shall feast for today, and rest tomorrow. The journey will begin in two days."

TWENTY

The Darkwood

AUTUMN 961 MC

By Anna's reckoning, it would take five days to cover the distance from the Orc village to the edge of the Darkwood. Chief Urgon led the party himself, accompanied by the Shaman Kraloch, and six hunters. They came out of the hills, crossing the vast plain that stretched to the edge of the Darkwood itself.

Their hosts said little during the march, for only Urgon and Kraloch could speak the common Human tongue, and their pace left little energy for discussion. Only in the evenings, as they rested, could conversations be carried out and even then, they were usually too tired to say much.

They set a fast pace, and four days later the Darkwood came into view; an extensive green forest stretching for miles in either direction. As they drew closer, the pace slackened until their hosts finally halted.

"We cannot take you farther," explained Urgon. "To do so is to invite death."

"Surely the Elves would understand," said Anna.

"The Elves defend their land with ferocity," the chief replied, "and there has long been enmity between our races."

"We shall wait here for your return," offered the shaman. "Good luck to you."

"Thank you," replied Anna. "You show us great honour."

They began moving toward the wood.

"I hope the Elves are not hostile," remarked Revi, "we'd be terribly outnumbered."

"There's only four of us," said Gerald, "surely they wouldn't see us as a threat."

"I wouldn't be so sure," said Anna. "Last time we contacted the Elves we had the ranger, Falcon, to introduce us. This time, we're just crossing their border without notice, they might not like that."

"All we can do is try our best not to look threatening," said Beverly, "and hope they're friendly."

They entered the edge of the wood and soon discovered how it got its name, for the branches of the trees formed a thick canopy, cutting light from the forest. The gloom was oppressive as they made their way deeper into the tree line.

They had been travelling for some time when Beverly suddenly stopped, her hands out to halt her companions. "Someone's here," she said, drawing her sword, her warrior senses on full alert. "Gerald, back to back, the princess in the middle."

"Where do you want me?" asked Revi, his face a mask of worry.

"To our side, we'll form a triangle," she replied.

A twig snapped, and then a thin figure rushed toward them brandishing a spear. Beverly stepped forward to gain some space to wield her weapon. Her opponent, a female Elf, stabbed forward, but the knight adeptly knocked the weapon aside.

She returned the attack on the Elf, but her adversary deftly leaped out of the way. Beverly, taking two steps forward, thrust with her blade, but the Elf, moving with lightning speed, avoided her attack.

Other figures appeared from the darkness of the wood, encircling the small group, their spears turned toward the Humans.

The Elf came forth again, and this time Beverly let the attack come, turning at the last moment to avoid the spear tip as it grazed past her. She struck down with her sword, slicing into the haft of the spear, chopping off the tip. The Elf cursed loudly, dropping the weapon and backing up.

"We mean you no harm," the knight said, but her opponent reacted by drawing a sword and dagger.

Beverly had trained for years, knew how to anticipate her opponent's actions, and so she waited, her eyes watching her enemy' feet; a foot twisted as the Elf prepared to launch herself forward. Keeping her sword low,

Beverly waited until the last moment and then dropped to the ground, her sword striking waist high as she did so. The Elf sailed past her as Beverly's sword cut into her foe, a line of crimson appearing at the Elf's waist.

Her attacker let out an Elvish curse and then moved to the right, beyond sword range. She turned, looking back at the red-headed knight in surprise, her hand covering her wound.

A shout from the darkness interrupted the melee, and another figure emerged, this one bedecked with expensive looking armour. The Elves forming the circle backed up, giving the small party room to breathe. The stranger came closer.

"You're Human," she said. "Why are you here?"

"We come from the north seeking Lord Greycloak's assistance," said Anna.

"Does she speak for all of you?" asked the Elf.

"She does," said Beverly. "She is Princess Anna of Merceria, and she fought alongside Lord Greycloak last year."

The Elf drew closer, her hands away from her weapons, "So this is the remarkable Human girl of which my father spoke."

"Your father?" asked Gerald.

"I am Telethial Greycloak," she said. "And Lord Arandil is my father."

"We came in peace," said Beverly, "but your warriors wouldn't listen."

"The Forest Wardens do not speak your tongue," offered the Elf, "but they take their responsibilities very seriously. Come, I will take you to my father, though it is some distance from here."

Gerald was concerned; the welcome here had not been what he had expected, and now he sensed danger. He held out his hand for Anna and then stopped himself; she was a young lady now, too old to be holding hands. He withdrew the offer, but Anna stepped closer, clasping his hand firmly.

"Together," she said quietly.

He nodded back at her, "Always."

The trek through the woods went on and on. Gerald had no concept of time here, for the sun couldn't penetrate the thick boughs. Finally, they halted in a small clearing.

"We will rest here," said Telethial. "Word has been sent ahead."

"Is Lord Greycloak coming?" Anna asked.

The Elven leader merely looked at her, her eyes unblinking, then turned her attention elsewhere, barking out orders in Elvish.

"What's happening?" asked Revi.

"She's posting guards," explained Anna. "I can make out a few of the words."

"I forgot you knew Elvish," remarked Beverly.

"Let's leave that knowledge between us," said Gerald, "it might be to our advantage for them not to know."

"Agreed," responded the knight.

They sat in silence for some time. Gerald looked around the wood, marvelling at the great trunks that stretched to such heights.

"It's impressive," he remarked. "I've never seen trees so tall."

"Agreed," said Anna. "When we visited the wood a couple of years ago, we never actually entered the forest."

"That's right," said Beverly, "we were only ever at the edge of the wood. These trees look ancient."

"And so they are," said Telethial, taking them all by surprise. "They have stood for thousands of years and shall survive till long after all the Elves are gone."

"What do you mean, gone?" asked Anna. "I thought Elves were immortal?"

"Our natural lifespan is endless," said their host, "but we can still die of sickness or in war. It is inevitable that our race should one day be gone from this land."

"Why would you say that?" asked Gerald. "Surely you have children?"

Telethial turned away. Gerald was about to say more, but Anna put her hand on his arm to forestall him.

"What is it?" he asked in a hushed tone.

"Remember back in Tivilton?" she asked.

"Yes, what about it?" he responded.

"Do you remember seeing any children?"

"Of course, in the village."

"Elven children?"

He stared back at Anna, the words sinking in. He looked at Telethial, seeing Elves in a new light, and suddenly felt an immense sense of loss, as if something wonderful had just passed into the Afterlife.

The distant sound of horses foretold the arrival of a group of riders. Gerald immediately recognized Lord Greycloak. The others, judging by their clothing, appeared to be Elves of consequence.

"It seems we have visitors," remarked the Elven Lord.

Telethial walked up to him, bowing deeply. "These interlopers were found entering the wood," she said. "They stand under penalty of death."

"Death," objected Gerald, "for entering the wood? Do you call that justice?"

The Elven leader looked at him, his face a mask. "I know you," he said, "I know you all. Tell me, why have you come here?"

"We are seeking you, Lord," said Anna. "A great calamity has come to Merceria, we need your help."

"As you needed it nearly two years ago. At that time you promised us access to your markets, but time has not been kind, and now we are returned to our previous situation."

"That was not my doing," objected Anna.

"There is a Necromancer at the court of Wincaster," burst out Revi. "Surely you cannot let such a thing stand."

"How do you know this?" asked Lord Greycloak.

"I saw her," the mage continued, "and she's an Elf."

The whole glade fell into an eerie silence.

"So," mused the Elven leader, "it has come full circle."

"What has?" asked Anna. "I implore you, tell us what you know."

"If what you say is true," said Lord Greycloak, "then I am truly sorry, but I cannot help you."

"What? Surely you can't mean that?" said Anna.

"Only once have we taken up arms against our kindred, and it almost destroyed us." Lord Arandil looked deep into her eyes, "Elf shall not kill Elf, it is our most sacred law."

"But you can kill anyone else?" exploded Gerald.

"Others are not our concern," said the lord. "I'm afraid you've wasted your time coming here. My decision is final. I will have the wardens escort you out of the forest."

"It is getting late, my lord," reminded Telethial.

"Very well," he said, "then show them our hospitality this eve, and they shall leave at first light."

He turned his horse, taking one final glance at the party before riding off.

Telethial watched him until he was out of sight and then turned back to the group of Humans. "Come," she said, "there are lodgings nearby. We shall see you fed. Let it not be said that Elves are not gracious hosts."

Gerald sat, staring into the fire. "We've failed," he said, more to himself than anyone else.

Anna seemed to be in the same mood. "So much for allies," she remarked. "I thought he'd be happy to help, but I guess I should have known better. No one wants to help a disgraced princess."

"That has nothing to do with it," announced Revi. "We didn't even get a chance to tell our story. There's something bigger going on here."

"Like what?" asked Beverly.

"I don't know," said Revi, "but there's more to this. He said Elf won't kill Elf, and he didn't seem surprised to learn a necromancer, more specifically an Elf, is behind the throne."

"You think he knew?" asked Anna.

"I don't know," he admitted, "but this reminds me of the Elves in Tivilton."

"Surely you're not suggesting they're all Death Mages?" said Gerald.

"No, but they're hiding something. There's some piece of the puzzle we're not seeing. Lord Greycloak was very friendly when he worked with us to suppress the rebellion. It's like he's been gutted."

"And what about Telethial's remarks?" asked Gerald.

"Yes," agreed Anna, "and the lack of children. Do you think the Elves are all dying off?"

"It might explain a few things," offered the mage. "But surely they're capable of having children. They can't all be thousands of years old."

Gerald shrugged, "We may never know, but from our point of view it makes little difference. They will not help us, perhaps our plan was too ambitious."

"No," said Anna, "I refuse to believe that. We're going ahead with our plan, it'll just need some adjustment. After all, we still have the Orcs."

"They never actually agreed to help us," reminded Revi, "they just said they'd consider it."

"Well, at least they seemed more enthusiastic about it than the Elves did," said Anna.

Gerald watched the fire slowly dying before them. "I suppose we should get some sleep, it'll be a long walk tomorrow."

"Agreed," said Beverly. "It would have been handy to bring horses through the gate."

"Yes," said Revi, "but I can't imagine the Orcs would have appreciated a warhorse coming through the flame."

"Oh, I don't know," said Beverly, "they didn't seem scared of them at Eastwood."

"A valid point," the mage confessed, lapsing into silence.

"Should we set a watch?" asked Gerald.

"I don't think it's necessary," said the mage, "after all, they've been watching us the whole time."

"After what happened at the banquet?" asked Beverly. "We'd be fools not to set a watch. I'll take the first shift, the rest of you get some sleep."

· · ·

Gerald woke to a sore back and complaining muscles, but at least his new teeth were still in place. He gently shook Anna awake.

"It's time to go, Anna, we've a long march ahead of us."

The princess stretched her arms, letting out a giant yawn. "I didn't sleep well," she confessed.

"No, neither did I," said Gerald. He was digging around their meagre bag of supplies. "I have some of that Orc meat here somewhere. He withdrew a shrivelled looking sausage. "Here it is."

"Ugh, that stuff is disgusting," said Anna, wrinkling her nose.

"Really? I find it quite tasty," he said, biting off a mouthful.

"That's because you have no sense of taste," she quipped.

Gerald laughed; it was good to see Anna's mood improving.

The Wardens marched them northward, toward the edge of the wood. As the trees grew thinner, they came across a second group of Elves. These were dressed in light armour, carrying bows and long knives, led by Telethial, who turned to their guides, whispering to them. A moment later their escort turned, vanishing into the recesses of the Darkwood.

"I'm coming with you," stated the Elf.

Anna looked up in surprise, "You are?"

"Yes," she insisted. "Not all Elves see things the way my father does. There are those of us that believe things must change, that the old ways must bend to the new."

"I don't understand," said Revi. "Are you saying you're going to help us?"

"These," Telethial continued, waving her hand to indicate the armoured Elves, "are young Elves determined to see our race emerge from our self-imposed exile. For too long we have hidden away while the land beyond our forest walls changes. It's time for Elves to resume their place in the world."

"And what place is that?" asked Gerald.

"It is time for us to emerge from the shadows to take our place beside the other races."

"How many Elves feel that way?" he asked.

She looked around at her group, "There are almost fifty of us. We would be honoured to accompany you on your quest."

"Our quest?" said Gerald. "That's hardly what I'd call it. More like a long and bloody war."

"Then so be it," said Telethial. "We shall stand with you until the end."

"And your father?" asked Anna.

"Perhaps, in time, he will see the wisdom of our choice, but for now we must act without him."

Gerald looked over the assembled Elves, "Fifty archers, it's not much, but I suppose we have to start somewhere."

"Yes," agreed Anna, "it's the start of our army. One day we'll have enough to take back the kingdom."

"We have more immediate concerns," said Gerald. "Now that we have an army we have the problem of paying them and feeding them. An army can't march on an empty stomach."

"My people can fend for themselves," said Telethial.

"That's all well and good, but it takes time to hunt."

"We will not slow you down," she said. "We carry food for two weeks." She held out her hand to reveal small, black lumps.

"Stonecakes," Gerald observed. "Aren't they a Dwarf invention."

"They are," said Telethial, "we trade with the Dwarves of Stonecastle."

Gerald was impressed; these Elves appeared to have planned carefully.

"What of the Orcs," asked Anna, "not to mention the Saurians? They might not like having Elves among them."

"An interesting situation," mused Revi. "I hadn't thought of it."

"Well, Telethial," said Gerald, "what do you say to that?"

The Elven archer stood silent for a moment before answering, "It is true that our ancestors treated both races poorly. Long ago the Elves destroyed the Saurian civilization and made war on the Orcish race, but none of us," she indicated her group with a wave of her hands, "were alive at that time. We are a new generation of Elves, perhaps the last, and we are determined to make amends for the sins of our ancestors."

"I cannot speak for the Orcs," said Anna, "but I think the Saurians might be difficult to talk to. I would be happy to act as mediator."

"An offer we most heartily accept," replied the Elf.

"Anything else we should know about?" asked Gerald.

"No," said Telethial. "We are ready to march with you, though we know not where."

"We're going into the Artisan Hills," said Gerald. "There, we will travel back through the gate to the Saurian Temple."

"Gate?" said the Elf in surprise. "You are using magic?"

"Yes," said Revi. "We have learned the secret of the ancient portals. We use them to travel great distances."

Telethial was speechless, standing perfectly still, staring at the mage, unblinking.

Revi shifted uncomfortably, "Naturally, it took some time to work it all out."

"You Humans are full of surprises," she said at last.

"Why do you say that?" asked Beverly.

The Elven maid turned to the red-headed knight, "You have such quick lives, and yet you accomplish so much. In the short time your race has been in this land, it has spread like a hurricane."

"It took us almost a thousand years to build this kingdom into what it is today," said Beverly. "I'd hardly call that 'like a hurricane.'"

"To an immortal, it is a short time. It seems like yesterday that we were fighting Humans, trying to prevent their incursions into our forest."

"When was that?" asked Beverly, a look of confusion on her face.

"Long ago," offered Anna, "when Wincaster was founded. Our capital was actually started as a military camp from which the Elves could be attacked."

"An interesting story," mused Gerald, "but we must get moving. We have many miles to travel before nightfall and Urgon will be waiting for us."

"A valid point," said Anna, "let us continue this conversation at another time."

"Very well," the Elf agreed. "Come, I will show you the way."

They met the Orcs on the northern plain, but if Urgon was surprised, he didn't show it. He merely nodded at the group, turned north and led the way. It wasn't until nightfall that Anna had a chance to talk to him. Campfires were lit, and though the Elves kept to themselves, Urgon came to join the small group of Humans.

"You're taking this extremely well," commented Revi. "I would have thought there'd be much enmity between Elves and Orcs."

"These are strange times," replied Urgon. "Your presence alone tells me so."

"You have to admit," said Gerald, "he has a point. It wasn't all that long ago that we were fighting the Orcs."

"Yes," agreed Anna, "but years ago we would have said the same thing about Weldwyn; we've been fighting them for generations."

"Nothing is permanent," observed Urgon, "our world is an ever-changing place. We must strive to make it the best that we can."

"And you bear no grudge against the Elves?" asked Gerald.

"No, but many of us are wary of the woodland race. What little interactions we have had with them has proven them to be disagreeable at best.

The Dwarves say they are a trustworthy people, but we have little experience with them as such."

"You deal with the Dwarves?" asked Gerald.

"Yes," replied Urgon, "we trade with the Dwarves of Stonecastle. Their weapons are highly prized." He drew forth his sword, holding it up to the firelight. "This very blade was forged for me by the Master Smith, Kalidor Bloodrock."

The blade glowed blue with magical energy.

"An impressive weapon," said Beverly.

"Take it," he said, "examine it up close, I think you will be even more surprised." He gave it to her, handle first.

"It's very light," she remarked, rising to her feet. She stepped back, swinging the sword from side to side to gauge its quality. "Very impressive, I can almost feel a small vibration as I swing it."

"Yes," said Urgon, "it hums."

"Hums?" asked Gerald.

"The magic it contains is great," the Orc continued, "the power of our ancestors."

"And a Dwarf made this?" Beverly asked.

"The blade was forged, as I said, by a Master Smith, but the magic was infused by our shamans."

She passed the sword back to the Orc Chief, who held it over the fire. As the flames licked their way around the blade, small symbols began to appear.

"Magic runes," observed Revi. "Very interesting. Tell me you didn't imprison an ancestor in it."

"No, of course not," decried the Orc, "but our ancestors gave it their blessing. It is imbued with the power of the hunt."

"Meaning?" asked Gerald.

"It gives the master of the blade immense strength and cleaves through metal. Only the best armour can resist its power."

"I'm glad we never had to put that to the test," said Beverly.

Urgon smiled, showing his ivory teeth. "It would have been glorious," he said, "but it will be a greater honour to fight beside you."

"Wait," said Anna, "does that mean you've agreed to help us?"

"Yes," he said. "Our shaman, Kraloch, has consulted our ancestors. We have agreed to join your cause. We ask only that when we are done, you recognize our claim to what you call the Artisan Hills."

"Agreed," said Anna, "though it may mean you have to work side by side with the Elves."

Urgon cast his glance to a nearby fire where a group of Elves sat in silence. "That will not be a problem, though I wish they were better at talking." He let out a laugh, a deep rumble that reverberated through the camp. Gerald couldn't help but join in, for the Elves were notoriously quiet.

Beverly was gazing up at the stars, deep in thought.

"Beverly?" said Anna. "What is it?"

Startled from her reverie, she looked across at the small group. "Sorry, Highness, I was trying to estimate strengths. From what we saw, the Orcs should be able to field, several hundred or so warriors."

"That would be consistent with what we saw at Eastwood," Anna replied.

"There were more than that," said Gerald.

"The village didn't seem that large," said Revi. "Tell us, Chief Urgon, how many warriors can you manage?"

"We Orcs are hunters, not warriors. Our villages can field large numbers, given enough time, but we need to leave some behind to guard our homes."

"So we could reasonably expect, say a few hundred hunters?" asked Gerald.

Chief Urgon looked at him with a confused expression, "Did I not say we were with you?"

"Yes," said Gerald, "we understood that."

"No," said Urgon, "I don't think you did. When I said we were with you, I meant all of us. All the Orcs."

"All the Orcs? More than just your tribe?"

"Yes," he replied, "I meant all the tribes."

"How many tribes are we talking about?"

Urgon glanced around the camp before answering. "If each person here, Human, Orc and Elf, were a tribe, then there would still be more."

Gerald stared back in amazement, "Why, that's thousands."

"Yes," said Anna, "though they're likely scattered throughout the land."

"Sadly, this is true," confessed Urgon. "Though all the tribes stand with you, only a handful are close enough to be of use."

"How many tribes lie within the borders of Merceria?" asked Anna. "We know so little of your people."

"At least six," replied the Orc, "though there are other tribes that could send help beyond your borders."

"Like the Orcs in the Greatwood?" asked Beverly.

"Yes, Redblade. Word of your accomplishments has travelled far and wide, the Orcs look forward to fighting beside you."

"Thank you," said the knight, "but I'm concerned we wouldn't be able to support such a large army. What do you think, Gerald?"

Gerald stroked his chin as he thought, a mannerism he had unconsciously taken from Baron Fitzwilliam. "We need to establish a camp," he said. "Some place out of the way."

"We have the Saurian city," reminded Revi.

"No, it must be out of the swamp. We'll need to train our allies to work together, harness their strengths, work on tactics."

"Yes," agreed Beverly, "they also speak entirely different languages, we'll need to organize a system of signals."

"And we'll need lots of food," said Anna. "I don't think the swamp would be able to support everyone, from what I've seen, the Saurians are barely able to feed themselves."

"There are other portal addresses," said Revi, "perhaps one of them will be suitable."

"We can't take everyone back to the swamp," said Anna. "What do you think we should do, Gerald?"

"Chief Urgon," asked the old warrior, "would it be possible for the Elves to remain in the hills with your people, for a week or so?"

"Yes," the Orc agreed, "perhaps it will give us a better appreciation for who they are."

"Excellent," said Gerald, "then I propose the four of us return to the Temple. We'll explore the other gates and hope at least one of them is remote enough that we can set up a camp."

"We will send hunters once you pick your final destination," added Urgon, "that they may take advantage of game in the area."

"We'll need to build shelter," said Anna.

"I believe the Dwarves might help with that," said Urgon, "they love building."

"That's all well and good," said Revi, "but don't you think we should find the destination first?"

TWENTY-ONE

Refuge

AUTUMN 961 MC

~

G erald lay back on the cold stone floor. Revi stood before the flame, atop the Saurian Temple, going through a series of incantations, while Anna, Hayley, Tempus and Beverly watched.

"How many of those is he going to try?" asked Gerald.

"He has to run through dozens of combinations. We still haven't cracked the code, it takes time," said Anna, stroking her dog's ears absently.

"I've found something," called out the mage.

They all rose, moving closer to the magical green flame.

"It's open," Revi continued, "but I can't see anything."

"Are you sure it worked?" asked Hayley.

"Yes, the runes all glowed and the flame enlarged, I have only to activate the last rune to allow passage."

Hayley stepped closer to the flame, her face almost touching it. "It's dark," she said, "but I see something there, some sort of strange shape. Should we go through?"

"We discussed this before," offered Gerald. "We send one person through first, and if it's safe, we follow. Who wants to take the plunge?"

"I will," offered the ranger.

"Very well," said Anna, "you know what to do."

Hayley grabbed her weapons, then picked up the small sack. They had all agreed that whoever stepped through should take some rations with them, for no one knew where they might end up, or whether they would be stranded. She took a deep, cleansing breath, then nodded at the mage.

Revi spoke the incantation, and then the familiar ripple appeared, momentarily disturbing the surface.

Hayley inched closer and then reached out, grazing the surface with her hand. The effect was instantaneous; she felt herself pulled forward and then, a moment later, she was standing in a small chamber, illuminated by a flickering pale green light. She closed her eyes, allowing them to adjust to the tiny glow of the reduced flame. The room felt small, and she reached out with her hands only to touch something in front of her; wood, branches of wood surrounded by dirt. It took a moment to register in her mind and then she realized they were roots. She must be in a cave of some sort, much like the temple at Uxley, but here, roots had broken through the ceiling from above.

The flame slowly grew, casting yet more light into the room. She drew her dagger and began cutting at the roots, which, though numerous, were not thick. Soon, she had cleared a small area of the obstructions, enough to hold half a dozen people or so.

The portal had enlarged again, and now Beverly stepped through, her sword at the ready.

"Trouble?" asked the knight.

"Roots," explained Hayley. "The chamber seems to be similar to what you described at Uxley. The floor is covered in dirt, but there's stone beneath. Once the others arrive, we'll start spreading out. There seems to be three corridors off of this square room."

"If the layout is the same," observed Beverly, "then the hallway opposite the solid wall should lead out."

"What's down the others?"

"One will lead to the living quarters, the other to a lab of some sort."

"I suspect Revi would like to take a look at that," said Hayley.

"Yes, and the princess too, especially now that she can read their language. We'll wait for Gerald to come through before we proceed any farther. In the meantime, we'll cut away some more of these roots."

They dug in with their blades, the work making them sweat heavily, while they waited for the flame to recharge.

Gerald stepped through with a lit torch in his hand. "The princess thought this might be useful," he offered. "She'll be along shortly. What have we got?"

"It looks just like Uxley," remarked Beverly, "though in worse shape."

"How deep do you think we are?" he asked.

It was Hayley who answered, "I don't think we're too far down. These roots would seem to indicate we're near the surface, but I can't tell for sure."

"I'll move down the corridor," offered Beverly, her hand out for the torch.

"I'd better come with you," said Gerald. "Hayley, you remain here till the princess comes through."

Gerald held the torch up, illuminating the long corridor. "I'll carry it," he said. "You'd best keep your weapon handy, you never know what might have taken up residence in a place like this."

They made their way forward, pausing to cut away more roots as they proceeded. Past a small corridor they went, keeping a straight line. Soon, they were at a four-way crossing. "Is this the same?" he asked.

"Yes," said Beverly, "I remember it well. The corridor off to the left loops back around to the flame. The right was some sort of sleeping chamber, at least that's what we assumed it was."

"Oh yes," he muttered, "I remember it now. We should come to the end of this hallway and then turn left. In Uxley, that led to the entrance in the well."

Beverly cut away another root and then moved forward, "Watch your head, there's not much clearance here."

Gerald ducked just in time, wood scraping the top of his head. Sure enough, the corridor ended in a hall that led left and right.

"The left corridor has collapsed," said Beverly, "right where the door should be."

A bark echoed down the corridor.

"I think Tempus just came through the gate," observed Gerald.

"This looks like a dead end," said Beverly.

"Not necessarily, we could dig our way out."

"But we might be deep underground."

"You're forgetting the Saurians. They're not a subterranean people. They live above the ground, remember? I think we'll find it's not too far."

"But we're not equipped for digging."

Another bark echoed down the corridor, and Gerald chuckled, "Some of us are."

Anna stepped through the gate to see Beverly waiting for her. "Where's Tempus?" she asked.

"There's dirt blocking the exit. Gerald has him digging us out. I'm afraid the light here is not great."

"Revi will be joining us shortly," said the princess. "He just has to wait for the flame to recharge. Once he arrives, he can cast his orb of light, that should give us a better idea of our progress. Is it very far, do you think?"

"I doubt it," said Beverly. "the layout here appears similar to Uxley. If the same holds true of the entrance, we'll only have to dig through ten feet or so of dirt."

"I'll go and see how we're progressing," said Anna, "while you wait here for our mage."

Anna made her way down the corridor to the flickering light thrown off from Gerald's torch. "How are we doing?" she called out.

"Tempus is making progress," said Hayley, "I wouldn't have thought he'd be good at this sort of thing."

"Why?" asked Anna. "He's a dog, isn't he?"

"Yes," replied the ranger, "but he's a fighter. I never imagined him being the type to dig up bones."

Tempus barked, backing up from the pile of dirt which occupied the end of the corridor.

"What is it, boy?" asked Gerald.

Anna moved forward, falling to her hands and knees to come up beside the large beast. "There's light here," she said, "he's broken through."

"What do you see?" asked Gerald as the princess pressed her face close to the small opening.

"Daylight, and a little bit of the sky. There's a nice breeze."

"Let's keep digging," said Gerald, "we'll take it in shifts."

Hayley dropped to her knees and began scooping the dirt out from behind Tempus. The corridor illuminated from behind them, and then a globe of light floated above their heads, the mage following calmly behind it.

"Beverly tells me we have an obstruction," he said.

"Just dirt," said Hayley. "We've already broken through, but we need to widen the opening, it shouldn't be long now."

Hayley was the first to crawl through the opening. She had volunteered, for though the princess was smaller, Gerald feared what might be on the other side.

The ranger stood, brushing the dirt from her clothes. She was on the side of a hill, her present location in the shadows, while before her she saw grassland stretching off to distant trees.

"It's safe," she announced.

"We don't know that for sure," said Gerald, passing through her weapons. "You'll have to look around while we open up this tunnel a little more. I'll never fit through it at its current size."

Hayley strapped on her sword and strung her bow, feeling more secure with it in her hands. "I'll poke around a bit," she said, disappearing from sight.

Beverly and Gerald continued with their work. There were more roots to cut, but the progress was helped now that they could push the dirt out, instead of pulling it back into the ruins. With the entrance way enlarged, they crawled through on all fours, emerging into the light beyond.

Gerald stood, stretching his back and Beverly came up beside him. The fresh air was pleasant across his face, and he took a deep breath, the sweat still dripping from his exertions.

Anna emerged from the deep, followed by Tempus, who surged forward to run into the grassy field. Anna laughed in glee at her dog, while Revi crawled from the temple, the torch still grasped firmly in his hand.

"It looks nice here," said Anna, "wherever here is."

Revi stepped into the sunshine, letting the cool wind wash over him. He closed his eyes, taking a deep breath. A moment later he opened them again. "I think I understand now," he said.

"Understand what?" asked Anna.

"The coordinates," the mage replied. "I think the coordinates represent the ley lines."

"Didn't we already know that?" asked Gerald, somewhat confused.

"Not exactly, no," confessed the mage. "You see, we knew there was some sort of reference being used, but I couldn't identify the names for each ley line. There are two sets, you see. One set that runs roughly north-south, the other east-west."

"Then what's the third coordinate?" asked the princess.

"That was the hardest one of all," said Revi. "I believe it represents altitude."

"Altitude?" asked Beverly.

"Yes," he admitted, "a measurement from the horizontal plane, if you will. Uxley is below the surface, but this gate is even. The gate in the Artisan Hills is above the absolute, if you like."

"What do you mean by absolute?" asked Gerald. "You're hurting my head with all this nonsense."

"It's not nonsense," the mage defended. "Imagine that the land is perfectly flat. Hills make the surface go higher. Their height is relative to the flat surface, you see?"

"You mean like being above or below water?"

"Precisely. The altitude is a measurement of how much above this flat line the gate it."

"So it measures distance above or below water?"

"Well, not necessarily water, no. But somehow they've come up with this system. It should make prediction more interesting."

"But how can you find other gates then, without knowing their altitude?" asked Anna.

"It will still be a guessing game," he said, "but at least I've confirmed the first two coordinate systems. Now we only have to try different combinations of the third rune."

"So where are we?" asked Gerald.

"If my calculations are correct," said Revi, "then we are in the northwest corner of Merceria. Bodden likely lies several days to the northeast, while Kingsford is to the south and east."

"That would put us close to the Weldwyn border," said Anna.

"Yes," Revi agreed, "likely a few days away at the very least."

"If I remember correctly, that area of the land is largely unexplored," offered Beverly.

"Correct," said Anna. "In short, it's a perfect spot for us to set up a camp."

Hayley called out from above, and they soon saw the ranger descending the hill, under which the portal lay.

"There's nothing visible in the area in terms of civilization, though there are plenty of animal tracks."

"What's the next step?" asked Revi.

"We'll bring through a few Orcs," suggested Gerald. "They will help scout out the area. We'll have Hayley coordinate things, and Revi can use his spell to allow her to speak to them."

"I'd forgotten about his language spell," confessed the ranger, "that will make it easier."

"It's called 'tongues,'" said Revi, a slight annoyance in his voice. "You should learn the proper name for things."

"I'd like to get Herdwin here first," continued Gerald, ignoring the mages protestation. "I think he'd have some valuable insight on where to build some shelter."

"Yes," agreed Beverly, "but we should still post lookouts. I thought a simple watchtower would be useful on top of that hill. It worked so well back in Bodden."

"Aye, it did indeed," agreed Gerald. "What do you think, Highness?"

"You're the General, Gerald. You get them started. I'm going to look around and begin making plans."

"Don't stray too far," warned Gerald, "I don't want you in any danger."

"Don't worry," she replied, "I'll keep you in sight. Come along, Tempus."

"You better go with them, Beverly, just to be safe."

"Aye, General," the knight replied.

Further investigation revealed an area most suitable for a camp; a stream nearby with an ample supply of fresh water, and two other hills, forming a triangle through which the water ran. There was also lots of exposed rock which Gerald suspected could eventually be put to use in the construction of defenses, should it become necessary.

The weather here was moderate, despite it being autumn, and they all had high hopes that shelter could be constructed before the onset of winter, which still lay some months off.

Princess Anna had taken to naming the various landmarks and so the hill, beneath which the gate lay, became known as 'Royal Hill'. The exit through which they had emerged faced south and to the southeast was 'Beacon Hill', while to the southwest lay 'Granite Hill'.

Lying between Royal Hill and Granite Hill was a small group of trees which eventually was named Elf Hollow, for it reminded her of the trees that grew in the Darkwood, though smaller in scale. The stream ran from the northeast, through the area within the triangle, and out to the south, between the two southern hills.

Revi and Beverly had returned to the swamp to retrieve the other members of the party while Gerald, Anna, and Hayley climbed to the top of Royal Hill. It was a magnificent view, and Gerald could see for miles in all directions.

"The perfect spot for a tower," observed Hayley.

"Or a castle," said Anna.

"I hardly think we're in a position to build a castle," said Gerald. "That takes years, and we'd need an engineer."

"It's a long-term plan, Gerald," she said. "I'm thinking to the future."

"I thought you wanted to take back the kingdom," he said.

"I do, but I have to be realistic. Look at the Norlanders, they've wanted to take back the kingdom for centuries."

"Agreed," he replied, "but we can't build a city here and expect it to remain hidden forever."

"Can't we?" she asked. "We're miles from anywhere, and the only way to get here is through the gates, which we control."

"True, but we're still tucked away in the northwest corner of Merceria. If King Henry sends out his rangers, they'll eventually find us. We can't hide a city, and anyway, we don't have enough people to populate a city."

"Eventually we will," she replied. "We'll have to recruit an army and bring them here to train."

"And how do we go about doing that?" he asked.

"We go to Weldwyn," she replied.

"If we go to Weldwyn, why wouldn't we just stay there?"

"Because this is where the gate is. We need it to travel about the kingdom."

"That makes sense, but what makes you think we can recruit soldiers in Weldwyn. They refused to help the rebellion last time, and we have no money to raise an army."

"I think we have a lot of goodwill at the court of Summersgate," she said. "We did save their city, not to mention the defense of Norwatch."

"All right, supposing King Leofric does agree to let us raise troops, how do we pay them?"

"I'm still working on that part," she admitted. "In any event, we still need to travel to Weldwyn. I have to tell them what has happened and return their ambassador's ring."

"Everyone is coming here; the Elves, the Orcs, even some Dwarves. We can't take them all to Weldwyn."

"I don't intend to," she confessed. "Once we're established here, we'll take a small party. Me, you, Tempus, Beverly, Hayley and, of course, Sophie and Lily."

"And Revi," added Gerald. "We're not taking you anywhere without a Life Mage."

"Agreed," she said. "I think I'd like to leave Herdwin in charge here while we're away."

"I suspect he will have some definite ideas on building a base of operations here, but what about Arnim and Nikki."

"It's a tough choice," said Anna. "On the one hand, I'm not sure I trust Nikki. If we leave her here, she might run off, and I can't risk her being found."

"Then we'll have to take her with us," said Gerald. "We'll put Arnim in charge of her. How soon were you thinking of leaving?"

"Not for a few weeks yet," she answered. "We have a lot of planning to do first, and it'll likely take quite a while for our allies to arrive."

Hayley looked south when she heard a whinnying sound; a black stallion erupted from the cave, to tear across the field.

"Looks like Lightning has arrived," the ranger mused.

Tempus barked at the sight, and Anna laughed, "That likely means Beverly's back."

"We'd best get down there and meet her. We need to know how many others are coming through."

They made their way down the hill while Lightning stretched his legs. Soon, the great beast finished his run, to halt and nibble at the wild grass. Beverly emerged from the cave, waving at them as she exited.

"I have news from Revi," she said as they approached.

"Who's coming through next?" asked Gerald.

"Herdwin will be along soon, they just have to wait for the flame to recharge. We weren't sure how long it would take after sending Lightning through."

"I would have thought a charger like him would use quite a bit of power."

"Actually," said Beverly, "it was remarkably little. Revi thinks that Humans take more because they have an innate magical ability that drains the ley lines."

"I suppose that means there are no horse mages," remarked Gerald.

Beverly shook her head at his remark. "Revi's made a discovery," she added.

"Not another one," said the ranger. "Let me guess, it's world-shattering."

"Not precisely," said Beverly, "but he did discover that while the flame is recharging, he can open another address. The reduced flame seems to be linked to the destination. "After Lightning went through, he reconnected to the Artisan Hills. It opened immediately. He brought through an Orc Hunter then returned to this portal and sent me through."

"Remarkable," said Anna. "The more we use it, the more incredible it seems."

"I marked out a camp earlier," said Hayley. "We'll sleep in the open tonight, but we should start building shelter at the earliest opportunity."

"We'll have to start chopping some wood to do that," said Gerald.

"Yes," said Beverly, "Revi's already seen to that. The Orcs will bring some axes with them. He's sending through six, to begin with, and he's hoping one of those will be Kraloch."

"Their shaman? Won't they need him at home?" asked Gerald.

"He speaks our language," Beverly reminded him, "but none of us speaks Orcish."

"But what about Revi's spell?" asked Hayley.

"He can't keep casting it," said Beverly, "and when he's not around, we'll still need to communicate with them."

"Yes, about that," said Gerald.

"About what?" the red-head asked.

"We're going to be moving on to Weldwyn in the near future."

"What about the camp?" she asked.

"We'll leave people behind to look after that," said Gerald.

"I have to get to Weldwyn," explained Anna, "and tell them what happened to their ambassador, not to mention everything that's happened to us."

"Surely that can wait?" said Beverly. "Winter's approaching, and we'll need shelter built before it hits."

"All things that Herdwin can oversee," said the princess, "but Henry told me Weldwyn was facing its own problems and I'm worried about them."

"How long before we leave?" asked Beverly.

"We'll take a couple of weeks to settle down and gather provisions, but I'd like to be on the way well before the snow falls; winter's not the best time to travel."

"On that, we're in agreement," said Gerald.

By the end of the first week, rudimentary shelters were complete. They resembled the Orc's huts, a frame made from branches with thinner branches weaved to form the walls and roof, all smeared with a liberal coating of mud.

Revi had been busy, ferrying travellers through the gate and now all of Telethial's Elves were through, in addition to more than thirty Orcs. The Elves kept to themselves, making their home in the nearby woods, while they contributed to the camp by hunting, a skill they proved to be most competent at.

Kraloch, the Orc shaman, was a valuable asset and once it was discovered that Herdwin spoke Orc, things became easier to manage.

Gerald couldn't help but admire the Orcs. They were a race that took people at face value, and though they valued skill at hunting, they did not denigrate others for their lack. Urgon had sent his most accomplished hunters, and they added to the Elves bounty. Soon, they had meat in abundance and a growing pile of skins and fur, necessary goods for the coming winter.

He was watching an Orc sew skins into a cloak as Tempus ran up and barked. He turned, scratching the great dog's ears when Anna approached.

"You look happy today," he commented.

"That's because we have some exploring to do," she replied.

"That's nothing new. We've had people out exploring the area since we arrived."

"Yes," she said, "but the scouts have discovered something."

"Oh? Now that you have my attention, are you going to tell me, or is it to be a surprise?"

"Haven't you wondered why the Saurians built a gate in the middle of nowhere?" she asked.

"Now that you mention it, it does seem a rather strange place to put a gate."

"That's what I thought," she continued. "We know the Saurians had a large trading empire. These gates, or Temples as we call them, were traveller's waypoints they used to get to their trading partners. It only makes sense that one of their trade routes came this way. There must have been something or someone out here to trade with."

"Yes, but who, and where, precisely? The gate at Uxley didn't show up near anything."

"Not that we're aware of," defended Anna, "but there may have been races that lived in the woods nearby, perhaps Orcs or some other creatures."

"So you think that someone lived in this area?"

"Yes," she said, "it makes sense, doesn't it?"

"I suppose so," he replied, "and you said the scouts had found something. Can you be more specific?"

"Some old ruins, far to the north west of here."

"How far?" he asked.

"It's close enough to ride there and back before nightfall."

"Then what are we waiting for?" he asked.

"There's a slight problem," she added. "We only have four horses, and one of those is really only a pony."

"We'll borrow Herdwin's pony," said Gerald, "I'm sure he wouldn't mind. We only need a small group, You, Beverly and I should suffice. Who found the ruins?"

"Some of the Elves. Telethial sent word, and they're standing by to take us there."

"How do they intend to do that? They don't have horses do they?"

"No," she admitted, "but Elves are very fleet of foot. They can jog as fast as we trot on our horses."

"Then we'd best get moving," he said, "while we still have daylight." He turned to give orders, only to find Beverly riding toward them, a horse and pony trailing behind.

"I might have already arranged things," admitted Anna, with a grin.

Telethial was waiting at the edge of the woods as the riders approached.

"You'll need to dismount," she advised, "for the undergrowth is thick here. I'll have some of my people look after the horses."

They followed the Elf into the woods, picking their way through the lush vegetation, Tempus trailing along behind. They had gone no more than an arrow's flight when they entered a small clearing where three Elves were looking over the remains of a stone column.

"What have we here?" asked Anna.

"We found this while we were out hunting," said Telethial. "It appears to be quite old."

The column was broken off at the height of a man's waist, and Gerald imagined that, had it been intact, he would have just been able to reach his hands around it to touch on the other side. The sides looked smooth but were overgrown with moss.

"It seems odd to see this in the middle of the forest," he commented.

"It was likely not a forest when this was built," said the Elf. "I would suspect this pillar is ancient, much older than the trees in this part of the wood."

One of the other Elves said something in Elvish and Anna perked up her ears.

"What was that?" asked Gerald.

It was Anna who answered, "She said there's more over that way."

"Wait," said Gerald, "we don't know what might live in the woods. Remember the ruins at Tivilton?" He looked at Tempus as the great dog let out a yawn. "Never mind," he said, "it appears safe."

They made their way over to the other Elf, who was pointing deeper into the darkness of the forest. They advanced only a few paces when Gerald saw, among the shadows, a wall of stone. It was fashioned out of bricks, cut and mortared together. He moved closer, running his hands over its surface. "It extends to either side, there's an opening just to the left." He shuffled sideways and peered through a gap.

"What do you see?" asked Anna.

"It's the remains of a building of some sort. In size, it's similar to your old room back at Uxley, but one wall has collapsed, and there's no ceiling."

Anna soon joined him, Tempus running past into the ruin while Beverly kept a safe watch. "There's writing on this wall," she said.

"Can you tell what language?" he asked.

"No, it's not Saurian, or Elvish for that matter."

"We've searched the area," offered Telethial, "there's no sign of anything dangerous, but there are more ruins like this scattered throughout the woods."

"We'll get Kraloch up here," said Anna. "Perhaps he could shed some light on this."

"You think it was an Orc city?" asked Gerald.

"I do," Anna said, "unless you can think of another race that might have built here?"

"How about you, Telethial," asked Gerald, "can you shed some light on this?"

"I'm afraid not," the Elf replied. "The great war was long before any of us were born. I have no knowledge of where the Orcs built their cities."

"What do you want to do about it?" asked Gerald.

"Our people are far too busy to worry about it now," confessed Anna. "Interesting as it is, we'll have to hold off on exploring it in more detail until after we've firmly established our camp. We'll at least get Kraloch and some of his Orcs up here to take a quick look, but a deeper investigation will have to wait. In the meantime, we have to get back to camp, before it gets dark. Come along, Tempus." The great dog barked and Anna hugged him.

Gerald smiled, it was good to see the old Anna breaking through.

TWENTY-TWO

Queenstown

AUTUMN 961 MC

~

A week soon became two, then three, and before they knew it a whole month had passed, but the camp was beginning to feel like home. Revi was kept busy funnelling people through the gate with the help of Hassus.

Near the end of the third week a group of Dwarves had arrived; a delegation from Stonecastle, including Begrin, an engineer. He took over the organization of the camp, planning out in great detail the future city. After a reconnoitre of the area, he declared there was sufficient stone in the region to construct a variety of buildings.

Anna had only sought to make a temporary camp, but the engineer's words had inspired her. Soon, she was obsessed with the details, listening intently as the Dwarf described a sewer system and fortifications.

"Surely these plans will take years," said Gerald one evening.

Anna sat beside him, nibbling at some fowl, but she held up her hand as she finished her mouthful. "The engineer, Begrin, said he should have a number of houses completed before winter."

"How does he expect to do that?" said Gerald. "We haven't the people."

"Oh," she said, "didn't I mention? There are more Dwarves on the way."

"Just how many are coming?"

"I'm not sure," she confessed, "but he thinks it'll be quite the flood. They haven't had a chance like this in their lifetime."

"What's that supposed to mean?"

"It means they love this sort of planning. They don't get much of an opportunity back in the mountains. Their cities have been built for centuries; very little new work is done."

"How's Herdwin taking all this?" he asked. "I haven't seen him around lately."

"He's been busy," answered Anna. "Revi sent him back through the gate, that's why you haven't seen him."

"Where did he go?"

"Back to the Artisan Hills and then overland to Eastwood."

"That's dangerous, Anna. He could be captured."

"He's a Dwarf, Gerald. No Human in Eastwood is likely to recognize him, and besides, he's already back. Revi brought him through this morning. He's setting up a forge even as we speak."

"I must say," said Gerald, "that I never thought this would work. I thought we'd just lay over a few days and then be off to Weldwyn. You still want to go to Weldwyn, don't you?"

"Yes," she admitted, "though it's hard to leave here just yet."

"We must be off before winter sets in, Anna, or we'll be caught in the snow."

"Yes, but we can't go without Revi, and he's needed to help work the gates."

"I would suggest we meet with all the major leaders. If we explain what's planned, we should be able to arrange all the necessary transportation before we go. Once we leave, they'll have to rely on Hassus to work the gates."

"We could leave Revi here," offered Anna.

"No," declared Gerald. "We're not taking you anywhere without a healer. If anything were to happen to you again, I couldn't bear it."

She hugged him, holding him tightly.

"What was that for?" he asked.

"That was me, being thankful that you're here," she said, wiping a tear from her eye. "Now, let's go and get something to eat, I hear they've managed to make up some sausages."

"Truly?"

"No, I'm afraid not, but perhaps we'll get some in Weldwyn."

"We have no money," Gerald grumbled.

"True," said Anna, "but that hasn't stopped us so far. I'm hoping that when we arrive in Falford, they'll look after us."

"We can only hope," he said. "Now, let's go find that food."

At Gerald's insistence, the camp had been organized into a criss-cross pattern of roads. This made it easier to navigate the area, and to find people. The Orcs adapted quickly to this method, but the Elves less so, for they still tended to remain separate from the other races, preferring to spend their time in the woods nearby.

Gerald had put Beverly in charge of the camp's defenses, and she had quickly organized patrols and pickets to keep them free from danger. They had erected a simple wooden tower on the top of the hill that sat above the temple cave. The view of the surrounding area was magnificent, and three Elves with bows were always stationed there to give warning should the need arise.

The centre of the camp had a row of fire pits on which there were constantly cooking various large animals. It had proven simpler than arranging regular meal times, for the work continued day and night. It was to here that they made their way, only to be intercepted by the Dwarf engineer, Begrin.

"Your Highness," he began, "I must see you on a matter of great concern."

"By all means, Master Engineer, how may I help you?" she enquired.

"We cannot carry out the blessing to the Gods without a name."

"Surely," said Gerald, "you'll bless it in the name of Saxnor."

"I'm afraid you misunderstand," said the Dwarf. "It is not the name of the Gods we lack, it is the name of the city."

"It's just a camp," said Gerald.

The look the Dwarf gave him indicated his displeasure, and then Begrin turned his attention back to the princess. "Please, Highness, tell us by what name you will have this city known."

She looked at Gerald for help, but he merely shrugged his shoulders. It was a voice from behind them that offered a solution.

"Queenstown," said Arnim, as he approached.

"I'm not a queen," objected Anna.

Arnim stopped in front of her, bowing before continuing. "With all due respect, Highness, this war is to be executed with the express aim of putting you on the throne, thus making you the queen. I can think of no more suitable name, can you?"

"Aye, a grand name," said the Dwarf, "Queenston it is." He wheeled about quickly, running off to join his colleagues.

"I don't think he heard me correctly," muttered Arnim.

"Close enough, I suppose," said Anna, "and Queenston has a nice ring to it, don't you think?"

"Cheer up, Arnim," added Gerald, "it's not every day you get to name a city."

. . .

Early the next morning Gerald made his way down to the stream along with Tempus. Anna was still asleep, but Beverly was watching over her, and he felt she was safe. The great dog ran ahead, wading in. A moment later he emerged, shaking the water loose and sending a large spray Gerald's way. It was a chilly morning, and the old warrior could see his breath as he came to the edge.

He knelt, cupping his hand to scoop some water, but Tempus barked, interrupting his concentration. He looked up to see Hayley approaching.

"Good morning," he said, as she drew closer.

"And a good morning to you too, Gerald," she replied. "How do you feel about taking a little trip?"

"What did you have in mind?" he asked, suddenly intrigued.

"Kraloch has been investigating the ruins we found."

"Understandable, but what does that have to do with me?"

"He's found something very interesting," she said, then smiled, standing expectantly, her hands on her hips waiting for his response.

"Well, get on with it then," he said, "tell me what they've found."

"It's a section of wall with carvings on it. It seems to tell a tale."

"What sort of tale?" he asked.

"A battle," the ranger replied.

Gerald's face broke out into a grin, "That sounds quite interesting, I think Anna would like to see that."

"I'm sure she's not the only one interested," said Hayley with a bemused look.

"What's that supposed to mean?" he asked.

"Oh, nothing," she responded, "but we need to get moving soon, it's a long trip and you'll... I mean she'll want time to look it over carefully."

"I'll wake her immediately," he said.

"Very well, I'll get some horses ready. I'll meet you by the north gate."

"It's not a north gate, Hayley. It's only a camp, and there are no gates."

"Tell that to the Dwarves," the ranger replied. "They've marked out locations for everything, including where the north gate will eventually be located."

"These Dwarves are driving me crazy. Why can't they be quieter, like the Orcs."

"You surprise me, Gerald. I never would have thought to hear you favour Orcs over Dwarves. Isn't Herdwin a good friend of yours?"

A surprised look crossed his face. "Of course, what's that got to do with anything?"

"I just would have thought you'd prefer the company of a civilized Dwarf over that of a wild Orc."

"The Orcs aren't wild. Just because they no longer live in big cities doesn't mean they're primitive. They have a rich culture."

"Fair enough," the ranger agreed, "but I'm still meeting you at the north gate, whether you want to call it that or not."

"Then be off with you, ranger," said Gerald. "I have to go and wake up a grumpy young princess."

"Grumpy? The princess? Why would you say that?"

"She was up late last night talking with that Dwarven engineer."

"How late?" she asked.

"Later than me," he replied.

Hayley chuckled, "That's not saying much, Gerald."

"What's that supposed to mean?"

"It means you retire quite early compared to the rest of us, on account of your age."

"I'm old enough to appreciate a good night's sleep, that's all," he defended.

"I meant no offense, Gerald, but you'd best get going now if we're to make it there by noon."

"Very well, I'll see you by the 'north gate'."

Gerald made haste to return to the camp, his morning wash completely forgotten. Tempus ran after him, eager to wake his mistress, but by the time they approached the makeshift shelter, she was already up, sitting on a stump while Sophie combed her hair.

"You're awake," announced Gerald, drawing closer.

Tempus ran over to her, nuzzling into her lap. She placed her hand on the great dog's head, rubbing it. "Of course, I've been up for some time. Where have you two been?"

"Down by the stream," he replied. "I ran into Hayley. She says they found something interesting up in the ruins. I thought we might go there and check it out, make a day of it."

"Sounds intriguing," she replied. "Have her get our horses, and we will meet her-"

"By the north gate," he interrupted, "she's already on her way."

"Well then," Anna replied, "we should get going immediately." She put her hand in the air, "That will be all for now, Sophie, thank you."

"But your hair's a mess, Highness. At least let me braid it. If you're going into the woods, it'll snag everywhere."

"Very well," she said, "but make it quick, we have a long way to ride. What are you chuckling at, Gerald?"

"You, Anna. Your hair's a rat's nest this morning. It reminds me of when we first met in the maze all those years ago."

The princess adopted a 'holier than thou' attitude to her voice, "It's simply the latest style. I'm becoming the very model of a fashionable princess." She couldn't hold the role for very long, however, and broke into a laugh. "I'll just be a moment, and then we'll be on our way."

They arrived to find half a dozen Orc hunters waiting for them. One of them called out in Orcish, and a moment later, Kraloch, the shaman, emerged from the ruins.

"It is this way, Highness," he said, sweeping his arm.

"Thank you," said Anna, "please lead on, Master Kraloch, we're eager to see what you've found."

The Orc led them through the woods, past an outcropping of stone. Soon, they were standing amongst more ruins, with sections of walls clearly visible.

"It's just through here," said the Orc, "where there are some stone steps. I think, perhaps, that it used to be a subterranean room, but the ceiling must have collapsed centuries ago."

Making their way forward, Gerald looked down to see the steps that Kraloch had mentioned. The tread was wide and deep, with a narrow rise, cloaked in moss, giving them an other-worldly look. Scattered about were stone slabs covered in weeds and grass.

"These must have formed the roof at some time," Gerald thought out loud.

"Yes," agreed the shaman, "but the real treasure here, is this." He pointed his staff at a vine-covered wall where someone had cut away the greenery, revealing images beneath.

Gerald stepped closer, his eyes absorbing the sight before him. "It's very intricate carving," he said. "These are obviously meant to be Orcs."

The shaman stood quietly before finally speaking, "We know our ancestors lived in massive cities. It is said, amongst our elders, that they fielded large armies during the Great War."

"I assume the 'Great War' was the war with the Elves?"

"Yes," Kraloch confirmed. "It is the war that destroyed our old way of life."

"And yet you hold no grudge against the Elves?" Gerald asked.

"Do you hold the Westlanders in contempt for the actions of their ancestors?"

"No," he agreed, "I see your point."

"Can we view more of this image?" asked Anna. "I think it might tell a story."

"Certainly," said Kraloch. "I shall have our hunters remove the vines for you. Perhaps, while they work, I could show you what else we have discovered."

"I would like that," said Anna.

"I'll remain here and help," offered Hayley, "while you two look around."

The rest of the ruins, while expansive, held little of interest for Gerald. Other than the occasional section of wall or bared floor tiles, there was not much left. It was clear that the Orcs had, at one time, had a rather large city here, perhaps even as large as one of the smaller cities of Merceria; Tewsbury or perhaps Kingsford. He wondered at the fate of these people. To his mind, it was a great evil that would completely eradicate an entire city from the map. His heart sank at the implications; surely the Elves were not that ruthless.

He was drawn from his dark thoughts as they returned to the wall, now revealed in all its glory. It was carved in relief, giving it an almost lifelike quality.

"It shows Orcs fighting Elves," said Anna. "The war must have gone on for years before this city was destroyed."

"Why do you say that?" asked Hayley, who, until this moment, had remained quiet.

"They wouldn't have time to carve this if the city was under attack," said Anna.

"What does it all mean?" asked the ranger.

"It means the war lasted for quite some time," said Anna. "What do you think, Gerald?" she asked.

Gerald was examining the details up close. "Yes, I'd have to agree, but it also tells us something much more valuable."

"Which is?" asked Anna.

Gerald stepped back to take in the entire image. "Look closely at the Orcs in this relief, Anna. What do you notice?"

She stared at it for some time before smiling, "I see it now. The Orcs, they're all formed up. It's almost like a shield wall."

"Yes," he agreed, "they must have been highly disciplined."

"They seem to be mainly armed with long spears," she continued, "while most of the Elves appear to be mounted."

"And yet," he continued, "the picture paints an Orc victory if we're interpreting it correctly. Doesn't it seem strange to you that there is no Orc cavalry?"

"So you're saying," mused the princess, "that they defeated Elvish horse by using their spears?"

"So it would seem," he replied. "Look at this panel down here." He knelt to point out the image.

"They're arranged in a circle," observed Anna, "with their spears pointing out like the quills of a porcupine."

"Yes," he mused, "a very interesting tactic, and one that would require a lot of training to perfect. This paints a very different picture of what we think of as Orc warfare."

"Agreed," said Anna. "Tell me, Kraloch, do the Orcs still use such tactics?"

"No," replied the shaman, "we are hunters now, and pride ourselves on individual accomplishments. Even when we went to war at Eastwood, we were a mass of individuals."

"The Orcs were dangerous adversaries at Eastwood," said Hayley. "I shudder to think what they could have done had they been in formations."

"Yes," added Gerald, "and armed with spears. Our cavalry would have been far less effective."

"An interesting observation," said Kraloch, "but this is the past. My people would not fight like this again, it requires them to surrender too much of their independence."

"It's a fascinating lesson in history," said Anna, "but beyond that, it is of little value to our existing situation. Perhaps when the war is over, we shall revisit this place and make it available for scholars to investigate further, with the Orc's permission of course."

"Why would you need our permission?" asked Kraloch.

"This city belongs to your people, Master Shaman. I would not wish to give offense by invading it."

"You are a curious one," the Orc replied. "Had we such allies during the Great War, perhaps this city would still stand."

"None of us are alone in this world," said Anna, "be they Orc, Dwarf, Saurian or Human. When this war is over, we will value our allies and together, make this a better, safer land."

The Orc nodded his head in agreement, "You are remarkable, Princess Anna of Merceria. We have not seen your like since the last Meghara."

"Meghara?" said Gerald. "You've heard of Meghara? Revi knows all about her."

Kraloch's face scrunched up in an expression they had learned was confusion. "Of course, all Orcs know of the Meghara, though I'm surprised you Humans have. The last Meghara was lost to us centuries ago."

"What do you mean, 'the last Meghara'?" said Anna. "Are you saying there was more than one?"

"Of course," the shaman replied. "Once every generation a shamaness would be revealed to us that is exceptionally gifted in the arcane arts. She is chosen by our ancestors to assume the position of Meghara; that of the all-powerful wizard, to use your Human terms."

"So you're saying," said Anna, "that Meghara was always an Orc female?"

"So say our ancestors," said Kraloch.

"You speak to your ancestors?" asked Hayley.

"Our shamans can contact the souls of our deceased," replied the Orc. "Is it not so with Humans?"

"No," said Hayley, "it is definitely not so with Humans."

"Does that mean," asked Anna, "that you could contact your ancestors that lived here in this city?"

"No," said Kraloch, "we can only contact those from the recent past."

"How recent?" said Anna. "Master Bloom will be interested to know."

"It depends on the power of the individual shaman; the most gifted may communicate with those that passed many decades ago."

The implications hit Gerald like a brick wall. "Can you talk to anyone who's passed?"

"No," the Orc refuted, "only those that answer the call. I'm afraid it's not a very selective spell."

"Still," said Anna, "I'm sure Master Bloom will be most intrigued."

"Yes," agreed Gerald, "and then he'll be on the verge of yet another great discovery." He looked at Anna, and they both laughed.

"What is it that you find so amusing?" asked Kraloch.

"Our mage," explained Hayley with a smile.

After another week passed, Anna called an assembly to deal with a growing problem. The large hut was noisy. All around the fire pit arguments broke out as Orcs, Elves, and Dwarves kept raising their voices to be heard. Gerald let out a yell to get everyone's attention, and the hut fell into silence.

"We're getting nowhere," he started. "We need to hear from you, one at a time. Let's start with the Orcs, Master Kraloch?"

"Thank you," replied the Orc shaman, moving to the edge of the fire to be more clearly seen. "The Elves and Orcs have both agreed to come here to help her highness set up the camp. Naturally, food is a critical requirement for such a situation, and so we have both agreed to provide such by hunting. This is where the problems arise."

The Elves' voices rose in disagreement, but Gerald was quick to intervene. "Silence!" he yelled. "You'll have your chance to speak after Kraloch is finished." He waited for the noise to die down and then nodded to the Orc, "Please continue."

"Perhaps my people are more far-sighted than the Elves," he continued, "but we must think long term. Winter is fast approaching, and with it, a scarcity of game. It is therefore in our best interest to capture and pen what we can, such that they can be used for an ongoing food supply."

"That sounds reasonable," agreed Gerald, "but how do you intend to do this?"

"There are wild boars hereabouts. Our hunting methods have worked for thousands of years. We cooperate on the hunt, driving game toward our catchers."

"Are you saying you wrestle boars?" asked Gerald in astonishment.

"Not the word I would have chosen," said Kraloch, "but essentially the same thing. Our hunters will physically restrain them. Usually, it takes two or three of us to tie them, and then they can be brought back to the pen."

"That sounds very dangerous," added Anna. "Are you sure it's the best course of action?"

"As I said, we've been doing this for thousands of years; it is an art we have perfected."

"I see," said Gerald, "but how is this a problem for the Elves?"

Telethial was about to speak, but once more Gerald forestalled her. "I'd like to hear Kraloch's opinion first, and then we'll hear out your side of the story."

The Elf bowed her head in acknowledgement, "Certainly, my lord."

"I'm not a lord," said Gerald in irritation. "If you must call me something, then call me general."

"Very well, General," said the Elf.

"Please continue, Master Kraloch."

"The Elves," continued the Orc, "disagree with the entire concept. They do not like the idea of keeping the creatures in confinement. They would rather starve out the winter months, letting the sick and injured die from lack of food."

"I must object," said Telethial. "You are misinterpreting our beliefs. We never said we would let anyone starve."

"And yet," continued the Orc, "the effect is the same. The Orcs have spent generations roaming the land in search of game. We are hunter-gatherers, moving where the food takes us. We understand the ways of nature. Survival is the most important issue at stake here, not the beliefs of a declining people."

Gerald held up his hand, halting the dialogue before things could be said that could not be undone. "Telethial," he beckoned, "may we have your take on things?"

The Elf maid stepped forward once again. She was on the opposite side of the fire pit from Kraloch, and Gerald immediately noticed the defiance on the usually unreadable face.

"Enslavement is not the answer," she started. "Wild animals need to roam their homeland freely. Once they are penned, their meat is tainted in the eyes of the Elders and cannot be consumed."

"Who are the elders?" asked Gerald.

It was Anna that supplied the answer, "They believe in different gods than us. The Elders are the Elves that gave up their lives in this world."

"So they worship their ancestors?" he whispered. "That's the same as the Orcs, isn't it?"

"Remarkably so," she agreed.

"Sorry, Telethial," said Gerald, "please continue."

Kraloch held his hand up, indicating a question.

"What is it?" said Gerald, again in an irritated tone.

"I find it odd that she says the Elves don't believe in enslaving animals," the Orc said, "for during the great war they enslaved Orcs by the thousands."

"That was different," defended Telethial. "That was a very long time ago. We do not agree with the decisions of our ancestors, but we are unable to change the past. Going forward, we must learn to live in peace and harmony with our allies as well as nature."

"I've heard something similar before," said Gerald. "The White Witch, Albreda, often talks of the balance of nature. Tell me, Telethial, what do you propose?"

"Elves hunt in pairs, with the bow. We have no objection to killing game, for that is the natural way of things; the strong feeding on the weak. Our hunters track each animal, assessing its benefit to us, before launching an attack."

"A time-consuming process," added Kraloch.

"You've had your say," said Gerald, "now let the Elves have theirs.

"If it is the will of the Elders," continued Telethial, "then they will provide. Failure to take such precautions will result in a depletion of available game." She turned her attention to the Orc, "Your methods will depopulate large areas of the wilderness and interfere with the food chain."

"Food chain?" asked Gerald. "What in Saxnor's name is that?"

"The Elves learned, long ago, that when you hunt out an area, you destroy the natural food for the predators. These predators, in turn, will become more aggressive in their hunt for food, attacking settlements and killing innocent people."

"And how do you prevent that?" asked Gerald.

"As I said, we hunt in pairs," repeated the Elf. "Each hunter maintains their own balance, hunting a variety of animals for their meat."

The room lapsed into silence as they all considered the words.

It was Anna that broke the quiet. "I understand that you have different views on hunting but can't you just hunt in different areas?"

"Yes," agreed Gerald, "that would easily settle the situation."

"But which areas should we hunt?" asked Kraloch.

"You hunt to the north," suggested Telethial, "and we will hunt to the south."

"No," denounced the Orc, "the Elves are trying to control us, just like their ancestors. We did not submit to their rule then, neither will we now!"

Telethial's face grew red in anger, "We will not bargain with such a pig-headed race as you. While I do not condone what our ancestors did to your people, I can understand the frustration that led to it. You are being entirely unreasonable."

"You are the one being unreasonable," argued Kraloch. "We came here to help the Humans, not to be subjugated by Elves!"

Tempus barked; a deep sound that brought the room back to silence. "Enough," said Anna. "I think that perhaps we need to take a break. Go and get some fresh air and we will resume our mediation once cooler heads prevail."

They began silently filing out of the hut.

"Herdwin," said Gerald, "a moment, if you don't mind."

The Dwarf waited for the others to disperse, "What is it?"

"I was curious as to your opinion. How do the Dwarves feel about this?"

"It's a tricky situation, I'll grant you that," said Herdwin. "It's all well and good to worry about the balance of nature, but the cold hard fact is that we need to eat. My people will build you a city..."

"It's a camp," interjected Gerald.

"Yes, a camp," continued the Dwarf, "but we're doing a lot of manual labour; cutting trees, hauling stone, digging and so on. There are a lot of us here in camp, and the few hunters have to supply food, enough for everyone."

"What do you suggest we do?" asked Anna.

The Dwarf thought a moment before replying, "I'm afraid that's a decision you must make on your own. You're in a difficult situation here, and the only solution may be to choose between the Orcs and the Elves."

"Which would you choose, if you had to?" asked Anna

"I won't answer that," he replied, "but I'll back whatever decision you make. Now, I'm going to go and talk to my fellow Dwarves and see what they make of this mess."

The smith left, his heavy footsteps receding into the distance.

"What do we do, Gerald?" asked Anna.

"I really don't know," Gerald admitted. "This is completely foreign to me."

"You have to find out what they want," came the voice of Nikki. She had entered the hut carrying two small wooden plates. "Arnim sent me in with some food for you."

Gerald looked down at the proffered meal, "What is that?"

"It's a cereal made from wild grain. The Orcs made it, it's actually quite tasty."

The old man drew his knife and used it to carefully taste the food. "Not bad," he said. "A little dry, but not too bad at all."

Anna smiled, releasing the tension that had been built up during the meeting. "Nikki, what did you mean when you said 'find out what they want'?"

"Sorry, Highness, I couldn't help but overhear your discussions. I might not have dealt with Orcs and Elves before, but if you overlook the physical differences, they're not so different from us. Everybody wants something. If they were truly at an impasse, they wouldn't have come to you for help."

"Yes," agreed Anna, "but how does that help us?"

"You have to discover what they want, what they truly want. When I lived in Wincaster, I had to balance my own freedom with that of the gangs that ruled the slums. Once I knew what motivated the gang leaders, the rest became relatively easy."

"But they just want to hunt," said Gerald. "Surely there's an easy solution?"

"I heard them arguing," said Nikki. "I think there's more than hunting at stake."

"Like what?" asked Anna.

"The Orcs," continued Nikki, "despite their supposed indifference, still fear the Elves. Or perhaps, to be more precise, they fear the re-emergence of the Elves as a power."

"That makes sense," said Anna. "The Elves used to be the dominant power in this area before the Great War."

"Yes," agreed Nikki. "Think of the Elves as the old gang that controlled the streets. Now the new gang, the Orcs, have arrived; each is jostling for power."

"But how?" asked Gerald. "We're only a small outpost, far from anywhere."

"You're wrong, Gerald," said Nikki. "You're not seeing the big picture. This might be just a camp in your eyes, but they both see it as the future. Humans rule this land now, they both know it. The race that gains the most favour with you will benefit in the long run, possibly at the expense of the other."

"You surprise me, Nicole," said Gerald. "I never saw you as such a diplomat."

"But we don't want them fighting," said Anna. "I want them to get along, all of them."

"Then you need to convince them that all will be treated equally," explained Nikki. "And like it or not, you need to drive home that Humans will always be dominant in the region."

"Surely not," said Anna. "I want all of us to be equal."

"You can't," said Nikki. "There must always be someone strong in charge, or else they'll fall to bickering again. The Great War they speak of was a fight for dominance. Even the history of Merceria tells us that a strong ruler is key to holding the kingdom together. What happens when a weak king rules?"

"The nobles start plotting," said Anna.

"And so," continued Nikki, "you must remain strong as a ruler. Humans vastly outnumber the Orcs and Elves. They know we could finish them off if necessary, so we need to show them that they add value to us. Each has something to contribute, and each should be rewarded with our friendship, in different ways."

"But how do we do that?" asked the princess. "We have no real power?"

"Give them a seat at the table," Nikki continued. "They both believe you'll win this war. Promise them a seat on whatever council you form when this is over. Make sure they're equal to each other in status, but keep your own control."

"What if you created an Earl's Council like they have in Weldwyn?" offered Gerald.

"Yes," said Anna, "and I'll give a seat to the Orcs and Elves, ranking each the same."

"But you have dukes as well," reminded Nikki. "How would that work?"

"While it's true that dukes traditionally had more influence, a lot of that has changed in recent years. It's actually the earls that have the greatest influence. Eastwood, Shrewesdale and Tewsbury are the most powerful men in the realm, after the king. Once I'm on the throne, we'll give each a single vote on the council. They will retain their titles, but they'll effectively all be made equal."

"There'll likely be opposition," warned Gerald. "The current system has been in place for hundreds of years."

"Things have to change, Gerald. We have a long war ahead of us. I'll not fight this war only to keep things the same." She turned to back to Nikki, "You've been a great help, Nicole. You've proven to be quite resourceful. I'm sorry I doubted your dedication."

"Your Highness, there's no need for an apology," said Nikki, bowing her head. "I'm just pleased I could finally be of use."

TWENTY-THREE

Summersgate

AUTUMN 961 MC

I t was a cold day as the party finally assembled for the trip to Falford. Gerald looked over the group as Anna finished giving instructions to Herdwin. Beverly rode Lightning, with Sophie, Anna's maid, sitting behind her. Gerald and Anna would ride the horse that Herdwin had procured for them, while Arnim and Nikki shared the Dwarf's pony. Revi sat behind Hayley on her nimble horse, looking uncomfortable in the saddle, while Lily clung on behind him. Tempus, of course, ran circles around the mounts, eager to begin the trip.

At last, Anna turned from the Dwarf, walking toward Gerald, who held out his hand for her.

"All set?" he asked.

"Everything's taken care of," she replied, taking his hand and climbing into the saddle behind him. "We should be on our way."

He nudged the beast forward, and the little column began making its way westward, toward the River Alde. As near as the mage could calculate, Falford lay across the river to the south-west. They planned to head almost directly west, and then follow the river bank south until the city came into view on the far side.

They had only just got out of sight of the camp when Anna spoke up, "I'm nervous, Gerald."

"Why would you be nervous, we've been to Falford before."

"Yes, but last time I was arriving as a representative of the crown, now I'm just a beggar asking for help."

"You're not begging, Anna, you're asking them to aid you in your rightful claim to the throne."

"Yes, but last time someone came asking, King Leofric refused them. How do we know the same thing won't happen again?"

"Because Alric is there, waiting for you. Do you think it matters to him whether you're a princess or not?"

"No, I suppose not," she agreed, but he sensed the hesitation in her answer.

"What's the worst thing that could happen, Anna?"

"The king might refuse to help," she confessed.

"Yes, but I can't see him throwing you out, so the worst case would be living a life of comparative comfort in Weldwyn. It wasn't so long ago that you and I planned to run away together and live our lives there as commoners."

"Sometimes I wonder," she said, "if we wouldn't have been better off to do so. My decision has cost you a lot, Gerald, you deserve better."

"I'm happy where I am, Anna. You rescued me from a life of misery, and I'll be there with you to the end, whatever happens. Now, I'll have no more of this maudlin talk. Let's say we find something more interesting to occupy your thoughts."

"What do you have in mind?" she asked.

"Well, why don't you recite the lineage of the kings of Merceria."

"Oh, that's easy. You could at least make it challenging."

The trip to the river took them two and a half days, but though the weather remained brisk, it was dry. By noon of the third day, they were gazing across the river into Weldwyn.

Gerald knelt by the river, splashing his face, as Anna came up beside him. He waited till she, too, knelt down, and then splashed her with water.

Not to be outdone, she splashed back, and soon the pair of them dissolved into laughter as Tempus charged into the river to join in the fun.

They were interrupted by Beverly, who called out, "There's a boat coming downriver."

The game was instantly over as they gazed upstream to see a small, single-masted sailing ship round a bend in the river, its decks crammed with soldiers. They wondered, at first, if it might have been a Norland vessel intent on raiding, but the flag of Weldwyn could clearly be seen flying from its mast. They watched as it drew closer, waving their hands in the air to the people on its deck. A few moments later, the ship lowered its sails and dropped anchor. Someone called out, but they couldn't understand, and they watched as a small boat was lowered over the side. The small group of men rowed ashore, pulling the boat up onto the bank.

"Are you all right?" a bearded man called out. "These are dangerous times to be out in the middle of nowhere."

"Why," asked Anna, "what's happened?"

The bearded man came closer, leaving his companions by the rowboat. "Weldwyn has been invaded," he explained, "by a massive army that crossed the western frontier late this past summer. We're transporting troops from the northern towns to the capital."

"The Clans?" asked Gerald.

"Aye, the Clans and then some. I've never heard of a force of such size."

"Who commands the men you're carrying?" asked Gerald.

"Captain Patterson, but the company will fall under the command of the Earl of Falford, or whomever he appoints."

"Please," said Gerald, "let us not delay you, you are on important business."

"There is no hurry," the man replied. "Many troops are gathering at Falford. It will be a week or more before they are ready to march. Who are you, if I may ask, and what are doing out here?"

"This," said Gerald, "is the Princess Anna of Merceria, though you'll have to excuse our rough clothing."

"Then you must be General Matheson," said the bearded man.

"I'm afraid you have the advantage of me," said a surprised Gerald.

"I'm Captain Sawyer, the master of the Otter. I've heard the stories of what you did in Riversend. You have the thanks of the kingdom. Can we give you some supplies?"

"Actually," said Anna, "we're on the way to Falford. Can you tell us how close we are?"

"You're a day's sail away. I'd offer to take you, but I'm afraid I have no room for horses. It'll likely take you two days overland, but you'll have to cross the river. Do you have enough supplies?"

"We do, thank you," said Gerald, "though I wonder if you might be able to take a message from us to the Earl of Falford?"

"I should be delighted," the man replied. "Would you like to come aboard and write such a letter, or maybe a verbal message?"

"I believe," said Gerald, "that a verbal message will suffice. Please tell His Grace that Her Royal Highness, Princess Anna of Merceria, wishes to visit his city."

The captain bowed deeply, "It shall be my honour, Highness, for everyone knows the great service you did our country. I will hurry back to Falford, no doubt the earl will send a ship for you that will accommodate your needs."

"That won't be necessary," said Anna, "please have him meet us across the river in two days time, we shall need to be ferried across."

"Of course, Highness," Captain Sawyer replied. "And now, with your permission, I shall excuse myself."

"Of course, thank you, Captain," said Anna.

They watched him hurry to the rowboat, yelling at his men to get back to the boat as quickly as possible. Soon, the sail was hoisted, and once again the ship was gracefully sailing down the river.

"That bodes well," said Gerald.

"Surprisingly well," added Anna.

"It seems they still remember you," he said with a smirk, "even if you are dripping with water."

She turned to him, wearing the most regal look she could summon. "I doth think it suits me," she said, and then burst out laughing.

Two days later, Anna, Gerald and Beverly were escorted into the Great Hall at Falford. Lord Erick Landford, the new Earl of Falford, stood as they entered.

"Your Highness," he said, "I am pleased to welcome you back to Weldwyn."

"Thank you, Your Grace," replied Anna. "Your men have been most courteous."

"I'm sorry to hear of your current predicament. Judging by your clothes you have been in the wild for some time. Would you let me do you the courtesy of finding something more suitable for someone of your station? I'm sure my wife would be delighted to assist."

"Thank you," replied Anna, "we would be pleased to take you up on the offer, but before we begin, what can you tell us of the invasion?"

"All in due time," the earl replied. "Can I suggest we settle into more comfortable surroundings? The great hall is drafty at times, perhaps the living chamber?" He waved his hands to indicate the door to his left.

"Yes, thank you," she replied.

They followed the earl through the door to the room beyond. Comfortable chairs were arranged around a fire that spat out warmth. The earl took a seat, waiting while his visitors made themselves comfortable and then launched into his explanation.

"I'm afraid the invasion came soon after you left us. The Twelve Clans must have been planning it for some time, for they came in large numbers. They bypassed Loranguard, crossing the river to the south and then curling up to take the city from the east."

"Do you have any idea of numbers?" asked Gerald.

"I'm afraid not," he replied. "It's clean across the kingdom, and the news we have is sparse. There was fear that the capital was in danger so Prince Alric has issued a proclamation in his father's name to raise what troops we can. We've been gathering them for almost two weeks in preparation to march them to the capital, reinforcing the garrison there."

"Did you say Prince Alric?" asked Anna. "I thought the king commanded the army."

"He does," explained the earl, "but there are two armies that have to be dealt with. Leofric headed north, and as far as we know, Prince Alstan took another force westward to protect the route south. The last I heard, he was marching to Walverton."

"What of Prince Cuthbert?" asked Gerald.

"I'm afraid we haven't heard any news. He was in Loranguard when the attack began. He may still be sieged in that city, or the city may have fallen, we just don't know."

"These men you're sending to the capital," asked Gerald, "who commands them?"

"They are an assortment of companies. Each commanded by a captain. Whoever is senior will take them to Summersgate."

"Might I suggest an alternative?" said Anna.

"I'm open to suggestions," said the earl.

"General Matheson here is quite experienced. I'm sure he would have no objection to commanding the expedition if that would be of help to you. He did, after all, command the defense of Riversend this past spring."

The earl rose from his chair, making a show of walking to the fire to warm his hands. "It would be highly unusual for a foreign general to command the soldiers of Weldwyn," he said, "but under the circumstances, I think it would be advisable." He turned away from the fire, extending his hand. "I accept your offer. Will you take command, General Matheson?"

Gerald rose to shake the earl's hand. "I would be honoured," he said.

"Excellent," continued the earl. "You have, Your Highness, provided an outstanding solution to our problem. I, myself, would have led the troops, but I'm afraid I'm not suited to a military life and lack the experience."

"How many men have you gathered?" asked Gerald.

"I'll have to see the final count," he said, "but there should be five hundred or so."

"With your permission, Your Grace," said Gerald, "I should like to appoint my own officers."

"Of course," said the earl, "I will draft a notice immediately giving you the authority to act as commander of the expedition."

"The General," corrected Anna. "If he is to command, he must be the senior leader. I'd hate for him to be outranked by another officer when he arrives."

"But surely the crown outranks all?" defended the earl.

"Of course," replied Anna. "If one of the princes wants to assume command, we shall not argue, but in the meantime, Gerald must have absolute authority over the troops."

The earl looked slightly uncomfortable with the situation, but he took a deep breath and relented. "Very well," he said, "the orders will be drawn up immediately."

"How soon until they are ready to march?" asked Gerald.

"My aide tells me they can be on the road by week's end. We'll find you a change of clothes, and then he will show you to the troops. No doubt you'll want to see them with your own eyes."

"Thank you, Your Grace," said Gerald.

"Rest assured," added Anna, "the general will do all that he can to help in these trying times."

"I only pray he is not too late," replied the earl.

By the end of the week the troops, organized into rough companies, were ready to move out. Most were armed with light padded surcoats and spears, but Gerald had managed to find enough with chainmail to form a company of heavier foot. The earl had provided a supply train that stretched for miles behind them. Beverly rode up to Anna and Gerald, who sat mounted on fresh horses.

"They're ready to move, General," she said.

"Surely you can call me Gerald," he replied.

Beverly smiled before answering, "I remember well the lessons of my father. I'll use your rank when in the field if it's all right with you."

"Very well," he relented. "You take the lead with the cavalry, Dame Beverly. Arnim will march with the spearmen, while the heavy foot brings up the rear. I'll keep Hayley with me as an aide."

"Aye, General," the knight responded, turning her mighty Mercerian Charger and riding off.

Anna, now dressed in more suitable clothing, rode up beside him. "What are our final numbers, Gerald?"

"I have five hundred and fifty, all told. We managed to scrape together 100 horsemen, Beverly is commanding those."

"And the rest?" she asked.

"Only fifty men with decent armour, the rest are spearmen. Unfortunately, we have no bows."

"This small army is almost the same size as the one we had at Kingsford when we won our first battle."

"Yes," he agreed, "though the enemy is likely far larger this time."

"But," she added, "we're only reinforcing an existing army. Once we meet up with King Leofric, there should be a much larger force."

"Let's hope so. In any case, I mean to drill the men each day after the march. It wouldn't hurt to give them some extra training."

"We should arrive in Summersgate in ten days," said Anna, "provided the supply train keeps up."

"Oh, it will," promised Gerald. "I've put Arnim in charge of it. The carriage that the earl provided for you is just behind the troops."

"Yes, I saw it," she said. "Tempus is inside with Lily, Sophie and Nicole."

"Where's Revi?" he asked. "You'll want to keep him close, remember what happened last time."

"Don't worry," she said, "he's just chatting with Arnim. He'll join us once the column is moving."

"You should get back to the carriage," he said, "it's a long ride ahead."

"Oh, I'm not riding in the carriage, at least, not yet, anyway."

"Why is that?"

"I'm going to ride with you, General, unless that would be inconvenient."

"No, of course not," he said, obviously pleased. "Would you like to give the command to march?"

"Can I?" she asked.

"Of course," he said.

"How should I do it?" she asked. "I want it to look proper."

"Wave your sword and stand in your stirrups," he suggested. "That always makes an impression."

"But there's too many to hear me."

"Don't worry, the word will be carried for you by the company commanders."

She drew her Dwarven blade, then stood in the stirrups. Gerald watched her rise, surprised by how mature she looked.

"Army, march!" she yelled, her thin voice echoing in the early morning air.

The shouts were repeated down the line, and then, like a giant snake, the column began to creep forward. Beverly led the cavalry in the front, though a small group had been detailed to bring up the rear. Soon, the spearmen moved, and Gerald and Anna watched as they filed past. At first, the only sound was the crunching of stone as the feet of the army advanced, but soon, another emerged, that of cheering as the troops marched past Anna.

"The men are in fine spirits," said the princess.

"Yes," agreed Gerald, "let's hope they still feel the same after marching for ten days."

On the way to Summersgate, they were joined by more forces raised in Kinsley and Mirstone. A hundred archers swelled the ranks, along with a small company of fierce Dwarven arbalesters from the Obsidian Hills.

Gerald and Anna joined Beverly at the head of the column when it came time to enter the capital. As they rode towards the gates, a group of horsemen approached to meet them. Anna broke into a smile the moment she recognized Prince Alric of the Royal House of Weldwyn among their number. Beside him rode Queen Igraine, along with some household troops. Alric was armoured, and Gerald was surprised by how much older he appeared, looking more like a seasoned warrior than the young prince they had left only a few months before.

"Take the column directly to the tournament field, Beverly," he said. "The princess and I shall greet our hosts."

"Aye, General," she responded.

They rode over to Alric and his mother, who waited patiently.

"Welcome," said the queen. "Had I known you would be arriving with the troops, I would have arranged something more fitting for you."

"Your Majesty," said Anna, bowing her head deeply, "it's a pleasure to see you again."

"No doubt it's a greater pleasure to see my son," the queen said. "He's been hopelessly maudlin with you gone."

"Mother," said Alric, "I hardly think this is the place to speak of such things."

She smiled at her son's discomfort as he turned crimson. "Shall we retire to the Palace? We can catch up on news, and no doubt you have many questions."

"Indeed," said Anna. "You remember General Matheson?"

"Of course," said the queen, "he did us a great service at Riversend."

"He was placed in charge of the reinforcements by the Earl of Falford."

"He was?" commented the queen. "Then we have lots to talk of. Now let us retire to more intimate quarters where we will discuss such things in complete privacy, shall we?"

The queen turned her horse, leading them to the Palace. Gerald looked back to see Beverly marching the troops towards the tournament field, knowing they were in good hands.

"Your entourage has shrunk since the last time you were here," commented the queen.

"Yes," agreed Anna, "much has happened since we last saw you, but I'm afraid little of it is good."

The queen looked back at her in surprise, "It appears time has not favoured either of our kingdoms, then. You must tell me more once we are inside."

They entered the courtyard of the Palace and dismounted while servants scurried to take their horses. Queen Igraine led them inside, with Alric and Anna in her wake. Gerald started to follow and then heard a noise from behind him. He looked back to see Tempus running toward them, followed closely by Sophie and Nicole, who were trying to catch him.

"Come along, old fellow," he said, patting the dog's head as he arrived. "You were almost too late." The strange group passed into the Palace with the two women following, their footsteps echoing down the long entrance hall.

Igraine took them to the left, into the same room they had sat in on their very first visit. Just as Anna was about to enter, Alric grabbed her hand, staying her. He stared into her eyes for a long moment, and then they embraced tightly.

"I missed you, Alric," Anna said at last. "I have so much to tell you."

"I'm so glad you're here," he replied. "We'll find some time for a private moment later, but a lot has happened while you've been away."

"We better head inside," said Anna, looking over his shoulder, "the queen is waiting for us."

"Yes," he said, "of course."

They entered the room, and Anna immediately made her way to the long wide chesterfield she liked. Gerald dutifully sat beside her, while Tempus curled up on the floor at Anna's feet. Sophie and Nicole waited patiently just outside the room.

Igraine addressed Gerald first, "I understand you've had significant military experience."

"I've been a soldier all my life," said Gerald.

"Good," she replied, "for I fear my husband marches to his doom."

"Why is that?" asked Gerald.

"The army that opposes him is vast, much larger than the Clans have ever mustered before. I would like you to lead a relief column north to help him."

"I only commanded the reinforcements," objected Gerald, "and now you want me to command an army?"

"Yes," she said, "does that surprise you? I know what you did in Riversend. The kingdom needs your help, and we're willing to pay you a king's ransom to do so."

Gerald, surprised by the turn of events, began to object, "That won't be necess-"

"His price," interrupted Anna, "is support for my claim to the throne of Merceria."

Alric and Igraine both looked on her in surprise.

"I'm afraid I don't understand," said the queen.

"As I said earlier," Anna continued, "much has happened. When we returned to Merceria, we were arrested and thrown in the dungeons. When we managed to escape, we discovered that a Necromancer now controls the throne."

"A Death Mage," said Alric, "on the throne of Merceria?"

"My brother, Henry, is the king now, but I fear he's being controlled. Master Revi thinks the old king's mistress is the true power now. Apparently, she's been plotting this for centuries."

"How is that possible?" asked Alric.

"She is, in fact, an Elf," interjected Gerald.

"You have proof of this?" asked Igraine.

"Only the word of Master Bloom," said Anna, "but I did manage to recover this." She pulled out the folded up paper, passing it to the queen.

Igraine slowly unwrapped it, revealing the ambassador's ring. She paled at the sight, then her eyes began scanning the document. "This is the wedding proposal," she said, "and my nephew's ring."

"Your nephew?"

"Yes, my husband's sister's son, Cedric. He went to Merceria to fulfill the agreement. We had wondered why he did not return when you left, but with all that has happened here, we did not have time to investigate further. This is unfortunate news indeed."

"Yes, it is worse, I'm afraid," said Anna. "When it was given to me, it was still on the ambassador's... I mean your nephew's finger."

"Where is this mage of yours?" asked the queen, changing the subject.

"He's gone to the Arcane Wizards Council to inform the mages of his discovery."

"He'll have a hard time finding them," offered Alric. "All the mages marched with the armies."

"Armies? There's more than one?" asked Gerald.

"Yes," confirmed the queen. "King Leofric took the main army and began the march to Abermore. Prince Alstan commanded the second, taking the road north through Middenfield to Faltingham, though I'm afraid we've had no word from either of them for almost a week."

"I thought the crown prince moved westward?" asked Gerald. "We were told he wanted to guard the road that heads south through Walverton."

"That was his original intention," said the queen, "but events in the north moved quickly and he was forced to redeploy."

"I'll take the army," said Alric.

"No," insisted the queen, "absolutely not. You are needed here, Alric, to protect Summersgate. Should your father be defeated, you must resist the inevitable siege."

"I will accept your offer to command," said Gerald, "and you can decide whether to accept the princess's request when we return."

"Thank you, General Matheson," said the queen. "You must march immediately. Alstan's army is on the northern road and has a week's head start on you. The king is somewhere to the west of that, the last we heard. The Clans have been tearing across the north, laying waste to everything in their wake. You must hurry."

"I shall march the troops first thing in the morning," said Gerald.

"We," corrected Anna.

"You should stay in the capital," he warned, "it will be dangerous."

"We're in this together, Gerald, remember?"

"Very well," he replied, "but we'll have to find you some armour, you can't go into battle in just a dress."

"I'll see to that," promised the queen. "Our armoury is well stocked, I'm sure we have something she can wear."

"That being said," continued Gerald, "if we are to march at dawn, we have much to do."

He rose, prompting the others to do likewise. "I shall report back in the morning before we march, Majesty."

"Thank you, General," said the queen. "Is there anything else we can do to help?"

"As a matter of fact, there is," continued Gerald. "It would be helpful to know what forces the king has under his command, along with those of Prince Alstan."

"Why would that matter?" asked the queen. "Surely the number of men is all you need to know."

"We are potentially fighting an enemy that outnumbers us, Your Majesty. Knowing what we have at our disposal will help us develop tactics to take full advantage of them."

"Then I will do all I can to find the information you need," she promised.

Gerald bowed deeply, "Thank you," he said, then turned and made his way to the door, followed by Anna.

As they exited, Alric called out. Anna paused in the doorway as Alric came closer, grabbing her hands and holding them in his. "I just barely saw you, and now you're marching off without me."

"It can't be helped," she said. "My place is with Gerald, he needs my support."

"You're facing impossible odds," said Alric.

"Yes," she admitted, "but Gerald and I have overcome obstacles before. I can't believe that after all we've gone through, Saxnor would see fit to let us fail now."

"I can go with you," he offered. "I'll disguise myself as a common soldier."

"No, your mother's right. You're needed here. You may not see it as glamorous, but the protection of the city is of paramount importance. Be safe, Alric, I can't be victorious in battle to return to an empty heart."

"I promise you I shall do my duty," vowed Alric. "And then when you return I will convince my father to sanction our marriage."

"I'm not an heir to the crown anymore, Alric. I'm just a pretender to the throne now."

"I don't care," he retorted, "I love you, no matter who you are and I won't marry any other."

She smiled at him then leaned forward, kissing him tenderly on the lips. "Till I return," she whispered.

After witnessing the tender moment, Sophie turned to Lady Nicole, only to see Nikki wiping a tear from her eye.

"It's beautiful," observed Nikki, "how someone can love another so deeply."

Sophie looked on her with surprise, "I never took you for one to be overly emotional, Lady Nicole."

"Perhaps we should all prepare to say our final goodbyes," was all that Nicole answered.

Arnim Castor unbuckled his belt, laying his sword and scabbard onto the table. It had been a long, gruelling day and he had to look forward to rising early in the morning. He was just preparing to climb into bed when he heard a faint knock at his door.

"Who is it?" he called out.

"Nikki," a voice replied. "I need to talk to you, Arnim."

He walked to the door, opening it to reveal Nikki. Her eyes looked red as if she had been crying, and he sensed she had something important to say. "Come in," he said at last, stepping aside.

She entered the room, casting her eyes about, wringing her hands nervously. Arnim recognized the habit from long ago.

"What is it?" he asked.

She looked at him a moment before replying, "I'm leaving."

"You can't leave," he said, "you'd put us all in danger. If anyone found you, they'd extract everything you know about us."

"I can't stay, Arnim. I promise I'll remain in Weldwyn until the war in Merceria is over, but I can't be a part of this any longer, it's too painful."

"Too painful? What in the name of Saxnor is that supposed to mean?"

"It means I have to leave. Please, come with me, we can make a home somewhere..."

"I won't leave the princess," he declared.

"What about me?"

"What about you?" he responded with pent-up anger. "What is it you want, Nikki? Whatever it is, I can't give it to you. Perhaps once, long ago, I would have gladly run away with you, but you ran out on me."

"When you were part of the town watch," she started, "I was sent to spy on you. Yes, I was told to seduce you, to find some way of blackmailing you, but I had no choice, it was my life on the line. I never expected to fall in love with you." Her eyes began to tear up.

"I loved you with all my heart," announced Arnim, "but you betrayed me. You waited till I was gone and then robbed me blind, took everything except the clothes on my back."

"I wanted to stay," she said through tears, "but they wouldn't let me. Please try to understand, these were dangerous men, if I hadn't gone with them, they likely would have killed both of us."

"And so you left me to protect me?" he accused.

"No," she admitted, "I left you because I had to choose my life or your love. I've always regretted that decision, and I think to some extent, you did too. It was you that recommended me to Valmar, wasn't it?"

"To protect the princess," he responded. "I knew that sooner or later, someone would get close enough to her to try to kill her. If you'd been with us sooner, she wouldn't have been wounded last year. Besides, you certainly didn't come out any the worse for it; a nice, comfy job playing Lady-In-Waiting.

"Not hurt?" she said. She started undoing the front of her dress.

"What are you doing?" he asked. "Do you intend on accusing me of doing something untoward, or are you trying to seduce me again?"

"No," she retorted, "I'm showing you the price I paid."

She turned away from him, lowering the dress from her shoulders. He gasped in surprise at the whip-scarred back she presented to him.

"This is what your precious marshal-general and his minions did to me, to make sure I obeyed his orders."

"Nikki," said Arnim, "I don't know what to say."

She pulled the dress back up over her shoulders, retying it. "I never stopped loving you, Arnim, but I can't bear it any longer. I won't stand by and watch you and your band of friends kill yourselves. There's no future in fighting King Henry. If you continue on this path, you'll all die a slow and painful death, every single one of you. Come away with me, please, I beg you."

"I had no idea, Nikki. I'm so sorry, I never meant for you to suffer this way."

"Then you'll come with me?" she said, turning around in anticipation.

"I can't," he finally admitted. "But one day, when this is all over, I'll look for you. If you want to go, Nikki, I won't stop you, and I won't tell the princess until it's too late to find you."

She looked down at her feet, then back up, meeting his gaze, her eyes brimming with tears, "Then it's goodbye forever, Arnim."

She turned and left the room.

TWENTY-FOUR

Middenfield

AUTUMN 961 MC

⌇

T he army stretched out for miles, strung along the northern road leading to Middenfield. Gerald rode with Anna in the centre of the column that stretched before and behind them like a long snake. The cold of winter was just around the corner, the chill in the air forming a thin cloud of mist that hovered over the troops.

The pace had been relentless, and now, four days after leaving the capital, they were within sight of the town of Middenfield. He watched as a lone rider trotted back along the column, the distinctive horse easily identifying its rider; Dame Beverly.

She drew closer, finally falling into step with them.

"What is it?" he asked.

"We have news," the red-headed knight responded, "but it's not good, I'm afraid."

"Let's have it," he said.

"We've encountered some stragglers," Beverly continued. "They were part of Prince Alstan's army. I'm afraid there was a battle two days ago. The Weldwyn army was routed, and the survivors have been scattered."

"Any news of Alstan?" asked Anna.

"I'm afraid not, Highness. The people we've found so far have no idea of his fate, but they say there's a large army up ahead. We may encounter them before dusk if we're not careful."

"Pull the horses back," ordered Gerald, "and halt the column. Hand pick your best men, have them scout the area carefully, but they need to avoid contact at all costs. We must find where the enemy is camped and prepare for battle first thing in the morning. How many have you found?"

"Only half a dozen or so, but there are likely more in the area."

"Send out riders to try to find them," he said.

"We need some idea of the enemy's numbers," interjected Anna. "Perhaps the survivors can tell us more."

"Good idea," agreed Gerald. "Send those you find to us." He looked around the immediate area. "We'll set up the command area over there, by that large tree on the hill. It'll give us a good view of the countryside."

"Yes, General," said Beverly, "anything else?"

"Yes," he continued, "send word for Arnim, I'll need to talk to him."

"I'll do that," said Anna. "Beverly needs to get the pickets out."

"But you're the princess, not a messenger," objected Gerald.

"True, but Beverly's got enough on her plate. I'm here to help, let me do this, Gerald, you have a battle to plan."

"Very well," he agreed, "but be careful."

"Of course," she said. "Come along, Tempus, we're going for a ride." She urged her horse off the road, heading toward the rear of the army where Arnim should be.

The column began to halt as word was carried north and south. Gerald rode up the hill, stopping beneath the solitary tree to examine the terrain. He nodded his head in appreciation, liking what he saw. "This will do nicely," he said aloud, though none were present to hear him.

Shortly after that, he heard a bark, and he turned to see Anna, Arnim and Tempus approaching on foot. He dismounted and waited as they drew closer.

"This is it," he declared, "this is where we'll meet the enemy."

"You wanted to see me, General?" asked the captain.

"Yes, Arnim. I'm making you a commander. You see that stream at the bottom of the hill?"

"Aye," said the knight.

"I want you to line the spearmen up behind it. We'll need them shoulder to shoulder, all along the base of the hill. I want them right at the southern bank to the stream, so that the attackers will have wet feet, you understand?"

"Yes," Arnim agreed, "but that will make for a rather crooked line."

"I know, but I need the enemy attack broken up, and the stream will do that. We'll have some additional surprises that I'll tell you about after the men are deployed."

"What about the flanks?" Arnim asked. "We don't have a large force."

"I'm going to split the archers; half on each flank. I want the Human bowmen on the right flank, on the road itself. The Dwarves, with their heavy arbalests, will be on my left, at the base of the hill. The cavalry will form up to the south, out of sight of the enemy but ready to deploy to our left. I suspect that's where they'll send most of their strength."

"Why so?" asked Arnim.

"Because," answered Anna, "their line of communication runs west to their other army, the one Leofric is chasing down."

"Anna's correct," said Gerald.

"I learned from the best," said Anna, beaming.

"I want the men camped directly behind their lines," continued Gerald. "We need them to be able to get into position in a moment's notice, if necessary. I expect the attack to come early tomorrow morning."

"Do you know what we'll be facing?" asked the new commander.

"Not yet, but Beverly's rounding up some stragglers. I'm hoping they'll be able to give us more information."

"Then I'll get right to it," said Arnim, turning.

Gerald watched him descend the hill. The soldiers were sitting by the road, resting their legs after an arduous march, but at the approach of the new commander, he saw them rising to their feet. How many of them, he wondered, would still be standing this time tomorrow?

"Do you think it's their main army we'll be facing?" asked Anna.

"No, I don't," he replied. "I think the bulk of their forces are facing Leofric."

"What makes you say that?"

"Because that's what I would have done. I think the main army is trying to draw Leofric away from the capital or they would have made a stand by now."

"How do we know they haven't?"

"We don't," he replied, "but Leofric impresses me as a shrewd tactician. I think he was trying to lure the enemy into battle where Alstan could reinforce him. I would imagine the loss of the second army has thrown his plans into chaos."

"So what will he do now?" she asked.

"I think he knows he's outnumbered. He'll withdraw toward Summersgate, but the enemy will have heard of Alstan's defeat. I suspect a good portion of the army that defeated Alstan will now be rushing to aid in defeating Leofric. We might be able to use that to our advantage."

"How?" she asked. "Surely the Clans outnumber Leofric."

"Yes," he agreed, "but that means a weakened force against us tomorrow.

The enemy can't just abandon the road to Faltingham. I think they'll have left a smaller force behind, that's good for us."

"And then we march to aid the king?"

"Precisely," he agreed. "If we pull it off, we'll march to the west without banners. With any luck, we'll arrive to a confused enemy. They might even take us as allies from a distance."

"But we still have to defeat them tomorrow, and even though they don't know we're here yet, we don't know what their strength is."

"I can help with that," called out a voice.

They looked to see Revi Bloom riding up the hill, along with Hayley. They dismounted, coming to stand beside Gerald and Anna as they gazed over the countryside.

"Quite the view from up here," Revi commented.

"You said you could help?" prompted Anna.

"Yes, Highness. I propose using Shellbreaker to fly over the enemy and give us some idea of their strength."

"An excellent idea, Master Bloom," said Anna.

"Yes," agreed Gerald, "when can you start."

"Right now," said the mage. "If someone will take my horse, I'll begin casting."

Gerald looked down to the troops below. The warriors were beginning to move westward, and he caught sight of a group of men walking up the hill towards them. As they drew closer, he recognized one of the Weldwyn captains.

"Captain Sanderson," he said in greeting.

"My lord," the man replied, "Commander Caster sent us up to help you. He said you'd need to relay orders and such. I've brought a dozen men to assist."

"Thank you, Captain. You can start by detailing out some men to take care of our horses. I'll have orders for the others shortly."

Revi, relieved of his horse, stretched his arms and cracked his knuckles. He took a firm stance and closed his eyes. The rest watched in silence as he began chanting, the air briefly feeling charged. A moment later he stopped, his whole body pivoting as if he was flying.

"I've made contact with Shellbreaker," he explained. "He's heading north, I'll tell you as soon as I see anything. Please don't let anyone touch me while I'm in this state, it'll break my concentration."

"Detail three men to guard this perimeter, Captain."

"Aye, sir."

"What about the supply wagons and camp followers?" asked Anna.

"Have them move behind the hill," said Gerald, "that will keep them safe for now. We'll issue food tonight, but I don't think there'll be time for breakfast. We'll have to tell everyone to eat enough for two meals."

"What if we marched west right away?" asked Anna. "Surely we would be of more use to Leofric?"

"No, we can't leave an enemy behind us, even if it's small. We must clear them before proceeding."

"But they don't even know we're here," she implored.

"I'll take care of that tonight," he added.

"I see them," interrupted Revi. "They're to the north, just south of Middenfield. Less than half a day's march away, I would say."

"Can you estimate their numbers?" asked Gerald.

"From the size of their camp, I'd guess they outnumber us at least two to one."

"What kind of troops do you see?"

Revi's head bobbed left and right as his familiar weaved through the air. "Very few archers from what I can tell, but there's lots of horses. I would estimate almost a third of their force is cavalry."

"Can you see what their foot soldiers are armed with?"

"Yes, looks like swords and shields mostly. I don't see many men in heavier armour."

"It sounds like the Norlanders," said Gerald. "I would expect they'd use similar tactics. Can you keep an eye on them tonight?"

"I'm afraid not," said Revi. "Shellbreaker doesn't see too well in the dark."

"I thought birds saw well at night," said Anna.

"See, yes," said Revi, "but distinguishing people at night would require him to get uncomfortably close. I'd rather not risk him."

"It's too bad he's not an owl," lamented Gerald.

"Jamie's faster than an owl," defended Anna. "He's a very good familiar."

"His name's Shellbreaker, Highness," Revi reminded her, yet again, "not Jamie."

"Is the enemy moving?" Gerald asked.

"Not yet, Gerald," said Revi. "They've set up a camp."

"Good, sever your tie with Shellbreaker for now, have him return here to safety. I'd like you to find Beverly and give her the layout of the enemy camp. When she has a plan, send her to see me."

"A plan?" said Revi. "I thought you were the one with the plan."

"A good leader takes suggestions," said Gerald. "Anna taught me that. I'll let Beverly give me her thoughts before I make my decision."

"Very well," said Revi, opening his eyes, "I shall seek her out directly."

The mage disappeared down the hill, clutching his robes as he navigated the slope.

"You enjoy egging him on, don't you?" he asked.

"Someone has to keep him humble," replied a smirking Anna.

"What do you want me to do?" interrupted Hayley.

Gerald looked to the ranger, "For you, I have a special job. How much do you like Dwarves?"

Dame Beverly Fitzwilliam crouched behind the fallen log. To her left and right were two dozen men, hand-picked for this task. They peered out at the enemy camp before them as the sun was sinking in the west.

"It's as the mage reported," said an older soldier, who had been part of Alstan's army.

"Yes, Thomas," she agreed. "Do you remember what lies beyond?"

"Yes," the man replied, "the horses are picketed west of here, and farther north is the command tent, but we're to avoid those areas."

"How many did you encounter when Alstan made his stand?" she asked.

"We had twelve hundred," he replied, "and the enemy had at least twice that."

"Then we're lucky," said Beverly, "I suspect many of them have ridden off to join their other army." She gazed out over the camp as darkness fell, leaving the area lit by dozens of campfires. "You remember what to do?"

"Aye," Thomas replied, "we go in quick, kill as many as we can and then retreat. The entire attack is to last but a moment."

"Good, it's important you head straight back to this point. Once you cross this line of trees, make sure you split east or west, or you'll get in the way."

"I'll make sure of it, though I still don't know why."

"Better you don't," she said, "in case of capture. There's a full moon tonight, so you should have plenty of light. Are your men ready?"

He looked at the soldiers surrounding them; all eyes were trained on him. "Aye, we're ready to give the Clans payback for our defeat."

"Then good luck," said Beverly, "and may Malin's wisdom guide you."

As one, they rose in silence, making their way across the open field toward the enemy lines. Her eyes followed them as they got closer, the enemy still unaware of their presence. She looked for enemy pickets but saw none. Perhaps, she hoped, they didn't believe in such tactics.

She heard the sounds of distant shouts as the Weldwyn soldiers rose from the darkness and descended on the enemy camp. Clansmen ran in alarm, their shapes revealed by the light of campfires. The attackers advanced, striking down those closest to the darkness first. Everything was proceeding as planned and Beverly had to force herself to withdraw. Much as she would have liked to watch the action, she had to prepare for her role in this raid.

She made her way back south, to the waiting line of horsemen, where she grabbed Lightning's reins and pulled herself into the saddle. The men to either side of her were almost stirrup to stirrup, eager to begin their appointed task. She listened for the telltale sounds, ignoring the occasional horse whinny. Distant horns announced the enemy's response and she held her breath, hoping to soon see her own men returning to the tree line.

"Prepare to move," she said aloud. "Remember, stay at a trot till the last moment. We'll be in very close formation. Once we engage the enemy, strike quickly and then withdraw. I want no heroics today; our sole purpose is to bloody their nose and tell them we're here, is that clear?"

There were calls of confirmation down the line. She counted to thirty and then saw a large group break the tree line, dividing evenly east and west. She held her sword aloft, counting, again, to thirty, all eyes on her, waiting for the command to move.

The enemy footmen, in pursuit, swarmed past the trees, and then she sliced her sword down through the air, giving the signal. The line began to move, the jangle of the horses harnesses mixing with the clopping of their hooves. Lightning picked up the pace at her command, and soon the trot became a slow gallop. She had perused the field before nightfall, ensuring there was no uneven ground to injure the mounts, but even so, she was hesitant to risk a full-blown charge.

"For Weldwyn!" she shouted, and the men took up the call. Forward they rode, like the Gods coming to wreak vengeance on the denizens of the Underworld.

Into the mass of men went the horses of Weldwyn, their blades seeking the life of their enemy. Beverly nearly took a man's head off with a slash of her sword. She rode by him, a surprised look permanently etched on his face, then cut into the chest of another Clansman. Lightning ran one down, his screams suddenly cut off as the charger's hooves collapsed the man's rib cage. They kept moving, striking down any who opposed them. The enemy line was scattered; more of a mob than a military formation, and soon the riders broke through to the other side.

"We have them!" yelled a Weldwyn horseman. "Let's finish this!"

"No!" ordered Beverly. "Stop!"

A small group of Weldwyn cavalry was starting to advance toward the enemy camp, but Beverly knew they would be cut down. Even now the enemy cavalry was mounting; they needed to withdraw or risk losing their advantage.

She pushed forward, easily out-pacing her Weldwyn allies, cutting in front of them, forcing them to turn to avoid a collision. She stood in the stirrups, her bloody sword held in front of her.

"There will be ample opportunity to kill them in the morning," she said. "Now return to camp or risk losing us what little advantage we have earned this night."

"But they'll get away," said one of the riders.

"The enemy knows we are here," said Beverly. "Come morning, they will be arrayed against us in great numbers. We must stick to the plan if we are to win through."

"But we have a chance to kill more of them. Better now than tomorrow when they are expecting us."

Beverly moved Lightning closer, the great black Mercerian Charger responding to her silent commands. She lowered her blade, pointing the tip to the rider's chest.

"You will follow my commands or I will end your life," she said. "Which is it to be?"

It took only a moment for the man to come to his senses. He wheeled his horse around, making his way back toward the Weldwyn camp. Beverly watched the others turn and trail along behind him.

Would they follow orders tomorrow, she wondered.

TWENTY-FIVE

To Battle

AUTUMN 961 MC

~

Gerald looked out from beneath the oak tree. The sun had just risen, but he had been here for some time; the expected approach of battle enough to prevent him from sleeping. He heard the soft footfall of feet and turned to see Anna and Tempus approaching. Anna stopped beside him, sharing the camaraderie in the stillness of the early dawn.

Gerald looked down at the men of Weldwyn. They were lined up behind the stream, sitting in position, and resting themselves.

"Shouldn't they be on their feet?" asked Anna.

"The enemy isn't in sight yet. Let them rest while they can, it's likely to be a long day."

"What if they don't come?" asked Anna.

"They will," said Gerald. "We've stirred the hornet's nest. They'll be eager for revenge."

"Where are they?" she asked.

"Revi can tell us more when he arrives."

"I saw him on the way up, he should be here any moment."

A low bark from Tempus turned their attention to the approaching mage.

"Good morning, Master Bloom," said Anna.

"Good morning, Highness, General."

"I trust you slept well?" said Anna.

"I did," the mage admitted. "I am thoroughly rested, most important since I'll be healing people later. And you, did you sleep well?"

"I did," said Anna, "though I fear our general did not."

"Too many preparations to make," said Gerald. "Once the battle's over I'll likely rest. It's rare for a warrior to sleep before a battle. Any sign of the Clans?"

Revi took up a stance, closing his eyes. He muttered the incantation and then began weaving as he gazed through his familiar's eyes.

"I see them," he said. "The main force is coming from the north and slightly west. You should be able to see them approaching around that group of trees in a moment."

"What's their composition?" asked Gerald.

"I see their horsemen in front, the rest are marching in three loose columns."

"They'll likely want to form into line quickly once they're opposite us. How are the cavalry formed?"

"They're not," said the mage. "They're just a cloud in front of the main columns."

"Just like the Norlanders," said Gerald, "I should have guessed."

"Why is that?" asked Anna.

"From all I've heard about the Clansmen," said Gerald, "they're primarily raiders; they're not used to the discipline of a line of battle. They likely excel at raiding, but Beverly's horsemen will cut them to ribbons if we can get them close enough."

"You want them close?" asked a familiar voice. They looked toward the sound to see Arnim Caster approaching. "The men are ready. I'll have them rise once the enemy's nearer. How close, exactly, do you want them?"

"As close as we can get them," Gerald replied. "I've presented them with a weak flank. Hopefully, they'll take the bait and attack our western flank. Once they're winded and confused, Beverly can move around the hill and chew them to pieces."

"Then what?" asked Arnim.

"Then we can take care of the rest of them," Gerald responded, calmly.

"You sound very confident," said Revi, "and yet there are so many of them. How do we possibly kill them all?"

"Kill them all? What makes you think that's what we're here to do?" asked Gerald.

"Of course it is," said the mage, his eyes still closed. "Isn't that what war is all about?"

Gerald turned his attention to the princess, "You tell him, Anna."

"It's not about killing the enemy," she explained, "it's about breaking their will to fight. If we destroy their morale, we defeat them."

"And how do we do that?" asked Arnim.

"Watch and see," said Gerald, "watch and see."

The group on top of the hill watched as the enemy drew closer, turning eastward, their great columns forming up into a single opposing line, well out of bow range.

"They're overlapping our lines by a considerable degree," warned Arnim.

The sound of horns announced a swarm of enemy horsemen who rode into the gap between the two opposing armies.

"You'd best take up position, Commander," ordered Gerald.

"Are they attacking already?" Arnim asked.

"No, but they're getting their people fired up. It won't be long now before they make their first move."

Arnim rode down the hill. Soon, the spearmen were lined up, their spears at the ready.

"What are they doing?" asked Anna. "Why are their horsemen riding back and forth?"

"They're trying to intimidate us," explained Gerald, "by showing us their overwhelming numbers. I think it's time we responded with a surprise of our own. Captain Sanderson, the flags if you will."

The Weldwyn captain nodded his head and then raised a small blue pennant, waving it over his head. Down the bottom of the hill a similar flag was waved, and then some activity began behind the spearmen's solid line.

"What's happening?" asked Anna. "What are they doing?"

"I thought I'd surprise you, Anna. I've had Sophie working with some of the women in the camp. They've sewn up some new flags for us."

Anna watched in silence as the new flags were unfurled. Now, instead of the standard of Weldwyn, a new flag appeared. It consisted of two horizontal bars, one above the other. The top red, the bottom green."

"Tell me," he said, "what you think."

Anna clapped in glee, "The red flag of rebellion over the forest green of Merceria."

"Your colours now," he informed her. "After all, we need something to carry into battle when we return to our home."

"But the Clans won't recognize it," she said.

"No," he acknowledged, "but it gives our men something to believe in. All the enemy knows is that a strange flag has appeared over their adversary. It'll give them pause to consider their options. Look, even now their riders are returning to their lines, they have no idea what's going on."

A cheer erupted from their own men as the enemy horse withdrew.

"It's already working," said Anna. "Tell me, what other surprises do you have in store for today?"

"I don't want to spoil your fun," he answered, "you'll have to wait and see."

It took some time for the enemy to make up their minds. Gerald was chewing on a cold sausage when he was interrupted by the mage.

"They're moving," said Revi, "and sending their cavalry to our left flank, just as you predicted."

"Good," responded Gerald. "Send Shellbreaker to our right flank, I don't want to be surprised by a double envelopment."

"Is that likely?" asked Anna.

"I doubt it," he replied. "They're more of a mob than an army. They've been predictable so far, let's hope they continue to do so."

The enemy horsemen drew closer, a large swarm which threatened to overwhelm the small group of Dwarves defending their flank. The riders were soon within range, but no bolts flew forth. Instead, a solitary horseman left the Weldwyn ranks, flowing red hair beneath the helmet making her instantly recognizable to those who knew her.

"What's Beverly doing?" cried out Anna in alarm.

"Wait for it," said Gerald, "this must be timed perfectly."

They watched as Beverly halted. She sat calmly on Lighting, her eyes carefully tracking the approaching enemy. Even from the hill, they heard the Clansmen yelling out in triumph, then Beverly turned, shifting her mount to point directly back at the rise, yet still, she did not advance.

The enemy horses were only a few lengths away when the field was suddenly enveloped in a thick mist.

"Lily!" cried out Anna in surprise.

"It was her idea," announced Gerald. "Now, watch closely."

They stared, mesmerized by the spectacle unfolding before them. The enemy horse was thrown into confusion, and even from their vantage point on the hill, the sounds of horses tripping and colliding, of men yelling in fear at the unexpected change to the landscape was heard. The horses in the rear, in full gallop, were unable to pull up in time and careened into the mist at full speed.

Lightning burst from the mist, Beverly pushing her horse for all he was worth. A small figure clung to the back of her saddle, its diminutive arms around the knight's waist, as the great horse carried them back to the Weldwyn lines at a forty-five-degree angle.

Gerald saw the look of understanding on Anna's face. "She's leaving a clear shot for the Dwarves," she realized.

Sure enough, no sooner had the red-headed knight cleared the path, then the arbalesters let loose, their iron bolts plunging into the mist.

"Will it be effective?" she asked.

"I hope so," said Gerald. "Hayley is directing them. We'll know in a moment."

Anna watched the cloud of bolts fly into the mist. There was a moment of tense silence followed by a sound like hail as they struck targets.

"They're packed tight right now," said Gerald. "The Dwarves don't even need to see their targets, just keep up a withering fire."

Gerald watched Beverly; she had reached the lines now and lowered Lily to the ground. The petite Saurian jumped up and down excitedly and then started heading up the hill.

Beverly wasted no time as she wheeled her great warhorse about and was soon galloping back westward, behind the archers. The Weldwyn riders had ridden around the hill while the enemy's attention was diverted, and a moment later, Beverly took up her position at their head. She raised her sword in the air, pointing it forward. With a tremendous cheer from the ranks, a hundred Weldwyn horsemen surged ahead, led by the avenging knight of Bodden Keep.

The mist clung to the field for a moment, but as the riders charged forward, it began to dissipate, revealing an enemy in chaos. Horses and men lay on the ground, bolts sticking out of them, while others wandered about in complete confusion. Beverly was witness to horses with broken legs and men crushed to death by their mounts, but then her attention returned to the advance of her own cavalry.

Before the enemy even knew what hit them, the swords of Weldwyn descended, utterly destroying any remaining opposition; those still able, ran in fear. The action was brief, no more than the time required to finish a mouthful of food, and then the riders fled in all directions.

Beverly sounded the recall, her voice barely carrying through the air, and yet the horsemen responded and rode back to their own lines, their mission accomplished. They had broken the enemy horse; now it was the footmen's turn.

Gerald watched as the enemy infantry began their advance. Anna stood, fascinated by the spectacle before her, her mouth agape as the immense mass of the Clansmen made their way forward, threatening to swamp the paltry army of defenders. Even Tempus seemed fascinated by the display, his tongue hanging from his mouth.

Lily made her way to the top of the hill, her part in the battle now complete. Hearing her approach, Anna turned, hugging her friend and talking to her in her own language.

Gerald, momentarily distracted by their greeting, turned back to the battle. "How's the right flank?" he asked.

"Safe for now," said Revi. "They seem to be redeploying their troops westward."

"They'd have to," said Gerald. "They're worried about our cavalry taking them in the flank."

"And will they?" asked Anna. "Take the enemies flank, I mean."

"Not yet," said Gerald. "We need to break their line up a little first and give them something else to worry about."

The enemy line continued its inexorable advance. Gerald caught himself holding his breath and forced himself to breathe. A light wind picked up, a bracing cold blowing across his face.

"It's getting cold, Highness," interrupted the voice of Sophie. "I brought you a cloak."

The handmaid wrapped a warm cloak about the princess while they both stood, watching the approaching storm below.

"They're moving so slowly," said Anna, pulling the cloak tighter.

"It looks slow because there's so many of them," said the old warrior.

"How many are there?" she asked.

Gerald held up his thumb and finger, forming an 'L' shape and did a quick estimation. "You can estimate numbers by looking at one-tenth their number and making a guess. I'd say there's still about fifteen hundred of them, not counting whatever horse they have left."

"What about their archers?" she asked.

"Saxnor has seen fit to send us this wind. Their archers won't be as effective, but they've already decided that; see how their entire line is advancing? There's no room for their bowmen to let loose."

"Couldn't they shoot over their heads?" asked Sophie.

"If they were well-trained, yes," he replied, "but I don't think they have the discipline for that. They're primarily raiders, like Norland."

"But surely they'll overwhelm our defenders," she said.

"We've thought of that," he responded. He looked over to the young maid and saw the look of dismay on her face. "Fear not, Sophie, we have another surprise waiting for them. It still requires a little luck, but I think it's going to work. The enemy is eager to come to grips with us."

"And that's a good thing?" asked the maid.

"Yes, it makes them keen to close the range, precisely what we want."

The enemy continued its advance, the vast wave of soldiers flowing ever nearer. Closer it came until the lead men were entering the edge of the stream, then, for some reason, the line wavered.

"What's happening?" asked Anna.

"We staked the stream," explained Gerald. "Small stakes, driven into the stream bed beneath the surface of the water, enough to make them cautious. Now Arnim will carry out his part."

Suddenly the entire Weldwyn line stepped forward, their long spears lunged out, and the first line of Clansmen fell beneath the sudden fury. The spearmen quickly hurried back to reform their solid lines.

The enemy advanced again, pushing past their fallen comrades only to have the defensive manoeuvre repeated. Wave after wave of Clansmen attempted to break the defensive line, but the more they pushed, the more the bodies piled up, impeding their own progress.

"The nice thing about spears," explained Gerald, "is the reach they have over the sword. When they're tightly packed together, they're almost impenetrable."

He turned to Revi, "If you would be so kind, Master Bloom, please give the signal."

The silent mage snapped his eyes open, "Just a moment," he said, "it's a little disorienting when I break my connection to Shellbreaker."

He took a deep breath, letting it out slowly. He held out his left hand, gesticulating wildly with his right, while he traced arcane symbols in the air. A moment later, a small ball of light appeared, hovering over his open hand. He kept up the incantation, watching as he levitated it into the air. A moment later his voice changed, falling into a deeper register. The ball of light began to grow bright, far brighter than Gerald had seen before. Finally, his chanting complete, Revi took another deep breath. "It's ready," he said.

Gerald, who had been distracted by Revi's spell, gazed back down the hillside. Beverly had seen the signal, and now the reformed cavalry rode forth, curving around the field to take the enemy in its flank.

The Clansmen, their line in disarray, their cavalry dispersed, took only an instant to collapse. One moment there was a thick line of footmen attacking the thin Weldwyn line, the next there was sheer panic as the invaders realized their flank had been destroyed. From atop the hill, it looked as though an anthill had been upturned; men were scattering in all directions, some even throwing down their weapons and rushing to the safety of the Weldwyn lines.

"Shall we advance?" asked Anna.

"No," Gerald replied, "they could still beat us if we leave our prepared positions."

"Then what do we do?" asked Sophie.

"We wait," he said. "I think we'll see a parley soon enough."

The enemy formed a thin defensive line, well back from their previous position. Revi, who had resumed his connection to his familiar, was relaying events from Shellbreaker's eyes.

"A large portion has fled," he reported. "They're forming up for a final stand, but I'd say there's less than three hundred of them."

"We killed that many?" asked Sophie.

"No," said Anna. "We scattered them. They're all running for safety."

"It's time to go forward and accept their surrender," said Gerald.

"Why would they do that?" asked Revi. "They hate Weldwyn."

"They're not surrendering to Weldwyn," Gerald replied, "they'll be surrendering to a Princess of Merceria. They still don't know who they've fought today, remember?"

They left Sophie on the hill as they mounted their horses and rode down to the battlefield where Beverly was waiting along with a cavalry escort. They continued onto the field, halting before the thin Clan line.

Beverly rode forward, exchanging words with the enemy, then returned. "Their leader is a man named Horst," she said. "He's willing to surrender if you guarantee the lives of his men."

Gerald looked to Anna, "Well, what's your answer? It's your victory, Highness."

"Can we still destroy their army if we have to?" she asked.

"Yes," he replied, "but it'll mean more casualties. We'll need every man we have to march to Leofric's aid."

"Very well," she decided, "tell them to lay down their arms, and we will spare them."

Beverly returned to the enemy line to exchange more words.

"Do you think they'll agree?" Anna asked just before the enemy soldiers began throwing down their weapons.

"There's your answer," said Gerald, turning to the horsemen around him. "Take them into custody, but make sure no one is harmed. We will enforce the wishes of the princess."

TWENTY-SIX

Nikki

AUTUMN 961 MC

Nikki lifted the tankard to her lips, enjoying the aroma of the heady foam on top. She took a swig, knocking back half the cup, then wiped her mouth with a kerchief. She looked at the small cloth, amused that she still clung to the habits ingrained on her by Valmar. She shuddered at the mere thought of the marshal-general, then took another gulp to finish off her ale, this time willing herself to use her arm to wipe her mouth like she used to.

It felt wrong, and she chided herself for falling back into old habits, but what else could she do? She looked around the tavern, taking in its patrons. She had started using this as her base of operations four days ago, and now, with a few coins in her purse, she was feeling much better about her future. She was sad that Arnim hadn't left with her but hoped that, perhaps someday, he might see the error of his ways. In the meantime, she had made some contacts, for the Amber Shard was a tavern frequented by all sorts of people, especially the kind she was used to dealing with back in Wincaster.

Getting the word out that she was available for hire had been easy. She had to be quite adamant though, she would not sell her body, but break-ins or infiltrations were all on the table.

As she sat pondering her future, a man entered the tavern, speaking quietly to one of the barmaids and then was redirected toward her. He was in his late twenties, fit by the look of him, with black, carefully trimmed sideburns and a clean chin. He walked directly to her table and stood a moment before talking.

"Nicole, isn't it?" he asked. "May I sit?"

"I don't know you," she replied, "but feel free." She pointed at the chair opposite her, and the man sat down. "What can I do for you?"

"My name's Finch," he said. "You don't know me, but I've made some enquiries about you. You used to work for the Mercerian Princess, didn't you?"

"Yes," she admitted, "what of it?"

"Well," he continued, "it's obvious you work from here now. I can only conclude you've had a falling out. May I ask if there's any bad blood between you and your previous employer?"

"Why don't you ask her yourself?" she said defensively.

"You and I both know she marched north with the army."

"Pity," she retorted, "then I suppose you'll just have to take my word for it when I say there's no bad blood."

"I've heard you're a hard worker."

Nikki laughed, "Naturally. I would hardly admit to being lazy, now would I? What kind of stupid comment is that?"

"I see you like to get straight to the point," he said.

"I don't believe in mincing words," she replied. "How about you tell me what you want?"

"I would suspect you could procure employment almost anywhere if you put your mind to it."

"Yes," she admitted, "I suppose I could, what of it? Are you offering me a job?"

"Do you think you could get a position at court?"

"Is that what this is about? You want me to spy on someone at the Palace?"

"Keep your voice down," the man hissed. He looked around nervously, then content that no one had overheard them, returned his attention to Nikki, "I promise you my sponsor pays very well."

"How well?" she asked.

"Let's just say that money won't be an obstacle."

"I haven't named my price yet," she warned.

"And you haven't heard what he wants you to do."

She leaned back in her chair trying to judge the man. "You have me intrigued," she said, "but I'd have to meet this sponsor of yours. I don't work through intermediaries, it's come back to bite me in the past."

"I think that could be arranged, but there would have to be some conditions."

"Such as?" she asked.

"A blindfold, nothing more. My sponsor would like to keep his where-abouts confidential."

"And so we would walk about town with a blindfold on? Nobody would notice that."

"You'd be in a carriage, of course," the man confessed. "I assure you, you would be perfectly safe."

"And if I meet this sponsor of yours and decide I don't want to work for him?"

"You would be dropped off back here."

"How can I be sure you wouldn't have me killed?" she accused. "It's not every day a man wants a woman to jump into a carriage wearing a blindfold and then takes them to an unknown destination."

"True enough, but you can tell the tavern keeper we're going. I'll make sure he knows who I am. If you were to disappear, they'd know who to look for."

"I'll think it over," she promised. "I would also want some sort of down payment to meet your sponsor. If I choose not to work for him, the down payment remains with me. Think of it as a finder's fee."

The man grinned back at her, "You're a woman after my own heart. Very well, I agree to your terms." He reached into his jacket and extracted a small purse from an inside pocket. "Here's a down payment," he said, dropping it to the table, "or should I say a retainer? I'll drop by tomorrow after I've arranged the meeting place. If you change your mind, you can cancel and keep the retainer. Will that suffice?"

"That sounds reasonable," she replied.

A barmaid wandered over to the table, but the visitor waved her away. "I'm just leaving," he said.

"How about you, Nikki?" the woman asked. "Another round?"

"Thanks, May. Talking makes me thirsty."

Finch rose from the table, nodding his head at Nikki in acknowledge-ment and then wandered through the tavern, eventually making his way to the exit.

May returned to the table bearing a fresh tankard. "Friend of yours?" she asked.

"More like a business opportunity," replied Nikki.

"He seems like a nice enough fellow."

"Only time will tell, May, only time will tell."

The barmaid returned to her duties while Nikki held the small pouch in her hand, testing its weight. It was rather light for coins, and she wondered if she had been conned, but the thought soon vanished, for there was no profit in it. She untied the top of the pouch and emptied the contents onto the table. Out spilled an assortment of uncut gems and she wondered where such items had come from. She selected one at random and lifted it close to examine it. Years working for the gangs had given her an appreciation for jewellery. When one was going undercover in a well-to-do household, it was likely the most valuable thing in the place.

The gem was red, and though it looked like a rough cut piece of salt, she saw the striations inside that marked it as a fire gem, one of the rarest and therefore most valuable in the land.

She was impressed by the quality but was suddenly aware of her surroundings and hurriedly scooped them all up, placing them carefully back in the bag. Whoever wanted to hire her was spending a lot of money. A score like this would set her up for years.

Next morning found her sitting in the same seat, contemplating her future once again. She watched the man, Finch, enter the tavern, just as he had promised. He wandered over, nodding his head in greeting.

"May I?" he said, pointing to the empty chair.

"Please do," she replied.

"Have you thought over my proposition?" he asked.

"I have. You made quite an impression yesterday. I'm interested in learning more."

"Excellent," he replied, "I thought you might agree, so I went to the trouble of arranging some transportation. Whenever you're ready, we'll head out the back door. I have a carriage waiting outside."

"Very well," she said, rising from her seat. "I see no reason to delay any longer." She tossed a few coins on the table, then put her purse away. "Lead on," she said.

He led her out the back door where a covered carriage waited. Finch opened the door for her, and she stepped inside. She looked around at the interior, noticing the thick curtains which blocked the windows. Another man was waiting inside, a black hood in his hands.

"Make yourself comfortable," the new man said, "and I'll put the hood over your head when you're ready."

She sat down opposite him, fussing over her dress, carefully feeling the dagger that was tucked into her garter. "I'm ready," she announced.

The stranger leaned forward, dropping the hood over her head. It had a strange smell to it that made her think of potatoes, and then the carriage jolted forward. She sat in silence, listening carefully to the sounds of the street as they rode by. She heard the distinctive sound of a hammer striking metal and knew she was passing the smithy near Wilford Street. The carriage turned, and she calculated they were heading south. The neighing of horses, the calling of the fishmonger, all of these sounds meant something to Nikki, and though she wasn't as familiar with the streets of Summersgate, she was sure she could retrace her path if needed.

The carriage finally slowed to a halt, the horse's hooves echoing in a large room of some type. The hood was withdrawn, and the door opened.

"After you," her new companion indicated.

She stepped from the carriage. They were inside a large room, a warehouse by the look of it. Crates and barrels were stacked against the walls, and yet the place appeared largely abandoned. She looked again at the barrels; they were new and unmarked. Someone had gone to considerable lengths to make it look like it was in use.

They crossed the large room to a flight of stairs leading up to an office that overlooked the storage area. Two men in long cloaks stood outside the door, but upon her approach, one of them opened it. Entering the small office, she noticed a table at one end, behind which were bundles of paper. Her contact, Finch, was sifting through them as she entered.

"Glad to see you arrived intact," he said. "I apologize for the roundabout trip, but we couldn't take any chances. Please, take a seat."

The two men from the door entered behind her, one of them producing a chair from somewhere. She sat, once again making a show of arranging her dress.

"Is your boss going to join us?" she asked, falling into the old vernacular.

"He'll be joining us shortly," Finch replied. "In the meantime, may I offer you a drink? I assure you it's not drugged or poisoned."

"No, thank you," she replied.

The sound of footsteps on the stairs drew their attention.

"Ah," said Finch, "I believe my sponsor has just arrived."

The door opened, and a large, well-muscled individual appeared. He was wearing a chainmail shirt and had the look of a seasoned warrior. He stood in the doorway, taking in everything, then settled his gaze on Nikki. His eyes lingered on her for a moment, and then he entered, standing off to the side to allow another individual access.

The man following him was well dressed in expensive looking clothes. A fur-lined cloak hung from his shoulders, but he had pushed it back on the right to free his sword arm. The hilt of the weapon in his scabbard was jewel encrusted. He walked into the room slowly, keeping his eyes on Nikki.

"So this is the one you've been talking about, Finch," he said.

Nikki tried to appear calm, but her experience of Valmar came back to haunt her, and she shuddered involuntarily. Her eyes settled on the newcomer, and something jogged her memory. "You look familiar, have we met before?" she asked.

"Not face to face," he retorted, "but I've seen you from across the room, back in Loranguard."

"You're Prince Cuthbert," she accused.

He wore a surprised look, "You've a good memory. I'm surprised you recognize me."

"You're a prince of the realm, why wouldn't I remember you?"

He smiled at the accusation. "You're a remarkable woman, Nikki, or should I say Lady Nicole?"

"Either will do," she said, falling back into old habits.

"I'm told you have access to the Palace," he began.

"I don't work for the princess anymore," she replied.

"No, but I hear you're still in good standing. You could, no doubt, get a position there if needed."

"Why would you need that? Surely you can go to the Palace anytime you want."

"My family doesn't know I'm in town," he confessed. "I would rather it remain that way."

"You have me intrigued. What, exactly is it that you want me to do?"

"We'll get to that soon enough. Tell me, what do you think of my brother, Alric?"

"I'm not sure what you mean," she confessed. "He's a prince, how am I supposed to feel?"

"Do you like him?" he asked.

"I neither like nor dislike him. If this is some attempt to get me to seduce him, you're barking up the wrong tree. I'll rob people, even kill them if needs be, but I won't sell my body."

"Ah, I see you have some scruples, but you needn't worry. I don't want you to seduce my brother, and I don't think it would work, anyway. He's too besotted with that Mercerian Princess."

"Then what is it you want me to do? Steal something from the Palace? Why don't you go and get it yourself?"

The prince ignored her jibes. "Why are you here?" he asked.

"I was promised coins," she said, "and lots of them."

"Greed, an emotion I can identify with. Now we come to the crux of the matter. What would it take for you to take care of someone for me?" he asked.

"If by 'take care of someone' you mean murder, it would depend on how difficult it would be. Who is it you want dead? Alric?"

Cuthbert nodded, "He's in a position to interfere with my plans, you see. We've never really gotten along, and I fear his good nature is working against him."

"He's a skilled swordsman," she said, "and has a personal bodyguard. I'd never be able to knife him."

"Oh, I don't want him killed with a blade," said Cuthbert. "No, no. I want him poisoned. In fact, I want all his top people poisoned along with him."

"That's a big job," she said. "I'd have to get into the Palace and poison the wine. Escape would be almost impossible."

"I'll see to your escape," said Cuthbert, "you needn't worry about that. With Alric and his cronies out of the way, I'll march right in and take over."

"So this is your plan to seize power?" asked Nikki.

"Precisely, and once I control the throne, I'll have lots of money to pass out. Are you still interested."

"I'd be a fool to say no. How much are we talking about?"

"Name your price."

"Five thousand crowns," she said.

"You surprise me," he replied. "I was expecting more. After all, it isn't every day someone gets hired to kill a prince."

"I don't want to sound greedy," she said. "And five thousand would set me up for life. I'd never have to work another day."

Cuthbert leaned in close to look deep into her eyes, "You and I are not so different, I think. We're not from the same levels of society, of course, but deep down we have similar motivations; money and power. I agree to your terms."

"Surely not!" objected Finch.

"I will have the last word on this," said Cuthbert, turning on his underling. "Remember who you're dealing with." He returned his attention to Nikki.

"Half in advance," she demanded.

He smiled, "Of course, I wouldn't expect anything less. I'll arrange to have funds delivered to you tomorrow."

"When is it to be done?" she asked.

"First things first," he said. "You'll have to get a position at court. Once that's done, you'll gather what information you can and report back to Finch, here. I have a timetable I must keep, but there are other factors at work. I shall be in touch when it is time, Lady Nicole."

"Please, call me Nikki," she said.

"So be it. I look forward to working with you on this venture, Nikki." He turned to the armoured man that brought him in, "Would you be so kind as to take our guest back to the carriage, Rogarr?"

The warrior grunted an acknowledgement as Nikki rose to her feet.

"This way, Miss Nikki," he said, in a thick accent.

Nikki exited the door, thinking back to Loranguard all those months ago. The accent was bothering her, and she struggled to identify it. She descended the steps, the door closing behind her. As she made her way to the carriage below, her keen hearing overheard a snippet of conversation.

"Should we trust her?" asked Finch.

"We shall see," replied Cuthbert.

She crossed the bare floor of the warehouse and paused before climbing into the carriage. She looked over to the immense doors of the warehouse; one was partially open, and she spotted a sign across the street, 'Edson's Farrier', and smiled. She stepped into the carriage and sat, waiting for the hood to be dropped over her head once again.

She rode back in silence, no longer paying attention to the sounds of the city, secure in the knowledge that she could easily find her way back if needed. She thought again of the strange accent of the warrior, and the more she thought of it, the more she became convinced that it was that of a Clansman.

TWENTY-SEVEN

The Long March

AUTUMN 961 MC

~

Toby Whitaker sat by the side of the road. "I have a stone in my boot," he complained.

"Let's move off the road a bit," said Angus, an old soldier. "You don't want to get run over." He grabbed the younger man's arm, guiding him to a nearby rock. "Have a seat, here, and see to it." He pulled the sling bag from his back, fished out a bottle and took a swig.

Toby sat down, struggling to pull the leather footwear loose. "My feet are killing me," he said. "How much longer are we going to march?"

"Until we give them a good drumming," the old warrior answered as the Army of the Twelve Clans marched past.

"I thought we'd be in Summersgate by now."

"We'll get there soon enough, my young friend." Angus took another swig of the bottle, "Here, have some of this." He passed it to his young companion.

Toby took the bottle, holding it absently as he watched the riders trot past. "Damn mercenaries," he said, "I don't trust 'em."

"You don't need to trust 'em," replied Angus. "They're the bulk of our horsemen. They'll be the ones that do most of the fighting. Let the foreigners die, better them than us."

"But we don't need 'em," Toby continued. "We're twice the size of the enemy, even without the mercs. We just need to trap King Leofric and lock 'im up like his son."

Angus let his eyes drift down the column, catching sight of the horses drawing the cage that held the Crown Prince of Weldwyn. "Aye," he agreed, "that'll be grand. It won't be long now. Leofric's lost one of his armies, and now we'll crush him. Perhaps we'll let the Trolls eat 'im for breakfast."

Toby shuddered, "I don't like those creatures, they terrify me."

"What, Trolls? I'm not surprised, the stuff of nightmares, they are."

"How did we end up with Trolls?" asked the younger man. "I can understand the Kurathians, but those huge beasts just aren't natural."

"I don't rightly know," said Angus, "but word is they were driven out of their homes in the north."

"What in the Twelve Clans could drive out a Troll?"

"Beats me, best not to worry about it though, that's hundreds of miles away, and we have better things to do. Are you done with that bottle yet?"

Toby took a deep drink and passed the bottle back. The older man shook it, then turned it upside down, noting that nothing came out. "You didn't have to drink it all."

"There wasn't much left. Anyway, we need to get back to marching."

"Did you remove the stone?"

"I did."

"Good, then pick up your feet, youngster. It's time we were on the move."

A distant baying interrupted their conversation, and this time even Angus shuddered. "Let's be quick," he warned, "we don't want to be around when those things are nearby, they'd likely chew your legs off for looking at them funny."

They started trotting beside the column, intent on catching up to the rest of their company, but Angus halted, putting his hand out stop his companion.

"What is it?" asked Toby?

"If I live and breathe, I don't believe it," the old man said.

"What? What have you seen?"

Angus pointed at a distant tree, "See that bird over yonder?"

"Yes, what of it?"

"It's a rare breed," said the old man, "a black coaster."

"You're imagining things," said Toby. "It's just a blackbird." He reached into a pocket and pulled forth the stone that had troubled him so recently.

"No, it's a coaster," defended the older man. "They can stay airborne for days and ride currents across the sea."

Toby hurled the stone, but it went wild. The bird cawed, flapped its wings, and then flew off.

"What'd you do that for?" asked Angus.

"A blackbird is a sign of doom," said Toby. "Best to send it on its way or we'll lose the battle."

"Don't be ridiculous. We outnumber King Leofric by more than two to one. What could possibly go wrong?"

"I don't know," admitted Toby, "but after seeing that bird, I have a bad feeling."

Gerald watched as the spearmen went about their practice.

"Are you sure this is going to work?" asked Arnim. "They march all morning, and then you have them practising all afternoon. Shouldn't we be hurrying to Leofric's aid?"

"There's no point in getting there if we can't defeat the enemy. These movements will be our salvation."

"How do you figure that?" asked the knight.

"Have you ever pricked your finger on a thorn?" he asked.

"Yes."

"And didn't that make you more cautious the next time you came into contact with one?"

"Yes, but what has that got to do with these drills?"

"Think of the spears as thorns," suggested Gerald.

Shellbreaker came into sight, soaring across the sky, coming to land on Revi's outstretched arm.

"The enemy is marching south," announced the mage.

"I thought," said Gerald, "that they'd already taken Wandermere?"

"It appears they have, and then they marched north, likely to threaten Faltingham, but I suspect the presence of the king's army has lured them south again."

"How far away are they?" asked Gerald.

"Still a few days march."

"And Leofric?"

"He's marching north from Abermore, but it looks like he's outnumbered almost three to one."

"Why doesn't he withdraw to Summersgate?" asked Arnim.

"He can't," said Anna, coming toward them. "He can't let his people suffer. The Clans would burn Abermore to the ground; he has to make a stand."

"Can we get a message to Leofric?" Gerald asked.

"I could send Shellbreaker with a short message attached to his foot, but then we'd lose his eyes. We wouldn't know where the enemy was located."

"A fast rider could get to Leofric in a few days," said Anna. "Abermore is southwest of us."

"Let me go, General," volunteered Arnim. "I know the plan, we've been over it multiple times."

"And what will you tell him?" asked Gerald.

"To make a stand just south of Wandermere and we'll reinforce him there."

"Can we get there in time?" asked Anna.

"We'll get there or die trying," said Gerald. "I think they've got the manoeuvres down, now we need to force march."

"Force march?" asked Revi. "I don't like the sound of that."

"It means," offered Anna, "that we march till dark and rise early in the morning."

"And the men will do that?" said Revi in astonishment.

"Of course, their homes are at stake," explained the general. "The men are motivated. They've won a battle and now feel invincible. They'd march to the Underworld if they had to."

"I wish I had your confidence," said the mage. "We're still facing a very large enemy, and you need to persuade Leofric to make a stand. You'll have to be very convincing."

"I'll send a note with Arnim," said Anna. "I'm sure he'll listen to reason. At least he'll know it isn't a trap."

"How will he know that?" asked Arnim.

"First of all," said Anna, "he's met you, Sir Arnim, and secondly, I'll include a little tidbit of information about Alric that only he and I would know."

"Like what?" asked the mage.

"None of your business," replied the princess. "Gather your horse, Arnim, by the time you're ready, I'll have the note for King Leofric."

"You should take some men with you, for protection," added Gerald. "Pick half a dozen riders and have Beverly make sure the mounts are fresh."

"Very well," said Arnim. He turned and bowed to the princess. "Your Highness, General, with your permission, I shall be on my way."

"Good luck," said Anna, "and may the blessings of Saxnor be upon you."

They watched him disappear amongst the trees, heading toward the makeshift stables.

"Will he make it in time?" asked Anna.

"Hard to say," offered Gerald. "If we double our pace, we should be able to meet up with Leofric, but it all depends on the enemy's movements. If we're too slow, we may find ourselves arriving in the middle of a battle, or worse, after it's all over."

"Then we shall have to have faith," said Anna.

"I'm not sure the Gods pay attention to such matters," said Gerald.

"I wasn't referring to the Gods, Gerald. I have faith in you, we all do. We'll get there in time, I know it."

"I wish I were as sure as you are," he responded.

She reached out and took his hand in her own, "You've seen a lifetime of battle, Gerald. I know you have this in you. If I had any doubt that you could win this, I'd suggest we run away and live out our lives in peace. I would do that in a heartbeat if I thought your life was in danger. You will win this coming battle, I know in my heart you will. You must have faith in yourself."

Gerald stared down at her; no longer the young girl he had helped raise. "You're right," he said at last. "I never wanted this job, but if I'm going to do it, I'm going to do it to the best of my ability."

"That's the Gerald we all know and love," said Anna.

Gerald blushed at the compliment.

"Now, General," she continued, "where should we start?"

"We need to feed the men," he said, "they're rising early tomorrow for a long march, and they'll need all their energy."

"I'll send word," she said.

"And Revi," he continued, "keep Shellbreaker in the air till dusk. We don't want to be surprised by anything."

"Yes, General," said the mage.

"I'll want him to sweep west and north of us tomorrow, it's imperative that we keep a close eye on the Clans. If we're to have success on the battle-field, we'll have to leverage every advantage we have."

Arnim's horse splashed across the stream, and then they started climbing the opposite bank. He looked back to see his men, all six of them, strung out in a column. The distinctive sound of a bow letting loose pierced through the woods; the projectile embedding itself in the chest of the rider behind him. The unlucky soul toppled from his saddle, falling into the water, his blood running downstream as he lay, motionless.

"Hurry!" the knight yelled, scanning the trees for sight of the archer. He spurred his horse forward, turning right as he crested the bank, looking in the direction the attack had come from. A second thud greeted his ears as an arrow buried itself into his horse's chest, felling the beast. Arnim reacted quickly, launching himself free, with the help of his stirrups, to tumble to the ground, his horse missing him as it landed with a tremendous crash. Arnim rolled out of the way just in time, then stopped, lying still, face down in the dirt. He listened carefully, waiting for his prey to emerge. Sure enough, some muttering came from the tree-line, and then the snap of a twig told him someone was coming to investigate, likely to loot. He waited, his eyes closed, his body tensed for action. A hand caught his shoulder to turn him over, and he opened his eyes to a foot. He reached out, grabbing an ankle and pulling with all his might. The man toppled backwards, and a moment later Arnim was perched on top of the bowman, throttling him, trying to squeeze the life out of him. His target tried to fight back, but Arnim's grip was like steel as the man's face turned red, and then his struggling ceased.

Knowing he was in danger from the dead man's companions, he rolled to the side just as another arrow whizzed past. Rising to his feet, he sprinted toward the cover of a nearby copse of trees only to see another bowman notching an arrow. Arnim watched as the man lined up his shot and let fly, but the knight was quick and dodged, the missile shooting past him harmlessly. He crashed into the bowman, his leather gauntlet punching his target squarely in the face. The bowmen crumpled without any further opposition. Arnim paused a moment, catching his breath and drawing his sword in his left hand. He looked toward the stream where he heard more splashing; two of his men were down, another rode to the far bank with an arrow in his shoulder. The final two had dismounted to seek shelter on the far bank, but the enemy kept up a constant barrage, and it was all they could do to avoid being hit.

The knight moved forward, as quietly as he could, parting the leaves with his sword as he went. He knew he was nearing the other bowmen now, their voices becoming clear as they called out their shots. Pushing a branch out of the way, he saw a group of six men leaning against the trees. As some notched their arrows, another stepped out from behind cover, took aim, and let fly. The arrow sailed through the air, taking out the wounded man and dropping him; the body floating, lifeless, down the stream.

Next, a lanky black-haired youth stepped out from behind a tree, taking a bead on a target. Arnim screamed a challenge and charged forward, his sword before him. The youth prematurely fired in surprise, the arrow going wild. Arnim's sword sliced into the young man's neck, almost decapitating him before he tumbled to the ground in a heap.

The other archers called out in alarm. One of them was fumbling for a long knife, but Arnim stepped forward, jabbing his sword into the bowman's stomach. The enemy clutched at the wound, his fingers sliced off as Arnim withdrew the blade.

The knight was looking for his next victim when an arrow sunk into his right hand, penetrating his palm and pinning it to his leg. He whirled on this new attacker, but his opponent had turned to flee, and all that could be seen was the back of him, crashing through the trees.

Arnim pulled his hand up, wrenching the arrow tip from his leg but leaving the shaft through his hand. Blood gushed down his thigh, soaking his leggings, and he stumbled forward, swiping his sword in a wide arc. He clipped the arm of an archer, forcing his opponent to back up and drop his bow. The knight took another step and lunged, the tip burying itself into the man's chest. He felt the blade scrape a rib as he twisted it, and then withdrew the weapon.

As his target dropped to the forest floor, screaming, another attacked from behind, but he had heard him coming. He struck out with the pommel of his sword, smashing into the man's face, breaking teeth. The archer stepped back, blood gushing from his mouth, and Arnim swung his sword overhead, aiming for the head. The blade fell short, missing his intended target, instead burying itself into the man's shoulder, wedging itself into the collarbone.

The blade was dragged from his hand as it fell with the body. The knight pulled his dagger from his belt just as an arrow dug into his side; his chain-mail blocking it from sinking too deeply. He wheeled about to face this last attacker, a rough looking fellow with a weather-beaten face. His opponent notched an arrow, confident that his next shot would finish off the Mercerian.

Arnim threw the knife. It sailed through the air, striking the man in the groin, causing the bowman to double over in pain. A branch lay nearby, and Arnim grabbed it in desperation. The final opponent recovered quickly, drawing his long knife and readying it as the knight advanced, stumbling as his leg threatened to give way beneath him. The archer stepped closer, his knife seeking Arnim, who, blocking with his injured right arm, felt the blade slice into his flesh. He brought the branch crashing down onto the man's head, and they both fell to the ground, he atop the now lifeless body. He felt a surge of pain lancing through his leg, and then darkness enveloped him.

The youngster made his way through the kitchen, navigating the congested room with ease. He stopped at the counter, lifting the plate of food that sat, waiting.

"Hurry up with that, lad," said the cook. "You don't want to annoy the king."

He held the plate before him, as if his very life depended on it, and headed toward the great hall. At his approach, another servant opened the door so he could continue walking into the room full of noise and merriment. Finding his target and keeping him in sight, he wound his way around the celebrations, finally coming to his destination and setting the plate before King Dathen of the Twelve Clans.

"Good lad," said the king, "now fetch us some more wine."

The youngster hustled off to fulfill his new assignment, leaving the king to glance down at the meat before him.

Beside the monarch sat an older man with a long, flowing beard that almost touched his own plate. "What is it you have there, Lord?" he asked.

Dathen examined the food carefully before replying, "It looks like beef to me. Far better than what we've been eating of late, eh Carmus?"

"It looks a tad undercooked," the bearded man replied.

"Just the way I like it," said the king. He noticed the look of disappointment on his companion's face after he glanced at his own meal. "Oh, come now, you're a Fire Mage, surely you can just fire it up a little if it doesn't suit your palate?"

"You know full well my magic doesn't work that way," complained Carmus. "It would still take time to cook."

"Stop your grumbling, man. You have a belly full of food and hopefully, come tomorrow, we'll be rid of King Leofric and his paltry army."

"So he's finally decided to make a stand?" asked the mage.

"If we're lucky," declared the king. "Perhaps, by this time tomorrow, we'll have him in a cage. Either that or in a grave, it makes little difference to me."

"What of Thorne's army? Have you heard anything, my lord?"

"I haven't," the Clan King confessed, "but I'm sure he's defeated Prince Alstan's force by now. If we're lucky, he may show up just in time to watch us defeat the Weldwyn king. Our strategy worked brilliantly, Carmus. We divided their army. Now, with our Kurathian allies, we must outnumber what remains of them by at least two to one, possibly more, and that's not taking into account the power of your magic. A few streaks of flame from you and they'll be running away as fast as they can."

"I wish I were as confident as you, Sire. I hear Weldwyn is notorious for deploying mages of its own."

"You worry too much, my friend," said the king. "You and the other mages are far more powerful than anything the locals can throw at us, not to mention the Kurathian mages, or did you forget about them?"

"No," said Carmus, "indeed not, but I am loath to trust mercenaries, Sire, especially those that are not paid from our own purse."

"Relax," commanded the king, "there will be coin enough for all once the enemy is defeated. After we destroy Leofric tomorrow, the road to Summersgate will be open. A few days march and the women of Weldwyn will be prostrating themselves before us, begging for our protection." The king let out a laugh, a deep rumble that caught the attention of the other guests who dutifully joined in the celebration.

"Perhaps you're right, Sire," said Carmus, "I should never have doubted you. After all, you united all the Clans even when they said it couldn't be done. Who am I to argue the point?"

"There, you see?" said the king. "You're coming to your senses. Now drink up, my dear friend, for tomorrow will be a most glorious day; it will be the end of our enemy."

Arnim opened his eyes. He was still in the forest, the dead lying all around him. He rolled onto his back and stared up into the sky; the sun was past its zenith, telling him that some time had passed. Moving his right hand, he cried out in pain as the embedded arrow struck a root. Grunting with the effort, he gripped the arrowhead with his left hand, snapped it off, intensifying the agony of his wound while fresh blood poured forth. Gritting his teeth, he transferred his left hand to the tail of the arrow. Taking a deep breath, he hauled back on the shaft. The broken arrow came loose from the wound, blood now pooling on the ground below.

He tossed the shaft aside, his eyes searching the area for anything that might be of use. Spying a kerchief around the neck of his last victim, Arnim fumbled to remove it one-handed, then wrapped his wound as best he could. Finished, he struggled to his feet, despite his sore ribs, balancing mostly on his uninjured left leg.

He glanced down to the river where the dead bodies of his men lay, their horses wandering about loose; he resolved to try and catch one but must see to his other wounds first. He picked up a discarded bow to use as a staff, hobbling across the clearing to where his sword lay, still embedded in a dead man's shoulder. He grasped it, pulling with all his remaining strength, trying to loosen the blade. It was only by placing his foot upon the body that he managed to separate the sword from the corpse.

The edge of the sword was severely dented, and he swore at its condition. Had a smith been present, he would have been more than happy to have them put an edge to it, but there was no time for such matters. He'd been tasked with getting through to King Leofric, but now that very mission was in peril. He scabbarded the blade and looked around the clearing, his eyes settling on a discarded quiver. This he took, briefly examining the arrows it contained and then, satisfied that he was adequately armed, he made his way down to the water.

The horses were scattered, the closest nibbling on a tuft of grass that poked up through the stones that lined the little stream. He approached slowly, trying to soothe the beast with a calm voice. As he reached out, the creature, perhaps skittish from the fighting, trotted off, leaving Arnim struggling to stand once again.

Cursing his luck, he tried once more, his leg making even this simple task uncomfortable. After three such attempts, he managed to grab the reins. Now came the hardest part, for he must haul himself into the saddle, a task made all the more difficult by his current state. With only one arm and one good leg, he tried many, many times before he finally found himself astride the beast.

He turned his new mount west, pain lancing through his body with each step of the horse.

Slade Martin, a royal archer of Weldwyn, leaned back against the tree, staring off into the distance. His mate, Palmer, had just finished pissing and returned, looking across the ordinarily quiet field that lay to the northeast. They were on a hill, south of Wandermere, at the very edge of the Weldwyn lines.

The sound of arguing drifted toward them and they both turned to look, but the trees obstructed their view of the camp that lay behind them.

"Another fight," commented Slade.

"They're becoming more common," observed Palmer.

"Not surprising, morale is low, and things can only get worse."

"Why doesn't he make a stand," asked Palmer.

"Would you?" asked Slade. "Any attempt to fight them here would be disastrous. We'd all be dead men."

"But surely he's just prolonging the inevitable."

"Personally, I'd rather live another day than fight a hopeless battle. I expect the king will withdraw again, putting us closer to Summersgate. Perhaps we'll withdraw to Abermore and take up a defensive position. We could likely withstand a siege there for some time."

"It's hopeless," grumbled Palmer. "We've done nothing but retreat for days on end. Every time we look like we're making progress, he orders a retreat. What in the Four Realms is he doing?"

"King Leofric is doing what he thinks best," said Slade. "I don't know what that is, but I believe he has a plan."

"It would be better if he told us," grumbled his companion.

"It's not the job of kings to talk to commoners," defended Slade.

"Still," continued his friend, undaunted, "it would be nice to know we're doing something other than just staring off into the distance. Why are we here, again?"

"We're on the lookout," explained Slade. "The enemy is known to scout the areas they're advancing into. We're here to warn the camp if we see anything."

"What if we see just a single rider?" asked Palmer.

"Then we investigate," said Slade. "Why?"

"Because I just saw one," said Palmer. "Look!" He pointed to the field beyond where a single horse trotted across the open space, its rider hunched down in the saddle.

Slade immediately rose to his feet and began stringing his bow. "Get back to the camp and inform the captain," he said, "this may be trouble."

Palmer turned and ran, making a racket as he crashed through the undergrowth.

The horse halted, and now Slade watched in fascination as the rider slid from the saddle, coming to rest, face down on the ground.

Slade scanned the area carefully but saw no signs of anyone else. He descended the hill, moving ever closer to the fallen man. The horse shied away from him, but he ignored it, focusing his attention solely on the collapsed rider who lay face down, chainmail visible beneath his cloak. The archer leaned over, grabbing the fallen man's shoulder to turn him over, only to be startled as he spoke.

"King Leofric," the man stammered. "You must get me to King Leofric. I have important news." The rider's eyes fluttered closed, and then he passed out.

Arnim opened his eyes. He lay in a bed, his pain no more. He wondered if he had, perhaps, passed to the Afterlife, but then considered that he was weaponless; surely Saxnor would not take him without his sword.

His gaze swept the well-furnished tent trying to guess his whereabouts. Outside, somewhere, a voice muttered, and then the tent flap parted to reveal a woman peering through, her grey hair framing a familiar looking face.

"Ah, I see you're awake," the woman said. "I believe we've met before, I'm

Roxanne Fortuna, Life Mage. I once had the honour of healing your Mercerian Princess."

"I remember," stammered Arnim. "Where am I? I must speak with King Leofric at once."

"Relax," she soothed, "he's on his way. I was summoned when they found you; you've been brought to the king's tent. How did a Mercerian end up here, in the middle of nowhere?"

"How indeed," boomed a voice. King Leofric stepped into the tent, Lord Edwin Weldridge following him.

"Your Majesty," said Arnim, "I have been sent by General Matheson. He's marching to support you."

"General Matheson?" queried Edwin.

"The Mercerian General from Riversend," explained the king. He turned his attention back to Arnim, "I remember you; you were one of Princess Anna's people. What message do you bring, Sir Knight?"

"The general commands an army of Weldwyn, assigned by Queen Igraine herself," said Arnim. "He marches to aide you, but you must make a stand."

"Would that it were so easy," said Leofric, "but we are severely outnumbered."

"I have a message, in the princess's own hand," said Arnim.

"It's here," said Roxanne, "it was among his things. The seal is still unbroken."

The king took the note, looking at the folded paper. "There is much blood on it. You have, I think, paid a high price to deliver this message."

"It is of the utmost importance," urged Arnim.

"Then I suppose I better read it at once," replied Leofric. He moved closer to a lantern, breaking the seal to read the contents. His eyes scanned the writing, and then he passed it over to Edwin.

"You have done well, Sir Knight. Rest assured, though it will cost us greatly, we shall make a stand." He turned his attention to the mage, "Where is Mistress Harwell?"

"She is nearby, Majesty," she replied. "Shall I fetch her?"

"See that you do," he replied. "I want her to enhance this man's endurance, I need him on his feet for the coming battle."

"Is that wise, Sire?" Roxanne balked. "He has lost much blood. Despite the repair of his wounds, he is still weak."

"Her spell will give him the energy he needs, will it not?" asked the king.

"It will," she agreed, "but it will not last forever."

"It doesn't have to," he replied, "one day will be enough. After that, he may rest all he wishes, or we'll all be dead, and it won't matter. We need every man we have tomorrow if we're to face the Clans in open battle."

"Understood, Sire," said the mage. "I will send for our enchanter immediately."

"Thank you," the king replied, returning his attention to Arnim. "Once they've fed you and given you some energy, seek me out, I may have need of your skills."

Arnim nodded his assent as the king turned to leave. "Come along, Edwin, we've work to do if we are to make a stand in the morning."

TWENTY-EIGHT

The Banquet

AUTUMN 961 MC

~

P rince Alric, third son of King Leofric of Weldwyn, gazed around the formal dining room. A dozen of the king's closest advisors were here, ready to help plan the defense of Summersgate, should it prove necessary. They sat at tables arranged in an inverted 'U' with Alric and his mother, Queen Igraine, seated at the head. The feast was sumptuous, the wine flowed freely, and the young prince wondered, not for the first time, if all of this grandeur were strictly necessary. Surely, he thought, it would be better to meet while sober rather than plied with wine.

The room fell silent as the queen rose from her seat, holding a goblet before her. "Let us raise our cups in salute," she said, "to the fine horses that Lord Marlowe has brought to Summersgate."

The viscount bowed deeply, his cheeks red from the drink.

Beside Alric, Jack Marlowe, son of the viscount and Alric's personal bodyguard, raised his cup in appreciation. "Cheers," he called out, perhaps a little too enthusiastically. His father gave him a disapproving look, and Jack sat back down.

"Thank you, Your Majesty, for your kind words," the viscount called back.

Jack took another drink, the liquid dribbling down his chin.

"Not too much," chided Alric, "you need to be at your best, there's a lot of important people here."

"I know," he retorted, "that's why I need the drink." He raised his cup again, draining it dry. "My father and I have never seen eye to eye," he confessed, "even at the best of times."

"Surely he's proud of you," offered Alric. "After all, you're the champion of Weldwyn."

"My father," replied the cavalier, "is not overly enthusiastic about tournaments. He thinks they're a waste of time. He wants me to settle down, get married, and give him grandchildren."

Alric laughed, "And that makes you uncomfortable?"

Jack looked stricken. "Of course, I can't deny this," he pointed to himself, "to all the ladies of the kingdom. It just wouldn't be right."

"But you'll have to settle down eventually," said Alric.

"That's all well and good for you, Highness," continued Jack, "you've got a beautiful princess lined up, no doubt with a nice dowry."

"In truth, she's been cut off from the crown of Merceria," said Alric, "so she doesn't have anything."

Jack looked at him in disbelief, "I'm truly sorry, Highness, I didn't know." He poured himself some more wine, "Still, there are bound to be other wealthy ladies that would love to marry you."

"No, Jack," said Alric, "I'm going to marry Anna."

"Isn't that up to your father?"

"I don't care what my father says, it's Anna for me or no one."

Jack downed his drink in one gulp. "I hope you like the life of a Holy Father because that's all that's going to be left for you."

Alric stared at his goblet, rotating it in his hand. He took a sip, then tipped it back, draining it dry.

Nikki looked around the room from her vantage point near the door where she easily watched the guests. For all appearances, they were already deep into their cups, the wine flowing freely.

Once she had been installed in her new position in the kitchens, it had not taken her long to get the lay of the land. She really only needed to be here for a couple of days before the banquet to insinuate herself into the daily tasks of a servant so none would be the wiser to her true motives. Now, she watched as the most important people left in the capital consumed their drinks with reckless abandon.

She left the room, making her way toward the kitchen, stopping beside the urns of wine sitting in the hallway, waiting while another servant passed by. When the hallway was clear, she withdrew a small vial from her sleeve, pouring a carefully measured amount of the pale blue liquid into each urn. It soon disappeared, absorbed by the golden hue of the wine.

Returning the vial to her sleeve, she cast her eyes about once more to determine if anyone had witnessed her actions. Confident her activities went undetected, she stopped the next servant who entered the hallway. "Grab an urn, they're eager for more," she said.

The servant dutifully lifted an urn, Nikki doing likewise. "Let's be quick," said Nikki, "it's a thirsty crowd." She led the way back to the great hall, hearing the wine slosh as she carried it.

Calling for a refill, Alric noted that it was Lady Nicole that brought in a large urn of wine. She wandered by, filling the goblets of the royals and their guests. He held out his cup, watching the amber-hued wine slosh into it. Jack did likewise and then stood, banging on the table with his fist to get everyone's attention.

"My lords and ladies," he said, "if I may indulge your attention for but a moment." He waited for the chatter to die down, ensuring everyone had a full cup. "I would like to propose a toast to Prince Alric and the successful defense of the city."

"To Prince Alric," they echoed back.

Jack drained the cup and sat down to see the nobles of Weldwyn mimicking his action. He turned to Alric, ready again to toast his liege lord, only to find him, face down, unconscious on the table.

"Ah, well," he muttered, slurring his words, "it appears our young prince cannot hold his wine." Jack's chin fell to his chest, and he pitched forward, coming to rest on the table like the prince.

Nikki watched from the doorway as the guests fell, one by one. The view was all too eerily familiar, and she suddenly thought back to that day in Wincaster, when all her friends had fallen.

The great double doors to the hall swung open, six armed men striding through. They took positions up around the doorway at attention, and then Prince Cuthbert stepped through.

He looked around the room, letting his eyes, at last, linger on his younger brother. "Ah, such a sweet sight," he said, "the crown is now within my reach."

He noticed Nikki watching from the servants' entrance. "You have performed your task to perfection," he said. "You have my undying gratitude."

"I'll settle for the rest of my money," she said.

"Of course," replied Cuthbert, stepping forward. He pulled forth a small pouch, offering it to her. "This bag contains more diamonds," he said, "or if you prefer, you can wait until our plans are complete and I will give you coins. Which would you rather?"

"The diamonds will do," she said, taking the pouch from his hand. "But tell me, now that you've removed your brother, what will you do next? Your father still rules as king, and there's the matter of the Crown Prince."

"They will trouble me no longer," he explained. "The army of Weldwyn is vastly outnumbered and will soon be destroyed."

"And when the Clans come to the gates of the capital?" she asked.

"Then we shall welcome them as liberators," he replied. "I will marry the Princess Breda, and that will unite our two kingdoms forever."

"Aren't you already married," Nikki pointed out.

"A trifling inconvenience, soon rectified," he replied. "Now, Nikki, don't go too far. I may have need of your skills again."

"By all means," said Nikki, "I look forward to serving the crown once again."

TWENTY-NINE

Opening Moves

AUTUMN 961 MC

~

K ing Leofric of Weldwyn looked down on the troops taking up their positions below him. He was on a hill, along with his cavalry and bowmen, while to the west, there stretched a line of spearmen, anchored on their left by a group of trees. The enemy lay to the north, the Clan army spread out opposite his own.

He turned to look at Sir Arnim Caster, who sat on a horse to his left. "Are you sure they'll be here in time?" he asked.

"Yes, Your Majesty," the knight replied, "they should soon be in sight."

"What do you think of my deployment?" the king asked.

"I'm not the battle expert, Majesty, but it looks good to me, although I'm curious why you placed the bowmen so far out to the left in front of the wood."

"They'll pepper the enemy when they approach, then fall back into the safety of the trees. I expect the Clansmen may try to outflank us with their horse."

"If I may be so bold," asked Arnim, "the line that stretches across the road below us, why are the men not moved up?"

"Ah, yes," said the king, "you've likely not dealt with our mages before. If you look closely, you'll see our Earth Mage, Aegryth Malthunen. She will raise mounds of earth and then the spearmen will occupy them, it gives them a defensive advantage."

"Will the whole line be fortified?"

"No, Aegryth will have to conserve some energy for the battle, but she'll strengthen the centre of the line. I suspect that's where the enemy will strike."

"Have you other mages?"

"Of course. You've already met our healer, Mistress Fortuna, as well as our enchanter, Gretchen Harwell. Mistress Harwell has taken up a position with the archers on our right flank. If the enemy approaches, she'll enchant their volleys."

"A key advantage, I'll wager."

"Yes, they'll inflict a great deal of damage. Tell me, Sir Knight, what do you make of the enemy position?"

Arnim glanced across at the army of the Twelve Clans. "Their line is very similar to yours, Majesty, with the foot forming the centre and the bows split to either flank. I notice their cavalry is divided in a similar fashion, is that normal? I would have thought it better to mass the horse in one place."

"You have a keen eye," said Leofric. "I think our adversary, High King Dathen, wants to keep his options open. He's likely hoping for our line to break and wants the cavalry nearby to exploit it. Of greater concern to me are the Kurathians."

"Yes," agreed Arnim. "Our mage indicated there were hundreds of them, and yet I can only make out some footmen, far to the eastern flank of the Clansmen."

"No doubt the rest are behind the woods, yonder. I expect they'll make an appearance soon enough."

"How many troops do you have, Majesty?" Arnim asked.

"Close to eight hundred. The combined enemy is easily twice our size. If your friends hadn't taken out the eastern force, we'd be facing far more. For that, we must be thankful."

"How will you fight them?"

"We will fight defensively and hold our ground. We must trust that our allies will arrive in time, for if they don't, it will be the end of us all."

A distant baying drew their attention northeast.

"What's that?" asked Arnim.

Leofric visibly paled. "Kurathian Mastiffs, lots of them, by the sound of it."

"If they are half as powerful as Tempus, you may be in trouble."

"Yes, they'll tear through our cavalry, given the chance. Hopefully, they don't have a lot of them. Where is the relief to come from?"

"From the east," Arnim promised.

Arnim turned his attention back to the enemy forces before them, noticing the banners that marked the enemy commander. "This High King Dathen," he said, "what do you know of him?"

"Not much, I'm afraid," said Leofric, "but he managed to unite all the Clans, a feat we would have said was impossible. I have no knowledge of his tactics, but judging from the way he's deployed his line, I'd say he is predictable." The king paused, to look over the battlefield, then turned his attention back to Arnim. "You were in Loranguard, weren't you?" he asked.

"Yes," answered Arnim, "why?"

"You met his daughter, Breda, I believe?"

"Breda? The woman that wanted to marry Alric?"

"The very same," confirmed the king.

"I'm sorry," said Arnim, "I'm sure had she known the repercussions, the princess would not have interfered."

"It matters little. Sooner or later they would have betrayed us; they've been after our lands for generations."

"Why do they covet your lands so much, Sire?"

"The land west of the Loran river is desolate and windswept, a violent country. I'm told little grows there."

The Weldwyn King shifted his eyes to the northeast, "I don't like the look of those Kurathians."

"Should we rearrange the troops, Your Majesty?" offered Lord Edwin.

"No, it will only weaken our line. We must hold fast."

"I would like to help if I may," offered Arnim. "I have seen battle before."

The king sized him up before speaking, "I would take it as a kindness if you would command the centre of the line, Sir Arnim. I fear we are some-what lacking in leaders. Take up a position down there," he pointed with the tip of his sword, "and talk to Aegryth. She'll introduce you to the men, but you'd best go now, I think the enemy will soon begin moving."

"Aye, Your Majesty."

Arnim bowed his head and then turned his mount to descend the hill. He had fought before, of course, but never had he had such a commanding view of the battlefield. He picked his way down the hill, careful not to stumble his mount, then rode behind the line until he reached the centre, where the spearman had created a gap while they waited for the Earth Mage to complete her spell. He rode directly toward her, halting as he came close.

She was carefully examining the ground but looked up at his approach. "I see King Leofric has enlisted some help," she said.

"I'm Sir Arnim Caster, Knight of the Hound."

"Ah," she replied, "one of the Mercerians. I'm Aegryth Malthunen, one of the king's mages."

"Yes, I saw you preparing defenses."

"These mounds?" she asked. "Yes, well, I do what I can, but I must conserve power for later in the battle. One final earth mound and I shall be done. Would you like to watch me conjure one?"

"By all means, though I don't want to interrupt."

"Not at all," she replied, "but I'll need you to back up just a titch. Horses are sometimes frightened when I cast."

Arnim backed up until she held up her hand. "That will do nicely. Now watch, as I call forth the power of the earth."

She set herself into a firm stance and then raised her hands into the air. He heard strange words come from her mouth, and then the air around her lit up like a thousand little fireflies. The lights swirled about her, and then gradually coalesced into a ring of light that descended and sank into the ground. He thought she was done, but the chanting continued, and then, without warning, the ground beneath her started to rise, as if some massive creature was pushing the earth up. Up she rose, until the mound was higher than a man's chest. With a shudder the mound began widening, increasing in circumference until twenty men or more could stand atop it. The chanting stopped, and she lowered her arms, turning back to Arnim.

"Well," she said, "what do you think? Interested in learning magic?"

"Impressive," Arnim replied, "but I think I'll stick to fighting for now."

She descended the mound, nodding at the men nearby. They began filing into position atop the new defenses.

"Does the army always have mages with it?" asked Arnim.

"Of course, the mages of Weldwyn have always accompanied their king into battle. Is it not so in Merceria?"

"There are few mages in Merceria," said Arnim, "and the only one we have with us is a Life Mage."

"A valuable ally," said Aegryth. "I wish we had one down here, but the king insists she stay by his side. I suppose it makes sense, from that commanding position he can dispatch her where needed most. I suspect many of us won't live to see tomorrow."

"You think we're going to die today?"

"Of course," she replied, "but the big question is how many of the enemy we'll take with us. We'll sacrifice ourselves to protect the capital."

"Then why not withdraw to the capital?"

"You, of all people, should know that. The king was preparing to withdraw until you brought news of relief. He's gambling the fate of his entire kingdom on your band of souls. I only hope his faith is not misplaced."

"They'll be here," Arnim promised.

She reached into a satchel and pulled forth a small, yellow cube. "Would you care for some sustenance?" she asked.

"What is it?" Arnim asked. "Some sort of magic?"

"No," she said with a chuckle, "it's just cheese. I need to keep my energy levels up if I'm going to be casting a lot of spells."

~

The army of the east marched on. Gerald kept them at a brisk pace, fearful that he wouldn't arrive on time. They marched in three columns, close enough to come to each other's aid if needed. He, himself, rode at the head of the centre column but kept casting nervous glances north and south to the parallel troop movements.

"How long till we see the enemy?" he called out.

Revi Bloom, who sat astride a horse, closed his eyes, his mind drifting toward his familiar. "We're getting close," he answered. "Beyond that wood ahead of us is a hill. They've got some scouts on it, but the main army is farther back. Are we going through the woods?"

"No," said Gerald. "We'll head southwest. I want to come around the southern end of the trees. You said earlier there was a plain there?"

"Yes," confirmed the mage, "it's grassland, very open."

"Excellent," said Gerald. "It'll give us the chance to form up." He turned in his saddle to see his new aide, Captain Sanderson, riding up. "Captain, tell the archers to deploy into the woods. If they meet any opposition, have them withdraw. They are to take up position to provide covering fire."

"Dwarves too, General?"

"No, leave the Dwarves with us, I have the feeling we'll need their arbalests."

"Aye, General," the horseman turned, riding off, snapping orders as he went.

"What of the cavalry?" asked Revi.

"I'll send them north, around these woods. If we draw the enemy toward us and hold them at bay, perhaps our cavalry can get into the enemy's rear." He turned to look around at his small circle of friends, "Hayley, ride over to Beverly. Tell her to commence the plan we discussed, and stay with her, she'll need a sharp pair of eyes."

"Aye, General," responded the ranger.

"Is it wise to have them so far away?" asked Anna.

"We have little choice. This is not a battle of our choosing. We can't be defensive here, we need to press our attack, and Beverly's horse has the best chance of doing that."

"So we just keep them busy?"

"Yes, a straightforward concept in theory, but we need to pull as much of their cavalry toward us as possible. That will relieve the pressure from Leofric."

"But how do we defeat them?" asked Anna.

He pulled his mount to the side, his party following, and waited as the column marched past. "There's a very real possibility that we may be defeated today."

"Don't say that, Gerald. I know we will win."

"We are vastly outnumbered, Anna, on a battlefield that we cannot control. These Kurathians we will be facing are not the raiders we saw in Riversend. These are professional soldiers."

"Then we'll show them the mettle of Mercerians," she replied.

"Our men are from Weldwyn," he corrected.

"It matters not," she replied, "for they've been trained by our greatest general. They will win through today."

Gerald blushed at the compliment, coughing to hide his embarrassment. "When the fighting starts, I want you back by the carriage with Sophie and the rest."

"No," she refused. "My position is here, with you, where I can give the men hope. I will serve as an example for them, and you shan't dissuade me."

He tried to look stern, angry with her decision, but he couldn't help but be pleased. "Very well," he said at last, "then we shall fight together."

"Yes," she agreed, "like old times. I will be the warrior princess, and today we shall see such a victory that it will be sung about by the bards down through the centuries."

He looked at her as she dissolved into laughter, "What's so funny?"

"I was just remembering Uxley," she said. "Remember when you first started showing me how to use a sword?"

"It seems so long ago, now," he mused, "but I do remember cutting down those weeds, why?"

"You're the one that mentioned the bards, all those years ago. Who would have thought that we'd end up here, of all places? Perhaps I'll hire someone to write a song about us."

"I think there's the small matter of winning this battle first," he replied.

"We're together, Gerald. Saxnor looks kindly upon us when we're together. I have no doubt we will win through this day."

"I wish I were as confident as you," he said.

She adopted a serious look, "That wouldn't be you, Gerald. Your caution is what makes you a great leader. The men know you wouldn't throw their lives away. You look after them and they, in turn, look after you. When a leader stops having doubts, they become dangerous to their own men."

"You've become quite the philosopher," he said.

"They're the words of a great man," she said. "A man you know all too well; Baron Fitzwilliam. There's a lot of him in you, my friend."

"Nonsense," said Gerald. "The baron has years of experience leading men. He's studied the greats."

"So have you," said Anna. "You may not realize it, Gerald, but you've been leading men for decades. You've absorbed every morsel of information that Fitz could feed you. You're a natural leader, whether you want to admit it or not."

"If I'm such a good leader," he mused, "why is it you refuse to follow my advice and go to safety?"

"That's easy," she said. "For all intents and purposes, I'm your daughter. That means I'm supposed to disregard your instructions and generally annoy you."

"Hah, you've failed," he yelled.

"Have I? How?"

"You don't annoy me," he smiled in triumph.

"I concede the point, General. Now, let's get back to work. I believe you need to start moving men into formations?"

King Dathen sat astride his mount. It had been a gift from his mage, Carmus, and now, as he looked down at the white charger, he appreciated its excellent lines.

"I must say I'm liking this horse," he said, trying to sound calm.

"It is a fine beast," said the mage. "Imported from the far lands of Ilea."

"It must have cost a fortune, Carmus."

"It was somewhat expensive, Sire, but only the best will do for one such as yourself."

"You flatter me," said the king, suddenly overcome with the sentiment. "When this is over, I shall make you the king's personal mage."

"The Magisterium Primus?" said the mage. "I am overwhelmed, Sire. There has not been a Primus in the Clans for centuries."

"You deserve it, my friend. Now tell me, how are our plans unfolding?"

"Excellently, Your Majesty. We have formed up opposite the Weldwyn line as per your instructions. We shall simply make some demonstrations, pin them to their positions and allow the Kurathian cavalry to loop around their flank and take them in the rear. I suspect it'll all be over by noon."

"You seem quite sure," said the king.

"Of course, Sire. Why wouldn't I be? We outnumber them to such a degree, what could possibly go wrong?"

The High King of the Clans kept staring at the enemy line.

"Sire," asked the mage, "what is it?"

"Why would Leofric make a stand now?" he asked.

"He wants a fight, Sire."

"Yes, but we've been chasing him for weeks. Why now, of all times? Why hasn't he turned and withdrawn like he always does?"

"Perchance he expects help from the Crown Prince? He may not be aware that we have his son in chains."

"Perhaps you are right, my friend. Let us turn our attention to the matter at hand. Send the archers forward. If we are to hold them in place, then let us make them as uncomfortable as possible."

Leofric looked northward toward the enemy lines, watching as the Clan archers advanced, bringing their bows into range.

"Looks like things are starting," said Lord Edwin.

"The bowmen are a minor annoyance," said the king. "The real question is what are the Kurathians doing?"

"Over there, my lord," said Edwin. "The enemy has revealed their plans."

Leofric looked east to see a large group of horseman rounding the wood.

"Malin's wrath, there's a lot of them," said the king.

The troops trotted, conserving their horses, but even at this distance, the sight of the Kurathian horsemen was impressive.

"They're lightly armoured at least, Sire," noted Lord Edwin.

"They might only be wearing leather, but their numbers more than make up for it. Look at them! There must be more than five hundred of the beggars."

"They threaten our flank, Sire. They'll get into our rear and play havoc."

"Prepare the cavalry, Edwin. We'll have to commit them to the attack."

"Is that wise, Sire? Surely they'll be cut to ribbons."

"We have little choice. If we don't stop the Kurathians now, nothing will. Have our cavalry form up on the field south of this hill. Perhaps the very sight of them will act as a deterrent."

"Aye, Your Majesty." Edwin spurred his horse, rushing toward the waiting Weldwyn cavalry.

"Malin guide me," said Leofric looking skyward, "for this day we have more need of your services than ever before."

~

Dame Beverly Fitzwilliam rode at the head of the small cavalry detachment.

"You know what we have to do?" asked Dame Hayley.

The redhead turned her attention to the ranger. "Of course, Gerald's instructions were very clear; we are to avoid any direct contact with the enemy cavalry."

"Surely we should attack them?" asked Hayley.

"We would be overwhelmed. Gerald knows the enemy horse is the biggest threat to Leofric. He hopes to draw them away. While the enemy is busy attacking our troops, we'll break through the line and flank their foot."

"Are you sure this is going to work?"

"Nothing is ever sure in war, Hayley. We must stick to the plan until contact."

"And then?"

"Then we improvise," Beverly replied. "Remember, we're most effective against their footmen. If we can get among them, they'll break."

"What about their archers?" asked the ranger.

"We'll have to trust to our armour to keep us safe. Once we charge home, the archers will have to cease fire or risk hitting their own men. The most dangerous part will be the charge heading into contact."

"I hope you're right," said Hayley.

"Trust me," said Beverly, "I know what I'm doing, but on the off chance I should be killed, you must be prepared to lead the charge."

"Me? Why me?"

"You're a Knight of the Hound, Hayley. You're more than qualified to carry on in my stead."

"Well, let's hope it doesn't come to that," said the ranger.

They rounded the northern edge of the wood, turning west. In the distance, across the open land, was a line of soldiers marching south.

"The Clans?" asked Beverly.

"No," said Hayley, "but I can make out their banners, they're Kurathians."

"They must not be expecting us," said Beverly. "I think it's time for a little of that improvisation." She drew her sword, waving it in the air to draw attention to herself. She pointed it left then right, signalling the men to form up into lines. Lightning dropped to a light trot as the others fell into place to either side.

Opposite them, the marching enemy halted and now rushed to form a line facing the new threat.

"Still no sign of their cavalry," said Hayley.

"It's likely to the south, hidden from view," said Beverly. "With a little luck, we'll be in amongst their foot before their horse can react. Hold tight, Hayley, this is going to get hairy."

She swept her sword down, pointing straight west and the riders began to advance.

To Hayley's eyes, it was a slow pace, for the horses were doing little more than walking. It was important, she knew, to preserve the horse's energy for the final strike, but she felt so vulnerable as the Weldwyn cavalry slowly advanced on their enemy.

As they drew closer, the horses began to speed up, no longer a light trot, falling into a full-blown gallop. Hayley watched the lines wavering as the horses advanced at slightly different speeds. She turned her attention to the Kurathians before her. They had formed into a line and now stood, shoulder to shoulder, their shields and swords ready to repel their foes.

The thunder of the hooves grew to a deafening roar. Hayley dodged as axes and spears were hurled from the enemy line. A hatchet struck the man beside her, bouncing off his shield and then she was in amongst the enemy, her sword slicing down in the well-practiced manner of a knight. Her training took over, jabbing and stabbing as her horse advanced. She had a quick glimpse of Beverly, her massive charger pushing through the footmen as they gave way. There appeared to be Kurathians everywhere and all the ranger could do was to concentrate on the task at hand. A quick parry, a kick with her heels, followed by a swing of her sword. Up and down went her arm, blood flying everywhere. Her horse stumbled, but the Archon Light quickly recovered, nimbly sidestepping a spearman.

Hayley struck out with her sword once again, this time sending a man sprawling, giving her a moment to look around, to take her bearings. The enemy had fallen back slightly, a leader making a defiant stand. The ranger jammed the blood encrusted sword into her scabbard, grabbed her bow from her back and notched an arrow. She took a steadying breath, breathing out as she let fly, only to see the missile strike true. The enemy leader fell, the shaft lodged in his eye, his defense collapsing around him.

Groups of Weldwyn horseman were cleaving their way through the enemy ranks, and so she fired off shot after shot. Soon, the enemy was running, their morale broken, and then she saw Beverly riding toward her.

"Good work today," said the red-headed knight, "though there's still much left to be done."

"What now?" asked Hayley.

"We take advantage of our success. Even now, the survivors flee south, swelling their remaining ranks; we must follow them."

Beverly rose in her stirrups, holding her sword on high, "To me," she yelled out, "form on me!"

Slowly, ever so slowly, the riders returned. They were covered in blood, and many had wounds, but these men of Weldwyn had won the encounter, and they knew it. Beverly waited for the cheering to finish and then led them south, once more forming them into a line.

~

Gerald's forces marched into the open. Off to the west, he noticed a massive horde of cavalry, still some distance away, moving in a southerly direction. The Mercerian led army had caught the enemy on the march.

"Revi," called out Gerald, "what are they doing?"

"Just beyond them, out of sight of us, is the army of Weldwyn. Our allies have taken up a position on a hill. It looks like the Kurathian horse is heading south to flank them."

"We need to get their attention," proclaimed Gerald.

Revi held up his hand to forestall him. "We already have it," said the mage. "It seems our presence has not gone unnoticed. Their troops are halting their progress south."

"Keep an eye on them, Master Bloom. They have fast horses and will be able to close the range with us quite quickly. Any signs of their hounds?"

"None yet, General, but I can't watch everything at once. Shellbreaker's only one bird."

"Captain Sanderson, signal the army. Form up as planned."

"Aye, General," replied the Weldwyn officer, riding off.

Gerald halted as the men carried out their instructions. The two columns to either side turned away from the centre, the middle column splitting in half and moving to fill in the western and eastern sides of the soon to be formed square. The entire manoeuvre took an agonizingly long time, and he watched as officers chided the men for being too slow. After what seemed like an eternity, the formation began taking shape. They now formed a rough square, bristling with spears. Into the centre of this formation rode the supply wagons and camp followers.

"That was nicely done," said Anna.

"A little slow," complained Gerald, "but everything seems to be in order."

"They're coming," warned Revi.

"How many?" asked Gerald.

"All of them, General. It seems we did far too good of a job. We now have the undivided attention of the Kurathian horse."

"How many is 'all'?" asked Anna.

"I'd say the horse alone outnumbers us," said Revi. "I'm afraid we may have bitten off more than we can chew."

As the enemy drew nearer, Gerald felt the ground shake with the thunder of the horse's hooves. Closer they came, the glint of sun reflecting off of swords and armour. He saw men wavering, their spears dipping and called out, "Stand fast! Hold the line! Remember, they can't hurt you as long as you hold the line."

He looked to his reserve. He had formed the heavier armoured men into a small company. Their job was to plug any holes that appeared should disaster strike. His heart was pounding, and he felt an overwhelming sense of panic as he realized the full implications of drawing the enemy toward them. A sudden metal clanging noise had him whipping his head around, only to see Anna lowering her visor. He took a breath, steadied his nerves and waited for the slaughter to begin.

~

Beverly slashed down with her sword, cleaving through her opponent's helmet, felling him. She gazed around at the destruction they had wrought; two more companies of Kurathians had succumbed to their blades. Her men were tired, the horses blown, but they had inflicted far more damage on the enemy than she could have hoped. She raised her visor, peering south to the enemy lines.

"Saxnor's beard," she cursed, "they've unleashed everything they've got."

"We've done our part," said Hayley, riding up beside her. "The horses are worn out, we can't possibly push on any farther."

"Form the men," commanded Beverly, "they'll need to rest briefly and then push on."

"Surely you can't be serious," objected the ranger.

If Hayley was expecting an answer, she was sorely disappointed. Beverly was staring south, her eyes catching something.

"What is it, Bev?" asked Hayley.

"The mastiffs," answered the knight. "They're moving them forward. They'll play havoc with our troops once they're in range."

"I thought they were only used against cavalry?" said the ranger.

"Yes, that's where they're most effective, but they'll attack just about anything. Imagine trying to fend off a whole cartload of dogs like Tempus."

"I see what you mean." The ranger shuddered.

"Do you remember the plan?" asked Beverly.

"Of course, why?"

"You have command, Hayley. There's something I have to see to."

"What? You can't just put me in command."

"Of course I can," said Beverly. "You know the plan."

"For Saxnor's sake, Bev," said Hayley, "what are you going to do?"

A smirk crossed Beverly's face, "What I have to do to save the column. Take care of my horses, Hayley. I'll see you on the other side." She clapped the ranger on the back and then wheeled her great warhorse around, trotting off to the south.

Hayley was about to call out but was interrupted as a captain of horse appeared in front of her.

"What are your orders, Dame? Do we pursue?"

"No," said Hayley, "have the men reform, we must carry out our primary task. We ride west and then south, into the heart of the enemy."

"Aye, Commander," said the captain, returning his attention to the re-forming of the men.

Hayley turned her head, trying to find her friend. She could just make out Beverly in the distance, her great steed carrying her south at a gallop. Even from this range, something was wrong, and she stared in shock as Beverly slumped in the saddle, an arrow protruding from her side.

"Beverly!" she cried out, but her own men were starting to move. With no choice, she tore her eyes from the scene of horror she had just witnessed.

THIRTY

The Battle

AUTUMN 961 MC

~

K ing Dathen of the Twelve Clans read the note. He swore profusely, crumpling the paper and tossing it to the ground.

"Is something amiss, Sire?" asked Carmus.

"Yes," fumed the king, "those damned Kurathians have turned east, just as they were about to destroy Leofric."

"But why?" asked the mage.

"It seems there is a second army."

"Another army? Surely not, Sire," the Fire Mage protested.

"It matters not," dismissed the king. "We still have enough men to destroy the Weldwyn army. Form the men into a solid mass; we're going to punch straight through the middle."

"Is that wise, Your Majesty? Surely the losses will be tremendous?"

"Tremendous? What do we care, as long as we defeat Weldwyn once and for all? We've waited centuries for this opportunity, Carmus, I'll not wait any longer. Launch the attack."

"Which forces first, Majesty?" Carmus asked.

"The foot. Move the cavalry east to threaten the hill. It'll tie up Leofric's horse."

"Aye, Majesty," said Carmus. He began barking out orders.

"At last I have you, Leofric," said the king. "Now it's time to take what has been too long denied from me!"

~

The line of invaders drew closer, and Arnim ducked as an arrow whizzed overhead. Aegryth was beside him, conserving her energy, watching with fascination as the Clans closed the range.

The arrows stopped, and Arnim knew what it meant; the lines were about to clash. A strange whooshing noise alerted him moments before a streak of flame struck a man in front, causing the poor soul to call out in pain as he was engulfed in fire. The man fell to the ground, writhing in agony, and then went silent.

"They have a Fire Mage," Aegryth cursed, "keep your eyes open."

Arnim pushed forward to replace the burned man, readying his sword as he did so. He stared at the faces of the enemy, now echoing the look of terror that gripped all warriors in the moment before contact. They were at the base of the mound, preparing to climb up. He raised his shield. Feeling a weapon strike it, he plunged his sword forward only to scrape across his opponent's helm. The mound gave them a distinct advantage, for the enemy had to fight uphill. Arnim stabbed out again, lower this time, and was rewarded when his sword dug deep. He withdrew his blade, his enemy falling to the ground. Beside him the spearmen did their job, thrusting out with spears, their long reach dealing out death and destruction. The enemy responded with axes and swords, striking at the spears trying to make headway.

Out of the corner of his eye, Arnim glimpsed someone grasp the end of a spear, pulling a Weldwyn soldier from his perch. The victim was swiftly engulfed by the enemy. The Clansmen surged forward once more, emboldened by this success, but for every man of Weldwyn that fell, another stood behind, ready to take his place to keep the line secure.

Arnim's shield was knocked back, and he planted his feet to give him more stability. He struck beneath his own shield, feeling the sword slice into someone's leg. Beside him, a man went down, but the rest of the line kept fighting. Again and again, he struck, his arm growing sore. It was no longer a grand battle, but a desperate fight for personal survival.

~

The distinctive twang of an arbalest preceded the appearance of a bolt sailing through the air, the missile burying itself into the chest of an enemy's horse. The mount collapsed, sliding into the Weldwyn lines and smashing aside the defenders.

"To the gap," yelled Gerald, turning in the saddle, his own sword rasping free of its scabbard. The nearby Kurathians grasped the significance of the situation; they rushed in, their fleet mounts leaping over the dead.

A hail of bolts flew across the opening, dropping several, but the riders were too numerous, and the shots too few. The heavier foot formed up to charge the hole in the line, but Gerald knew they wouldn't arrive in time. He spurred his horse forward, seeking the enemy.

He careened into a Kurathian horseman, his sword stabbing with short, efficient strikes. His opponent fell, the horse bolting into the centre of the formation. Gerald pushed forward, using his horse to temporarily block their progress. He parried a thrust, holding onto his reins as he did so. Another strike drove his blade into an enemy's chest, lodging in the man's rib cage, where even a hard pull did not free it.

Suddenly, the general's horse fell, and he instinctively launched himself from the saddle. The injured Kurathian in front of him, also caught by surprise, tried to block this new attack. Gerald, with only a moment to react, grabbed the rider around the waist, dragging him from the saddle as he fell to the ground, his sword still lodged in the now unconscious man's chest.

Rolling to the side, Gerald narrowly avoided the crushing hooves around him as he stood up. He quickly stepped back to avoid a blow then caught his attacker's arm, yanking the rider from the saddle. The general struck out, his fist hitting his target squarely in the face, felling his opponent. He bent over and armed himself with the defeated man's blade.

A sound behind alerted him to danger, and he turned just in time to see another horseman bearing down on him. Unexpectedly, the horse tumbled without any warning but a loud snapping sound, throwing the rider from the saddle as Tempus dug into the unfortunate horse's leg. Gerald stepped forward, finishing off the Kurathian with an efficient stab of his sword.

The chainmailed men rushed to fill the gap, driving back the enemy and restoring the line. Gerald cast about, his eyes resting on a lone horse, wandering about the centre of the formation. He made his way toward it, hauling himself into the saddle.

Revi came toward him, a grave look on his face.

"What is it, Revi?" he called out. "What's wrong?"

"It's Beverly," he said, "I saw her go down. I'm afraid we've lost her."

"What? How?" he demanded.

"She was riding south when an arrow took her, she'll be torn to bits by the mastiffs by now."

"Saxnor's balls, that's a horrible way to go," said Gerald.

"What do we do now?" asked the mage.

"We do what we do best," he replied, a grim smile transforming his face. "We die here and take as many as we can to the Afterlife with us."

~

Masruk Dur pulled back on the leash. "I said hold the beasts steady," he yelled. "If you don't get a firm grip on them the dogs will become unruly."

The Kurathian handler pulled back on the leather straps.

"That's it," said Masruk. "Remember, you've got four of the brutes to contend with, so let them know who's in charge."

"Don't we want them to be unruly?" asked the trainee, Kratic.

"Not until the enemy is closer," said Masruk. "Once these dogs get fired up, nothing but blood and flesh will satiate them. They're the deadliest things on the battlefield, but they can only be used once, so we want to make sure it's the right time."

"How do we do that?"

"We wait until the enemy is close," the master continued, "then we rile them up. Remember your training; the sound of the whip cracking overhead or the smell of blood is all it takes, so control your beasts."

"But I can hardly move in this rig," came the complaint.

"Do you want your throat ripped out? That rig, as you call it, protects your arms, legs and neck. I know it's uncomfortable, but it's designed to keep you alive. Remember, the hounds are trained to go for the extremities."

"But what about the rest of me?" asked Kratic. "What if the men of Weldwyn attack us?"

"No one in their right mind is going to come anywhere near us."

"So when do we deploy them?"

"When we're told to," said Masruk, "and not a moment before. In fact, if we're lucky, we won't have to deploy them at all."

It began with a distant bark, and then the whole pack started baying and growling, creating a deafening roar.

"Whatever it is," said the trainee, "it's getting closer."

Masruk turned in irritation, calling out, "Baccus, keep those dogs of yours in check, they'll alarm the others."

"Too late for that," came the reply.

The trainee stared with an open mouth. Baccus had turned his head north, the eyes of Masruk soon spotting the subject of his gaze.

A lone horse, a rather large one, trotted toward them, its rider slumped in the saddle.

"Some damn horse is wandering toward us," called out Baccus.

"Well, see it off," ordered Masruk. "It'll send the dogs into a frenzy."

Kratic struggled to control his charges. The dogs were pulling now, their combined strength threatening to rip the leashes from his hands. He watched the strange horse. Even as Masruk and Baccus talked, the horse broke into a gallop, heading directly toward them. Suddenly, as if from nowhere, a rider was now sitting on the great beast. The trainee noted the smallest of details; the red hair, the arrow tossed carelessly to the ground. What did it mean? His mind struggled to make sense of it.

A moment later, the horse ran past the first handler, deftly avoiding the mastiffs who lunged and snarled at it as the handler struggled to control them. The rider's sword crashed down onto the head of Baccus, splitting it open like a melon. The corpse fell to the ground, the lifeless hands no longer grasping the leashes.

The barking grew in intensity, and suddenly the horse was coming directly for the trainee.

"Release your hounds, man," yelled Masruk as the rider drew closer.

All along the line of mastiffs the leather cords were released, and suddenly the entire mass of hounds rushed to the attack. The dogs were quick, but the Mercerian Charger was faster, changing direction suddenly and heading east. The rider sliced with the sword, taking another handler under the chin, cutting through his jaw. The Kurathian fell to the ground, clutching his face as blood gushed forth.

The trainee looked around a scene of utter chaos. The mighty Kurathian Mastiffs, the blood driving them into a frenzy, were no longer under control. He looked toward the body of Baccus, but the sight of two hounds tearing it apart sickened him. He turned to the side to vomit as three hounds rushed past him, intent on taking down their prey.

~

Beverly urged Lightning on. The great horse was struggling now, his breath coming in short gasps, his footfalls no longer steady. He stumbled slightly but quickly regained his footing. Glancing over her shoulder, she saw the bloodthirsty hounds strung out behind her in hot pursuit, snapping at her heels, each intent on the promise of violence.

She looked to the south, to where she knew the column should be, but there was no sight of it, only an endless sea of enemy horsemen that swirled about. The closer they drew, the more Lightning's stride started to shorten. A mastiff appeared to her side, and she swung her sword to drive it off.

A few of the Kurathian riders spied her. At first, they took no notice, after all, another horseman was nothing to worry about, but as she drew closer, the hounds came into view, causing panic. Soon, they were more concerned with trying to get out of the way, to get anywhere that might save them from the devastation that was about to be delivered.

Beverly crashed through their ranks, slicing with the sword as she rode. A Kurathian rider was felled, tumbling from his horse after Beverly's sword dug into him. Down he went, to be met by the ravenous mouth of an enraged mastiff.

The tearing of flesh, the screams of men and beasts surrounded her as she raced through the cloud of horsemen. Now, she stopped her swordplay, intent only on making her way to safety. A blade scraped past her head, narrowly missing her as she crouched low in the saddle, praying to Saxnor that the Kurathians were too busy to take notice of her.

Her mount balked, and she looked up to see a wall of spears blocking her. A voice called out above the din of battle, but she could not decipher the words. Lightning was done in; the great beast slowed to a stop, panting.

Beverly slid from the saddle, hefting her sword once more in her hands. She turned to face the riders who were beginning to encircle her, ready to sell her life for the protection of her horse, but voices were calling from behind her. She turned again to see Gerald. He had ordered the men to open the line, creating a small gap in the wall of spears. She grabbed Lightning's reins, urging him on to safety.

Hayley rode on, the men following. They were heading southwest now, clear of the enemy's line. Off in the distance, a line of Weldwyn foot fought their Clansmen enemies. She urged her mount to pick up the pace when suddenly a tremendous crashing sound thundered off to her right.

An explosion of dust and dirt flew through the air, and she wondered what in the Afterlife had caused such a commotion. A moment later she saw a huge rock, the size of a man's head, sail past, crashing into some nearby trees, splintering them.

She cast her eyes westward, looking for some sign of siege engines, only to witness a horrific sight, for upon a hill stood large, grey-skinned creatures hurling stones.

She had heard of Trolls before, but never, in her life, had she expected to bear witness such fearsome creatures. They stood over eight feet tall, hefting rocks above their heads as if they held no weight. They made grunting noises as they hurled their projectiles across the intervening ground. Hayley saw a rock strike a rider, knocking the horse from its feet, leaving a red smear where it struck the ground, its rider reduced to little more than pulp.

"Ride!" she yelled, for there was little else that could be done. She glanced back over her shoulder to see the horsemen trailing along behind her. Another rock sailed past, removing a man's head from his shoulders. It was almost compelling to watch; one moment the rider was pushing his mount forward, the next his head vanished altogether, the body falling from the saddle.

A man struggled, his horse had gone down, and he was running, eager to escape his fate. She watched the others ride by, now safely out of range, and then urged her mount toward the straggler. The Trolls, observing from their height advantage, redoubled their efforts, sending a hail of large stones her way. Her nimble horse dodged and turned, narrowly avoiding a rock the size of a shield as it struck the earth beside her.

She reached out, grabbing the man's forearm as he stretched his hand toward hers. He clung on as she spurred her horse forward, dragging the survivor along with her. Soon, they were out of range, and she halted, looking down at the man. He was limping, his arm bleeding, but glad to be alive.

"Thank you, Ma'am," he said. "I owe you my life."

"You have no horse," she replied. "Find shelter and stay here, out of range and I'll send someone to find you later. We ride to battle, and I can't take you with me."

The man nodded his understanding while Hayley turned to see her assembled men, waiting.

"We have been through a storm," she started, "and have emerged relatively unscathed. Now let us carry our vengeance to the enemy this day!"

The men began to cheer as Hayley rode forward, falling into place behind her.

~

Gerald surveyed the scene before them. With the mastiff attack on the Kurathian horse, the enemy's assault on the square had screeched to a halt. Now, littering the field before them, giant hounds fought over scraps of horsemeat while strong teeth rent the living flesh from the wounded and dying.

Anna looked pale as she scanned the scene before them.

"Are you all right, Anna?" Gerald asked.

"I'll be fine," she answered. "but the devastation is horrific."

"We owe it all to Beverly," he said. "If she hadn't lured them here, we would have been worn down and then picked apart by their horsemen."

"How is she?"

"She's tired," he said. "Revi is healing her, and Lightning too. It was an amazing accomplishment, she couldn't have done it with any other horse."

"What happens now?" she asked.

"We still have to get to King Leofric. Even without the Kurathians, he's still outnumbered."

"But how?" she asked. "We have dozens of mastiffs between us and our target?"

"Hmmm," mused Gerald, "I hadn't thought of that. I suppose we could move the Dwarves up. Their arbalests should be more than capable of dealing with them."

"Is there any other way?" asked the princess. "I'd hate to see all those dogs killed."

"They're vicious animals, Anna. They'd just as soon rip your throat out as sniff you."

"Tempus is one of those dogs," defended Anna.

"I understand," he agreed, "but Leofric is in danger."

Anna cast her eyes about as they spoke. "Where is Tempus," she asked, "I thought he was with you?"

"He was," said Gerald. "He took down a horse during the fighting. That was the last time I saw him."

Anna's calm demeanour quickly shattered. "There he is," she yelled. "He's wandered out onto the battlefield. We have to get him."

She spurred on her horse, quickly pushing her way past the spearmen.

"Wait! Anna, no!" he cried out, urging his horse to follow. "It's too dangerous."

She rode out only a short distance and dismounted. A mastiff turned its blood-soaked head in her direction, snarling menacingly, and then the others took up the growl. Anna stood where she was, frozen in fear. Tempus ran over to her, moving to face the new threat. The growling grew in intensity, and then the hounds started barking, whipping themselves into a renewed frenzy.

Gerald dismounted, walking slowly toward her, his hand outstretched. "Give me your hand, Anna. Slowly now, don't make any sudden moves."

A mastiff lunged at her from the side, and he rushed forward, his sword held at the ready. Instead of attacking, the beast lay low, its chin to the ground. Gerald grabbed Anna's hand, pulling her back towards him. Another mastiff came forward, it too, prostrating itself before them.

"What's happening?" he called out. "I don't understand."

"They're bowing down to you," called out Revi from behind the safety of the spear wall.

"Nonsense," responded Gerald, "they're just tired from all the blood-letting."

Anna, now snapped out of her fear, looked around the field. "No, Revi's right," she said. "Come with me."

She pulled him forward, leading him toward the largest concentration of hounds. At their approach, they all lay down, their great heads between their front paws.

"It's the grey wolf," said Anna. "Your spirit animal must dominate them."

"That's utter nonsense," said Gerald. "I don't turn into a wolf."

"You wouldn't know," said Anna. "The only time the grey wolf shows up is when you're unconscious."

"Those were dreams, Anna, nothing more."

"Tell that to Beverly, she saw it too, back in the dungeons of Wincaster."

Gerald walked about experimentally. The hounds began to move themselves toward him, abandoning their feast. Soon, they were sitting before him, waiting expectantly like Tempus waiting for a bone. "What do I do now?" he asked.

"Order them to move," said Anna. "Perhaps you can lead them to that area to the west of the woods."

"That would clear a path well enough," said Gerald, taking a deep breath. "Very well, here goes nothing."

He waved his hands, trying to usher the dogs forth, but they all stared at him in incomprehension. "Well, that didn't work," he said.

"Tell Tempus what to do," suggested Anna, "perhaps the rest will follow?"

"Tempus," he called out. "Over there, boy, go and fetch." He tossed a stone in the general direction and watched as the great beast ran after it. He started to follow, and soon the mass of hounds rose to accompany him.

"I'll lead them there, myself," he called back to Anna. "Tell Beverly to resume the march. I'll catch up when I can."

He looked down at Tempus, who had returned, stone in mouth. "It looks like it's you and me, my old friend," he said, looking around at his new pack, "and dozens of your relatives."

～

King Leofric gazed down at the battle below him.

"They're pressing us hard, Sire," said Lord Edwin.

"Will the centre hold?" asked the king.

"Hard to say, Lord. They still have more men to commit. If our centre breaks, it'll all be over."

"Send down the cavalry," said King Leofric. "No, hold on, I'll lead them myself."

"Is that wise?"

"If we are to die today, then let it be said that we died fighting."

"Aye, Lord," replied Edwin.

"Come," the king continued, "let us die in the company of good men."

"I would have it no other way," said Edwin.

The horsemen of Weldwyn were clad in chainmail and armed with lances and sword. Leofric took up a position at their head, Lord Edwin beside him. He turned to face his men, his helmet removed to allow them to see his face.

"Men of Weldwyn," he began, "we ride today to bring justice to those who would enslave our people. Let no man fall unbloodied and may the wrath of the Gods go with you." He placed his helmet back on his head, snapping the visor shut. The echoes of the men's cheers gave him hope, and he raised his sword to get their attention.

"All ready, Edwin?" he asked.

"We'll all join you in the Afterlife," said his friend.

Leofric swept his sword down, and the horses moved forward. He led the cavalry of Weldwyn, picking up speed as they descended and then broke into a gallop, heading directly toward the enemy commander's standard. The King of Weldwyn called out for King Dathen's death as he rode, but his voice was lost beneath his helm, overpowered by the thundering of hooves. The enemy troops looked on in fear as the mightiest warriors of Weldwyn crashed into their line. Leofric's sword rose and fell, powered by years of training. Onward, the cavalry rode, cutting through the Clan line of foot like an unstoppable wave. All before them fled, or died trying to resist the power of Weldwyn.

Lord Weldwridge struck down with his sword, cleaving an enemy archer. "We have them, Sire," he yelled out just before an enemy sword punctured his mail, driving deep into his side. "Sire," he called out, falling to the ground.

Leofric, though, had problems of his own. The Clans' horsemen now responded to the charge, and his small band of Weldwyn horse were engulfed by the finest the Clans could muster. The fighting grew intense, and the king looked around, his own force growing smaller by the moment. He saw King Dathen's standard, tried to push toward it, but the press of man and horse was too much.

～

Arnim stabbed forward one final time, his opponent falling beneath his blade. He looked up to see the enemy unexpectedly withdrawing.

Aegryth came over to him. "You are unhurt?" she asked.

"Yes, I'm fine," he said. "Just tired. What's happening?"

"They're pulling back to Dathen's standard. The fight is there, now."

"Where is that?" asked Arnim.

"Look to the north," said Aegryth, pointing. "You see that large standard with the wolf pelts?"

"Yes," he replied.

"That's him."

"Who's that fighting nearby?" he asked.

She peered into the distance, shielding her eyes from the sun. "It looks like Leofric's standard. He's ridden into the enemy lines."

"We must help," said Arnim. "Surely there is something we can do."

"I have an idea," she said. "Gather what men you can, while I begin to summon."

"Summon what?" he asked nervously.

"Wolves," she said. "They will clear a path for you. Now go collect your men."

He rushed off, the sound of her chanting diminishing as he searched. The defenders were worn down, many wounded or dead, but they all knew what fate would befall their kingdom, their home, if they didn't fight to the bitter end.

Arnim gathered those he could and soon stood before Aegryth with nearly thirty men. "This is all I could muster," he said. "Will it be enough?"

"It will have to," she replied. "Now, be ready to run, for the way will only be clear for a short period of time."

She uttered the words of command, and the air came alive with a buzzing sound. Small lights appeared, floating around her and then as she cast her hands forward, the lights disappeared into the ground. A moment later, a pack of wolves materialized into existence, each one a moment before nothing but a small spark of light.

She barked out a final word of command, and the wolves sprang into action, running northward toward the enemy lines.

"Run!" Aegryth yelled to Arnim. "Run as if the very hounds of the Underworld were nipping at your heels."

Down the mound ran Arnim, his newly gathered men following. His sword was out as he pumped his arms, willing his legs to carry him as fast as was Humanly possible.

Up ahead, wolves leaped onto Clansmen, taking them down with teeth at their throats. A bolt of fire streaked past him, exploding as it hit a warrior behind him, but Arnim kept running. He jumped over a body, rushed forward, absently striking down a Clansman who reached out for him. He was pure adrenaline now, a messenger of the Gods. The enemy line was ahead, Dathen's standard just behind it, surrounded by guards. The knight checked his pace slightly, slowing only enough to try and gauge the right moment.

A spear thrust out, and he sidestepped, bringing his sword down onto his victim's head. He kept moving, stepping over the body, using it to catapult himself over the enemy line. He landed among a group of mailed warriors. So stunned were they by his feat that they failed to react in time and he drove his sword into the stomach of one, withdrawing it in time to parry another.

He heard his volunteers as they clawed their way into the enemy line. Arnim blocked another thrust, swung his right fist into the man's face while stabbing with his sword. The Clan King's guard was at a loss as to how to fight this left-handed warrior and fell back, giving up ground. Arnim let out a yell, advancing in a rage, ignoring his wounds as swords surrounded him.

～

Leofric's head rang as the side of his helmet was caved in. He ripped it off, giving him a better view of the battlefield. Now able to see his attacker clearly, he struck out, driving his sword into the man's chest.

A strike landed against the king's lower back, but his mail stopped it from penetrating. He turned in the saddle, swinging out with a wide, arcing blow, but missed his target. He tried to pivot his horse to face this new attacker, but the press of soldiers made any defensive manoeuvre impossible. The Weldwyn King knew, in that moment, he was looking death in the face.

The enemy warrior, a huge bulk of a man, raised a large axe overhead ready to send Leofric to the Afterlife, and then the beast of a man stopped, staring blankly as an arrow pierced his throat. He toppled from the saddle, his horse bolting at the sudden change in weight.

Frozen there, shocked at his reprieve, Leofric's ears were greeted with the sounds of men calling out, "For Weldwyn, for Weldwyn!" He turned to see the Clansmen driven back as a new force of riders came into the fray. Unsure of what to expect, he prepared to battle once more when one rider broke off, coming directly toward him.

"Your Majesty," the newcomer said, "I'm Dame Hayley Chambers. General Matheson sends his regards. We've come to lend you a hand."

~

Arnim slashed out, his opponent trying to block the attack, but the blade only deflected the knight's blow; the sword slid down the length of the weapon to cut into the cross guard. Arnim flicked his wrist, sending the enemy's weapon flying. The Clansman whipped out a dagger, but Arnim was quicker, driving the point of his sword into the man's stomach. The enemy fell forward, clutching his wound.

Arnim didn't wait, he stepped forward to attack a man with a long beard, who was muttering something. Recognizing the magical language from Revi's past incantations, the knight dove to the side just as a streak of flame flew past him. He scrambled to his feet, pulling forth his dagger and let it fly. It raced toward the mage, causing him to duck as the blade flew past. Carmus, a sneer etched on his face, turned his gaze back to his attacker, but it was short-lived. Arnim had rushed forward as soon as he let his missile loose, and his opponent now found himself face to face with the Mercerian, even as his blade sought home. The mage crumpled to the ground, his long beard soaked with his lifeblood.

"You'll die for that," yelled a voice.

Arnim turned to see a large man with a mighty two-handed sword held at the ready.

"Many have tried," said Arnim, "but none have succeeded."

As the great sword came crashing toward him, Arnim ducked, feeling the weapon swish past his face. Armin knew that a two-handed sword was an awkward weapon to wield, requiring lots of room. He waited patiently for the next strike, backing up as the formidable blade sliced the air in front of him. He remained still, until his opponent's body was forced to follow the momentum of the massive swing, then stepped forward, driving his sword into warrior's leg. The weapon penetrated through muscle, his foe collapsing as his leg buckled. Arnim withdrew his blade and brought the pommel crashing down onto the man's head, ending any chance of retaliation.

The fighting around him grew more intense. A cry of alarm alerted him to someone struggling, across the sea of individual melees, trying to help a fallen warrior to his feet. Before Arnim could move, an arrow pierced the man's head, and he fell, his assistance no longer available. The fallen warrior stood, his eyes locking with Arnim's across the field of battle.

Arnim took in the man's armour; the rich gold tabard over the finely crafted chainmail left no doubt as to its owner. King Dathen of the Twelve Clans ran toward him, his sword raised high. Arnim stepped back, but his foot caught on a body, tumbling him to the ground.

The High King struck, the expectancy of an easy victory dashed as Arnim lifted his blade, blocking the attack, but his sword shattered beneath his opponent's ferocity.

King Dathen stood over the knight, his victory all but complete. "You fought well this day, my noble friend, but you'll die like all your Weldwyn brothers."

Arnim gazed back, defiance in his eyes. "I'm a Mercerian," he said, "and we don't fight fair." He drove the broken blade into Dathen's stomach, pushing himself forward as he did so, using all of his remaining strength to force it in.

Dathen staggered back, instinctively grabbing his attacker with a deathly grip as he fell to the ground, pulling the knight forward, to land on top of him.

Arnim felt the king's breath in his ear, heard words escape the man's mouth, "I have failed," he gasped out, "they'll never forgive me for this." The body went limp.

Arnim pushed himself off the king and staggered to his feet. Looking around, he saw that the enemy was broken, running in all directions. Soon, he was surrounded by Weldwyn horsemen, a familiar voice calling out to him.

"Arnim?" called Hayley. "Arnim, are you all right?"

He stood there, staring at the carnage that surrounded him, his energy all but spent. Voices swirled about him as he fell to his knees. He watched as the healer, Roxanne, rushed to the High King's body. A moment later she cast a spell while others tied the Clansman's hands before him.

"It's over, Arnim," said Hayley. "We've done it. We've saved Weldwyn. The battle is won."

Soldier's cheers erupted from all directions as Arnim, once more, descended into unconsciousness.

THIRTY-ONE

Alric

AUTUMN 961 MC

~

P rince Cuthbert turned to his aide, "Finch, go and unlock the armoury. You'll find the keys on my late brother. Once we're properly armed, we'll summon the watch commanders one by one. Either they'll join us, or be executed."

A man's voice carried across the hall, "Don't you think you're being a little premature?"

Cuthbert wheeled about to see Alric no longer unconscious. He had risen from the table and now, as he spoke, others were doing the same.

"What treachery is this?" demanded Cuthbert.

"You talk to me of treachery, Brother?" shouted Alric. "It was not I that conspired to poison the Royal Court."

"But how?" the elder brother replied. "Who betrayed me?"

"Lady Nicole came to us," said Alric. "It was her idea to play out this charade and lure you from your hiding place."

Cuthbert turned to Nikki, snarling, "You'll die for this."

He drew his sword, but Nikki was faster. She sliced through the air with her knife, carving a deep cut into the back of the Dark Prince's hand.

He cursed at the wound, stepping back momentarily, his blood dripping to the floor.

While all this was occurring, loyal Weldwyn soldiers entered the room, blocking all the exits. Cuthbert's men, seeing the futility in it, tossed their weapons to the floor, but their master remained resolute, holding his sword ready.

Nikki backed up, putting some distance between them. She watched the older prince looking about the room, slicing with his blade to keep the others at bay.

"Surrender, Cuthbert," said Alric, "or we'll be forced to cut you down."

"Go ahead and try, you little shit," spat out Cuthbert. "I should have taken care of you back in Loranguard. Well, if you want me, you're going to have to come fight me."

"Allow me, Highness," offered Jack, drawing his sword. The cavalier began to move, only to be halted by Alric's hand on his arm.

"No," declared Alric, "he's a Prince of the Realm and my responsibility." He turned to face his brother, "Very well, Cuthbert, this ends here, now."

Cuthbert sneered. The guards formed a loose circle, penning him into the centre of the room. The younger prince stepped forward, drawing his sword. "I should have known," he chided himself. "What was it they promised you, Brother? Money? Power? No, of course not, you already had that. The crown? That was it, wasn't it?"

"You couldn't possibly understand," said Cuthbert. "You haven't seen the power behind the Twelve Clans. Even as we speak the army of Weldwyn is being destroyed. You can defeat me, but the Clans will win out in the end."

"I think not, Brother. You forget the Mercerians!"

"What of them? Do you think a young princess can win the war for you? You're far more foolish than I thought."

The two opponents began circling each other. "You've missed much by being away, Cuthbert. It's not the princess that will save the kingdom, it's her general."

"What general?" spewed the older prince. "What are you talking about?"

"Of course," said Alric, keeping his voice calm, "I forgot, you wouldn't have heard the news. He defeated the Kurathian attack at Riversend this summer past."

The look of surprise on Cuthbert's face told him all he needed to know.

"You couldn't have heard of it, the invasion coming so soon afterwards. It's a pity you didn't learn more about our allies."

"Allies? What do you mean?"

"Merceria will be our ally," said Alric.

"You fool, Alric. You've been played like a fiddle. Do you think the Clans alone could organize an invasion this big? It's not King Dathen that planned this whole affair. You may well have won this round, but Merceria is now a bigger threat than you can imagine."

Now it was Alric's turn to be surprised, "What are you talking about, Cuthbert?"

"I'm saying," the elder prince continued, "that I'm willing to die for my masters." He lunged forward suddenly, committing everything to his surprise attack.

Alric knocked the incoming sword aside, reposting with a thrust, impaling his brother's heart.

Cuthbert's eyes rolled up into his head and then slumped to the floor.

"I taught him that," proclaimed Jack in the deathly silence that followed. "Round up the others and take them to the dungeons."

Alric tore his gaze from the body of his brother. He felt numb as he looked around the room, finally settling on his mother. There were tears in her eyes, having had to bear witness to his deeds.

"I'm sorry, Mother. I didn't want to kill him."

"You did what you had to do to save the crown," said the queen. "I know it was a difficult decision, but your father will understand."

The prisoners were escorted away while Alric stood, staring at his blade while his brother's blood slowly dripped to the floor.

"What do we do now, Highness?" asked Jack.

Alric snapped out of his stupor, "We round up his fellow conspirators."

"We have no idea where they might be found," said Jack, "and by the time we interrogate the prisoners they'll have long since fled."

It was Nikki that offered a solution, "I can take you to their hideout."

"I thought you said you were blindfolded," questioned Jack.

"I was, but I still had my other senses. They were using a warehouse across from Edson's Farrier."

"I know it," said Jack. "I shall take men there directly."

"You must hurry, Jack, before they have word of what has transpired here."

"What of him," asked the cavalier, pointing to Cuthbert's body.

"Take him to the crypt," said Alric. "He will lay with our ancestors."

"A traitor?"

Alric stared at the body a moment before responding. "I can't believe he was truly evil," he finally said. "Perhaps those behind this invasion had some influence over him, controlled him somehow. He wasn't always driven by a lust for power. I have to think, in the end, he was corrupted by them."

Two guards stepped forward, lifting the body, Alric watching as they bore it away. Jack ordered everyone else from the room, leaving the prince alone with his thoughts. How long, he wondered, had they controlled his brother, and who else may be under their influence? His thoughts were soon interrupted by a soft footfall. Lady Nicole stood, waiting for his attention.

He took a deep breath, letting it out slowly to calm his nerves for he still had a kingdom to serve. He turned to face the woman, "What can I do for you, Lady Nicole?"

"I'm sorry it had to end this way, Your Highness," she said, digging into the folds of her dress. "Your brother gave me this as payment, I think it should belong to you." She held out the bag of diamonds.

He stared at it, his mind a whirlwind of emotions. Cuthbert had been corrupted by this dark shadow, but here was Lady Nicole, who, more than anyone else, would have benefited by helping Cuthbert. Yet, in the end, she had done the right thing and saved them all.

"Keep it," he said at last. "You've saved the Crown of Weldwyn; consider it a gift from a grateful kingdom."

THIRTY-TWO

Aftermath

AUTUMN 961 MC

~

K ing Leofric looked down at the battlefield, tears coming to his eyes. "So many dead," he lamented.

"We had little choice, Your Majesty," consoled Hayley.

"Indeed, the Clans will rue the day they invaded our kingdom for generations to come."

"Are you injured, Majesty?" asked the ranger.

"No, just incredibly tired. It's been a very long day, and we yet have things to do."

"The prisoners are being rounded up," offered Lord Edwin, returned to health. "Surely you can rest now, Majesty."

He turned to the man beside him, "We owe much to the men who gave their lives for their kingdom this day. I would see them buried, and the graves properly consecrated. These warriors must rest in eternal peace."

"And the enemy dead, Your Majesty?"

"Burn them and let the dark smoke be a warning to our foes."

"I must thank you," he continued, turning his attention back to Hayley, "had your cavalry not arrived in a timely manner, I would be among the dead this day."

"You had them well in hand, Your Majesty," replied the ranger.

"Still, your help was appreciated. I must find some way to repay the debt."

Hayley patted her sure-footed horse, the Archon Light still lathered from the fighting. "I should see to my mount. With your permission, Majesty?"

"Yes, of course. It is an interesting breed you have there, Dame Hayley. I think our light cavalry would benefit from them. Perhaps one day we will import them to Weldwyn, I think they would command a high price."

"I'm sure Princess Anna would be most amenable to that," she replied, "but I fear much has yet to occur before we can consider such a thing." She turned her mount, picking her way through the dead and dying warriors strewn about the field.

Leofric noticed someone approaching him, another man struggling along behind. "Sir Arnim," the king called out, "I'm glad to see you survived."

"I did, Majesty," he replied, "and I've brought you a present. It seems all sorts of people can be found in a battle. I present to you, King Dathen of the Twelve Clans."

He tugged on the rope he was carrying, pulling the prisoner forward. The enemy ruler was covered in blood, his hands bound with rope.

Leofric looked down from his horse in surprise, "And here, I thought he'd managed to escape."

"Nay, Lord," said Arnim. "I almost killed him, but your Life Mage insisted he survive to face the king's wrath. He is here to suffer your judgement. Say the word, and I shall slay him for his offenses to your kingdom."

Leofric was sorely tempted, for the loss of life this day had been great. "No," he said at last, "we shall keep him hostage against the behaviour of his people. With the High King himself as our guest, they won't dare invade again." He stared down at his opponent, witnessing the look of utter defeat.

Arnim held up a sword, offering it hilt first, "King Dathen's sword, Your Majesty. A prize for you to exhibit."

"Keep it," said Leofric. "I'm told you defeated him in single combat. I can think of no man more worthy to wear it."

Arnim, stunned by the remarks, stumbled for words before finally answering, "Thank you, Your Majesty. I shall treasure it for the rest of my life."

"Captain Barker?" called the king.

"Yes, Your Majesty?" replied a nearby cavalryman.

"Take charge of the prisoner, see that he is properly confined. And find Sir Arnim a horse, we must ride over to our allies, there is still work to be done."

"Aye, Sire," replied the captain.

. . .

They rode eastward, down the hill toward a second great scene of carnage. Arnim had feared for the fate of his comrades, but it was soon obvious they had done well for themselves, for most of the dead were the Kurathian mercenaries. General Matheson was talking to the princess as they approached, but the old man quickly responded to the visiting king.

"Your Majesty," Gerald said.

"General Matheson, Your Highness," greeted Leofric, "it does my heart good to see you safe from harm."

"We have won a great victory today," said Anna.

"Indeed," said the king, "though I wish our own losses were not so high."

"It is ever the burden of leaders to mourn their dead," said Gerald.

"Wise words," agreed the king. "I wish more men would think such things before starting wars. Have you rounded up many prisoners?"

"Yes, Majesty," answered the General. "They are giving themselves up in droves. Even the dog handlers have surrendered themselves. Only the Trolls remain formed and ready to fight."

"I'm not surprised," said Leofric, "for they are a long way from home; they have little choice."

"What will you do with them?" Gerald asked.

"They shall be sent to Riversend and Southport. They'll man galleys to protect our shores from further incursions."

"And yet," said Gerald, "they have so far refused to surrender. I fear more lives may be lost this day, for they are a fearsome race."

"Perhaps," offered Leofric, "we should bring our archers forward to eradicate them."

"Their hides are thick," Gerald reminded him, "and your arrows would have little effect."

"Do you have an alternative?" asked Leofric.

"As a matter of fact, we do," replied the general.

"Yes," agreed the princess, "I'd like to talk to them."

"And how do you propose to do that?" asked Leofric. "No one here speaks their language."

Anna smiled before continuing, "Not an insurmountable problem. Our Life Mage can cast the spell of tongues."

"I'm not familiar with it," said the king. "Do tell me more."

"It allows a person to understand the rudiments of a language. It's how we first spoke with Lily."

"Ah, yes," said Leofric, "your Saurian friend. Very well, if you think it advantageous then, by all means, try it. But what is it you expect to learn?"

"Don't you think it strange," mused Anna, "that Trolls would march in an army. Have you ever heard of such a thing before?"

"No," admitted the king, "in all our history, it has never occurred."

"Nor ours," said Anna, "and yet, something has compelled them from their homes."

"We know so little about them," said Leofric, "perhaps they are simply mercenaries."

"I don't think so," said the princess, "but I intend to find out. We'll go and talk to them directly, would you care to accompany us?"

"I shall leave that to you," said Leofric, shaking his head. "You seem to have far more experience with other races."

"Very well, Your Majesty," said Gerald, bowing his head. "We'll talk to these creatures and report back our discoveries."

They wheeled about, riding toward the distant unit of Trolls.

"You're all set," said Revi, completing his spell. "Now remember, Highness, you'll only be able to discuss basic concepts."

"I'm fully aware of the limitations of your spell, Master Bloom. Perhaps one day you'll be able to increase its effectiveness."

"Magic doesn't work that way," the mage complained. "I can extend the duration with more power, or even affect more people, but I cannot change the effect."

"Understood," said Anna. "Will you accompany us?"

"I think not," answered the mage, "there are still wounded that need my help; if only Aubrey were here."

"Let us hope she is still alive and well," said Anna. "In the meantime, it will be us three." She turned to Gerald and Beverly, who had just returned to their camp, when a loud bark echoed across the field.

"Us four," corrected Gerald, watching as Tempus charged toward them.

"Yes, of course," said Anna, "just as it should be."

They had formed up the troops opposite the Troll position. The impressive creatures stood well over eight feet tall, towering above even the tallest Humans. The spearmen were there to safeguard against the Trolls attacking, but during the battle the mighty creatures had contributed little, save for acting as a deterrent.

The group stepped forward, forgoing their mounts. They walked four abreast, Anna between Gerald and Tempus, while Beverly stood to the great beast's right. They closed the distance quickly, then paused well within earshot.

"*We come in peace,*" called out Anna in the Trollish tongue.

"*What do you want?*" replied a deep voice.

"*We wish to see your leader,*" she said. "*Send him forth, and we shall talk.*"

The Trolls soon parted, and an immense individual stepped forth, his stone-like skin a darker grey than his companions. He strode across the distance, halting just short of them. "*I am Tog*," he said in a deep rumbling bass. "*I speak for my people. Talk, and I will listen.*"

"*Why have you come here?*" asked Anna. "*Why have you come in war to this land?*"

"*We had no choice,*" Tog answered. "*Our land is lost to us, we must keep moving or die.*"

"*Where do you come from?*" she asked. "*Tell me of your home.*"

"*The swamp is our home, far to the north, west of the great wood, but a darkness has come there, and we have been forced out.*"

"*Tell me of this darkness,*" she said. "*How were you forced out?*"

"*Death and sickness came. The very swamp which gave us life began to sicken. In a short time there was no food to sustain us, even the plants withered and died, and so we came south.*"

"*To the Clans?*" she asked.

"*We were met by a wizard,*" said Tog. "*He gave us promises that if we helped with the war, he would return with us to our home and remove the blight. Now, it seems, we have failed. Our home will never again see the feet of our people.*"

"*What if I could promise you a new home?*" asked Anna.

"*How?*" the intimidating creature replied.

"*I am from Merceria,*" she said. "*A great kingdom that lies far to the east. To the south of our realm is a great swamp that sits empty. What if I could give you a home there? What would it be worth to you?*"

"*It would mean a future for my people,*" Tog said, "*but why would you do such a thing?*"

"*I have no wish to kill you,*" she replied. "*I would rather we be friends.*"

"*And what would you want in return?*" he asked.

"*That you help us. We fight for our home, much as you fight for yours. Like you, a shadow has taken over the land of my birth. Help us reclaim it, and you may take a portion of the swamp for your own. Once the war is over, we'll help you settle the area, bring trade and assist you in whatever way we can.*"

Tog scratched his chin, giving him a somewhat Human look. "*Very well,*" he answered, "*on behalf of my people, I will agree.*"

Anna turned to Gerald, reverting to the common tongue, "He's agreed to help us. We're going to give them a portion of the swamp in exchange."

"What about the Saurians?" asked Beverly. "The swamp is their domain."

"The Saurians are far to the east," she replied. "I was thinking about the area south of Colbridge. Perhaps, with a little encouragement, they might be able to clear up the river and open trade to the sea."

"You've thought this out carefully," said Gerald.

"I have indeed," she admitted, looking at the troops formed up behind them. "Now, we have to diffuse the situation before someone gets scared and starts fighting."

"I'll move the troops farther back," said Beverly. "I would suggest you disarm the Trolls, at least for now. That should help put the men at ease."

"Thank you," said the princess, returning her attention to the leader of the Trolls.

"*We will move our men out of range,*" she said in the ancient tongue, "*but you must put down your weapons. They will be returned to you later.*"

"*Very well,*" said Tog, "*we shall do as you wish.*" He turned to march back to his companions but stopped, returning his gaze to the small group, "*Who are you?*"

"*I am Princess Anna,*" she said, "*and these are my companions. Welcome to the army of Merceria.*"

King Leofric was relieved to see the situation resolved. He called them all to his tent that evening to thank them for their assistance in defeating the threat to Weldwyn. The king set a modest table, but after the busy day, they were thankful for the chance to relax among friends, free from the obligations that had so consumed their time of late.

They ate in relative silence, each consumed by their own thoughts. The king ate sparingly, as did they all, save for Tempus. The great mastiff accepted all offerings and ended the evening lying in satiated slumber at Anna's feet.

Gerald was starting to drift off to sleep, the day's actions finally taking their toll, when Anna spoke up.

"I was thinking," she mused, "that perhaps the solution to our problem lies right here." She stabbed her finger down on the table for emphasis, riveting Gerald's attention.

"What's that?" he asked.

"You have all these prisoners," she continued, "but surely, even with manning galley's, there are large costs involved."

"Meaning?" asked Leofric.

"Well, they must be guarded, and fed, for that matter. They also need to be marched south to the great ports of Weldwyn, even while the army is still needed."

"We defeated the enemy," said Arnim, "surely there is no further need for the army?"

"Actually," observed Gerald, "Anna's right. There are stragglers on the loose, from both sides, and they still need to march to Loranguard and find out what's going on there."

"True enough," added Leofric. "You've returned Alstan to me, but I have another son in that great city that I am worried about."

"How is the Crown Prince?" asked Arnim.

"He is doing much better," replied the king. "The mages have seen to his injuries. I'm afraid the Clans were not gentle with him. He had been beaten and starved when we liberated him from the enemy camp."

"He's strong," said Gerald, "he'll recover."

"Yes," admitted the king, "but he blames himself for losing the battle. If you hadn't come north with reinforcements, I'd have been locked up with him and paraded around the Clans as a trophy."

"We mustn't dwell on what might have been," added Anna. "Instead, we should focus on the future. I mean to take the throne of Merceria, Your Majesty. I know you haven't been one to support such a bid in the past."

"Circumstances were different then," said Leofric. "You have now come to the aid of our kingdom on multiple occasions, the least we can do is support your claim."

"Thank you, Your Majesty," she said. "That is most reassuring."

"While I support your claim," he continued, "I am left in a difficult situation. Our losses have been high, and I have too few troops left to lend to your cause. You were talking about the cost of these prisoners; are you suggesting they fight for you?"

"I don't trust the Clansmen," said Anna, "they fought for their kingdom, but the Kurathians are a different matter. They're mercenaries, much like our ancestors. They'll honour a contract, I'm sure."

"Well," admitted Gerald, "they are currently unemployed."

"Yes," agreed Anna. "I propose we hire them on. We will grant them land in exchange for their service."

"It still takes money to hold an army together," interjected Arnim.

"Money is the one thing I have in abundance," offered Leofric. "I will supply the funds as long as you take the Kurathians from Weldwyn. I'd be helping you to recover the crown and getting rid of one of our problems at the same time."

"That's most gracious of you," said Anna.

"When we return to the capital," the king continued, "we'll swear them into your service. The mercenaries will have to remain outside of town, but their leaders will need to take an oath."

Gerald raised his cup in salute. "A most excellent solution," he said. "Both kingdoms get what they want. I promise someday we'll repay you, Your Majesty."

"It is I that owe you, General," insisted the king. "Now, it is getting late. Tomorrow we march for Summersgate, and I'd like to check in on my eldest. Good night to you all."

They filed out of the tent quietly, Gerald halting outside, stretching his arms and looking at Anna. "You did well tonight," he said.

"Yes," she admitted. "The future is looking promising and yet there's still more work to do."

"Meaning?"

"Meaning, we still have to recruit Mercerians. We can't return to the kingdom leading a bunch of foreigners, people will naturally turn against us."

"I have some thoughts on that," he offered.

"Oh? Do tell," she pressed.

"I think the Duke of Kingsford would support us," he said. "After we saved his city last year, he said as much. It would give us a strong base to recruit from."

She looked at him in surprise, "I thought the planning was my job."

He chuckled at her response, "Remember, you instructed me and Beverly to come up with plans for a campaign."

"That was back when we were in the swamp," she said. "So much has changed since then."

"Yes, but we've updated our plans along the way. I've got an idea how we might accomplish things, but we need a better sense of what sort of shape the kingdom is in."

"We'll find out soon enough," she replied, "but let's not get ahead of ourselves. We must get back to Summersgate first, then we'll worry about the spring offensive."

"Spring?" he asked. "I thought we might take the first step in the winter."

"You can't march an army in the dead of winter," she replied, "everyone knows that."

"Can't you?" he said. "I have some ideas on that too, but you're right, we have other things to worry about for now. You'd best get off to bed, Tempus looks exhausted, and you know he won't settle till you're safe."

She rubbed the great dog's head. "You're right," she said at last, returning her attention to Gerald, "but I'm a little upset with you."

"Why's that?" he asked, shocked by the statement.

"You expect me to go to sleep after teasing me with the idea of a winter attack. I'll be fussing over it all night long."

He suppressed the laughter that threatened to erupt from his mouth, "Good night, Anna."

She hugged him tightly around the waist. "Good night, Gerald."

THIRTY-THREE

Celebration

WINTER 961 MC

~

The first snow of winter fell, sending cold winds blowing across the land as the army arrived back in Summersgate to great applause and ceremony. The queen insisted on welcoming home the heroes of the kingdom with a parade. Leofric rode at the head of the troops, Anna and Gerald beside him in a place of honour.

The festivities continued indoors with feasting and celebration in abundance. King Leofric requested that the Mercerians stay at the Royal Palace, even going so far as to give over an entire wing of the grand structure to the princess's entourage.

Now, three days later, a consequential assemblage of the kingdom's most important people arrived to bear witness as the Kurathian leaders swore an oath to serve Anna's cause.

Leofric and Queen Igraine sat off to the side, giving Anna centre stage. She sat upon a majestic chair, Tempus to her left while Gerald, in his battle-worn armour, took his place to her right. Dame Beverly stood in front, between her charge and the rest of the crowd, her sword drawn and planted, point down, onto the floor.

The Kurathian leaders were at the front of the crowd, looking nervous. Only four of them had agreed to the terms for their people, the rest having been marched off to imprisonment.

Princess Anna rose, the room falling into silence as she did so. "We are gathered here, today," she began, "at the gracious invitation of King Leofric of Weldwyn. Let all, here, bear witness to the great affection and friendship that exists between our people."

She paused while the crowd applauded. They were in a good mood, and well they should be. The recent victory spelled an end to the Clan threat and promised a bright future for the Kingdom of Weldwyn, but for Merceria the future still looked bleak and grim.

"With the approval of the king, we will, this day, swear into service, an army of warriors who will help us march into Merceria and liberate it from the darkness that has so plagued my people. Let there be no mistake, the campaign will be long and hard, and many will die, but in the end, we will be victorious."

Once again the pause as the audience applauded.

She nodded to Gerald.

"Captain Lanaka," he announced, "Leader of the Kurathian Light Cavalry. Step forth and take your oath."

A thin, middle-aged man approached, his skin darkened by time at sea gave him a weather-beaten look. He stepped up to Beverly, removed his sword and handed it to her.

The red-headed knight took the blade, then stepped aside, allowing him to come face to face with the princess.

He lowered himself to one knee, bowing deeply. "I swear, on behalf of my people to honour the terms of our agreement. To follow your orders and to assist you, in every way, to recover the throne that is rightfully yours. I swear this by all the Holy Saints."

Anna briefly looked to Gerald, who nodded slightly. "I accept your oath," she said. "Take back your sword that it might serve me."

Beverly moved up to the Kurathian, returning his blade to its scabbard. Lanaka turned, nodding to her in acknowledgement, and then backed away from the princess, repeatedly bowing as he did so until he was back amongst the crowd.

Gerald called forth the rest. An ancient man named Montak spoke for the mastiff handlers. Anna had been most impressed with the dogs and had visited their makeshift kennels repeatedly since their return. She absently stroked Tempus's ears as the man came forward to swear his oath.

A very polite Kurathian named Jaran commanded the archers. He was well educated and spoke the common tongue fluently. He too, took the oath, sounding very earnest as he pledged his allegiance to their cause.

The last one to step forward was short and portly, an enchanter by the name of Kiren-Jool. Revi had already held numerous discussions with the man and insisted that the presence of such a mage would be advantageous.

Their oaths complete, each took their places back amongst the crowd and fell into quiet discussion. Anna held up her hands for attention, and the room fell silent once more.

"It would be remiss of me," she continued, "not to mention the accomplishments of one of our own. I call on Lady Nicole Arendale to step forward."

Nikki, caught by surprise, gasped. Arnim, standing beside her, prodded her to make her way forward. This she did, halting in front of Dame Beverly, still surprised at being called out by the princess.

Beverly looked her in the eye and smiled. "Well done," she simply said, stepping out of the way.

The former Lady-In-Waiting was beckoned forward by the princess, coming to stop an arm's length away. Nikki bowed deeply, feeling a flush of embarrassment come to her cheeks.

"Lady Nicole," began the princess, "Prince Alric has informed me of the extraordinary service you performed for Weldwyn. We are forever in your debt for the selfless assistance you have provided our closest ally. I would grant you a boon. Please tell us how we might reward you for your deeds."

Nicole took a deep breath before answering, "Being able to serve you is the only reward I wish. Through my time with you, I have come to understand what it means to have friends and loved ones."

"Then so be it," Anna declared, "for I will gladly take you back into service."

"There is one more thing," said Nikki unexpectedly. "I would give you a gift."

"A gift for me?" queried the princess. "Surely you have already granted us the greatest gift by saving the life of my betrothed."

Nikki pulled forth the purse, holding it to the side for Beverly. The knight stepped forward, taking the bag and emptied the contents into her hand, the diamonds twinkling in the light.

"These are of great value," noted Anna. "Surely you could use this yourself?"

"No," Nikki insisted, "I want you to have it to help pay for the army."

Anna stared back for a moment and then nodded, "Very well, I most graciously accept your gift."

A lone figure broke from the crowd, moving forward to present himself. "I ask a boon," he called out.

"Step forward, Sir Arnim," replied Anna. "and have your say."

He crossed the floor to stand beside Nikki, his face fixed on the princess.

"Well, Sir Arnim, what boon do you seek?"

"I would like your permission to marry Lady Nicole Arendale, Your Highness," he said, turning to face the woman beside him, "provided she will have me."

Nikki's eyes began to tear up as she nodded her assent.

"Very well," pronounced the princess, "I give you leave to do so and ask Saxnor for his blessing of their upcoming nuptials. Now, let us call forth for wine and celebrate this happy turn of events."

The crowd began cheering as the couple turned to face them. Arnim and Nikki stepped forward to be greeted by well-wishers shaking their hands.

Anna, her moment of glory over, held out her hand to Gerald. He took it, leading her down into the crowd where Prince Alric stood, waiting patiently. Gerald placed her hand in the prince's, nodding his approval and then backed up to give them some privacy.

Anna looked into Alric's eyes, her attention riveted on the face she loved so dearly.

"My father has given his blessing to our union," said Alric. "We can be married before the spring."

Anna leaned forward and kissed him, pulling back to look into his eyes once more. "Would that it were that simple," she started, "but I cannot marry before the throne is secured. Until that time, I need to concentrate on the task at hand, with no distractions. The darkness that is behind my brother's rule must be rooted out and destroyed. I dare not rest until I have eliminated this shadow of the crown."

"I understand," he said in reply, "and I will wait however long this takes, knowing that in the end, we will be together."

"As will I," she responded, kissing him once again.

Epilogue

WINTER 961 MC

A well-dressed man walked through the Palace halls in Wincaster, his cape fluttering behind him, to come before the immense double doors, halting at the presence of two knights.

He nodded in greeting as one of them turned, opening the door to the great hall. At the far end sat two chairs, and the man walked with purpose toward the occupants, his footsteps echoing throughout the large chamber.

He halted, kneeling before them, waiting for acknowledgement

"Arise, Captain Fraser," said Lady Penelope.

Standing, the captain turned his attention to the other occupant, King Henry of Merceria.

"Your Majesty," he said, bowing his head.

"You forget your place," said Lady Penelope, "it is to me you report."

Captain Fraser took a deep breath, the sweat trickling quite visibly down his neck.

"What of Weldwyn?" she commanded. "Give us your report."

He took a deep mouthful of air, "I'm afraid the plan came to naught, Your Majesty."

"Your plan," she corrected.

"Yes," he admitted, "my plan."

"Just as your plan failed at Riversend," she added.

He stood in silence, his hands and legs beginning to tremble in fear.

"This is the second time you've failed us, Captain Fraser. There will not be a third."

He opened his mouth in protest, but as he did so, she raised her hands, uttering something he didn't understand. A green streak emanated from her fingers, striking him in the chest, paralyzing him. He felt himself being drained of energy and looked at his hands in abject fear as they began to shrivel up before him. Soon, they dissolved into dust, and as he tried to scream, the rest of his body began transforming, ending his life. The shrivelled body hit the floor, releasing a green cloud of mist that lingered briefly in the air before he was no more.

King Henry looked to her in annoyance. "Wasn't that a bit extreme?" he asked.

Lady Penelope Cromwell swept her gaze from the floor to that of Henry. "You may be the King of Merceria," she said, "but never forget who truly rules here."

Share your thoughts!

If you enjoyed this book, share your favourite part! These positive reviews encourage other potential readers to give the series a try and help the book to populate when people are searching for a new fantasy series. And the best part is, each review I receive inspires me to write more in the land of Merceria and beyond.

Thank you!

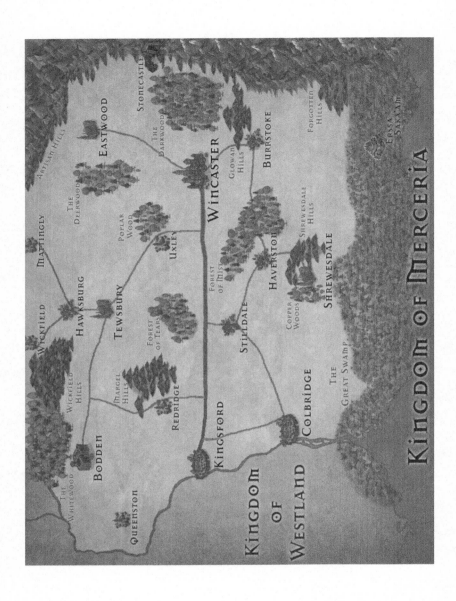

Kingdom of Merceria

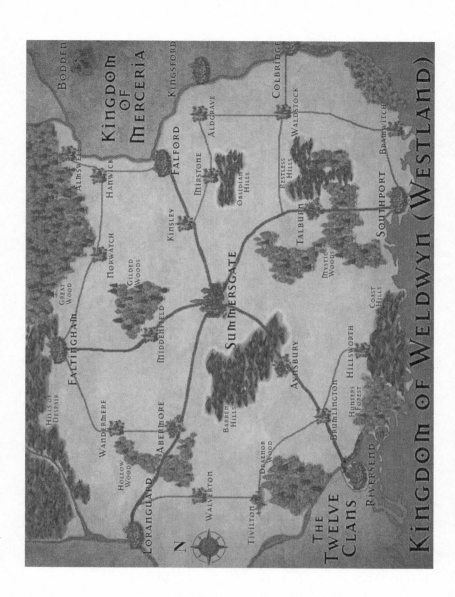

Kingdom of Weldwyn (Westland)

How to get Battle at the River for free

Paul J Bennett's newsletter members are the first to hear about upcoming books, along with receiving exclusive content and Work In Progress updates.

Join the newsletter and receive *Battle at the River*, a Mercerian Short Story for free: PaulJBennettAuthor.com/newsletter

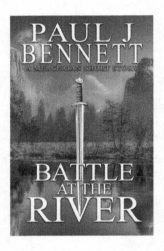

An enemy commander. A skilled tactician. Only one can be victorious.

The Norland raiders are at it again. When the Baron of Bodden splits their defensive forces, Sergeant Gerald Matheson thinks that today is a day like any other, but then something is different. At the last moment, Gerald recognizes the warning signs, but they are outnumbered, outmaneuvered, and out of luck. How can they win this unbeatable battle?

If you like intense battle scenes and unexpected plot twists, then you will love Paul J Bennett's tale of a soldier who thinks outside the box.

A few words from Paul

When I first started writing Shadow of the Crown, I knew I wanted to reveal more about Nikki's background. In the first draft, I used flashbacks to tell the story of Arnim and Nikki's past, but I found it dragged the story down. After all, readers were left hanging after the epilogue to *Heart of the Crown* and I wanted to jump right back into the narrative. I eventually settled on the final method, revealing little tidbits about their past throughout the book. It is much more about Nikki's redemption now and I find that more satisfying. Of course there are lots of other things happening and everything is building to the next book, *Fate of the Crown*, where the matter of the rulership of Merceria will be settle once and for all.

I often find, as other authors do, that the characters tend to take on a life of their own. Gerald is becoming a more accomplished leader, Anna is becoming a serious young woman, and yet they still have moments of fun and playfulness. Revi has now found his lucky charm and is ready to take on the burden of great power, even Nikki and Arnim have sorted out their past differences and are ready to join the others in overthrowing the shadow that grips the throne of Merceria. The path will be arduous and now the group must face a new challenge, not just a battle, but an entire campaign to win back the kingdom.

There are many people that have taken this journey with me and allowed me to tell this tale. I should like to acknowledge the talents of Christie Kramberger, who created an incredible cover with a suitably dark theme. I would also like to thank the following Beta Readers who gave so much valuable feedback, from simple spelling mistakes to plot inconsistencies: Stuart Rae, Rigel Chiokis, Tim James, Mark Tracy, Rachel Deibler, Don Hinkey, and Paul Castellano.

In addition, I must once again thank our Alpha reader, Brad Aitken who not only brought Revi Bloom to life, but made sure we didn't forget him in the storyline. In addition, the following people have contributed in their own way: Jeff Parker, Stephen Brown, Amanda Bennett, Stephanie Sandrock.

Last of all, but certainly not least, I must thank my wife, Carol Bennett for her support and suggestions. She has been my editor, marketer, promoter and social media coordinator, in addition to being my 'Lucky Charm.' I am so happy that we are taking this journey together.

Finally, thank you, dear reader, for without you there would be no *Heir to the Crown*. It is your feedback that has kept me motivated to write more about this wonderful world I have created and the people that inhabit it.

About the Author

Paul Bennett emerged into this world in Maidstone, Kent, England at the beginning of the 60's, then immigrated to Southwestern Ontario with his family six years later. In his teen years, Paul discovered military models, leading him to serve in the Canadian Armed Forces. Around the same time, he was introduced to role-playing games in the form of Dungeons & Dragons (D & D). What attracted him to this new hobby was the creativity it required; the need to create realms, worlds and adventures that pull the gamers into his stories.

In his 30's, Paul started to dabble in creating his own role-playing system, using the Peninsular War in Portugal as his backdrop. His regular gaming group were willing victims, er, participants in helping to play test the new system. A few years later he took his role-playing system and added additional settings; including Science Fiction, Post-Apocalyptic, World War II, and the all-important Fantasy Realm.

The beginnings of Servant to the Crown originated three years ago when he began a new fantasy campaign. For the world of Merceria, he ran his adventures like a TV show; with seasons that each had twelve episodes, and an overarching plot. After the campaign ended, he was inspired to sit down to write his first novel. He knew all the characters, what they had to accomplish, what needed to happen to move the plot along. 123,000 words later, Servant of the Crown was written!

Paul has mapped out a whole series of books in the land of Merceria and is looking forward to sharing them all with his readers over the next few years.